Praise for Julia Bryant's novels:

'A rich first novel conjuring up a vivid and realistic portrait of Portsmouth in the final years and aftermath of the Great War . . . A pulsating and heart-warming saga peopled with human and compelling characters and with convincing dialogue.' *Yorkshire Post*

'Here's a great excuse to put your feet up and escape into a world which celebrates Portsmouth's past . . . It's really well worth the read.' *Portsmouth News*

'Packed with interesting people living what might appear to be mundane lives, but of course they are not. We get an insight into the lives of the families of sailors, their good and bad fortune, their ups and downs. Decent people who we want to win through.' Betty Burton

'A family saga full of rich characters and intertwining stories . . . well written, real dialogue and real people.' *Huddersfield Daily Examiner*

By the same author

Waiting on the Tide
Written on the Tide
Borne on the Tide
The Restless Tide
The Spirit of Nelson Street

About the author

Julia Bryant was born in Portsmouth: her step-father and husband both served in the Navy. She trained as a nurse, then after her three children grew up, earned an honours B.A. in English and history. She and her husband now live in Portsmouth once more.

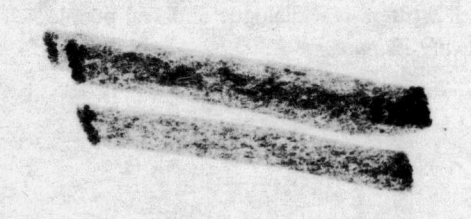

JULIA BRYANT

The Water is Wide

HODDER

First published in Great Britain in 2005 by Hodder and Stoughton
A division of Hodder Headline

A Hodder paperback

1 3 5 7 9 10 8 6 4 2

A CIP catalogue record for this title is
available from the British Library

ISBN 0 340 81964 2

Typeset in Plantin Light by Palimpsest Book Production Limited,
Polmont, Stirlingshire

Printed and bound by Clays Ltd, St Ives plc

Hodder Headline's policy is to use papers that are natural,
renewable and recyclable products and made from wood grown in
sustainable forests. The logging and manufacturing processes are expected
to conform to the environmental regulations of the country of origin.

Hodder and Stoughton Ltd
A division of Hodder Headline
338 Euston Road
London NW1 3BH

For my sister Marj and brother Stephen
with love

JULIA BRYANT

The Water is Wide

HODDER

Copyright © 2005 by Julia Bryant

First published in Great Britain in 2005 by Hodder and Stoughton
A division of Hodder Headline

A Hodder paperback

1 3 5 7 9 10 8 6 4 2

A CIP catalogue record for this title is
available from the British Library

ISBN 0 340 81964 2

Typeset in Plantin Light by Palimpsest Book Production Limited,
Polmont, Stirlingshire

Printed and bound by Clays Ltd, St Ives plc

Hodder Headline's policy is to use papers that are natural,
renewable and recyclable products and made from wood grown in
sustainable forests. The logging and manufacturing processes are expected
to conform to the environmental regulations of the country of origin.

Hodder and Stoughton Ltd
A division of Hodder Headline
338 Euston Road
London NW1 3BH

For my sister Marj and brother Stephen
with love

ACKNOWLEDGEMENTS

I should like to thank the following people for their patience, kindness and unstinting help in my research for this book.

Alan Norman Gibbs, Royal Marine Bugle Major, retired

Matthew Little of the Royal Marine Museum

Richard Brooks, author of *The Royal Marines 1664 to the Present* (Constable)

The Royal Marine Barracks, Eastney by Andrew Lane (Halsgrove) proved to be an invaluable resource book.

As always, Peter and Audrey Rogers for history, cooking, accounting and friendship

Pamela Fontana for her encouragement and proof-reading assistance

Graham Bennett and the staff of the Ventnor Heritage Museum

The staff of Portsmouth Libraries and the Museum and Records Office

Christopher and Margaret Seal of Sealpoint Computers

I

September 19th 1902

As HMS *Terrible* steamed into Portsmouth cheers, tears, and hullabaloo broke out on the jetty. Her paying-off pennant ribboned out across the sky, and music from the band floated towards the waiting crowd. In response hooters whooped their welcome from the ships in the harbour. Fledgling sailors on HMS *St Vincent* hailed the returning heroes of Ladysmith and Mafeking. Wives yearned to see their husbands and harlots braced themselves for the thrust of business. Families watched the iron-walled cruiser inch towards its mooring, and yearned to swarm aboard.

Nineteen-year-old Fidelis searched the top deck for a sighting of her father, Drill Sergeant Jack McCauley, returning home after three years' foreign service. As she shielded her eyes from the sun's glare, a playful breeze lifted her hat and dropped it in the water between the ship and the shore.

'Bosun, look lively there, get a boat-hook,' barked a voice above her, on the ship.

A sailor leapt down a gangway, rescued her soggy hat and presented it to her on the end of the pole.

'Thank you,' she said, holding it away from her dress and blushing at being the centre of attention.

'Pay no heed to me, Ma'am, 'twas the lieutenant what spotted it.' The bosun pointed to where a Royal Marine officer stood at the rail, his helmet raised in greeting.

Gazing up at him, Fidelis was dazzled. For a moment,

the sun haloed his blond hair, and the gold frogging on his sleeve gleamed at her. She stared until her eyes watered, then he was gone. It was an instant of enchantment. Would she ever see him again? She very much hoped so. Fidelis wanted to cut through the protocol separating officers from lesser ranks and have him notice her again. From the look of that particular lieutenant, life was one long, glorious adventure.

As the officers' gangway was lowered, she hurried back to her place in the crowd. A great cheer went up as they spotted their hero at the head of the gangway.

'Would you look at him, like a great cockerel, bedizened in all that gold braid?'

Beside her, Aunt Shamrock pointed her parasol to Captain Percy as he strode ashore to meet the port admiral. Giving him the benefit of her cleavage and the Prince of Wales feathers trembling on her hat, she cried, 'Welcome home, sir.'

Amused at her sauce, Captain Percy raised his hat to her and the crowd roared their approval.

Laughing at her, Fidelis had a vision of Shamrock as a ship's figurehead, her bold brown eyes striking fear into the enemy. A star at the local music hall, all bosom and fancy hat, auntie was such fun to be with.

'Oh, Fee, I'm ravaged for the sight of him,' she said, grabbing her arm.

'Who is he?' she asked, knowing such excitement was not for her aunt's brother Jack.

'My sailor, wasn't he a Samson in strength and a dove for delicacy? You'll get to treasure a man who takes his time, Fee.'

Fidelis laughed. Her aunt's amours were always short-lived but intense, while her own experience of love was so far limited to letters. Her fiancé, Bugler Harry Dawes, was stationed in the West Indies – they had become engaged by letter. He had gone away just before her seventeenth birthday and would return next year, in July, a few months after her twentieth. The Dawes family were her next-door neighbours, Auntie Ruby and Uncle Norman with their three lively sons. She and Harry, the youngest, had been pals for ever; going fishing with hand-lines, scrumping apples from the officers' gardens and playing draughts on winter evenings.

'I love you, Fee,' he had whispered that last time. 'Write to me, tell me what you're thinking and I'll tell you what's happening to me.' He bent to kiss her. It had been a shy, fumbled effort that would have to last her for the next three years.

Love at a distance was so unsatisfactory. She could not remember how his lips felt on hers and sometimes looking at his photograph he seemed a stranger to her. What did love feel like? How did you know when it was real? The womanly counsel she had had so far had been contradictory. Ma hinted at endurance, rather than pleasure, and Shamrock filled her head with writhing bodies in unbelievable contortions.

The second gangway was secured and the families surged up its slope, eager to see their loved ones. Once aboard, Auntie disappeared. Among the waiting sailors, in straw sennet hats and striped collars, were men in the blue uniforms of the Royal Marine Artillery, with the distinctive red stripe on their trousers. She searched anxiously for her father. Where was Pa? All of a sudden she was being whirled around in his arms and having the breath squeezed out of her. Laughing and crying, Fidelis looked up at him. Tall, dark and blue-eyed, he crackled with life.

'Fee, darling, is it really you? When did you turn into such a beauty?'

She blushed. 'It was just yesterday, especially for your homecoming. Oh, Pa, it's so good to see you again.'

'Where's your mother?'

'She's not very well.'

'No surprise there,' he said, his gaiety quenched. 'I'd forgotten about her delicate constitution.' He struggled to recover himself. 'Did she send her love?'

Fidelis remembered her mother's words.

'Fee, I have a migraine. If I can just lie still it might settle. Tell your father there will be steak-and-kidney pie, and trifle to follow. I have it all ready prepared.'

There was no fond message of love. Nineteen-year-old Fidelis could no longer pretend that her parents' marriage was anything other than mutual sufferance. Ma had not had a single headache in all the time her husband had been away.

'Ma said there would be a hot meal waiting.'

Pa shrugged. 'Thought my sister would have been down here flaunting herself.' His expression turned to one of tolerant amusement.

'I expect she's met her sailor.'

He father laughed. 'Poor fellow, he'll have been in lover's knots all morning.'

Fidelis sensed that 'lover's knots' were not afflictions discussed in polite company. 'When can you come ashore, Pa? I'm dying to hear all about your adventures.'

He shook his head. 'Never mind all that, I'm avid for all your doings. Fancy, you're a nursemaid now I hear. Next thing you'll be the housekeeper with the key to the cellar in your pocket.' Taking her arm, Pa said, 'Let me set you down for'ad with the other families. Leave will be piped at noon, then I'll be a gentleman of leisure.'

Fidelis stood among the women and children gazing at the curious world of men. There were whistles shrilling, barked commands, sailors rushing to stow ropes or salute haughty-looking officers. It was all iron walls, scrubbed decks and gleaming brass-work. The ship's band began to play 'A Life on the Ocean Wave'. Children were swept up in their fathers' arms and wives kissed and petted. She walked up and down the deck searching for Shamrock. She found her with her sailor man, perched between a ship's lifeboat and one of the four funnels. Her aunt kept touching him, smoothing his collar or stroking his beard. He in turn patted her hand or whispered in her ear. 'Intimacy,' Fidelis whispered, and felt her body stirring in response.

Moving to the ship's rail she looked down at the throng of people ashore, crossing the bridge from the pubs and shops on the Hard to the railway station for London or to the ferries for Gosport and the Isle of Wight. Far below on the harbour mud-flats urchins slithered for pennies tossed to them from passing travellers. She sniffed the seaport bouquet of seaweed, burning coal and salt water.

'All present and correct,' said her father, swinging his kitbag up on his shoulder. 'Let's be away to Eastney and your mother's cooking.' He drew her hand through his arm. 'Ooh! Fee, there's no place like home.'

After he had saluted the officer at the head of the gangway they were back on dry land. It took a while to escape the hubbub around the dockyard. Everywhere the crew of the *Terrible* was cheered and welcomed. Young women rushed to touch the sailors' collars for luck. Old men slapped them on the back and mothers cried.

'I'll treat you to one of the new electric trams, Pa. See the poles on their roofs connecting them to the power supply?'

'Let's go up on top, when it comes. I want to re-acquaint myself with Pompey.'

Fidelis smiled. It was only the strangers that called the town Portsmouth. While theories abounded as to the origin of the name, it had never been discovered.

'Just think,' she said, when they were seated upstairs in the front seat, 'you went away in one century and returned in another.'

'I went away in Queen Victoria's reign and have come back under King Edward's. What do you make of the fellow?'

'He's big and jolly and intent on enjoying himself from what I can tell. Shamrock saw him at the Alhambra in London, after the show, and he winked at her.'

Pa threw back his head and laughed. 'I think my sister would get a reaction out of a corpse. But you, Fee, what do you want out of the new century?'

Fidelis smiled. She had forgotten how interested Pa was in new things. 'I want to drive a car, fly in an airship, do the cakewalk and go over the Niagara Falls in a barrel.'

'That's Jack McCauley's daughter talking. You have my hunger for change and invention. I envy you being on the brink of things. It's a big wide world with so much to discover. Now tell me, are you happy at your work? You haven't talked of it at all in your last few letters.'

She frowned. 'I think I told you before, Mrs Allen is ever so pretty but it's like she's in a doll's house, playing at being married. You never know how she'll be – one minute nice as pie and the next she's screaming at you. When the nurse-maid left she wanted me to help with little Sophie, now the maid's left I'm doing everything.'

'Why d'you think the nursemaid and the other girl left, Fee?'

Fidelis was silent for a long while. Her father tamped down the tobacco in his pipe, while she stared out of the window, lost in thought. There was something terrible about to happen at the Allens' house, she was certain of it. When her friend Molly, the previous nursemaid, left in tears, Phoebe Allen had screamed at her; 'Never darken my door again, you slut.'

The following week, Molly's father had come around, crashing at the knocker and demanding to see Mr Allen. Even when Phoebe had insisted that Fidelis shut the door in his face, the man stood about in the front garden, stamping and cursing. When Mr Allen returned, money was thrown at Molly's Pa from an upstairs window.

Still he stood there shouting. 'You gotta give my girl a good character, she slaved for you,' the man shouted.

Only when the Allens called the police did he go away.

Pa nudged her arm. 'You're wool-gathering, girl. I was asking why you thought the other maids left?'

'I suppose they had their reasons,' Fidelis lied. 'I think Molly left to get married, she's got a little girl, now.'

'What line of work is he in, this Mr Allen?'

'Goes out at night, in evening dress, and comes home ever so late. I don't know what he can be doing. Doesn't get up 'til dinner-time. Mrs Allen's mother is very rich, I think.'

'I hope you're getting extra money for what you're doing. You got to watch these jumped-up people, it's all show and no substance with them.'

'Yes Pa, and I got the day off.' Pride wouldn't let her admit that her day off and night at home were the first free time in months.

'You'd better be looking out for a new position. Once things are on the slide they'll go from bad to worse.'

'Eastney Barracks stop, look lively on top,' called the conductor.

Her father hauled his kitbag from the bus and lifted it onto his shoulder. 'Let's go around and look at the old girl,' he said, crossing over to Cromwell Road.

There behind the thick flint-dressed walls was the Royal Marine barracks complete with Union Jack and clock-tower. It had always dominated their lives, with Pa drilling recruits on the parade ground and Ma taking in washing for the colonel's lady, while Fidelis ran to the school there with the other rankers' children.

Once he had satisfied himself that it was still standing, they turned towards Gibraltar Street. The little houses showed well-scrubbed doorsteps and immaculate net curtains to the world – none more so than number seventy-two. At the first rap of the knocker Ma appeared. Pale and elegant, with hair as red as her daughter's, Mary McCauley gave her husband a wintry smile.

'Welcome home, Jack.' She rested her hands on his jacket as if to ward off any closeness. He bent towards her and she suffered herself to be kissed.

'It's good to see you, Mary.' Their awkwardness with one another was overshadowed by the joyous barking of Ebony, the family dog, who flung himself through the back door at the sound of his master's voice.

'Hello boy, well, aren't you the lively one, and what a welcome.'

'Jack, you will want to wash your hands, now. There's water in the basin upstairs. I'll pour your ale and Fee and I will have lemon cordial.'

Once they were seated, Ma closed her eyes and made the sign of the cross before taking a knife and cutting into the pie. As she spooned the gravy onto his plate Fidelis saw the flicker of irritation in her father's eyes. His physical presence filled the house. Fidelis had thought the living-room pleasing, with its lace frontal to the mantelpiece and embroidered antimacassars on the armchairs. But now it seemed cramped and fussy. This was a world of women, and Jack McCauley was an invader.

Conversation was made in nervous rushes.

'Mary, the house is a credit to you, girl. You have it all splendid.'

'Jack, are you keeping well? Have you got over the malaria you told me about?'

'I'm in the pink, fit as a flea.'

'I thought Shamrock was coming with you.'

'She had a prior engagement.' Pa reached across the table for a slice of cake.

Silence throbbed with unspoken thoughts. In her eager looking-forward to her father's return Fidelis had glossed over her parents' differences. They were oil and water. Pa was warm and outgoing while her mother was distant and disappointed with life. She had looked forward to seeing them together again but wishful thinking had clouded her memory. Smiling awkwardly she got up from the table. 'I'll go and take off my best clothes then I'll wash up while you and Ma catch up on things.'

'I'll unpack my kitbag later, and I'll share out the spoils. One of the officers talked me into doing some sketching, while we were in China. You might find them interesting, Fee.'

In her room, as she unbuttoned her jacket, all the joy of Pa's homecoming drained away. She paced about the room in her chemise and drawers, feeling restless. Anticipation was never the same as the reality. Self-deception smoothed over uncomfortable truths, and then came the day of reckoning, when the hard facts smacked you in the face. Never mind her parents, what were her own true feelings? Did she really love Harry, or was she using him to escape from them? She sat on her bed and drew out the scent bottle from beneath her pillow. It had lain for days in the waste-paper basket in Phoebe Allen's bedroom, where she had thrown it after a screaming match with her husband. Fidelis had wrestled with her conscience. She knew her mistress had not meant to throw it away. But surely, among the litter of bottles on her dressing-table, she wouldn't miss just one. The word, *Ensorcelée* was written on the label in curling script. What did it mean? Closing her eyes she stroked the stopper over her neck. The perfume whispered to her of experiences she had yet to taste. An image from earlier in the day floated into her mind. It was of the lieutenant from HMS *Terrible*, smiling down at her, golden and self-assured.

* * *

Hurrying to work the next morning, Fidelis thought about her first weeks at Clarendon House. The Allens had seemed the last word in elegance and sophistication, like characters from *Pride and Prejudice*, her last school prize, with James as the handsome Darcy and Phoebe as the wilful Lydia. Working for them had quickly tarnished their lustre.

'Things is going from bad to worse. We'll be lucky to see our wages, I'm thinking,' Cook had said, only last week.

'My sister, Nellie, writ me from Brighton. Says I should pack me bags and go down and live with her.' The big woman's jowls shook with anxiety, as she whisked the eggs for baking. 'It's the trades-folk what I'm sorry for. They gives credit to get their customers then has ter come round the back door, cap in hand, to get their money. Poor man in the cheese shop shot hisself 'cos of all his debts.'

Over a mug of cocoa each, they decided to give it one more month. Cook would write to her sister and Fidelis would scour the pages of the *Evening News*. As she opened the back gate she could feel her temper rising. Why should the Allens sponge off their staff? What was it the Bible said? '*The labourer is worthy of his hire.*'

If Pa got to hear of it he would be raging. But she would fight her own battles; it was a matter of picking the right strategy. She found the door locked, curtains drawn, and the house in darkness. Cook must have packed and gone.

She should have seen the signs. Why had they suddenly given her the time off, when they had held out on her for weeks before? There was she, riven with guilt over taking that scent, when they were thieving her wages. She thought of Phoebe Allen's coaxing, last time, when she had got up her courage to mention money.

'Fidelis, you are a treasure. I don't know what I would do without you. Here have this last violet cream.' Her brow wrinkled. 'If you could be patient with us a for just a teensy-weensy bit longer you shall have your money in full.' And then, there was that conspiratorial grin just like a naughty child. 'Aren't these chocolates heavenly?'

There was nothing for it but to get in through the kitchen window. Fidelis got her fingers through the gap at the bottom and hefted up the lower pane. Her feet slithered on a slimy dishcloth left in the sink. Stepping down onto the stone floor, the gloom and the silence unnerved her. Where were the Allens? Feeling her way across the room she searched out the matches and candle-stub in the dresser drawer. The sound of a lavatory being flushed in the bathroom overhead had her creeping up the stairs.

A light gleamed under the Allens' door. She kicked it open and found the room in chaos. There were drawers torn from cupboards and jewellery strewn on the floor. Sitting on the bed was Phoebe, dressed in her coat and hat, with Sophie in her arms. They were both crying. The toddler held out her arms, and without thinking Fidelis picked her up. 'Hush my pet, I've got you. Let's go and find your rabbit.'

'Fidelis, thank God, you are going to save our lives.'

James Allen's face was the colour of putty and his chin unshaven. Yet he still thought he could sway her with his buttery smile. I've walked myself into a trap, she thought angrily. 'Why should I help you?' she said, picking the velvet rabbit from the floor and giving it to the little girl.

'Because you care for Sophie and don't want her to be distressed.'

'Please, dear sweet Fidelis, we're depending on you,' added his wife unctuously.

Why had she ever admired Phoebe? She was a greedy child. 'I want my money that's owed me, that I worked for. I won't be tricked into doing nothing wrong.'

'You shall have it. All I want you to do is to take Sophie over to Mummy's in Heron Grove, number sixty-four. I've a letter for her that explains the whole vile business. Sophie's all ready and James will get out the pram for you.'

They were wooing her into doing what they wanted, banking on her affection for the child. She slipped the letter into her pocket and carried Sophie downstairs. Her employer was in the hall waiting for them.

'Goodbye, my sweet girl,' he said, leaning over the pram, as she settled his daughter beneath the covers. 'Hurry, hurry, there's not a moment to lose.'

'What about my written character?' Fidelis demanded, sensing this was the last time she would see James the pretender.

He looked at her as if she were speaking double Dutch.

'I need a reference so that I can get a new position.'

'God, d'you think I have time for that? Go!' He shoved her towards the front door.

At his touch her fury coalesced. Drawing back her arm she punched him in the mouth. Staring at her in disbelief, James Allen sank onto a chair. Before he could say anything, Fidelis bumped the pram out of the door and down the steps. She hurtled down the road, as far and as fast as she could from the odious Allens. Footsteps thudded behind her and voices shouted at her to stop.

What did they want? Was it the police? Would they lock her up? Hitting your employer was a heinous crime, she was certain.

A man stepped into her path. Gasping, she looked into his face. Where had she seen him before? And then, it came to her that she knew him. It was the wine merchant from one of the posh shops in Palmerston Road. He removed his bowler and wiped the sweat from his face with the back of his hand.

'It ain't her, Charlie, we've been had.' Turning to Fidelis he demanded, 'You tell me where they've gone or it'll be the worse for you.'

Still overwrought, she snapped at him. 'You stop that roaring, this minute. Whatever you want them for, it's nothing to do with me.'

'Where is he, that deceivin' tyke?'

'Gents, don't you see? It's the oldest trick in the book,' said the wine man. 'They sent her off out the front door, while they takes to their heels down the back alley. We bin had.'

The Allens had made her their decoy.

Fidelis ran through the Southsea streets to the seafront, past the big white hotels overlooking the beach, on past the South Parade Pier, bouncing the pram in front of her. She turned right past the Canoe Lake, a park beloved by visitors, and paid it no heed. By this time her temper had been replaced by fear. What would happen to a servant that punched her master? Could she be sent to prison? Her hand throbbed with the contact. What must James Allen be feeling? With a jolt she realised she had raced along without a thought for Sophie. She looked into the pram and said, 'We're going to see your Grandma, won't that be fun?'

The baby was fast asleep, her face streaked with tears and mucus. She had no bonnet and her coat was not buttoned properly – poor little one being dragged from pillar to post.

On reaching the green-tiled mansion that was Kelmscott House, Fidelis pushed the pram to the front door and rang the bell. 'May I speak with Mrs Mount?' she said to the sour-faced woman who opened it to her.

'And who might you be?' The maid sniffed. 'Go around to the back door, at once.'

'This baby here is her granddaughter. I thought relations were let in the front door.' She could feel her temper simmering. 'You can take your time, I'm in no hurry.' Bending over the pram she took the sleeping Sophie up in her arms.

'You better come in.'

'I've got a letter from Mrs Mount's daughter. No, I'm to give it only to her.'

'Wait there, while I speak to Madam.'

Fidelis got a hankie out of her pocket and spat on it. Gently she rubbed it over Sophie's face and cleaned her runny nose.

'Mrs Mount will be down in a minute. You're to give me your name and wait in there.'

'Fidelis McCauley,' she said, refusing to be humbled by the maid's snooty manner.

Glaring at her, the woman held open the door to the sitting-room. Fidelis paced around the room. Its walls were covered in patterned wallpaper in shades of green and blue. She went closer to study the grapes clustering on their vines. She sniffed the air, scenting roses. Moving towards the window she found the source of the perfume in a brass bowl set on a polished table. It was filled with dried petals and leaves and seed-pods. Surreptitiously, she slid some into the pocket of her jacket, wanting to carry something of the room away with her. Her teacher once said that it was the space between things that was as important as the things themselves. This would be the effect she would strive for in her own home, wherever it was. 'If wishes were horses beggars would ride.' Wishes! She was a spendthrift in wishes.

'Good morning, Miss McCauley.' Mrs Mount smiled at her before reaching out her hand and stroking her granddaughter's cheek. Turning to the resentful maid she said, 'Take Miss Sophie upstairs, and put her in my bed, for the moment. Thank you, Eileen. Please ask Cook to send us in a tray of tea and biscuits.'

Eileen's face softened as she held out her arms to receive the little girl.

Mrs Mount seated herself in an armchair and indicated that Fidelis should take the seat beside her. 'My daughter has given you a message for me. May I have it please?'

When she had finished reading, Mrs Mount folded the letter back into the envelope. 'Fidelis, I must apologise to you for the distress of the last few weeks. I shall give you your wages and reimburse you for your lost employment. My daughter will be away for some time. Will five pounds be satisfactory to you?'

Relief, anxiety and rage churned inside her. The money was far more than she had hoped for but there was something else. The sound of tapping at the door startled her.

'Come in, please.'

The maid was back with a tray filled with gilt-edged china. She set it down on the coffee-table between them. 'Thank you, Eileen,' Mrs Mount said, taking up the teapot. 'Now, Fidelis, please help yourself.'

She couldn't swallow a crumb. 'Please, I want a reference.' There, it was out.

'Most certainly you shall have it, but first do have some refreshment. It is a long walk from my daughter's house, you must be hungry.' After pouring them both a cup of tea she went over to the desk by the window. 'I shall write one for you this instant. Please, help yourself to whatever takes your fancy.'

Fidelis tried to drink her tea without slurping, but her hand shook. As she set it back on the saucer a clock somewhere chimed ten. There was the day just started, and yet she felt as if she had lived a lifetime since leaving home that morning.

2

Phoebe Allen had been terrified when the tradesman burst through the gate and demanded to see her husband. For his part, James seemed to have lost his reason, punching the grocer and smashing his glasses. Alerted by all the commotion, one of the neighbours had telephoned the police.

Only hours before, James had confessed to putting up the deeds of Clarendon House as collateral against his latest gambling debts.

Phoebe was incredulous. 'What deeds? You know the house doesn't belong to us. It comes to me when I'm twenty-five from Daddy's estate. We'll be summonsed for false pretences.'

'It isn't the police we have to worry about,' her husband said, his face chalk-white and voice shaking. 'When Monty Vaughan finds out I've welshed on him he'll come around with guns blazing.'

'He wouldn't shoot you would he?' Phoebe had whimpered.

'We'll be long gone, darling. What we'll do is go up to London and make a new start. We'll get Fidelis to take Sophie to your mother's and then we'll make a run for it.'

After the fight, he was at the police station all night. Phoebe had paced about the empty house waiting for him to return, sick with worry, imagining every creak of a floorboard or rattle of a window-pane to be Monty Vaughan come to get them.

James did not come back until late the next morning, after a night in the cells and a severe caution from the duty sergeant for ungentlemanly behaviour.

'Jumped up fellow,' he raged, brushing his sleeve as if to remove all taint of the police contact. 'Put a nobody in uniform and they get ideas above their station.'

'What about Monty Vaughan?' asked Phoebe. 'He could come around at any minute.'

Her husband's earlier bravado vanished. 'What money have you got? And don't forget to pack your jewels. Now Sophie's taken care of we must go. Don't just stand there wringing your hands, get your things together.'

She had taken the sum set aside to pay back Mummy for her last loan to them, only a week ago.

Now, sitting opposite her in the train in a shabby overcoat, James looked positively seedy. Her own outfit had come out of the dressing-up box: a feathered hat and a jacket in a horrid shade of brown, making her look like a bedraggled sparrow. Never had she worn second-hand clothing before. When they got a few stops along to Havant Station he changed his mind.

'Leave that book in the carriage, it'll put them off the scent.'

And so it was that *Silas Marner*, Mummy's Christmas present last year, laid a false trail. The plan was to sell Phoebe's jewels and make for America.

'We'll get through this dreary patch and then we'll be in a new country. In a few weeks you'll be the belle of New York. We'll have made a new life for ourselves.'

Brighton had always been such a treat, staying at the Metropole and strolling down the whole length of the pier with Daddy. Now, with money in short supply they were obliged to see the seamier side of things. Mon Repose in one of the side streets well off the seafront was a disappointment to say the least.

'We're on the run, darling. Slipping through the net,' he'd whispered, as they sat in the dining-room sipping tepid Windsor soup.

The reality of their situation wasn't nearly as exciting as the detective stories he used to read to her. Being the quarry now, herself, worked her to such a pitch she could hardly swallow. Looking at the clock, Phoebe realised it was the time when she would have been called up to the nursery to say good-night to her daughter.

'What about Sophie?' she had asked, missing her baby.

For a moment his *joie de vivre* paled. He wouldn't meet her eyes. 'We have to make sacrifices if we're to grasp our chance. Your mother adores the child and she'll have the best of everything. In a few weeks she'll have forgotten us. Face it, you were never the doting Mama.'

'But I did love her in my way,' Phoebe said, stung by his bluntness. She remembered the wonder she had felt at holding Sophie for the first time, and saw the perfection that was her child. Feeding her, having her at the breast, drawing nourishment from her alone had been so satisfying. 'She was so pretty,' Phoebe pleaded. 'I looked forward to dressing her up and watching her grow. And she loved us. Look how excited she was to see you whenever you went into the nursery.' The thought of being so quickly forgotten brought on the tears. Sophie loved her unreservedly and called her Mummy, now. The thought that she would soon be replaced, in her daughter's affection, by Grandma was unbearable.

James wouldn't meet her gaze. 'If you haven't the pluck to see this through, if playing dolls with Sophie is more important to you . . .' He shrugged.

Phoebe wilted under his scorn. She hated it when he sulked, it could last for days. Leaning forward she touched his arm. 'Why don't we do something for fun? Let's just have one day here when we forget everything.' She watched his mood change. He could always be wheedled away from the glooms with a treat. 'Nobody will be looking for us here, after all. What's one day?'

'And what shall we use for money?' he asked.

She could tell that the thaw was setting in. 'I found a ten-shilling note in the pocket in my old handbag. It's almost as if it was waiting there for us. Tomorrow we'll go down the Lanes to the jewellers but now let's have a frivol.'

At dinner that night, in the tawdry hotel, she sparkled for him, laughing at his jokes, drinking too much and later, in the bedroom she was abandoned. Not since before her pregnancy had she allowed James such liberty over her body.

'Being on the run suits you, my darling,' he whispered, before taking her again.

She lay in the darkness afterwards, feeling glutted with sex. And then, suddenly, the thought of Sophie asleep in Grandma's house stabbed at her. Tears leaked from under her lashes. Her dear little girl, she might never see her again. Tiptoeing across the floor she took a tooth glass out to the bathroom and filled it with water from the tap. It tasted like warm antiseptic lint and left her as thirsty as before. Climbing back between the sheets she lay curled around her husband, listening to him breathing in and out and tried to time her breaths with his.

He awoke the next day in a foul mood and complaining of a headache. Knowing how long he could maintain a sulk, she did not look forward to the day. In spite of his professed pain James polished off a fried breakfast, drank two cups of tea and sent for extra toast. They spun out an hour sauntering down to the Palace Pier, looking in all the shops on the way. James insisted she have her fortune told by Madam Zaza.

The booth was dim and smelled of cigarettes and cheap scent. The Russian fortune-teller's fingernails were bitten to the quick and her voice had traces of the East End of London rather than Moscow.

'You have an interesting hand, my dear. What a restless

soul, always drawn to beauty. Like a butterfly, you flitter, flitter, flitter—always searching for love.'

Something in her voice frightened Phoebe, and she withdrew her hand.

It began to rain and they left the pier, drawn to the blaze of lights across the promenade at the Brighton Aquarium. The clock-tower and the roof were studded with blazing bulbs advertising the 'Electric Exhibition'.

Like eager children they paid their sixpences and walked through the turnstiles. At first they were dazzled by the variety of exhibits, not knowing which to choose. Laughing, James accepted an invitation from a salesman to have his boots cleaned by an electric bootblack. He sat up on a chair amid a crowd of onlookers watching the brush on a metal rod whirr around his feet. Phoebe was fascinated by an electrically operated frying-pan, and watched the edges of a rasher of bacon crisp in the smoking fat. From there they watched a model train whiz along a track through the Scottish Highlands. In another exhibit they saw a replica of the King's bedroom, with all sorts of heating and lighting devices.

'Isn't it all splendid,' she said, grabbing his arm and walking down a long corridor between the marble pillars and potted palms. Flanked on each side were huge glass reservoirs filled with coloured rocks and gallons of bubbling water. In these fairy palaces swam hundreds of fishy inmates. The largest crystal cages contained porpoises and sea lions darting and diving, then reclining on the rocks. There were mackerel, seahorses and even tiny silvery sprats.

'Ooh look, there's an arrow pointing to the anemone gardens.' Phoebe was entranced. The colours astonished her. Waving purple tentacles hung from the rocks, feathery golden fern-like structures draped themselves around a stone mermaid, and tiny lime-coloured flowers sat amid the pebbles.

A sudden shock of pink caught her eye, as a fish she could not identify flew from side to side like an express train.

'Let's top it off with tea at Hanningtons.' James squeezed her fingers. 'I think an afternoon nap is required.'

Phoebe blushed. It was like a second honeymoon, but even better because she wasn't so frightened. She had acquired a taste for swivel-diggle as he called it. He flirted with her outrageously in the tearooms, kissing her hand and playing footsie. She pretended outrage when he wrapped up two buttered scones and slid them into her handbag for later.

The next morning, they quarrelled when Phoebe awoke to find him searching through her handbag. 'I hate you doing that,' she stormed. 'Why can't you ask me if you want something?'

'Because you always make me feel like a naughty schoolboy, indebted to Mummy.'

Again his sulking ruined her breakfast. She sat in the hotel dining room, opposite him, on the verge of tears, hardly able to swallow. Yet it had not affected his appetite. James sat there, his newspaper folded on the corner of the table, oblivious to her, wading through a vast amount of sausages and bacon, studying the sports page.

Back in their room he continued to read, ignoring all her pathetic attempts at conversation.

'Please Jimmy, don't shut me out, you know it frightens me.' Phoebe could hear the cringing tone in her voice and hated herself for it. 'Let's go down the Lanes and see what my treasures are worth. Daddy always bought me the best.' She bit her lip, knowing James hated having his nose rubbed in her father's money.

He erupted out of the seat and flung her jewel-box at her. 'Here take it, I'll make my own way. Never let it be said I lived off your father's earnings,' he snarled, dragging on his coat.

Panic-stricken she ran forward, sinking onto he▮

grasping his legs, terrified of being abandoned by him. 'Jimmy, please, please don't leave. I'm sorry, I'm sorry, I didn't mean it. Let's go and have coffee at Hanningtons again and take our time. You know that none of it is mine now, truly, it's all ours. Let's go up to London as soon as ever we can. We're in this together, every step of the way.'

'That's my brave girl.' James turned and carried her back to the bed.

Phoebe sighed. He really did love her, it was just that he was so highly strung. After he had locked the door, she closed her eyes and gave herself up to his practised seduction. Always, at the peak of pleasure she cried out and then he would hold her in his arms until sleep came.

Awakening later in that poky little room, even though they had been there for three days, was still a sickening shock. The sun seeped through the dusty slats of the Venetian blind and revealed all the shortcomings of the third-rate Brighton hotel. It was then that she pined for her bedroom in Southsea: the satin quilt and the lace-edged pillowcases. She had only to reach out for the bell-cord and Fidelis would come and run her a bath, tipping in the lemon verbena crystals. Keeping warm on the rail would be the fluffy towel, and later would come the tray of tea and ratafias.

Phoebe thought of Sophie, her face all rosy in sleep. She did love her, she did! Suppose when she went back again later, Sophie didn't know who she was? Tears welled in her eyes.

Living with James was such an up-in-the-air existence. He demanded every minute of her time and attention. There were moments of intense joy and deserts of loneliness. Waking up each morning she never knew to which point of the compass his mood would swing. Being made love to in the morning was disorientating. Phoebe ran her hand over the bedside table for her watch.

She opened her eyes. James had gone and with him her

jewellery and her watch. He would be in the Lanes, now, setting her pearls on the counter. Would he part with her garnet earrings? How about the gold locket? Her father had given it to her on her twenty-first birthday. It had been just before he became ill and the nurses moved in. Poor Daddy. Phoebe drew the matted blanket around her. She wrinkled her nose at its smell, a stale blend of other people's breath. What would he think of his darling girl getting herself in such a fix? No, if she thought any longer about her father she would be done for. Her mother would probably be relieved to be shot of her troublesome daughter. She had certainly been a disappointment to her. Being pretty had never impressed Marcia Mount. She could hear Mummy's voice ringing in her head.

'Phoebe! For goodness sake, stop primping and preening. Why did you put that cake on your plate if you had no intention of eating it? There are children in this town in poverty and want while you squander what's put before you.'

Once in a tantrum she had answered back. 'I'll post it to them, then. They can have the Battenburg slice, and the lemon-curd tart and the chocolate sponge.'

Her nanny sent her to bed with no supper. Worse was to come. Worse than a smack, Mummy had given her best party frock to Cook's daughter. How was it that mother and daughter were so at odds with one another – could she have been adopted? And yet, the maids loved Mummy. She was always so interested in their lives. Phoebe was ravenous for her mother's love, desperate to be taken on to her lap and cuddled. Even a lecture was better than her indifference.

Her life changed when she met James who was as greedy for fun and pretty things as she was. Life suddenly sparkled. It was only when she had Sophie that doubts wormed their way into her mind. It was ages afterwards that they resumed lovemaking. He said she smelt of stale milk and that she had let herself go. It was rarely that they went out together any more and he took to coming home later and later. Their money melted away. When she humiliated herself by asking her mother for help, it was refused.

'Phoebe, there are a hundred and one economies you could make. When I see that you are taking your position seriously I will see what I can do. In the meantime, I suggest your husband cancels his account with his tailor and settles your debts.'

James had been furious. 'The penny-pinching gorgon, does she want her granddaughter to starve?' He had flung out of the house and not returned until the next day.

Then there was that business with Molly. He had sworn that nothing was going on. She had seen the girl some months later, in Palmerston Road, just as it was getting dark. She was arm-in-arm with her father and heavily pregnant. Everything had gone from bad to worse. Phoebe bit her lip. It was when she was alone that fears rustled around her like falling leaves. Would they be able to start a new life in America? Could one really step away and leave the past behind?

She got up and padded barefoot to the window, and peered out at the clock on the church tower further down the street. It was only half-past eleven. Should she go and meet James, in the Lanes? There was the risk they might miss one another. Having missed breakfast Phoebe began to feel hungry. Perhaps she could have a tray sent up to her room. Instinctively she reached for the bell-pull. But in Mon Repose room service was not provided. She would have to go downstairs and face Miss Fullick at the desk by the front door. The owner had a way of withering you with a look, and an irritating habit of clicking her tongue when asked for favours. When she had asked for an extra blanket that first night she had sighed.

'I'll send Phyllis up with the blanket when she's finished serving dinner. Perhaps if you closed your windows at night you would not need extra bedding.'

Phoebe had slunk up the stairs feeling like a naughty schoolgirl.

No, she would not put herself through that humiliation. James would be back at any moment in triumph. They might even dine out in some out-of-the-way restaurant. She poured herself a glass of water and opened the wardrobe.

The shock drove the breath from her body. His clothes were gone, his suitcase and her jewel-case. Panic clenched at her stomach. She rushed along to the lavatory and vomited thin brown acid into the bowl. Back in her room, Phoebe locked the door and cocooned herself in the blankets. He was not coming back. James had made love not because she had aroused him but to stupefy her while he made his get-away. For the first time since leaving boarding-school she sucked her thumb.

It was cold when she awoke. At first Phoebe was in a muddle and then it came to her: James had abandoned her. Dragging on her dressing-gown she went to the window and once more checked the time – it was half-past two. There was still half a glass of water and the scone in her jacket pocket. The water tasted warm and the scone was stale and hard to swallow.

'We will make a new life for ourselves.'

James's words had sounded wonderfully exciting. Now she wanted her life back, to be his spoilt darling. Phoebe knew she couldn't do it on her own. Always when faced with unpalatable facts, other people had smoothed her path. She was accustomed to floating on the froth and now the plug had been pulled. There were no rescuers. It dawned on her that she might not have enough money to settle the bill. Other people, not her sort of people, did moonlight flits. Tipping her purse onto the table she counted out twenty-five shillings. Three nights' accommodation with breakfast for the two of them amounted to fifteen shillings. What could she do? How long could she live on ten shillings? If she paid her bill she would be entitled to breakfast tomorrow. But for now she would go into Brighton and have tea somewhere, perhaps visit the aquarium again. Eating alone would be a rehearsal for what might come later.

Gathering her washing things, she crept out onto the landing. The toilet was engaged. In the bathroom the tap made alarming noises and she filled the basin with tepid water. Standing in her petticoat she soaped herself before cleaning her teeth.

A man burst in. 'Why didn't you lock it?' he growled, banging out again.

Red-faced, Phoebe rushed back to her room. Fully dressed, she attempted again to visit the toilet. As she turned the handle the man in the shiny suit shuffled out. The stink sickened her and to compound her shame there was no lavatory paper. She sacrificed one of her lace-edged handkerchiefs and flushed it away.

After dressing in the least crumpled blouse in her case, Phoebe combed her hair and dabbed a spot of perfume behind each ear for Dutch courage. She buttoned her coat and left the sanctuary of her room.

On the promenade, the wind from the sea made her eyes water. Once inside the aquarium her spirits lifted – they had had fun here, together. But it was difficult to recapture the gaiety of yesterday. In the tearoom she tipped too generously to offset her awkwardness. Even the anemone garden failed to enchant her. Outside again, Phoebe shivered. The sky was grey and the sea the colour of over-cooked cabbage.

An empty evening lay ahead of her. In lieu of dinner she bought herself a bag of caramels and a penny novel to fill the empty hours. On the way up to the hotel she tripped over a paving-stone. Shocked and limping and with her knee burning, she made her way up to the hotel.

'Your husband not with you, dear?' Mrs Fullick asked, as Phoebe attempted to sneak past her desk.

3

It was the fifth of October, well into his leave period, and Lieutenant Daniel Herrick, late of HMS *Terrible*, was aching to escape the confines of home. He helped his mother down from the carriage and stood with her outside the Crinoline Church. It was an eccentric twenty-sided wooden building. Looking up at its domed topknot he smiled. 'It's for all the world like a tea cosy.'

'A tea cosy complete with staircase and minaret,' laughed Mother. 'Mrs Crinoline is an odd character, I grant you. Yet she has served her country well. Practical and fanciful, an amazing combination.'

Daniel remembered his father telling him how the church had been taken to pieces, and packed up and sent off to the Crimea to act as a field hospital. He wondered if her present resting-place would become a permanent fixture. Perhaps she was destined for yet another evolution.

By this time, his colonel father had alighted and acknowledged the adjutant's salute.

'Alicia, come along with you,' he said taking his wife's arm. The two of them entered the church with their son following behind.

Now, seated in the front row between his parents, Daniel prepared himself for an hour of tedium. Around him the congregation's faces assumed piety. As they knelt on the lumpy hassocks he saw his father, staring straight ahead. On his other side, Mama's eyes were closed and her lips moving in fervent prayer. They were like the lion and the lamb. Jasper wanted to rule his son and Alicia to indulge him. It seemed to him that most church-going was a matter of the carrot and the stick. God goaded man on the path to righteousness with the threat of hellfire and the promise of heaven. What do I feel, he asked himself? Was God a bearded Englishman, with a huge ledger, forever recording the failings of his creatures? And what of heaven and hell? It was all so implausible. Since service in China he had seen the suddenness of death, had lost his best friend Gregory Fox to a sniper's bullet. The only reality was what you could see and touch in the present moment. Then there was the puzzle of the Christian and the pagan. He had witnessed more humanity amongst the cursing lower ranks than amongst some of the clergy and professing believers. Were he not on leave his attention would have been taken up with the intricacies of Church Parade: the marching-in and marching-out, inspection and dismissal. Having the commanding officer as his father meant that he could never escape the chafing routine of regimental life. He looked around the church at the row upon row of blue tunics: all individuality suppressed beneath the King's uniform.

Drowsy in the early autumn sun, a bee droned past him. Daniel followed its flight around the congregation. Some women cowered as it approached, others nudged husbands to rescue them from the furry intruder. It landed on the front pew opposite, and a girl with red hair let it rest on her gloved hand. Calmly, half-way through the Creed, she got up from her seat and walked over to a brass jug that was full of flowers. Scarlet dahlias, they were. She set the bee down among them before resuming her seat. It was the girl on the jetty. Daniel willed her to look at him.

The congregation rose. The band took up their instruments and played the introduction to the second hymn: '*Fair waved the golden corn in Canaan's pleasant land When full of joy one shining morn went forth the reaper band.'* That incident of the hat, two days ago, had been over almost as soon as it began, but while it lasted they had sparked with mutual attraction. As he continued to gaze at her, she blushed and looked away. All pretence of following the service was gone. He must speak with her. As the vicar climbed into the pulpit and began his weekly castigation, Daniel studied her. It was her colouring that first drew the eye, all that glorious red hair. But there was something else – an independence and lack of pretence. Although tall, she had none of the round-shouldered shrinking that most women affected to minimise their height. She was like a long-stemmed lily. It was the same hat, he was sure of it. But there was a new ribbon with trailing ends that almost reached the collar of her jacket. He wanted to peel back that glove and kiss her hand. Again he stared at her and she stared back, challenging him to look away first. He had never seen such eyes – were they green or turquoise? He wanted to kiss the sprinkling of freckles on her nose – and then his mother prodded him with her parasol. It was time to bow his head for the blessing: the service was at an end.

He cursed the protocol that demanded his father leave first and he and his mother follow afterwards. Outside, the aide-de-camp was waiting beside the carriage to convey his colonel to the dais at the parade ground to take the salute. The band had formed up behind them, and the adjutant was primed to give the sergeant major the signal to march. Freed from company inspection Daniel walked the few yards back home.

'We must look sharp,' said Mother, tugging his arm. 'Arthur Palmer will be here with Maude at twelve-thirty on the dot. Darling, do stop dawdling, Pa wants you to be especially kind to her. Poor child, she lost her mother last year. I think she finds these social occasions something of a trial. For my sake, Daniel, be your most charming.'

Arthur Palmer was the Admiral Superintendent of the dockyard and a great friend of his father. He knew Pa entertained hopes of him paying court to Maude. Sometimes he felt like a prize bull being led into the breeding-pen. As they approached the officers' gate leading towards their residence, he looked back at the Crinoline Church. Those not involved in the march-past were hurrying towards St George's Road to watch the band, and the Royal Marines set off towards the seafront. He searched the figures milling about but the tall redhead was not among them.

Fidelis barely heard what Auntie Ruby was saying. Unconscious of what she was doing, she followed her neighbour back to Gibraltar Street.

'That sergeant in the band weren't a patch on my Norman for playing. He was all fuzzy. I don't reckon he can blow his nose let alone a bugle. Of course, that was what drew me and Norman together. He could melt a heart of stone with his bugling. You heard from Harry lately? He was that thrilled at getting engaged. It'll be the making of him. Young lads need a woman to steady them.'

With a start Fidelis realised that Harry's letter was still unopened on the mantelpiece. She couldn't marry him now. Almost without thinking she had drifted into saying yes. They were pals and she had wanted to please his mother. When she had spoken of Harry's proposal, Auntie Ruby had burst into tears and Uncle Norman had hugged her soundly. There was a whole world of feeling that she had not known about when she had said 'yes' to the engagement.

'I'm that glad, Fee. What a party we'll have when my boy gets home. Push the boat out good and proper.'

They were the parents she wished were hers. Mr and Mrs Dawes always looked out for one another. They kissed and hugged, laughed and teased. It was Auntie Ruby she had gone to when the curse had come when she was thirteen. Walking home from the barracks school, terrified she was bleeding to death, it was her homely features she looked for.

''Tain't nothing to be worked up about my pet, it's a stepping-stone to being a woman. Your mother will give you some cotton squares to wear each month.'

'Every month,' she had gasped. 'Can't it be stopped?'

Auntie Ruby had hugged her, dried her tears, and promised to tell Ma for her. Now something even more momentous had happened, but this time Aunt Ruby was the last person she could confide in.

She wanted to be on her own to relive the moment when Lieutenant Herrick looked into her eyes. He had remembered, she was sure of it. It was like the sudden fizz when a branch catches fire. The air had crackled between them. As he and his mother walked through the gate to their house, he had turned and looked for her. This was what fate had in store for her and she must be dauntless in pursuing her goal. There were always obstacles in the path of true heroines, and looking at the colonel's son, Fidelis recognised the scale of her challenge.

Daniel held out the chair for Maude Palmer then seated himself beside her. Poor girl, she was paralysed with shyness. A nervous flush stained her neck, and his attempts at conversation seemed to intensify her discomfort. At one end of the table sat Father and at the other Admiral Palmer. Both of them, used to commanding attention, were not natural listeners. They boomed away at one another like cannons across a battlefield.

'What d'you think of this Selborne Scheme, Jasper? Common entrance and training for Royal Marines and our naval cadets?'

'Capital, old man, badly needed, that Jacky Fisher of yours

is a fellow to watch. He's going to put scientific gunnery on a proper footing at last. It'll give Royal Marine officers a better understanding of seamanship, when they're on board, and our fellows more respect for your gunners.'

'Dining with me, next week. Care to join us? Percy from the *Terrible* is coming too.'

There was a pause as the steward served the admiral his soup from the silver tureen. Daniel's mother set down her spoon and smiled at their female guest. 'I believe your home is in Kent, Maude?'

'Yes.' The girl stared at the tablecloth. 'We have a farm near Cranbrook, and orchards.'

'You must miss the countryside,' Daniel said, endeavouring not to look at her.

'I miss the trees and the fields and my dog, Russet.'

'Could you not have brought him with you?'

'He's a farm dog,' she said, crumbling the bread roll on her plate. 'The dockyard would be far too noisy and strange for him.'

And for you, thought Daniel, feeling sorry for the motherless girl thrust into a world of men and ships.

As if reading his thoughts, she said, 'I miss my friends and my painting. Father is frightfully busy.'

Mother smiled at her. 'Maude, you must come to one of my teas with the wives, here. They are such a merry lot of young women.'

Daniel passed her the bread sauce after the steward had helped her to roast beef and vegetables. 'What sort of painting do you do?' he asked, without much interest.

She looked at him for the first time. 'I'm recording all the fruit and flowers that are native to Kent. It will take me ages.'

He smiled at her, having no idea what to say to keep the conversation going. The meal staggered towards dessert.

Father and the admiral continued to boom away at one another. And then he was put in the spotlight.

'So, Daniel,' asked Palmer, 'what d'you think of your Captain Percy? Splendid fellow, what?'

'Indeed Sir, I was not part of his crew, just a super-numerary given a lift home from Hong Kong.'

'What's your next posting?'

'I don't know, Sir. I have three weeks leave and then, perhaps, further gunnery instruction at HMS *Excellent*.'

'Hrrmph! We are going down to Kent next month to the farm. You must look us up. The shooting's first-class.'

'If I'm free to do so, Sir,' Daniel replied, praying that a posting would rescue him from spending time with the red-faced old buffer. He had no interest in Maude but felt sympathy for her, closeted with her father in that huge house in the dockyard. But experience had taught him not to offer his company to women he felt sorry for. They so easily mistook his intentions.

'Arthur, I have requested that cook make you a treacle pudding, I know it is your favourite.'

'Alicia.' Palmer clasped her hand in his meaty paw. 'You indulge me. I have not had such a treat since last we dined together.' He smiled. 'And custard, I trust?'

Daniel felt a wave of affection for her. Dear Mother, she always kept a record of her guests' partialities. She was effort-lessly kind to everyone.

The dessert was cleared away and the Stilton and port were brought in. Maude was taken into the sitting-room with Ma, while he was left to endure the dialogue of the deaf between his father and Arthur Palmer.

'Daniel,' said Pa, 'get your journal and show our guest your account of the defence of the legations at Peking. A joint operation with the American Marines, you know, Arthur. Makes interesting reading.'

Daniel got to his feet knowing any argument would be useless. He went to his desk by his bedroom window and took his journal from the drawer. Some whim made him look out across the beach. There was a black dog bounding across the shingle with a girl behind him. He reached for his binoculars. Focusing on the girl as she fastened a lead to the dog's collar he realised it was the redhead from church. Cursing his father and Admiral Palmer roundly, Daniel picked up his journal and slammed the door.

West Indies
Sunday August 31st
My Dearest Girl,
I think Sundays are when I am most homesick for you and Ma and Pa and all my friends at Eastney. If I close my eyes I can almost see you all sitting down to dinner. Funny things you miss, really, Ma's runner beans and her apple dumplings. I can picture her stood talking to me as she ran the iron over my shirt, then disappearing behind a cloud of steam. She always believed the best of me and I always wanted to make her proud.

What larks we had, didn't we Fee? Scrumping apples and fishing across from Hayling. Then there were the fierce draughts matches and card games with your Pa. We have always been the best of pals and I hope we shall become even closer when we are married.

Life here is a never-ending routine of: gunnery, band practice, bugling and cleaning. I am sick of the sun and long for an English winter, chilblains and all. It's strange that I left England thinking of you as my pal and now you are my sweetheart, yet we have hardly kissed. We have a lot of catching up to do.

I am counting the days until July next year. Won't that be a time for celebration?

Please, please, write soon. I am starved for a letter.
Ever your loving Fiance,
Harry.

Fidelis put the letter back in its envelope and slipped it in her hankie drawer beside the box containing the engagement ring. She didn't know how to reply. One look had changed everything. It had shown her that what she felt for Harry was not love but sisterly affection. If she were his sister she could write and tell him about the moment when she looked at Lieutenant Herrick and forgot to breathe. He would understand her alarm at finding out that his father was the colonel commanding the barracks. But even if he were still only her brother, Harry would not have understood that she wanted this man regardless of the consequences. That she was willing to overturn her life on the basis of two charged glances and one dazzling smile. Staring at the lieutenant across the church that morning, she knew he wanted her. It was just a matter of time before they met. Nothing had been said yet, but already they were conspirators. His eyes had spoken to the wildness that was in her for all of Ma's careful training. If Pa had not been so adamant that she be brought up in the Church of England in spite of her parents being Catholics, she would have had to go to confession once a week. Those charged glances this morning and her fevered thoughts would have had to be whispered into a priest's ear. If she had been a Catholic she would have been down the road to St Swithun's and not seen Lieutenant Herrick at all.

'It's guilt, guilt and more guilt,' Pa had said to her once, when she had asked him why they didn't all go to church together. 'I had the catechism beaten into me in Holy Ireland and I'm not having your soul interfered with by any priest. I changed my faith soon after you were born and I want you to grow up to love the Lord, not fear Him.'

Ruby and Norman had been her godparents and she had been happy to go to the Sunday service in the barracks. In spite of nothing being said in front of her, Fidelis knew it was a bitter thing for her mother to go to church alone. Sometimes when Pa was away she and Ma would say the rosary together or she would wait for her outside St Swithun's and they would walk home together. It was a wound that lay between the three of them with no hope of healing; something she did not want to think about today.

Fidelis stood at her bedroom window watching the marine, high up on the balcony of the clock tower, lowering the flag as the bugler sounded the sunset call. It seemed to signal the end of her girlhood. She held the scent bottle and whispered the name written on the label. '*Ensorcelée, ensorcelée.*' It pulsed through her like a magic spell.

Yet, it was absurd, the stuff of penny magazines. If she could only re-assert the sane, matter-of-fact side to her nature and pop this bubble of fancy, she would be saved. If only she could be her mother's daughter.

4

Her father's gasps and mother's groans awakened her, followed by the rhythmical banging of the bed against her wall. Dragging her clothes from the chair Fidelis crept downstairs. She stood at the kitchen sink scrubbing at her skin with a cold flannel, trying to wash away her knowledge of their intimacy. There was no joy in it and what followed was shaming to all of them. She dreaded the silent breakfast with her father's excessive politeness and her mother's open dislike. Pulling on her clothes, she clipped the lead to Ebony's collar and stole from the house. It was just light, with the October morning cold and clear. Fidelis broke into a run. In minutes they were crunching over the shingle of Eastney beach. This was the natives' part of the shore, no trippers ever ventured so far from the promenade. It had its own peculiarities. Clumps of cabbage and sea-kale grew on the stones, and in the summer there were blossoming weeds like mallow flowers and dandelions. The vegetation stopped well before Southsea and the piers.

She was the only witness to the rising sun streaking the sky with red and gold. Taking off her boots, she tied them together and parked them beside a rusty clump of weeds. Fidelis pulled the back of her skirt through to the front and tucked it into the waistband. Together she and Ebony ran down to the water's edge. Gasping, she advanced into the sea, her toes tingling. Shivering, she gazed and gazed at the unfolding day. Moment by moment her pulse steadied and her breathing slowed. Her mind emptied of painful thoughts and she recovered herself. It was now into the second week of October, almost three weeks since she had stormed out of the Allens' house. Three weeks of idling her time away between helping Ma around the house, and waiting and hoping for a glimpse of Lieutenant Herrick. The *Evening News* had not yielded any work vacancies that interested her. There were heaps of jobs for scullery maids, ladies' companions and cooks. She seemed to fall between two stools, being too experienced for the scullery and not skilled enough for the kitchen. With the tension between her parents she wanted a live-in position, but Ma cautioned her about leaping from one disaster to the next.

'Fee, you've got that few pounds in reserve and can afford to be choosy. What you want is a well-established place where you can build on what you've learnt already. Somewhere with a woman who knows how to run her household.'

Today she would present herself at the Servants' Registry in Commercial Road and see what they had to offer. Beside her, Ebony splashed and wallowed then plunged back onto the beach. Fidelis turned and laughed as he shook himself, sending out a million drops of water. He took off down the beach and she settled herself on the shingle to dry her feet and wait for his return. Concentrating on buttoning her boots, she did not hear the footsteps approaching her.

'Good morning.'

Startled, her eyes travelled up, past the polished boots and the blue uniform, into the face of the lieutenant from the *Terrible*.

'I thought you were a mermaid.'

Fidelis shook her head. She'd prayed for a glimpse of him and now, when she least expected it, he was here, stunning her into silence.

'May I sit down?' he asked, as if he were standing in her drawing-room.

It was wonderfully ridiculous. Nodding she said, 'Pull up a chair.' Then he laughed and she blushed. Close to, he was even more beautiful. The blond hair was familiar but the blue eyes and full lips were new discoveries.

'Who are you and where do you come from?' He pushed his hair from his forehead, revealing a white stripe hidden from the sun.

She could taste his voice like rich chocolate in her mouth. 'I'm Fidelis McCauley and you're Lieutenant Herrick.'

'Fidelis, what a wonderful name, how did you come by it?'

'It was my Irish great-aunt's name. She was a nun. I think my mother thought it would buy me into heaven.'

'I don't believe in heaven. Do you?'

Shocked, she looked away. Of all the words she had thought to say to him or the replies she had fancied to hear, this was beyond her wildest imaginings. Questioning heaven! 'I haven't ever thought about it.'

'I think that there is no hereafter, it's all here and now.'

'How? What d'you mean?'

'We get glimpses, don't you think? I saw a girl once, from the deck of a ship. The breeze lifted her hair and set it rippling out behind her like a glorious satin banner. A taste of heaven, if you like.'

Fidelis blushed. 'How about hell?' she whispered.

Now it was his turn to look away. 'The death of my brother Roderick, when he was seven. I came home from school and found his room empty. They hadn't told me. He died of measles and had been buried the week before. All the things I was going to tell him, the games we were going to play, melted away.'

Her hand flew to her mouth and he drew it into his own, curling his fingers over hers. 'How awful not to be able to say goodbye,' she said. 'I would be so angry.'

He squeezed her hand. 'I haven't spoken of it for years.' And then he smiled. 'And you Fidelis, what are your glimpses?'

She closed her eyes, savouring the warmth of his hand enclosing hers. The most recent was, of course, sighting him from the deck of The *Terrible*, but she would not admit to that. 'I think, winning the prize for singing when I was twelve. My mother and father came to the barracks school and I sang, all about being a pilgrim. I could see the tears in Pa's eyes and my voice just soared up into the ceiling.' Fidelis smiled. 'There was just one thing though, I wanted to sing, "She who would valiant be", instead of "he".'

'And what was the worst thing?'

'When I realised my mother and father didn't love one another.'

'When you're little your parents are the whole world, aren't they?'

Fidelis nodded, staring down at the stones, acutely aware of him kissing her fingers one by one. What other liberties might he take and would she let him?

'You taste salty,' he said licking the inside of her wrist, 'like a sea creature.' His tongue peeled back her defences, stirring her appetite. She felt exposed, found out, laid bare, unable to meet his eyes.

'I have told you my darkest secrets but not my name. It's Daniel.'

Fidelis was startled by his change of tack. 'I saw you in church with your mother and Colonel Herrick. I put two and two together. My Pa is a drill sergeant.'

'Aren't we more than our job titles? You think so, or you wouldn't be sitting here talking with me. We can be friends, Fidelis. I knew it when I saw you in church rescuing the bumble bee.'

'What sort of friends?' she challenged him. 'Will you invite me home to tea?'

'I wouldn't want to share you with anyone. I'd take you to Mulberry's in the High Street, opposite St Thomas's Church. The hot chocolate is superb. Come tomorrow, I dare you.' He got to his feet and brushed the sand from his trousers, then stretched out his hand and pulled her up beside him. 'Isn't there something in the Bible, about making the stranger welcome then finding you have entertained an angel unawares?'

'If you don't believe in heaven how can you have angels?'

'We could be fallen angels. Come tomorrow, and I might let you touch my wings.'

'Then you would be Lucifer,' she said, striking sparks from his argument. They stood together almost touching, trading word for word. At any moment the spell would be broken, a bugle call would ring out or someone walk onto the beach. It was Ebony leaping and barking across the shingle that drew them apart.

'Hello, boy.' Daniel patted his head. 'Oh, you're a handsome dog, yes, yes. Will you come too, old boy? There are railings outside, we could tie you up there.' He grinned at her. 'I'll see you at eleven on Thursday, unless you are afraid.' And then he ran from her, up the beach towards the gate leading to the officers' quarters.

Fidelis rushed to the water's edge and let loose a fusillade of stones. He had left her on the simmer and she didn't know how to reduce the heat. She wanted to run and run and run. Ebony returned to her with a drool-laden length of driftwood. She wrestled it from his mouth and raced across the beach. They ran and fought one another until her fever cooled. Taking the lead out of her pocket she called the dog and clipped it to his collar. Walking down from the beach she heard the bugle call for second breakfast at a quarter to seven, and was pulled back into her life. Pa would be cooking breakfast and her mother laying the table, her face unreadable.

As she got to the top of the road, Fidelis drew level with a woman in a large hat. 'Auntie, what are you doing out here?'

'Went out last night and never got home. I thought I might be lucky and charm a bit of breakfast out of Jack. I've a powerful fancy for a bit of bacon between me teeth.'

'I'm so glad to see you,' she said, hugging her fiercely. 'Where have you been?'

Shamrock laughed. 'You tell me your secret and I'll tell you mine?'

Fidelis smiled, hugging her conspiracy to herself. 'Look who I found on the beach,' she called, stepping indoors.

Her father laughed, 'Must of smelled the fry-up. What you doing this time of the morning? Thought you theatricals didn't climb out of your beds 'til dinner-time.'

'Jack, me darling, I haven't never been to bed. Was at a party in Southsea and you wouldn't believe the drink-swilling that went on.'

'That's off your territory. Doing a bit of social climbing?'

Fidelis felt the knot of unease begin to loosen. Whatever had happened last night between her parents would now be swept under the carpet. Shamrock would be star of the breakfast table and no one would question her movements.

'Good morning, Shamrock.' Her mother came out of the kitchen with a tray of tea. 'How are you? Let me take your coat, sit by the fire for a minute. It's a cold morning.'

'Grand to see you, Mary, looking neat as a new pin you are. I'll just get me hat off, that's it.' Looking a foot smaller without her elaborate headgear, Shamrock sat in the armchair warming her hands. 'I hear me pal Jimmy Allen has come unstuck. Wasn't that where you were, Fee, working for the family?'

'Until three weeks ago, I was. Now I'm looking for something else.'

'He needs a good thrashing, playing the Champagne

Charlie at the expense of ordinary working men and women,' Pa stormed. 'Getting stotious, while honest traders are trying to settle their bills. Thank God, you're out of there, my Fee.'

'There are plenty of good houses that would be pleased to employ you. You're a good laundress now, and from what you say I should think work with young children might suit you.'

Fidelis smiled at her mother. Compliments were rare. It was so easy to please her father and he was always lavish in his praise. What must her life be like, she thought. What does she feel, having all her values dismissed and her beliefs ignored? 'I'll lay an extra place for Auntie,' she said, going out into the kitchen.

When she came back Pa was reading to Shamrock from last night's paper.

James Allen, who had been arrested on the 21st of September after assaulting the grocer, Samuel Hogben, appears to have left the area owing several tradesmen considerable sums of money. When a police constable called yesterday, neighbours said they had not seen the Allens for several days. From the signs of disorder in the house their departure would seem to have been a sudden decision.

'How well did you know him, Auntie?' Fidelis asked, setting down the cutlery.

'Everyone knows Gentleman Jim. A dab hand at the devil's prayer-book that fellow. But he met his match with a friend of mine. Didn't he promise to put up the deeds of his house the other week? My pal called his bluff. Now, Jimmy's vamoosed 'cos the house was never his in the first place.'

'What's the devil's prayer-book?'

'Cards, Fee, you know, your clubs, spades, hearts and diamonds. Who'd guess that Jimmy's Pa was church minister?' She stirred her tea noisily. 'Strange creatures gamblers,' Shamrock said. 'I've seen hundreds lost and gained. Chancing everything on the one turn of the card. Not my idea of pleasure, not by a long chalk.'

Fidelis thought of little Sophie. What a disturbed life she had had, for a baby barely fourteen months old. Perhaps she was better off with her grandmother. She had seen the affection in Mrs Mount's eyes, and even the sour-faced Eileen had softened at the sight of the sleeping child.

Shamrock set about her breakfast with gusto, and talk between them came to a halt. Once the second cup of tea was finished she wiped her mouth with her handkerchief.

'We can do each other a favour, Fee. You're at a loose end and I'm in need of someone to set me house straight, get it on to an even keel, so to speak. I can give you five shillings a week. I can't say fairer than that.'

Pa laughed. 'You'll need a pitchfork to clean up that midden, I'm telling you my girl.'

Shamrock glared at her brother. 'Well, she'll be better off with me than she was with gentleman Jim and his missus. Least she'll be sure of her money.'

'There won't be any gentleman callers will there? I don't want Fee to mix with any, or there to be any.' Her mother's voiced trailed away in confusion.

Fidelis stared at her plate, knowing how her aunt would respond to such fears.

'You can be sure of that, Mary. Fellers there may be, but gentlemen, never.'

Refusing to respond to the bait, her mother concentrated on clearing the plates.

Shamrock turned and smiled at her. 'What d'you think, Fee? I'm not saying as you'd want it to be permanent but it would tide you over. I'd throw in some tickets for the show, and your tram fares.'

It would get her out of the house and she could certainly do with the five shillings. The disapproval of her parents always acted as a spur for her to take the opposite path. Her only anxiety was when she would be required to start. Pretending to have her mouth full, she delayed answering. She would not, could not, give up her meeting with Daniel Herrick for anyone. He was the most exciting thing ever to have happened to her. She must have the chance of knowing him better.

'When would you want me, Auntie?'

'Soon as you like, why don't you come back with me, now? No time like the present.'

'I'll put together a few things for Fee to take with her,' said her mother. 'A scrubbing brush, carbolic and washing soda, I've a spare iron and some cleaning rags. Fee, go up and get your aprons.'

'I'm not a savage, you know. I have all that stuff,' Shamrock bridled.

'It's just getting them out of the cupboard and using them, that's your trouble, girl,' teased Pa.

'Come on, Fee, get your things together,' said Shamrock, ignoring him. 'You can work your magic and turn my hovel into a little palace, so you can.'

They stood at the tram-stop chatting away. Fidelis had not laughed so much in ages.

Up on the top deck going down into the heart of Portsmouth, she watched the town come alive. Men in caps and working-boots pushed carts through the streets, some filled with cheap-jack furniture for a house removal, others with paint tins, putty and decorators' tools. Gangs of young girls hurried to the corset factories. Women in pressed clothes and polished shoes stood at the bus stops, waiting to go to the shops and offices in Southsea and Commercial Road. Sailors hurried towards the dockyard. On the pavements paper-sellers yelled the headlines, and flower girls filled their buckets with tight-curled chrysanthemums.

As Shamrock opened the door and took them straight into the kitchen of number seven Buckle Street, Fidelis set down her basket and gasped. How could anyone live like that? There was hardly an inch of space to set her foot, not a chair that was not draped with clothing or stacked with paper. The table was a stew of ill-competing ingredients. A bag of onions sat next to a crumpled pair of satin drawers, and a congealed pork chop sat on top of a sheet of music.

Shamrock laughed. 'I'm a thorough-going slut, I'll not deny it, but there's always better things to do than setting it straight – places to go and people to see. But I've done the circuit now and I'm drowning.'

'Done the circuit?'

'I move round the house from top to bottom. When I've lost track of one room, don't I move next door? I know, Fee, I should be disgusted with myself.'

'Ma would have a fit.'

'I would not let her come within a mile of the place. Already she looks at me like I'm something the cat's dragged in. But you're a real woman of spirit.'

'I don't know where to start.'

'Well, I let you into the tidiest room, it's all downhill from here.'

'How can you live like this? How do you ever find any-thing? What about your things for the theatre, your costumes and stuff?'

'That's in the care of Mrs Fitzroy. It's all kept in the Palace. I tell you what we'll do. I'll go to Carmenatti's and get us a cream cake apiece, and I'll come back and brew up some coffee and we'll have a council of war.' The door slammed behind her, and Shamrock hot-footed it to Commercial Road and the Italian pastry-cooks.

Fidelis rushed to the window and flung it open. Taking off her coat she went out into the garden and pegged it on the line. Fetching her basket, she poured some soda crystals down the blocked sink, riddled the ashes out of the range, re-lit it, and set a kettle of water over the hob to heat. Amassing all the dirty washing in a pillowcase she bundled it on the bottom of the stairs, and went in search of a tray to gather the unwashed plates. By the time Shamrock had returned, Fidelis was on her knees scrubbing out the kitchen.

'Fee, you're a jewel and no mistake,' she gushed, setting the ribboned cake-box on the mantelpiece. 'I'll just find the coffee and we'll be in business.'

'You'll open all the windows in the house,' Fidelis burst out. 'Wrap all these food scraps in newspaper, then you can scrub that table.'

'Jesus, Fee what's got into you?'

'It's you Auntie Shamrock, thinking we can sit here in this shambles and eat anything. Standing there, buttering me up, letting me slog away, and not offering to do a hand's-turn to help me. There's not one plate, cup or saucer fit to use.'

'I'll eat them meself. Aren't I paying you handsome to do it?'

'You pay me the money now and I'll stay the day. Tomorrow I'm busy.'

'Let me guess,' her aunt said. 'Would you be having a little tête-à-tête with that handsome officer I saw you talking to on the beach, this morning? You'd better be careful, my Fee. Playing under your father's nose. You're turning into a gambler.'

'It's nothing to do with you,' Fidelis flared, furious at having been spied on.

'Jimmy Allen lost everything because he couldn't leave the table, even when ruination was staring him in the face.'

'What's he got to do with it? I'm just having a cup of chocolate and talking.'

'You're fooling yourself, and I can well see the attraction, my darling. He's a gorgeous fellow – wouldn't I eat him up meself if he gave me a minute of his time. But I know when the stakes are too high. I know when the party's over and how to put it all down to experience.'

'I'm going, you can't stop me,' Fidelis blustered, to cover her fright.

Shamrock shrugged. 'A word to your Pa would do it. I wouldn't enjoy ratting on you, Fee, but it might be the best course before you're really smitten.'

It was too late. Now she had seen him she couldn't draw back. She was a gambler, risking everything on his golden smile. She was between the devil and the deep blue sea and her auntie knew it. Shamrock had all the cards in her hand, and wasn't she enjoying it. Secrecy was essential if Fidelis wanted to see him, and secrecy would have to be bought. 'I'll come early and come back afterwards and finish up.'

Shamrock hugged her. 'I think we're beginning to understand one another, Fee.' Picking up her handbag, she laid two half-crowns on the mantelpiece. 'I think there's a pretty little outfit upstairs, somewhere. One of the singers left it behind. Tall slim girl, she was. Would fit you a treat.'

5

Fidelis shivered as she walked up the High Street to Mulberry's Tearooms. The morning was fresh as a cut apple and everything seemed pin-sharp under her gaze. The leaves on a Virginia creeper became a scarlet shiver, and high up on the tower of St Thomas's church the golden galleon weather-vane winked in the sun. Gulls screeched overhead and a tram trundled past. She slowed her steps, not wanting to seem eager. There on the corner of Pembroke Street was Mulberry's, just as he had described it: flaking gilt paint and mullioned windows. As the bell tinkled on the door, she saw an officer's pillbox cap with the gold braid around it. He was there waiting for her. Putting down his newspaper, Daniel came towards her.

'Fidelis, hello.' He smiled and took her arm. 'Over here by the fire.' He helped her out of her coat then held out a chair for her. 'What will you have?' he asked. 'The teacakes look good, and the muffins. Hot chocolate or coffee, you choose.'

'Hot chocolate and a teacake please.' She let out her breath and felt her anxieties fall away. The smell of baking wrapped itself around her. Daniel reached across the table for her hands, warming them between his own. It was a grown-up treat and she was going to enjoy every crumb of cake, every grain of sugar and every second in his company. The waitress disappeared behind a curtain. They were alone.

'What have you been doing today?' he asked, kissing her fingers.

'Housework and riding along on the top of a tram. Oh, and probably wasting my time with a royal marine who thinks he is Casanova.'

Daniel grinned at her. 'He must be devilishly handsome.'

'He's got a mirror like the step-mother's in Sleeping Beauty, and it lies and lies.'

'I am meeting a real beauty with a cruel heart. She has a golden pin and sticks it into proud young men. The hissing of deflated pride follows her wherever she goes.'

Fidelis could not help giggling. This was the most fun she had had in ages.

'Where have you been? Working for your mother?'

'No, my Aunt Shamrock, she's a singer at the People's Palace.'

'How exciting. Do you go and see her there?'

'Sometimes.'

'I love the music hall. It has such energy. She must be big and brave to go out there on the stage and tame her audience.'

Fidelis laughed. 'Shamrock's bold and brassy and they love her. But she's got a beautiful voice when she's not clowning about.'

'Can you sing? I'm tone deaf.'

She didn't believe him. His voice was poured honey, coating her skin. 'Yes, I sing with Pa sometimes and Shamrock, mostly Irish songs.'

'Would you sing for me?'

Their words lay along the surface, like dealt cards, but underneath was wildness.

'Your chocolate, Sir and Madam.'

She was startled when the waitress appeared with the silver tray and the steaming cups. The teacakes were set in front of them with a dish of butter curls. There were miniature knives and forks with ivory handles, like doll's-house cutlery.

'So would you?'

'Would I what?'

'Sing for me?'

'You'll have to come to the concert, at Christmas in the barracks theatre. Though I expect it's too amateur for you,' she said, trying to sound indifferent.

'Why would you think that?' He challenged her. 'You don't know me. I'll be in the front row and I shall stare at you until you drop your music.'

'I would close my eyes and shut you out.' She had paid the concerts no heed, until that moment, scorning them as embarrassing homemade affairs. In taking part she would be playing a game, performing in front of everyone yet singing only for him.

'Will you close your eyes when I kiss you?'

She trawled the spoon through the sugar crystals, trying to hide her blushes. 'What have you done today?' she asked primly, beginning to cut into her teacake.

'I took my dog Tusker for a walk, I went into barracks and had my hair cut, and I accepted an invitation to go to Kent for the weekend. And, then I walked all the way along the seafront to an assignation with a beautiful woman.'

Fidelis smiled. Whatever the game, she was beginning to pick up the rules. 'I'm working for Aunt Shamrock at the moment. I used to work for a gambler,' she said. 'He ran off owing me my wages. But I gave him something to remember me by.'

'And what was that?'

She could tell he was eager to know. Now the action she had been so ashamed of became a daring deed of defiance. 'I punched him in the mouth.'

He roared with laughter. A couple entering the tearooms stared at them. Daniel straightened his face and pretended fear. 'I shall have to mind my manners, I can see. I've never taken tea with a lady prize-fighter before.'

'He deserved it.'

'Did he pay you after you had terrorised him?'

'No, his mother-in-law gave me my money and a good reference.'

Daniel smiled lazily at her, then, taking his napkin, leaned forward and wiped the chocolate froth from her lips. 'Eat up your teacake. I want us to have time for a walk, and there is a favour I have to do.'

'What's that?'

'I'll tell you later. How's the chocolate?'

Fidelis wrinkled her nose. 'A bit too sweet.' Now that the tearoom was filling up with customers she wanted to leave.

He called the waitress and paid the bill, tossing a sixpenny tip into the saucer. Setting his cap on his head, he held open the door for her and they walked up the High Street. Solid as the Empire, the town walls stood between them and the sea. High up on a niche the bust of Charles the Second stared down at them. Daniel took her hand and they stepped through the sally port and down to the wooden pier. The last time she had strayed this far from home had been with her father. Now, she was with whom – an acquaintance, a friend, or was he a lover? Fidelis shivered.

They sat on the bare boards swinging their feet above the water. 'Close your eyes and let the sun warm your face,' he said, lacing his fingers in hers.

She knew he would kiss her. She waited and waited, and when she was sick with waiting, his mouth closed over hers. His tongue traced the shape of her lips then darted between them exploring her, drawing out sweetness. 'You will see me again, won't you, Fidelis? We will be such friends.'

She opened her eyes, aware of two women on the beach, fishermen approaching the pier, and soldiers on duty at the Round Tower a stone's throw away. 'There are people watching us,' she whispered.

He chuckled. 'Let's steal away. I have to go to St Thomas Street, just behind the church.'

Her mood was changing from moment to moment like the arrow on a barometer. She swung from modesty to bravado, uncertainty to exhilaration. As if sensing her uncertainty Daniel said, 'Have I been too hasty? You are just so beautiful I couldn't help kissing you. Don't say you didn't want me to, for I won't believe you.'

'I'm saying nothing.' She looked away, not wanting to own up to anything.

They walked down to the small inner harbour at Camber Quay, watching the seagulls flocking as a man tossed fish-heads into the water. She revelled in the luxury of frittered time. At the Allens' she would have been feeding Sophie her lunch, ironing Phoebe's clothes or any of a multitude of tasks.

'Here we are,' Daniel said, stopping at a tall house with a dolphin doorknocker. 'I have to collect the mail for Captain Sellick. You don't mind waiting, do you?' he said, taking a key from his pocket. 'You can snoop around, it's quite empty.'

She swallowed, wanting both to step forward and draw back. It was curiosity that eventually drew her over the doorstep. Her footsteps sounded loud on the bare floorboards and the air was chill. Inside the hall were pictures of men in naval uniform, while a sword in its scabbard hung on the wall beside the stairs. Holding open the door into the front sitting-room was an elephant's foot. Fidelis shuddered. Daniel gathered up the letters from the mat and stowed them in his briefcase.

'I shan't be a moment. I must just go upstairs and check the windows and make sure no leaks have developed since last night's rain.'

From the open doorway she peered into the room. Sunlight was filtering through a gap in the curtains and shining on one end of a cracked leather sofa. In the fireplace a copper coal-scuttle gleamed. The house smelled of pipe-smoke and neglect. Turning back to the hall she saw a newspaper on a side table, and spread it on the bottom step of the staircase and sat down to wait. Had he really needed to come here today or was it too good an opportunity to miss? The edge of danger excited her. What would she do if he dragged her upstairs and ravished her?'

'Gloomy, isn't it?' he said, sitting beside her, his voice loud in the empty house.

Fidelis blushed at her thoughts. 'This is an old man's house and he doesn't care for it much,' she whispered, acutely aware of the heat from his leg seeping through her skirt. She felt as she had at barracks concerts, dry-mouthed and fearful.

'Poor Fidelis, let me warm you up.'

He held her face between his hands and kissed her eyelids and then her mouth. The kisses were appetizers, teasing her palate. She wanted more and more and more. He stroked her neck while his tongue slid into her mouth, stealing her breath. She was drowning.

'Take off your hat, Fidelis,' he whispered, 'I want to touch your hair.'

She drew out the pearl pin and set it with the hat on the dusty table.

Daniel took out her hairpins one by one, then combed his fingers through her hair until it hung loose around her shoulders. Slowly, rhythmically, he began massaging her head. 'You are a glorious present,' he whispered. 'I want to unwrap you and enjoy every morsel.' They kissed again, deep drenching kisses. He stroked her neck, walking his fingers along her collarbone, having them disappear beneath the neckline of her jacket. Teasing, advancing, retreating, he wooed her.

She was floating without thought, cast adrift, in thrall to his touch.

Rat-a-tat-tat! Fidelis leapt from the step, sinking down again dizzy from the sudden movement. 'Someone's coming,' she whispered, panic-stricken.

'No, no, Fidelis, shh! shhh! The second post, that's all it

is.' He put his arms around her and she leant against him, waiting for the world to stop spinning.

'We ran away with ourselves, caught fire, and now we have been rescued.'

It was all moving so fast. Relief and disappointment surged like tides inside her. What if they had not been interrupted? Feeling foolish, she picked up her hairpins. 'I want to tidy myself,' she whispered, avoiding his eyes.

'There's a mirror on the first landing by the oriel window. I'll go and check the back door and the kitchen.' He came back into the hall and looked up at her.

Fidelis was flushed and her eyes fever-bright. His presence made her clumsy, her hair slippery under her fingers. As she set her hat straight she could not look in the mirror and face herself. Little had happened beyond kissing. But she wanted more. He had set her alight and she was still smouldering.

'Are you all right, my sweet girl?' he said, coming across to her and kissing her lightly on the cheek. 'Next time we'll have a picnic and I'll bring some cake and wine. You would like there to be a next time, wouldn't you?'

Fidelis delayed answering, busying herself re-buttoning her coat. 'I'll have to see. I may be working somewhere.'

'It will have to be Wednesday fortnight, in the afternoon. If you can't come, post me a letter to this address. We'll say two o'clock, I'll wait until three.'

'How will I know if you can't come?'

'I'll write to your Aunt Shamrock and I'll keep an eye open for you walking on the beach. Now just one last kiss to seal our friendship.'

He drew her down onto the first step of the staircase, kissing her softly, making her want to cry. She pressed her fingers over his lips, tracing the contours of his mouth, smoothing the blond hairs of his moustache.

'I want to run away with you,' he said, 'but now we must

go before you steal my wits.' He sprang to his feet and pulled her up beside him. 'Come on Fidelis, let's walk and talk. Where shall I leave you?'

'At the tram stop on the Hard. I have to go back to Shamrock's and change into my own clothes. I don't want my ma to see this outfit or she'll ask questions.'

'Are you good at keeping secrets?' he asked, holding the door open for her.

'I will have to be,' she said, stepping onto the pavement. Coming out of the gloom the autumn sun seemed dazzling. There was a more companionable feeling between them now and they talked easily together. 'What will you do with the rest of the day?' she asked, as they neared her tram stop at the Hard.

'I shall lunch with Mother and play billiards with some of my chums. Tonight I'm off to a dinner in the dockyard. What will you do at the magnificent Shamrock's?'

'She'll be at rehearsals now. Then she'll come back and run through her songs on her own piano. Would you like to see her? I can always get tickets.'

'Would you come with me?'

Although the Peoples' Palace was miles away from Eastney, they still ran the risk of being seen together. What if one of Harry's friends saw her with Daniel? Guiltily she thought of her engagement ring sitting in her bedroom. 'Yes, I might do that.'

With the arrival of the tram the morning was gone.

Daniel squeezed her hand. 'Until we meet again,' he said.

Shamrock watched her niece coming towards her. By God she was a beauty, just on the verge of all that life had to offer. The girl had that special ingredient, style. It was in the way she held her head and how she moved. It was something inborn; a natural grace. Looking at her, that young lieutenant must have thought himself dead and gone to heaven. Now was the moment for her niece to draw back and no harm done. It was sure as shooting that he would want more than kisses. What he would not want, not in a month of Sundays, was to marry her. Shamrock sighed. It was a risky time for a woman, with your body telling you one thing and your head another. You believed that moonshine would last and honeyed promise be kept. As Fee drew nearer she stepped away from the window, not wanting to be caught snooping.

'Thought you had a rehearsal, Auntie.' The girl was in a daze.

''Twas only a dress-fitting, tomorrow we run through the new numbers. Wednesday's a quiet night. Had a good morning? I'd say someone's put a glow in them cheeks. Was our Romeo waiting for you with his breath on fire?'

Her niece blushed and looked away.

'If he's got anything about him he'll be counting the hours 'til he sees you again.'

'Shall I get us something to eat? There's that salt beef left over from yesterday and some of Ma's pickles. I'll put the kettle on.'

'Change out of that frock, don't want to get food down it. I'm giving it to you. The colour and cut of the jacket is made for you. Now, off you go upstairs, chop-chop.'

'Auntie, d'you really mean it? Can I keep it up here? Ma would never— Oh it's lovely.' She hugged Shamrock then darted away to change.

Later, as they sat over their sandwiches Fee surprised her. 'D'you think you could teach me to sing? I want to do something for the Christmas Concert at the barracks.'

'You can sing already, my chick. If I remember the last time I went to that tin-pot theatre it was a real ragbag affair. Why would you want to waste your time with them? Unless of course our Romeo is putting in an appearance.'

Fee's guilty look told her she had hit the target. 'What's it worth to me?'

'I'll give your bedroom a clear-out, a real dockyard job, and I'll clean the windows. Didn't you say the sailor man was coming on Friday?'

'Fee, you're a chip off the old block,' she chuckled. 'It's good to have you as my pal. You go and light the fire in the front room and I'll have a look through my music and see what I can find to suit your voice.' Riffling through the song sheets, Shamrock was lost in thought. If he knew the half of it, her brother Jack would be raging. But Fee thought herself in love with this fancy marine and would not be talked out of him, that she did know. It would end in tears, but the heart-stopping power of first love was something she remembered all too well.

'This room, Auntie, it's clean and polished as if it's in another house.'

'Ah, well, this is where I work at my profession. I have a voice to look after and words to learn. I am a performer. People pay money to see me and I never send them away disappointed. If you want me to help you, Fee, you've got to do as I say. It'll be practice, practice, practice. I don't want you going out at the barracks and making a show of me. Are we in this to the finish?'

Fee laughed. 'Do or die, Auntie. I want to be the best that's in me.'

'Grand! Now, give me a song and let me see what we're working with.'

Shamrock was impressed. 'You're lucky Fee, you have perfect pitch but you need to work on your breathing. Simplicity's the thing with Irish songs, and feeling. You work on those scales and you'll be soaring above all the others.'

Her niece laughed. 'It's all so different to how I thought it was going to be.'

'Fee, it's all suck it and see at your age,' she said, knowing

Fee was talking about more than singing. 'If you want something you've got to pay the price and not just in money. You'll likely make a show of yourself and shed a few tears, but don't waste your time in bitterness or hanging back or blaming.' She struck the tuning-fork on the piano top. 'Hear that, a second ago there was silence, a few more seconds, silence again. We're given our lives moment by moment, and have to squeeze out every drop of loving and learning, for there's no second go.'

'You're my best pal, Auntie,' said Fee hugging her soundly.

''Bye Fee, see you tomorrow. We'll conquer the world, you and me.' Shamrock sighed. Wouldn't she adore being nineteen again, with all her hard-won experience?

> *Dear Miss McCauley,*
> *My granddaughter Sophie is in need of a nursemaid and I feel you would be ideally suited to the task. Please call on me tomorrow morning at 9.30 to discuss the matter.*
> *Sincerely Yours,*
> *Marcia Mount.*

After reading the letter aloud Fidelis looked up to see her mother crying.

'Oh, Fee this is your chance, a proper position in a well-run household.'

Seeing Ma so happy she couldn't disappoint her. 'I shall have to write to Shamrock. It's a good thing I left her tidy.' She would miss being with her, they had had such fun together, but she needed a job that would last. At any time Auntie could be off on one of her tours and not be back for weeks. Fidelis sighed. She would have to live in, probably in the nursery, and how would she get on with the other staff?

'If you ask me, Fee, it's a good thing you've finished with Shamrock. Skivvying for her would teach you nothing.'

Fidelis laughed, to cover her irritation. 'Oh Ma, if you could see your face. There's no harm in her.'

'That's as maybe, but it's not the atmosphere I want you to be exposed to.'

'You make me sound like an orchid,' she said, taking the cup of tea poured out for her. 'I'm a servant when all's said and done. Sometimes you talk as if we're gentry.'

'It's a question of character and personal substance.'

'Oh, Ma.'

'Don't you dare condescend to me, madam.' The anger in her mother's voice startled her. 'You and your father mock my standards, laugh at my efforts to live according to my beliefs. I will not have you setting me at nought.'

'I'm sorry,' she whispered. 'I don't understand.'

'I want you to live up to your name, Fidelis, to be faithful in small things as well as the larger matters. You have it in you to be such a fine woman, yet lately you seem giddy and aimless. What is the matter with you?'

'Nothing Ma, I was only teasing,' she mumbled. Not since she had stolen the sweets at the Sunday school outing had Ma been so angry. It was not her fault that the Allens had flitted away, leaving her without any work.

'You've got yourself engaged to Harry without the least idea of what such a promise entails. Have you answered the letter he sent you?'

'I suppose you think I'm too young and Harry's not good enough for me,' Fidelis snapped, frightened at where the conversation was taking them. She could always charm her way out of difficulties with Pa, but her mother would not be diverted.

'I do think that. You are too young and careless of others' feelings. But it's the other way around, Fee. You are not good enough for him. He's loyal and kind and hardworking. What sort of wife would you be? I hope that he finds someone more worthy of him, and that is the truth.'

6

Phoebe had just enough money to buy a train ticket home. It had been a horrid, horrid time. She hated Brighton, or the part of it she had been forced to inhabit for the last three weeks. Sinking down the social scale, trying to stretch the few shillings in her purse, it was as if the girl who had stayed with her father at the Metropole, all those years ago, was a complete stranger to the wretch she had become. If she could just take hold of herself this seaside nightmare could all be forgotten. By teatime she could be at Kelmscott, soaking in a hot bath, with Eileen in the kitchen laying her a tray of little delicacies. She could go back to her old bedroom and sleep till morning. Sophie would be there, waiting to see her mummy, chuckling with glee to see her. But it was facing her mother that was the stumbling-block to Phoebe. What it all boiled down to was a question of loyalty. If she chose Mummy, it meant she must give up on James.

In rational moments she knew he wasn't coming back for her. All she had been to him was a fine house and a fat purse. It was holding to that belief that was so hard. There was no earthly reason to suppose he would return to her, yet she had not been able to relinquish their room in Mon Repose in spite of Mrs Fullick's veiled scorn.

'Your husband still not back yet, Mrs Burne-Jones? Whatever do you think has happened to him?'

'I believe he is staying with friends in town, and will be back as soon as he has concluded his business.'

'I dare say. But in the meantime there's the little matter of your bill.'

And there it was, that horrid sceptical sigh of hers.

'I shall pay it in full this afternoon,' Phoebe had said, trying to affect outrage at being asked. But she had not her mother's dignity nor her bank balance. Waking in that room, now, brought her to tears of defeat. It was so vile. And even the chambermaid seemed to scorn her. She just dragged the covers over the bed with no effort at neatness. The sheets had not been changed for days, but she dare not complain.

In the library reading-room she held up the newspaper to hide her tears, as she relived last Thursday. She had wandered into the less salubrious streets of Brighton and found a pawnbroker's shop. Without the least idea of how business was transacted, she entered and approached the counter. Phoebe had had to wait while a woman with a coughing baby pulled off her wedding-ring and settled for a shilling. With head cast down and the child clutched to her, she shuffled out.

'What you got there?' he asked, with not an atom of respect. But why was she surprised? Her shabby clothes and lack of confidence gave no clue to her earlier life.

His tone altered when he examined the locket Phoebe placed before him.

'A beautiful piece, ma'am, fine workmanship,' he said, turning it over in his fingers. 'Look at that clasp, and hallmarked Birmingham. How much were you looking for?'

'The chain and locket are both hallmarked twenty-two carat gold. I think twenty pounds at least,' she said, mumbling the first figure that came to mind.

He raised his eyebrows at her, and smiled as if he were doing business with a child. 'I couldn't advance you more than ten pounds, the market being what it is.'

'I am in difficult circumstances,' she whispered. 'If you

can't give me at least fifteen pounds I shall have to go else-where.' She reached across the counter but the pawnbroker snatched the locket up.

'I need to look at it more carefully on my workbench. I shan't be more than five minutes.'

Phoebe had found the shop frightening, with its heaps of old clothes and blankets. In the glass cases lay every con-ceivable item of jewellery: necklaces, mourning bracelets woven from the loved one's hair, brooches with stones missing, pocket watches and, worst of all, wedding-rings. This was a warming of what lay ahead of her. In here was the smell of poverty: sweat, urine and panic. Hysteria flut-tered in her chest. Why was he taking so long?

The curtain separating the shop from the workroom twitched, and the man in the grey shirt and fingerless gloves laid the locket back on the counter. 'Ten pounds is my final offer. You won't get more round here. 'Course, you could go up the Lanes, but that's a tidy walk from here.' He smiled at her, his voice oily with sham sympathy, knowing her des-peration.

'Can I have the pictures from inside?' she whispered.

He shook his head. 'Wouldn't be able to get them out my dear, without them tearing. Besides, people likes a bit of history. Seeing folks better than themselves fallen on hard times. It gives them comfort.'

Phoebe was like a snail without its shell, smarting under his careless cruelty. Blinking, she stared at the locket Pa had given her, trying to draw from it his warm accepting love. Bereaved, she nodded her head.

'Ten pounds then, my dear. It can be redeemed up until December the twenty-second. After that it will be placed in the window for sale.'

She bit her lip.

'What name is it, for the receipt?'

'Mrs Burne-Jones.'

'And the address?'

She couldn't think. Were James's horrid gambling cronies still looking for them, and what about the police? Would she get James into trouble if she gave the name of the hotel?

'My customers' details are confidential,' the pawnbroker said.

'Walnut Cottage, South Harting, West Sussex,' she whispered. It was Granny Mount's house.

'You're a long way from home, my dear, a very long way.' He tried to press the notes and the receipt into her hand, but some fibre of pride made Phoebe hold out her purse rather than have him soil her fingers.

The encounter made her yearn for cleanliness and fresh linen. Her efforts at washing had resulted in her having to wear damp un-ironed drawers and camisoles. The hotel soap irritated her skin, and Mrs Fullick objected to wet things hanging from the window.

'It lowers the tone, Mrs Burne-Jones. We have a reputation to keep up. I can arrange for your things to be laundered if you wish.'

What reputation, she had thought, as she refused the woman's offer. Perhaps she could allow herself some new underwear and a bar of nice soap: what was the one she had at home? Rose geranium, that was it: she could see it nestling on the scallop shell beside the brass bath taps.

Her relief at settling her bill at Mon Repose had been enormous. She had discarded her old drawers in a copy of the *Brighton Argus*, and left them behind a hedge in the park. Her morocco leather suitcase was exchanged for a pair of woollen gloves after she lost her suede ones. Now, in the library reading-room, she was almost back where she started. The money from the locket had simply dissolved. Having managed a hot bath at Mon Repose and changed into her new garments, she had treated herself to a cream tea and a replacement copy of *Silas Marner*, along with a bar of her old, familiar soap. It had made her feel close to her mother. Those were the times when she had felt completely secure: tucked up in bed with the fire crackling and Mummy's voice bringing the story to life. But the happy moments were all in her early childhood. Once she began to challenge her mother, the affection was withdrawn. Marcia Mount's love was conditional. Her many accomplishments defeated her daughter and stopped her from even trying to emulate her. All Phoebe had was a doll-like blonde prettiness that made men smile and want to pet her.

It had been Mrs Fullick's bill that had taken the wind from her sails.

'Ten days' bed, breakfast and evening meal amounts to thirty-five shillings, Mrs Burne-Jones.'

Phoebe was left with three half-crowns and a farthing.

'I have a reservation for your room from tomorrow evening, so we must part company,' she said briskly.

In the sharp features of the hotelier Phoebe read scorn.

'I will gather my things and trouble you no further,' she had said, after forcing herself to eat a cooked breakfast and sneaking two pieces of buttered toast into her handbag.

'Shall I send the porter to fetch your luggage?' The woman smiled, knowing full well she had only a paper parcel to her name. 'If your husband comes back, where shall I say you've gone?' There was triumph in her tone.

'I will be with my mother in Southsea.' Phoebe had gathered her pride and just managed to sweep out of the door of Mon Repose before the tears came.

She couldn't understand herself. Here she was in the library with her bag under the table, still undecided. There was nothing to keep her here. In fact, she could not keep herself at all. It was that foolish, vain hope that, even at the eleventh hour, James would come and rescue her, that hobbled her attempts to rescue herself.

Phoebe had to decide. It was now five o'clock: either she went home to her mother or found enough money for a night's lodging. The thought of seeing Sophie again gave her courage. Her child's face swam before her, the dark eyes and the roguish smile and little pointed chin. Did she remember her? Would she hold out her arms to be carried? 'Sophie,' she breathed.

Sitting on the toilet in the Ladies she stared down at the green mosaic floor, and began to count the tiny squares as she tried to calm herself. The toilet paper was hard and scratchy and left her wet and uncomfortable. She sacrificed another handkerchief, terrified that she might smell of stale urine. In the mirror over the washbasin she combed her hair, and wished that she had taken the trouble to wash it. If only she could be certain she was doing the right thing. Out on the platform, Phoebe perched on the edge of her seat and stared down the track. She wanted two separate outcomes with equal desperation: James to come back to her and her mother's forgiveness. Anxiety fluttered against her ribs and her hands were slippery with sweat. If only there were a sign to indicate the path: something like God's voice from the burning bush speaking to Moses. Perhaps on Brighton station it could be a seagull with a frond of seaweed in its mouth. And then, belching steam, the train came towards her. Without volition she was caught up in a knot of passengers getting on and off. A man held the carriage door open for her, and she stepped aboard, then he had disappeared behind his paper. The whistle blew and, as the train began to move, Phoebe grabbed the handle and leapt out onto to the platform. The porter was too intent on slamming the door to notice her limping away. The pain in her ankle made her feel faint; she could hardly bear to put her foot to the floor, but she must get away. The noise and urgency of the station terrified her. Mixed with the fear was shame. She had panicked – let herself down, and Sophie. If she could just sit and rest somewhere, have a glass of water perhaps, then she could think what to do. It was only later, as she limped towards a chemist's shop in Queen's Road, that Phoebe realised she had left her handbag on the train going to Portsmouth.

7

Prompt at seven, wearing the black dress Phoebe Allan had given her, Fidelis left home. She took a battered valise, packed with a few clothes, in case she needed to start straight away. The upset with her mother had left her bruised and sad. When she and Pa fell out their grievances were soon forgiven, but with Ma reconciliation was slow in coming. Things had got worse lately, and her mother often frightened her with constant talk of death.

'I won't be here to be your conscience for much longer. You'll be on your own, and have to remember what I taught you and be a woman of your word.'

When had Ma become so pale and thin, she wondered? She had always had a cough, in the winter, but now it was there all the time. Ma had never been one for kisses and cuddles, but they had been close. She had told her stories about her life in the orphanage and the kindness of Sister Frances. Fidelis thought there was much that was glossed over but had never felt able to enquire more deeply. At twelve years old her mother had gone as a skivvy to a huge house along the seafront called Walburton, and worked until her marriage for Lady Gordon. She had the gift of storytelling and brought the house to life for her imaginative child. There were the dinner parties, with the starched linen napery, the heat from the candles flickering in silver sconces, ruby wine winking in crystal glasses and the swish of satin skirts as the ladies took their places. The air would be filled with the scent of roses and stephanotis. There was even a minstrels' gallery, and it was rumoured that a ghost violinist had been heard to play on winter nights. It became their place of enchantment – an escape from their routine lives in the married quarters at the barracks. If ever her mother was listless and distant, Fidelis had only to say, 'tell me about Walberton,' and her mood would lift immediately. Now, having worked for some years in service herself, she saw the stories for what they were – flights of fancy. Poor Ma was such a wise woman in many ways, and yet foolish and difficult to love.

Fidelis walked through the Eastney streets full of little terraced houses filled with sailors, marines and dockyard men's families. There were men in working-boots and shabby caps off to labouring jobs on buildings in the town; there was a window cleaner loading his cart with buckets; and some, more eager, housewives on their knees scrubbing their doorsteps. There was a liveliness here, with people whistling, singing or gossiping to their neighbours, that was absent in the more salubrious areas. Westward towards Southsea were the guesthouses in Festing Grove where skivvies washed the steps. She turned the corner near the seafront into Heron Park, full of villas owned by the wealthy such as Mrs Mount. Fidelis smiled. There should have been a hill between Eastney and Southsea to indicate the rise in fortunes from one district to the next. This time she approached Kelmscott by the back door. Walking through the yard, she remembered being frosty to the maid when last they met. For once in her life, humility was called for.

'Oh, it's you.' Eileen stood in the doorway and sniffed.

Fidelis smiled at her. 'Good morning, I've got an appointment at half-past eight with Mrs Mount. It's about the nursemaid's job.'

Grudgingly, Eileen stepped aside.

'Hope you're taking it,' said a red-faced woman standing at the table, spooning meat into a pie-dish. 'We bin run off our feet, not known if we was coming or going. Sit down, girl. There's tea there, help yourself.'

'I'll be pleased to have a place here,' said Fidelis, pouring herself a cup from a large brown pot. 'I was told Mrs Mount is good to work for. When I was at her daughter's house the cook reckoned she was top-notch.'

'What was her name?'

'Sarah Gibbons.'

'She a big woman with curly hair and eyes brown as boot-buttons?'

Fidelis smiled. 'The very same.'

'Knowed her I did from the Methodee church up on Highland Road. Voice like a bullfrog but that kind, give away her last farthing – got a wonderful light hand with pastry. Where she gone to, now?'

'Gone to Brighton to be with her sister.'

'Take off yer coat and get warm. Eileen'll tell madam you're here.'

She tried another winning smile on the mournful maid and the woman sniffed, in a more encouraging way, before closing the door behind her. In the scullery she could see a small figure standing at the butler sink and swathed in a sacking apron. She was washing saucepans.

'This here is our Midge,' said Cook, giving her an affectionate glance. 'She come from the orphans' home, a year since, we're knocking her into shape, ain't we gal?'

'Yes, Cook.'

'Step down and say hello, then.' She turned to Fidelis before lifting a circle of pastry via the rolling-pin and resting it over the top of the pie-dish. 'What's your name? I knowed it was something fancy 'cos madam told me last night.'

'It's Fidelis, after my great grandmother, means faithfulness.'

'That's sommat to live up to,' the woman chuckled. 'I'm Mabel Hobbs, but mostly I'm Cook 'cept for madam, she always calls me Mrs Hobbs. Bin here the longest, knows the place from top to bottom. Anyfink you wants ter know if it's in me powers I'll tell ya.'

'I'm Midge for midget,' the girl smiled. 'Cook's trying to fatten me up, to see if I grows any.'

Fidelis shook their hands. Cook's was warm and floury and Midge's wet and slippery, like a fish. 'How old are you?' she asked, thinking that she couldn't be above twelve.

'Fifteen on Christmas Day. Pleased to meet ya.'

'Madam's ready for you,' said Eileen, giving her a sceptical glance before setting down a tray.

'We got off on the wrong foot, last time,' said Fidelis, getting up from the chair and holding out her hand. 'Call me Fee, everyone else does.'

'Right ho,' a smile flitted across the maid's mournful features. 'Madam's with the baby giving her a bath. It's up the top floor, first door on the right. Reckon she'll greet you with open arms.'

'Fidelis, good morning to you.' Mrs Mount's voice came to her from behind a screen. 'Bring a chair around with you.'

She was astonished to see her employer in a nursemaid's apron, with Sophie on her lap swathed in a towel. Instinctively she took the bath and emptied it down the nursery sink. 'Good morning, ma'am,' she said, taking her seat. 'Hello Sophie, you look lovely and clean, has your Grandma given you a bath?'

'Gamma.' The child smiled up at Mrs Mount, giving no sign of having recognised Fidelis.

'As you can see, we are badly in need of assistance. These last weeks have been disrupting for everyone. Lie still darling, while Gamma fastens your napkin. I hope you have come to accept your old position. That will be the first step towards normality.'

While she was talking, Fidelis handed her Sophie's petticoat and dress hanging over the fireguard. 'Yes please, ma'am. When would you want me to start?'

'Would tomorrow be at all possible, Fidelis?'

Watching her, she saw that Mrs Mount was no longer the composed madam of the household, but a weary grandmother unused to the demands of a fretful baby. Her mind raced. How could she use the situation to her advantage? 'I could start today, madam, but there's just the question of my music lesson on Wednesday the twenty-ninth.'

Mrs Mount smiled at her, unaware of her barefaced lie. 'I'm sure that can be arranged. I shall leave Sophie in your charge. Eileen will bring you both some breakfast. Shall we say ten o'clock in the sitting-room? Then we can talk about the conditions of your employment.'

'Hello Sophie, you and me are going to be pals, just like last time.'

The child stared at her. One cheek was flushed and she tugged her ear.

'Have you got a nasty toothache?' She stood up and held Sophie in her arms as she toured the room. It had the look of being hastily pressed back into service. The carpet was worn and the curtains faded. The bed assigned to her had been made up with fresh linen but the quilt looked as if it had been pensioned off years ago. 'Let's see if we can find some toys in that cupboard. Then I'll sit you in your cot and we can set this place to rights. What d'you think?' She found a hairbrush on a battered trolley and sat down to brush the child's hair, all the while keeping up a flow of reassuring chatter.

'We used to dance and sing, Sophie, you and me. I'll just tidy those goldy curls then we'll take a peek in the mirror. Bo!' She showed the child her reflection in the glass, held her away, then showed it her again. 'Bo,' she cried and was rewarded with a chuckle.

The door opened and Eileen came in with the breakfast things. 'See you got her laughing. Madam's bin run ragged with her. I brought you her bottle, and porridge, a pot of tea and toast and jam. How that suit you?'

'Thanks ever so much, I'm starving.' She settled Sophie into her feeding-chair and tied a muslin napkin round her neck. As she began spooning porridge into the baby's mouth, Eileen perched on the bed.

'Where d'you think Miss Phoebe got to? Can't understand no one running off and leaving a little angel like her.'

Fidelis shrugged. 'They could be anywhere.'

''Course,' the maid said with some relish, 'that husband of hers could've done her in.'

Whilst they were digesting the possibility, a bell rang somewhere in the house and Eileen darted away.

Fidelis washed Sophie's face and gave her a couple of spoons to play with while she ate her own breakfast. So far so good, she thought, remaking the cot with fresh sheets. 'Come on, my pet, let's give you your bottle. The sandman is coming to take you off to dreamland.' She carried the baby around the room singing a song Pa taught her. 'Blow the man down boys, blow the man down.' Soon Sophie's eyes began to close. For a moment Fidelis thought of Phoebe holed up somewhere, lonely and frightened. In spite of the warmth of the nursery fire, she shivered.

Midge tapped on the door and crept in when Fidelis beckoned to her. 'Eileen sent me up ter say as madam's ready for yer.' She peeped over the bars of the cot at the sleeping Sophie. 'Ain't she a pretty little thing. I'd like to hold her, but Cook says I'm too clumsy.'

'I'll let you know when she has her bath and you can help me. That's if it's all right with Cook.'

'Ooh, ta ever so much, I looks forward to that.' She smiled shyly. 'Best get back or Cook'll fetch me one.'

'Enter,' Mrs Mount called. 'Ah, Fidelis, sit down, will you please. Is Sophie asleep? Ah, that's good.' She smiled encouragingly. 'You must have seen some changes in my grand-daughter since last you saw her. It must be over a month, now.'

'Lots, madam – Sophie can stand ever so firm, she'll be walking any minute.'

'Splendid. Now, I shall want you to get her into a sound routine of sleep, exercise and play. You will, of course, have one afternoon a week for yourself and one Sunday a month to visit your parents.'

'Yes, madam.'

Mrs Mount sat facing her, with her back to her writing-desk. She looked immaculate in a cream silk blouse and long black skirt. Her fingers fidgeted with a silver-topped pencil.

'Now as to your uniform,' she frowned. 'That dress is most unsuitable, black is very draining for a young girl. I have some green striped Viyella that would suit you well. I will get Eileen to bring it down from my studio. Can you sew, Fidelis?'

'Yes, but my mother is very good, madam. She would be pleased to make the dresses for me on her sewing-machine.' She thought quickly. 'When Miss Sophie wakes up, I could take her for a walk around to my house and drop the material in to my mother and she could measure me up and get started.'

'Excellent. I shall leave you to your duties and to get acquainted with the others. Please bring Sophie to me at five o'clock. I like to have an hour with her before her bedtime.'

'Thank you, madam, good morning.' Fidelis paused at the door. 'May I bring my quilt from home and some books and pictures please, madam?'

'Certainly. I wish you to regard the nursery as your home. We will redecorate it when Dorcas comes, she has an eye for such things.'

Who Dorcas was she would discover later.

Fidelis bounced the pram to the end of Heron Grove and across to the Canoe Lake. All the while she chatted to Sophie.

'This is a pretty place in the summer. Little boys float their boats here and the swans come. There are lots and lots of flowers and blossoms on the trees.'

It had all gone so much better than she had expected. Fancy Madam thinking about her having a uniform that suited her, and a proper winter coat. She had worn black frocks all her working life, and hated them. And then having the nursery redecorated by the mysterious Dorcas. Suddenly everything had come right. And the cherry on the cake was her meeting, in a fortnight's time, with Daniel. Thoughts of him lay enticingly in the back of her mind, as she walked around the lake and threw the stale bread that Cook had given her to the ducks. 'Quack, quack, quack,' she said, and Sophie laughed. 'We'll go round the lake one more time and then we're off to see my Mummy and Auntie Ruby.'

She saw them before they saw her. They were standing on the pavement waiting for the knife-grinder to sharpen her mother's dressmaking shears.

Ruby spotted her first and hurried towards her. 'Lovely to see you, my cherub,' she said, hugging her warmly. 'And who is this little darling? Aren't you a bonny girl, have you got a smile for me?'

'Hello Fee.' Her mother's greeting was cool. 'So you have been taken on?'

'Yes, and I've got some stuff because Mrs Mount wants me to have some uniform dresses. Could you make them for me?'

'Bring the child in, Fee. It's cold out there. Of course I can, let's see the quality of the material.'

While they were talking, Sophie watched the sparks flying from the knife-grinder's stone, then became distracted by the milkman's horse passing by.

'You go indoors with her, Mary. I'll see to the knives and such,' said Ruby, smiling at the child.

Fidelis edged the pram through the narrow doorway, hoping that Sophie would charm Ma into a better mood.

'Hello young lady,' her mother said. 'We must take you out of that coat or you won't feel the benefit. Fee, go and get your old chair from your bedroom.'

When she came downstairs, Auntie Ruby had stepped over the garden wall from her own house and walked in through the kitchen. 'I went and found Harry's old rabbit. Here you are darling.'

After settling Sophie into the chair, Fidelis took the parcel from under the pram mattress and began to untie the string.

'Ruby, will you make us all some tea? There are some biscuits in the barrel. I'll get my sewing-box.'

Watching her unfolding the cloth, she could see her mother's mood lifting. Mary McCauley was impressed. 'This is wonderful quality. It will handle beautifully and be so comfortable, and even better it will launder well.' She turned and smiled at her. 'So, how do you like your new position?'

'I think I shall be happy there. The cook and the maid are nice and they've been there years, and there's a little orphan girl that they make such a fuss of.'

'How about Mrs Mount?'

'She's what you'd call out of the top drawer, Ma. Really elegant, and her sitting-room is so pretty.'

'Here we are,' said Ruby, handing a cup to Fidelis and a piece of biscuit to Sophie. 'I was thinking of you today. Got another letter from Harry. Tickled pink he is at the thought of getting married. Just think, less than nine months now 'til he's back. If you made yer mind up we could have an autumn wedding. What d'you think?'

Fidelis saw her mother looking questioningly at her. 'I don't know, Aunt Ruby, I feel as if I've only just got engaged. What with the upset with my job and settling into a new one, I haven't really decided.'

'Harry's been away a long time,' said Ma, riding to her rescue. 'They will need to get to know one another all over again. And Fee will want to get a few things together for her home, let alone think about her wedding clothes.'

Ruby's round, rosy, face creased into a smile. 'Hark at me, rushing you along, Fee, poking my nose in. You gotta forgive my impatience. You're such a lovely girl, I'm frightened you'll slip through my fingers. Always wanted a daughter and you're tailor-made for my Harry.'

'We'd better get you measured up for these dresses, Fee, I expect there are things you need to do back at Heron Grove.'

She stood with her arms out while her mother unrolled her tape-measure and Aunt Ruby chatted to Sophie. Talk of marriage alarmed her, it was all too soon. Daniel filled her thoughts. She knew it was foolish and dangerous but was not yet ready to relinquish her daydream.

'When they're ready, I'll pop them around to you, Fee.' Ma gave her a flicker of a smile and then it was gone.

Relieved, Fidelis kissed her cheek. 'I know you'll make them look so smart, I'm really looking forward to wearing them.'

She sat Sophie on her lap and buttoned her into her coat. 'We better give bunny back to Auntie Ruby.'

'Oh, she can have it, Fee and welcome. Now don't forget to send Harry your new address. He so looks forward to your letters.'

Fidelis settled the baby in the pram and hugged her future mother-in-law. 'Mrs Mount is ever so busy so I won't be home 'til a week on Sunday. I'll see you all soon.'

She dawdled back to her new home, enjoying the late autumn sunshine, promising herself a rummage through the nursery cupboards, determined to set her stamp on the place. As she neared Kelmscott, and saw Eileen showing a policeman out of the front gate, Fidelis felt a stab of fear.

8

'Please sit down, sergeant. How may I be of assistance?' Marcia Mount felt a flicker of irritation at having her first child-free morning interrupted. But, judging by his demeanour, the policeman was the bearer of bad news.

'We have some information about your daughter and her husband.'

'Have they been found?' She stared at the scarlet fringe on the turkey rug, counting the threads in an effort to concentrate her mind. If her son-in-law were dead, it would come as a relief – he had cost her dear in money and temper. What she felt about her daughter was uncertain.

'We believe that Mr Allen has gone to London. However, in response to the newspaper drawing of your daughter and her husband, we know now that they were in Brighton. A jeweller in the Lanes contacted us with a positive identification of Mr Allen and a list of jewellery that he bought from him.'

'Did the jeweller say whether he was with anyone?' asked Marcia, recognising the items on the list the sergeant gave her.

'He was on his own, Mrs Mount. Early this evening we had a message from Sussex police reporting that a jewel case was found in the cloakroom in the Brighton railway station. We have no way of knowing how long it has been there.'

'My son-in-law can survive by his wits and charm, but my daughter Phoebe – she is totally unused to fending for herself.' Marcia wanted the man gone. It was only by concentrating on driving the nails of one hand into the palm of the other that she stopped herself from screaming. The sergeant coughed. Dredging up the last remnants of good manners, Marcia said, 'May I offer you some refreshments?'

'Tea would be welcome, Mrs Mount.'

The prompt response to her tug on the bell-pull indicated her maid's ear had been pressed to the door. 'Eileen, bring some tea for the sergeant and myself, if you please. I'm afraid your name has gone completely from my mind.'

'Hankins, madam, that's very kind, thank you.'

Later, with the tray at her side, Marcia felt more in command. 'Milk and sugar, sergeant?'

'Yes, please, ah, thank you.' The man smiled and seemed less forbidding.

She watched him settle his trilby on the carpet and spoon the sugar into his cup. Marcia took up the silver tongs and set a slice of lemon afloat in her cup. She prided herself on living a useful, ordered life, keeping abreast of events and supporting causes with more than her cheque-book. It was November next week, and she was due to address the local branch of the National Union of Women's Suffrage Societies. Banners were needed, and armbands. The speech was as yet unwritten. Her niece, Dorcas, was supposed to be arriving soon to lend her weight to the campaign. After sipping her tea for some moments she returned to the problem in hand. 'Have you any information regarding my daughter?'

From behind his chair the man drew out a handbag. 'Is this familiar to you, ma'am?'

Marcia covered her face with her hands while she fought for control. 'It belongs to my daughter.' How had she not seen it when he came into the room? She, who was normally so observant, had noticed nothing.

'I am sorry to upset you, madam. Shall I ring for your maid?'

Drawing a handkerchief from her sleeve, she shook her head. No, she must not give way. 'Do you believe that Phoebe is still alive?'

'Our only certain information is that Mrs Allen bought a ticket at Brighton intending to travel to Portsmouth, a few days ago. From our enquiries it seems that a woman jumped out of the train as it was leaving Brighton station and was lost in the crowd before the staff could detain her. They believe she may have injured her ankle. A porter remembers that she was limping.'

'So she is alive?'

'Almost certainly,' Sergeant Hankins nodded. 'We've had to open the handbag to find the identity of the owner. I would like you to examine the contents, please.'

Marcia wanted the man to be gone, and she wanted to be alone. It felt like trespass to search Phoebe's handbag but, since the policeman had asked her, she had no choice. The contents were in chaos, with everything coated in face-powder. Wrapped in a paper napkin was a stale cheese sand-wich. Marcia tossed it into the waste-paper basket. She drew out a crumpled copy of a railway timetable, a bottle of smelling-salts, a bar of soap and her daughter's purse: inside were a silver sixpence, a three-penny bit and a farthing. She clamped her mouth shut to stifle the scream rising in her throat. In the pocket of the lining was a pawn ticket made out to a Mrs Burne-Jones for a gold locket.

That Phoebe had pawned the last present her father had given her disturbed her mother far more than the paltry con-tents of her purse. Raphael Mount had loved his daughter with a warmth and acceptance that always shamed Marcia. Careless with possessions, the locket was the only gift that Phoebe valued. What was the significance of the name on the pawn ticket, written in Phoebe's handwriting? Was it a coded message?

'Mrs Mount, do you know a Mrs Burne-Jones?'

'It was probably the first name to pop into Phoebe's head. The locket was given to her by her father – he was a great admirer of the Pre-Raphaelite brotherhood. Burne-Jones was one of their most revered artists.'

'It sounds as if your daughter wants to be found, madam. After all, she had bought herself a ticket to Portsmouth; why she didn't complete the journey is the question we need to answer. What does your husband think? May we speak with him?'

'My husband died three years ago, sergeant. He was irreplaceable.'

'I am sorry, Mrs Mount.' The sergeant's grey eyes registered sympathy.

'Thank you.' Marcia bent her head over the handbag, praying not to cry. She craved silence and her own company. Inside an inner pocket was one of Phoebe's calling-cards. *Mrs Phoebe Allen, Clarendon House, Clarendon Road, Southsea.*

'What do you suggest that I do, Sergeant Hankins? Should I offer a reward for her whereabouts?'

'No, madam, not at this stage. The Brighton police will be visiting all the hotels and guesthouses. They will question doctors, vicars and the Salvation Army. Give us until Monday to see what we can uncover. Oh, there was one other thing. The pawnbroker said that she had given an address in Sussex, South Harting, I believe.'

'It was where her grandparents lived until they died some years ago.'

'Have you the least idea, madam, why Mrs Allen should change her mind at the last minute, about returning home?'

'Fear, I believe, fear that she would not be welcome.'

The chemist had been most kind. He had bandaged her foot and given her a glass of water. It had embarrassed her not to be able to offer some payment for his kindness. She pretended that her handbag had been stolen, but when he offered to summon the police she took fright.

'May I get you a taxi, Mrs Burne-Jones? You've had a nasty fall, you should rest at home for a few days.'

'That's very kind but I have friend in the next street. I shall take refuge there a while.'

'Can my assistant walk with you, madam? Even a short distance is likely to be painful.'

Phoebe shook her head. 'Please don't worry on my account. You have been most solicitous. I shall be fine.'

'Let me lend you a stick to lean on. Your friend can return it to us later.'

She hobbled away without the least idea what to do. She arrived at the park by the Royal Pavilion, after an interminable and painful walk punctuated by stops at various public benches. Seated on yet another bench, she wondered what one did for food when one was without the means of paying for it. The afternoon wore on. The nursemaids gossiping across the path began to drift away. Phoebe was frightened. It was getting dark. She knew that she could go to the police and she would be rescued and taken home to Mummy, but some stubborn loyalty to James prevented her from taking that step. It occurred to her that the park might be locked at night. The thought of sleeping in the open in the dark terrified her. With the aid of the walking-stick, she managed to find her way onto the promenade and a seat in a beach shelter. A vicar walked by and raised his hat to her.

She thought about Pa and how he used to take her to church at St Thomas's in Old Portsmouth. When she became bored with the interminable prayers and the choir's fluty singing, he would slip a treacle toffee into her hand. Phoebe would make it last until the end of the service. If she closed her eyes she could feel the warmth and largeness of her father's hand, the gold ring on his little finger, the lines tracking across his palm. His hands smelt of sandalwood soap, and his neck of the special cologne he bought from Trumper's in Piccadilly. On fine days they would walk home together by the sea. When she was tired they would rest in a shelter like the one she was in now. And then he would say the words that always made her feel safe. *'Come to me all you who labour and are heavy laden and I will give you rest. My yoke is easy and my burden light.'*

Repeating it to herself, it felt like a message from her father. She would find a church and seek refuge. If she could just have something to eat; a bath and a bed for the night perhaps, tomorrow a plan might come to her.

'Robbed, you say how unfortunate, do please come in, Mrs—? I didn't catch your name.'

It was then that the idea came to her. 'I don't know my name. Everything that happened before I was attacked has gone completely from my mind.' Phoebe gave the vicar's wife her most winsome smile.

Harassed, with a baby in her arms and a child tugging at her skirts, the woman held open the door. 'Please come in, my husband will be home soon. You must eat with us and then we will see how we may help you.'

The smell of stew of some kind made her mouth water. She was shown into a bare-looking room with a table and two chairs. Phoebe shivered.

'Paul won't be long.' The woman disappeared.

Her surroundings were devoid of interest. She felt as if she were sitting in an old gravy-boat – everything was brown, from the furniture to the curtains and the decrepit tomes in the glass-fronted bookcase.

Why had she drawn back at the last minute? If her courage had only lasted for a couple more hours she would have been safely home at Heron Grove. What was it that distressed her

most, Phoebe wondered. Was it that James had never loved
her? Or was it her mother's continual disappointment? The
fear that nobody believed her worth loving still cowered in
the pit of her stomach. Only Pa had been able to dissolve
that anguish. In his company it was possible to see herself
as a person of value. If Pa had been waiting for her she would
have stayed on the train.

At last the front door close behind Sergeant Hankin. In spite
of sitting in front of the fire, Marcia shivered. It was as if
her life was a piece of needlepoint, and moment-by-moment
the stitches were being unpicked. All her achievements, all
her crusades, would mean nothing if Phoebe came to harm.
If Raphael were alive, he would be out searching for his
daughter, and if he were alive she would have come home.
What was the matter with her that she could cry over the
plight of an orphan in Africa, yet be unmoved by her own
child's pain? She realised that the churning in her stomach
was shame.

. What did she really know about her daughter? As with most
mothers in her position, Phoebe's baby milestones were
unknown to her – Nanny took care of all that. Her child existed
on the periphery of her life, presented at tea-times and for
family photographs. An unexpected parent in his forties,
Raphael Mount had been devoted to his child. Marcia had
felt shut out. While she tried to educate and discipline Phoebe,
her husband indulged the girl. Her daughter's marriage had
come as a relief. Only after the wedding had she regained
Raphael's attention. But their time together had been brief.
Within a year cancer had withered him and made her a widow.

'You were my life,' she whispered to the framed sketch she
had made of him on one of their holidays. 'You astonished
me. Taught me to paint and draw and made me see what
injustices and cruelties there were around me. Do you

remember, after that party when we were sitting in the conservatory, what you said to me? *"Marcia, you are the most ignorant and beautiful woman I know. This state of affairs must not be allowed to continue."'*

She put the drawing back in its place on the mantelpiece. Of course she had been lucky to have had all those years with him, but she wanted more. If Raphael were with her now he would guide her into doing the right thing. Marcia sighed. How did you love your child without reservation, as he had? Always with Phoebe she was coaxing, cajoling and threatening, wanting her to share her values, have her talents. What had it been like for her daughter? One moment she would be petted and the next ignored. Only Raphael had had time and patience. She stood in front of his picture trying to absorb the essence of him, that wise simplicity.

Satisfied that something had been achieved that morning, Marcia drew up her chair to the desk. Yes, she had been impressed by Fidelis McCauley: the girl had dignity and self-possession. If only the problem of her daughter could be so easily solved.

Phoebe shivered in the narrow bed. She had been the recipient of the vicar's charity and had paid for it in prayers and humiliation. The soup was tasteless and the bread stale. His children stared at her and his wife was clearly resentful.

'You can help Peggy wash up and clear away. Tomorrow you'll have to be gone.' The woman looked strained and exhausted.

When it was clear that she did not know how to wash up, Peggy set her to drying the plates.

'Where you come from? Looks to be a toff's missis, did he beat ya?'

'I have just been unfortunate,' she'd said. 'I was robbed at the station and fell, twisting my ankle.'

'Where was you going?'

'If you don't mind I'd rather not say.'

'No good bein' snooty with me. And them knives and forks is all wet, get them out the drawer and start again. There's the china to put away. Prayers again later.'

'Is it possible that I could have a wash?'

It was a struggle up the stairs with the can of water. By the time she had washed herself with a sliver of soap and emptied the water into the slop pail, she was trembling with weariness.

'Madam, you may stay the night with us but in the morning I must insist on calling the police. We have not the resources for your care.'

'Thank you, Vicar. Once I am recovered I am sure my relatives, whoever they may be, will want to reimburse you for your kindness.'

She was awoken by the cold. Peering out of the window she saw it was just getting light. Frost rimed the roofs and stiffened the grass in the back garden. With teeth chattering, she peeled away the sheets and set her foot on the icy floor. If she was to make her escape before the household stirred she must be quick. Dragging on her clothes she saw that her drawers were bloody and unwearable – the curse had come. In the kitchen last night she had noticed clothing hanging from wooden bars pulled up and down by a rope. Perhaps she could help herself to a change of underwear.

The pain in her ankle stabbed at her as she limped down the stairs. Phoebe filled a basin with water, warm from the kettle left all night on the range. She washed herself with a dishcloth and carbolic. The drawers and petticoat were loose but clean. Last night she had noticed a collecting-box for the overseas missions on the table in the vicar's study. She snatched it up before her conscience got the better of her, and crept out into the yard. The family dog leapt at her from his kennel, barking madly. Desperately she hit him with her stick and he retreated, howling. Phoebe hobbled to the end of the alley and looked about her. Over the course of her stay in Brighton her choices had been whittled away. All she wanted now was a seat in the park out of the wind, where she could rest a moment before deciding what to do. She struggled across to a seat away from the entrance and shook the mission box repeatedly until it was empty. It accrued her two shillings in pennies and halfpennies. Once, she would have tossed the money into a little china dish on her dressing-table without a second thought. Now she must portion it out carefully across the day. Once she had been fun-loving and lively; now she must use all her energies to simply stay alive.

9

Daniel Herrick sat in the train watching the Kent country-side sweep past the window. It was hilly and thickly wooded. There were sheep in some fields and every so often barns with round towers topped by conical white cowls. He would ask Maude about them. The rural landscape was new to him, his only acquaintance with the county being his time in the barracks at Deal. A weekend with the Palmers was not enticing. He would be hard pressed to extract any enjoyment from it.

'Good man, Admiral Palmer; useful to you, Daniel,' said his father. 'A young officer needs to make contacts, put himself about a bit. You've proved your mettle in China, now's the time for some diplomacy in home waters.'

'Darling, it will be a tonic. Maude is a dear girl, she just needs encouragement. Country air will do you good. I've sent you with a fruit cake for Arthur and some of Cook's lemon curd.' His mother kissed him. 'Do your best Daniel, it's only three days.'

It was what would be read into his visit that worried him. Promotion through influence tasted sour on his tongue. He wanted command, but through his own merit. Being the only child intensified things. Away in China he had been his own man. Who his father was cut no ice with the rankers; what he did and what confidence he inspired in the men was what mattered. Perhaps he could volunteer for service abroad, the West Indies or South Africa, anywhere away from the emasculating influence of his father. Even his mother saw him as a dangerous creature – the handsome bachelor on the loose. In her own gentle way she wanted to steer him towards the right woman, but Daniel wanted more than a dutiful virgin.

'Crossways, Crossways, change here for Canterbury.'

He stepped down from the train and looked about him. The country station was almost deserted. A man in gaiters on the opposite platform was pacing with a bulldog on a lead. Maude had said someone would come and meet him with a pony and trap. As he stood outside the station staring up the road, Daniel realised he was starving. Whatever else happened, he would probably be well fed.

'Mr Herrick, that you, sir?' The wheels on the trap rattled over the cobbles.

'Yes, good afternoon to you.' He held out his gloved hand and it was taken and shaken vigorously by the driver, a spare red-faced man in rough brown tweeds. The dog gave him a malevolent look and snarled at him.

'Name's Ash, give us yer bag and I'll stow it for you. Sit along side me, sir, it won't be above ten minutes 'for we fetches up at the farm. Kipling! You get up there in the back and shut your noise. Don't heed him, sir, he's all bark and no bite.

'Miss Palmer be pleased to see you. Got a feast cooked up for you. The Admiral's looking forward to a bit of shooting. He scares up the rooks no end.'

Daniel smiled. Ash had the confidence of a man long in the job.

'Tells me you're a man of the sea, sir, been off fighting in foreign parts.'

'Yes, China and South Africa mainly, gunnery's my field. Have you served your country, Ash?'

'Only as a landsman, I'm a grower of things. Been at

Crossways Farm nigh on forty years. Ain't a lot I don't know about fruit trees and their rearing. Nearly November, it's the back end of the year, not much to see. You wants to come in April, when the cherry blossom's out. That's when Kent is in her glory.'

Daniel looked about him as they drove through the town. The buildings fascinated him. Some were black-and-white timber structures while others were of small red bricks, and many were faced with white boards. 'It's very different from Hampshire,' he said. 'What are those towers I've seen out in the fields, some square and some round? They're attached to barns as far as I can see.'

'Oast houses, sir, for the drying of hops, the square ones is Sussex oasts and round ones are our native Kent. Later you'll see the hop-poles in the fields. As I said, there's not much the eye can settle on this time of year.'

'I like the red roofs around here, in Hampshire it's all grey slate or thatch.'

'Kentish peg tiles, fixed on oak battens with wooden pegs.'

They came over a hill and down into the valley. Against the backdrop of the setting sun stood a farmhouse.

'We're here, sir. This is Crossways, been in Miss Palmer's mother's family for generations. Graceful old lady ain't she? I'll stop for you to look at her awhile.'

Entranced, Daniel walked down the path towards it, taking in the tall brick chimneys, the broad sweep of the timbers and the studded oak door. Never had he been so drawn to a building. It stood in a fold of the valley as if had grown there, every shape, texture and colour mellowed by the years. 'Looks as if it was planted rather than built.' He spoke his thoughts aloud.

'So it has in a manner of speaking, the bricks are baked Kentish clay and the timbers from the trees hereabouts. Local materials makes for harmony.'

Looking down from the hill, he had thought the oast-house chimneys were attached to the farmhouse but now, drawing closer, he saw they were part of a large barn. As Ash brought the trap over the path, the front door flew open and a liver-coloured spaniel bounded towards them. That must be Russet, he thought, as the dog leapt up at him. Kipling left the trap from the other side, and skulked away. It was some while before Daniel extricated himself from Russet's friendly greeting.

'Hello, Daniel.' Admiral Palmer, looking every inch the gentleman farmer in gingery tweeds, strode out to meet him. 'Welcome to Kent.'

Feeling that some comment was expected of him, he gripped his host's hand and said, 'Good afternoon, sir. This is a fine-looking farm. I come to you in a state of total ignorance, I know nothing of the countryside.'

'We shall have to teach you, my boy. Come you in and Maude will make us some tea. Russet, get down sir.'

'Hello, Daniel,' and there she was, still flushed with shyness but without the desperation of that afternoon in Eastney. 'Please come in.' She turned from him to Ash who had thrown a stick for Russet and was watching him as he sped after it. 'Back bedroom, please, Ash. I'll have a cup poured for you.'

He realised that Maude was on her own territory and more at ease. 'I'm looking forward to you showing me around and teaching me all about apples.'

She smiled and held open the door into a large kitchen. 'You'd need a lifetime for that. Mummy was the expert, she knew the taste and colour of nearly two hundred different varieties. But perhaps you could scratch the surface.'

Daniel set down the parcel that Ma had pressed on him. 'The fruit cake is from my mother and I've brought you some of her lemon curd. I have a letter for you, too.'

'That's so kind. Put it over on the dresser, will you? Mrs Ash has taken some hot water to your room. You probably feel a bit dusty after all that travelling. The lavatory is to the right down the passage. We'll have tea waiting.'

Walking up the creaking wooden stairs towards the back of the house, some of the tensions of the day began to fall away. Maude and her father seemed to have a far simpler way of living at Crossways than their life in the naval dock-yard. So far as he could see, they managed with the minimum of servants. His room pleased him. It had a large bed with plenty of blankets and a patchwork quilt in bright orange, red and green. The floor was bare save for a rag rug beside the bed. He poured some water into the basin and washed his hands, then stood looking out of the window as he dried them. The trees were huge, some thirty feet he guessed, bare of apples but still here and there a leaf clung to a branch. He thought of Ash, and wondered how must it be to live a whole lifetime in one place – to be rooted like the trees. After combing his hair, he found his way back over the creaking boards and down the stairs. Following the sound of voices, he arrived in the main room of the farmhouse. It was spec-tacular – wood-panelled and dominated by a huge fireplace with logs heaped in a basket by the inglenook.

'Sit you down, Daniel,' the admiral boomed, 'you must be famished, it's a tidy step from Portsmouth.'

Once he was seated, a fresh-faced woman nodded towards him.

'Good day to you, sir, I'm Mrs Ash.'

He held out his hand and she shook it firmly. 'Good after-noon,' he replied. 'Daniel Herrick, I'm glad to meet you.'

'Mira and Jonathan have known me since I was a baby,' said Maude, smiling up at her.

'I'll leave you to your meal,' the woman said. 'There's hot water there in the jug, Miss Maude, for to top up the pot, and plenty more pie in the kitchen.'

The easy relationship between the couple and the Palmers

was so different from the formality at home between his family and the staff. But at Eastney they were not in a home of their own choosing, and the servants came and went.

'Dive in, Daniel,' said the admiral, waving his hand across the table, 'we eat hearty in Kent. Afterwards I'll show you around the place. I hope you've brought stout boots, it's muddy at this time of year.'

He needed no second bidding and helped himself to thick sliced ham, cheese and pickles. Maude sliced a brown loaf and poured them all tea from a silver pot. He smiled at her. 'I can see that you would miss being here.'

'I'm a fish out of water. But Father has promised when his time in Portsmouth is over I can come home.'

'I don't know where my home is. As a child it was in the Isle of Wight, in Cowes, but Pa sold it when my grandparents died. My mother lived there, too, but my uncle has it now. When Pa's service time is over, then they will decide where to settle.'

'How strange,' she said. Russet had lain down on the mat beside her and she stretched out her hand to stroke his head. 'I know wherever we go that Crossways is here waiting for me. It has been in Mummy's family for generations. But, Daniel,' she asked, her grey eyes searching his, 'where do you think you would want to be?'

He smiled. 'I have become a rolling stone since growing up. There doesn't seem to be anywhere that exerts a particular pull. My grandparents have gone, and in the service one is constantly on the move.'

'Kent has much to recommend it,' said her father. 'Great rolling hills, woods, and on the coast wonderful fishing. The people are open and friendly. Rattling around from place to place has lost its attraction. The navy is a young man's game. I won't be sorry to settle down here and try my hand at squirearchy.'

'Try some of Mira's scones with apple butter from our orchards.' Maude poured another cup of tea.

The admiral opened the parcel and began spreading the lemon curd on a slice of the fruit cake. 'Splendid – a wedding of acidity and sweetness.'

Daniel pushed back his chair. 'I think I shall burst,' he laughed. 'Thank you, it was a feast.'

'Good man, now you go and get your country togs. We'll take a turn around before it gets too dark. The days are short as it gets towards November.'

'Thank you Maude.' He smiled at her. 'I'll see you later.'

'I hope you're good at draughts,' she said as she cleared away the plates. 'I am the Crossways champion, at least according to Pa.'

The air was chill and different somehow from the sea breezes he was accustomed to in Eastney, more penetrating. His boots slithered over the muddy fields. Maude's dog ran ahead of the two men, wallowing in puddles, and coming back from time to time to check their progress. Daniel laughed apologetically. 'I am a complete foreigner to the countryside, sir. You will have to forgive me if I seem ignorant.'

Palmer gave a great laugh. 'By God, boy, we shall have to set about your education. Kent is famous for its sheep and there was a great wool industry around here. We have wonderful forests with all manner of timber and then there are the hops and the apples. This county is the drunkard's dream. We're the garden of England.'

'What are those little huts for, over in the next field?'

'Housing for the pickers. Mostly they come from London in September to harvest the hops. Mothers, fathers, children, even grandmothers come, and Romanys too. My wife loved them coming. Wouldn't miss the Hop Supper for the world. A real countrywoman, and Maude is the same.'

'I can see the attraction,' Daniel said, looking around him.

'We'd best get back, it'll be pitch-black soon.' The admiral gave a low whistle. 'Russet, come here, sir,' he called.

Back in the warmth of the farmhouse, the evening passed pleasantly between the three of them. Admiral Palmer sat reading by the fire while Daniel and Maude played several games of draughts; at each one Maude trounced him.

On the Saturday morning, after they had lingered over a late breakfast, she took him up to the storehouse and he was drenched in the scent of apples. She showed him the different varieties lying on the slatted wooden shelves; Bramleys, pippins, costards and russets, she knew the names of all of them.

'They're like my family,' she said. 'I know their flavours and uses, which ones are for dessert and which for cooking. Here, have this Autumn Pearmain, it's one of the oldest apples in England.' It was a slightly lopsided apple, a dull gold and orange. He took out a penknife and cut it in two, offering half to Maude. The flesh was firm and creamy and he was surprised at how juicy it was. It dribbled down his chin.

'Here,' she said, offering him her handkerchief.

He mopped his face, then returned the favour, dabbing at her chin. Maude stood there like a trusting child. He bent and kissed her lightly on the lips, more from affection than desire. She flushed and moved away. Unbidden thoughts of what Fidelis would have done in the same situation stirred in him.

'Life here is good,' he said, wanting to soothe her embarrassment. 'There's a real sense of the changing seasons. You must miss it here, when you're away.'

'Living in Admiralty House is an ordeal,' she confessed. 'I don't have Mummy's gift of conversation and knowing how to mix people so that they balance each other. It's the naval wives I find difficult. They try to manipulate things so that they talk about their husband's promotion chances, and want to use me to get to Daddy. The parties are deadly. I get stuck with the plainest girls in the fishing fleet, desperate to trawl a spare commander or captain if they're lucky.'

Daniel laughed. 'I've never heard them called that before. It must be a horrible predicament.'

'I'm a person, outside of whether I marry or not. I have ideas, and talents and wishes of my own. Daddy has promised when he retires in a couple of years, we'll come back home.'

He was surprised at her intensity. But since meeting Fidelis he had hardly given Maude a thought. How shallow he was. 'Let's meet up more often when we're back in Pompey. I know Mother would love to see you.'

She gave him a fierce look. 'I want *you* to want to see me. Not to be your good cause.' She stamped away and hurried across the fields before he could catch her.

Cursing his ineptitude, Daniel wandered back to the farm-house, at a loss how to occupy himself. In the kitchen Mrs Ash was busy turning bread out of loaf tins onto the table. The hot yeasty scent made his mouth water.

'You take off your boots, and go along into the sitting-room. Mr Palmer's there with the paper. I'll bring you in some sandwiches and tea by and by. Miss Maude off with her dog?'

He nodded, not wanting to be drawn into talking about her. His only hope was that she would walk off her anger with him. It was a relief to spend time with her father, a man with whom he had some common ground.

'Come and sit by the fire, my boy,' the admiral boomed. 'Tell me what you think of these automobiles that are springing up all over the place. Think they're our future?'

They were deep in discussion when Mrs Ash came in with a loaded tray of ham sandwiches.

'Welcome dear lady, welcome indeed, what a feast. Daniel,

will you separate that nest of tables, then we can eat in comfort. Thank you, thank you indeed.'

'I'll bring you in some cider,'

'I'll come with you and fetch it back,' Daniel offered, seeing Maude coming towards the house with Russet bounding behind her. He wanted to smooth over any awkwardness between them before it clouded the weekend.

'Here you are, sir, jug of cider and two tankards.'

'Maude, are you going to join us?' he asked, as she came in the back door. 'I would like it if you did.' He wasn't just trying to ease himself out of a sticky patch. He wanted her friendship. She attracted him in a way he had not met in a woman before. There was an honesty and inner confidence that drew him to her. He felt the desire to live up to her in some way, to be more than the easy charmer.

'Yes, I will, but give me a moment, I want to get my boots off and have a word with Mira.' She smiled, and he felt immeasurable relief.

Later they were companionable, all three of them. Her father asked her if he should buy a motor car and she surprised Daniel by saying yes.

'You've adapted from sail, Daddy, to steam turbines. Why not a petrol engine?'

'I hope this won't see the end of the horse,' he said, staring into the fire. 'Fine animals, don't you think?'

When they had eaten their fill, Admiral Palmer promised Daniel, 'A good stride out around the boundaries.'

Maude excused herself and agreed to see them at dinner.

That evening, they feasted on a massive pork and cider casserole followed by apple dumplings. Another evening of draughts and then the admiral surprised him by playing the piano. Not the usual nautical rumpty-ti-tum shanties but classical pieces that soothed and enchanted. Maude stood by the piano, turning the pages and smiling at her father.

Daniel lay in bed that night replete and well content with the day.

After Sunday dinner it was she who drove him in the trap to catch the train back to Portsmouth. They stood on the platform, suddenly shy with one another.

'It has been one of the happiest weekends I've ever spent,' he said, bending to kiss her cheek. She blushed a pretty pink and he felt a surge of affection for her.

'I've enjoyed it too, Daniel. Give my love to your mother, thank her for the cake.'

He leaned out of the window and waved to her. 'We'll meet up in Portsmouth,' he promised. 'Let me know when you get back.'

Sitting in the train Daniel reviewed his weekend. It had been far less of an ordeal than he had anticipated. On the smaller scale of his home territory, Admiral Palmer became human and welcoming. Their walks together had been full of anecdotes and tales of country life and local characters. He had felt comfortable in the older man's presence, even liked him. As for Maude, in the time they had been together he had felt – what? It was difficult to free himself from the hidden pressure, from both his parents and hers, to hot-house his emotions. If he had been required to be her brother nothing would have been simpler. To be her husband and lover was another matter. He had seen too many marriages come to grief – everything fine on the surface yet, in the background, hidden affairs. Could he come to love her? He couldn't be sure.

The train was stuffy and the rhythm of the wheels soporific. Unbidden, a face floated behind his eyes: the cheeks were flushed and lips open, and the eyes – such eyes. He could feel the texture of her hair, smell her perfume and beneath that her particular female scent. Even the thought of her aroused him. Daniel stared out of the window. With her there were no questions. Even before he had spoken with her or known her name, his body had alerted him. Fidelis McCauley, the drill sergeant's daughter, was an impossible marriage prospect. Everything in his background warned him against her. Conducting an affair with a ranker's daughter, within the barracks community, was madness. Yet, he wanted her with an intensity that woke him fumbling and excited in the early hours with her name on his lips.

She wanted him, Daniel could feel it. Would she be there next Wednesday, waiting for him? Of course, hers was the greater risk in seeing him. If things went too far it was always the woman who paid the price. Perhaps she wouldn't be there and he would be rescued from himself. Or, he could be posted to Kent, and in time he might grow to love Maude Palmer.

Instead of alighting at Fratton, the nearest station, he went on to the Harbour Station, wanting to walk home along the sea-shore to clear his head. It had come to him in the last few weeks that life in the Royal Marines was a matter of practise and experience. He enjoyed the company, pitting his wits against his fellows and larking with them when off duty. He liked the men. Pa had counselled him never to ask them to do something he wouldn't tackle himself. China had tested him to his limits, physically and mentally. Combat taught him as much about himself as about the men. Keeping one's nerve, being decisive, rallying everyone when they were weary or frightened – facing death. Reading the men: who could be relied on, who was a bully and had to be faced down, who was windy and needed to be encouraged. Their respect mattered to him. All of it was a sight easier than managing his private life.

Daniel walked along the ramparts towards Clarence Pier. The Isle of Wight was clearly defined in the cold air of late afternoon. Would he like to return there to set up home, he wondered. At boarding school he had longed for the house in Cowes, his mother, his dog and brother Roderick. He would have been nineteen, the same age as Fidelis, and been a companion at home to confide in; Roddy would have diluted the expectations placed on him.

Still he vacillated on what to do about his high-spirited redhead. There were two days in which to decide. The following week he would likely be sent to Hythe on a gunnery course, back in Kent. Common sense told him that calling a halt now was the wisest course. It had been a lively flirtation but when he was with her he wanted more. She excited him and he knew the feeling was mutual. But their circumstances precluded anything permanent. He was still uncertain when he arrived back at the barracks.

'Good evening sir, madam and the colonel are dining out this evening. What are your plans for this evening?'

'I think a tray in the sitting-room will be fine. A sandwich and perhaps some cake, whatever Cook has to hand. I will unpack and be down in an hour or so. Could you bring me up some tea now?

'Certainly, sir.'

Smiling, he set down the jar of apple chutney that Maude had insisted he bring home for Ma, and saw two letters on his desk. One was an invitation to a mess dinner in Chatham in November. The other was addressed in handwriting he didn't recognise.

> *Dear Daniel,*
> *I will be able to meet you on Wednesday the twenty-ninth as I have been given the afternoon off from my new employment. Please contact me by letter at sixty four Heron Grove. I am now a nursemaid. I do not want to waste my time if you have changed your mind. Please meet me at Mulberrys it is not my style to hang about in the street.*
> *Fidelis*

He laughed out loud. She had such assurance. In his mind's eye he could see her standing to her full height, looking about her before dropping the envelope into the box. And then that fluid long-limbed way she had of walking. His body stirred at the thought of Fidelis McCauley. What would it feel like to lie naked beside her, skin to skin? He wanted to know. Flinging his case on top of the wardrobe he sat at his table and dashed off a note. After he had bathed and eaten his supper, he would walk around to Heron Grove and drop it through the letterbox.

10

'That Midge has got herself a follower,' Cook said. 'She brought him in the other night, big shy lump of a marine. Don't look old enough to be let out on his own, let alone courting. Can't half eat, that boy, he polished off half a loaf and a great lump of fruit cake. Midge sits watching him like he's a god or something.'

'It's called square-pushing,' laughed Fidelis, as she took the iron from the range and set about her best blouse. 'In the barracks the last meal's at four and the next one's not 'til six next morning. The young lads are starving after all that drill. They survive by following a cook or maid and come scrounging round the kitchen door. It's how my Pa met my mother.'

'You got a follower?'

She could feel the two women's eyes on her, their curiosity razor sharp.

'I'm engaged to a bugler. He's out in the West Indies.'

'Got a photo?'

'I've pasted it up on my side of the nursery screen. I'll show it to you next time you're up there,' she said, giving them just enough information to dampen their appetite.

'When's he back home?' asked Eileen, not willing to let go of a sniff of romance. Unmarried and nearing fifty, she drew nourishment from the small change of other people's lives.

'Next July. I haven't seen him in three years.'

'Good job you gotta snap of the lad, else you'd forget what

he looks like.' Cook took off the lid and dropped the dumplings into a bubbling saucepan. A rich, meaty aroma filled the kitchen. Fidelis hoped her blouse would not smell of stew. Today she was meeting Daniel, and everything had to be perfect. The thought of him and what they might do together simmered below the surface all the time. It was there as she fed Sophie her egg custard and sat with her looking at a picture-book.

'What's this? It's an apple, does Sophie like apples?'

She nodded vigorously.

'And what's this?' She pointed to a liver-coloured spaniel.

'Bow-wow,' said Sophie, smiling.

After nursery lunch, she settled Sophie to play in her cot while she dressed for the afternoon. Buttoning her blouse she wondered if, after one of his kisses, Daniel would unbutton it for her. Would he stroke her neck as he had last time? Fidelis left her hair plaited across her head, imagining him taking out the pins and threading his fingers through it. The finishing touch was to rub the stopper from her scent bottle on her neck and between her breasts. *Please let him be there waiting*, she thought, as she held Sophie's hand and walked her downstairs to the sitting-room.

'Good afternoon, my young lady,' said Madam, taking charge of her granddaughter. 'See, I have made a little play-room for you. What do you make of it?'

Sophie settled on the rug in the triangle created by the joining of the two armchairs back-to-back with the sofa. Mrs Mount perched on the arm of one of them, and watched her examining the toy bricks and jug of silver coffee-spoons.

'Thank you Fidelis. I believe Eileen is taking her out later on this afternoon, and you will be back here by half-past five?'

'Yes, madam.'

'I hope your music lesson is successful. You will have to

let me hear you sing. Perhaps you might perform at one of my little entertainments in the future?'

'I would like that, madam,' she said, affecting modesty yet all the while seething with impatience. To lend validity to her outing, she went back upstairs and picked up the old leather music case she had had at school.

'You looks done up like a dog's dinner,' said Cook, sitting by the range with her feet up. 'You sure it's singing what you're going to?'

''Course I am,' Fidelis said, hoping she sounded suitably indignant.

'Looks ever so pretty,' sighed Midge, from her chair at the table, where she was breaking up a block of salt with a rolling-pin before filling all the salt cellars.

'Have to give us a song,' sniffed Eileen. 'I ain't heard nothing but them scales so far.'

'I'll give you a kitchen concert when I get back,' she promised. ''Bye.'

With time to spare, Fidelis dawdled along, savouring the hours ahead of her. Moment by moment she was drawing nearer to him. A line from a poem she had seen in a book sprung into her mind. '*It is the birthday of my life, because my love is come to me.*'

The words repeated themselves over and over like a charm. On reaching the High Street she stepped over the cracks between the paving-stones, just for luck.

He was there, waiting for her. She could see him through the window, seeming intent on rearranging the cutlery on the table.

'I didn't know whether you would come,' he said, taking her coat then holding out the chair for her.

'I didn't know either, for sure,' she said, delighting in his uncertainty.

'What will it be this time, tea and crumpets?'

Fidelis studied the menu, not knowing whether she would be able to swallow anything. 'Tea and fruit cake would be nice.' She smiled at him, and he held her hand and kissed it. Ooh! If only she could stop time and have the afternoon last forever.

He gave the order and then once more took her hand. 'It feels like a long time since we last met and yet it's only a fortnight.'

'A lot has happened to me. I've a new job and a new place to live, and my singing.'

'Yes, I noticed the address on your letter. How are you settling in?'

'Think I'll be happy there, the others are friendly and Mrs Mount is firm but fair. I'm looking after the same little girl I told you about, but in her grandmother's house. The other day a policeman came round with Phoebe Allen's handbag. Eileen, that's Mrs Mount's maid, said Madam was ever so upset about it. Policeman reckons that her husband has left her in Brighton, on her own, and gone off with her jewels.'

'Eileen must have a very hot ear from pressing it to the door, I should think.' He laughed. 'It sounds like a case for Sherlock Holmes.'

'It's strange. If I went missing like that my Pa would be frantic, probably go off to Brighton and walk the streets 'til he found me. I don't get the feeling that she and Phoebe got on very well. She loves little Sophie.'

'It's likely Mrs Mount has offered a reward and even hired a private detective. Ah! Nourishment.' He smoothed his napkin over his lap and then changed tack. 'How is the singing coming along?'

She laughed. 'That's where I'm supposed to be, now.'

'I have been to Kent, among the cider apples, and now my leave is over. Next week I'm off to Deal and a gunnery course.'

'How long for?' she asked, with a lurch of disappointment

'It will be just under a couple of months, right up until the night before your concert when my Christmas leave starts. Do you like Christmas, Fidelis?'

How easily he spoke of going away. In that time he could meet someone else, in that time he would forget her. She stirred the sugar into her tea, trying to swallow down her disappointment. All her energy had been focused on this meeting: his being posted had not entered her mind. How stupid she was.

'Fidelis, did you hear me?'

'Ah, Christmas,' she floundered. 'I used to love it, with the presents and the service in church and Aunt Shamrock coming around, and then the pantomime. It's different when you're working in someone else's house. Everything is organised for their enjoyment. Last year Sophie was a tiny baby, and Mrs Allen was tired and ratty all the time. It just flew by in a sort of fog.'

'I loved it on the Island with my brother. Sometimes we had snow and could toboggan down the hill, behind our house. Some of the villagers would come around and sing carols. Pa and I built a snowman once. But always there was school looming in the background, knowing that the days were running out. And then, when Pa got further up the ladder and we moved from barracks to barracks, it wasn't the same.'

'I just hated waiting for Father Christmas. I made Ma leave a mince pie for the snowman and a carrot for the reindeer.'

'Waiting is so much of life, isn't it?' he said, 'I think we have to make the most of the red-letter days when they come, don't you?' He seemed to look right into the heart of her.

Fidelis put down her cup, afraid that he would see that her hand was shaking. 'Is this a red-letter day?' she asked, staring at a stray sultana on her plate.

'I think today is getting better and better, don't you?'

She nodded, not trusting herself to speak. Around them couples talked and laughed while she and Daniel gazed at one another. Beneath their teasing lay desire.

'We shall have to call in at St Thomas Street. I know it's a bore but I promised.' He put down his napkin and smiled at her. 'Are you ready?'

The question was like a stone thrown into a pool, leaving ripples of possibility. She let him help her on with her coat, and they slipped out of the tearoom. Outside, he held her hand and they walked together to the old captain's house. As he turned the key in the lock, Fidelis looked around her to see if they had been noticed. The street was deserted.

'Come in,' he said, holding the door open for her.

When it was closed she stood with him in the gloom of the hall waiting to be kissed. His face was in shadow, the only sound their breathing. He held her by her shoulders and covered her mouth with his, dizzying her with deep, languorous kisses.

They lingered outside the front room tasting each other until he pushed the door into the sitting-room open with his foot. The curtains were closed and a fire burned in the grate. The light from an oil-lamp on the table cast a softening glow.

'I came here earlier,' he said. 'I wanted us to be warm and private.'

Fidelis smiled. 'It's like a dream.'

'We're dreaming with our eyes wide open,' he whispered.

She stood like a child while he unbuttoned her coat and drew the pin from her hat, then perched on the edge of the settee while he took off his own cap and jacket.

'To us,' he said, handing her a glass.

'To us.' At first it was sour, but after some experimental sips it became smooth on her tongue.

'Do you like it?' he asked. 'It's claret.'

'It tastes of fruits,' she said, 'currants, plums and raspberries.'

'This is our secret kingdom, Fidelis. We keep everyone else outside. In here we are spellbound. *Ensorcelées.*'

'How do you spell that?' she asked him, liking the way the word sounded as he whispered it to her. 'Will you write it down for me?'

He took a scrap of paper from his pocket and a pencil and wrote it down for her. It was the name of the perfume she had stolen from Phoebe Allen, but it sounded so different from when she had said it to herself.

'Arrnsorcellaay,' he whispered again, 'it is French for "spellbound".'

She stared into the fire, watching the flames flicker and blur. When his glass was empty he began to undo her plaits, setting the pins on the table between the glasses. His fingers loosened her hair until it was hanging around her shoulders in a thick banner, then he stroked her head and neck. It was as if she were being cast adrift, floating away from herself.

'Rapunzel, Rapunzel, let down your golden hair,' he whispered against her neck.

Fidelis turned and kissed his mouth.

Daniel began to undo her blouse. The air was cool on her neck as he released the buttons. With every movement she was moving into deeper waters. He looked at her as the last one slipped from its mooring, then pulled the blouse free from the waistband of her skirt and slid the sleeves down her arms. It lay on top of his coat, in waiting for whatever else was to be discarded. She was drifting, drifting . . . In the silence it was touch that spoke for them. His fingers untied the ribbons on her chemise and released her breasts from their covering. At his stroking her nipples hardened, and he bent to kiss them. She felt a tenderness that was almost pain as she stroked his hair.

'Fidelis,' he whispered, 'I want to run away with you. To lie with you and know you entirely.'

She was in a fog, confused by his wishes and her own. 'I don't know,' she whispered.

'I want to stroke your belly and your thighs to bring you alive. To lick you with my tongue in all your secret places.'

His words tugged at her, drawing her away from the feel of his mouth on her skin, the heat of his breath in her face. Her body was still alive to his touch but caution insinuated itself between them. 'No,' she cried, drawing away from him, sinking onto the floor and reaching for her clothes. Anger, shame, confusion swirled in her. What had she been thinking of? Her fingers trembled in her haste to cover herself.

Daniel stood up. 'It's all right, Fidelis, please, just sit down, I'm not going to hurt you. I'm sorry I rushed you. Listen, I'll go upstairs and leave you to dress. Don't worry, there's no harm done.'

It had all been so fast. She had wanted to be swept away by him. It was what he said that frightened her. The putting his desires into words had somehow distanced her from the tide of feeling. He must think her very stupid or worse. There was a word for girls that led men on. Molly back at Clarendon House had told her. Sitting huddled in her coat, she began to cry.

Daniel came back into the room, and took a handkerchief from his pocket. 'Fidelis, my sweet girl, don't cry, please, please sit down. It's my fault.' He put his arm around her shoulder. 'I feel all sorts of things now: relief, regret, anger and sadness. Darling, you are just so, so tempting. What shall we do? Would you like to go back to Mulberry's and have more tea?'

'How can I? I must look a sight.' The last thing she wanted was to be among people, subject to their judgement, their pointing and sniggering. 'I need to cool down and tidy myself. Don't look in the least like I've been to music classes.'

He smiled. 'It was a music of sorts. Anyway my love, I go down to Kent on Saturday – then there will be time for us to cool down. We'll see how we feel then.' He touched Harry's ring, hanging from the chain around her neck.

'I think there is someone serious in the wings, isn't there?'

She nodded, unwilling to talk to him of Harry.

Daniel smiled ruefully. 'Ma and Pa are nudging me towards an engagement to this girl called Maude. I don't love her but I think we could be chums given time.'

'So what is this, with you and me?' she asked, angry with both of them.

'Enchantment, pleasure?'

'I want it to be more,' she said, knowing she was being ridiculous.

'Fidelis.' He held her face between his hands. 'I want to be honest with you. I can't ever be your lover in a proper way and you know that, don't you?'

She nodded, too miserable to speak.

Fidelis got to her feet. 'I want to go, now,' she said. 'I want to be by myself.'

'Are you sure? I'll walk with you to Heron Grove, if you like.'

'No, Daniel, I don't like.'

He hung his head. 'I'm so sorry. The last thing I wanted was to make you unhappy. I wanted us to enjoy each other, to be warm and loving and now I have offended you. Will you be all right?'

'I am a grown-up, of course I shall be all right. Thank you for the tea and the wine.' She felt like a child thanking her hostess at a tea-party. 'Must go now.' Before he could say anything, she rushed to the front door and slammed it behind her. Thankful for the rain to cover her bedraggled appearance, and too impatient to wait for the tram, Fidelis ran through the streets. Her body felt like an over-wound clock.

Gasping and crying, she struggled on until she reached the back gate of Kelmscott House.

'Cripes, you looks like the wreck of the Hesperus,' said Cook, as she stepped into the kitchen. 'Best go upstairs and get out of them wet things or you'll be taking a chill. Here, take this cup of tea with you.'

'Thanks, Cook,' she managed. 'Where's Sophie?'

'She's in with madam and Miss Dorcas. You'll like her. She's an artist. Mad as a hatter. Went off to Africa with her Auntie, was sommink about starving children in the war, out there. She's a rare one, she lives on the Island now. She takes lovers, bold as you like she is. Showing off her grandchild to her, is madam.'

'Don't let them know I'm back yet,' she pleaded.

'They're chattering away in there like sparrows. I doubt they've noticed the time. Oh, and you had a caller. Your Ma, it was, ever such a nice lady. Brought you a parcel and your letters. Didn't seem to know about your singing lessons. I left it all up on your bed.' Cook winked. 'Singing lessons, that's what they're calling it nowadays.'

In the nursery, Fidelis stripped off her clothes and scoured her skin with a towel. Standing in her chemise and drawers, she untied the parcel. The care with which her mother had folded and pressed her frocks made her cringe with guilt. What a thankless, deceitful creature she was. Once she had put on one of her frocks and replaited her hair, she felt calmer. Sitting in the nursing-chair, she drank the tea before opening Harry's letter.

HMS Ramillies,
West Indies
September 1st 1902
My Dear Girl,
By the time you get this, your Pa will be home again. I

*can remember the excitement when I was a little lad,
down at Farewell Jetty waiting for my Pa. He was always
such a hero to me and I remember feeling small and shy
with him. Then he walked down the gangway and swept
me up on his shoulder. I was king of the castle.*

*I expect your letter telling me all about it is in a
mailbag somewhere waiting for me. Life potters on hot
and steamy and full of routine and cleaning, cleaning,
cleaning. Being on the flagship means being under the eye
of the admiral. Being a humble bugler I am just a
number in the scheme of things.*

*Letter are not the same as talking are they, Fee? We get
disconnected. When you're with me I can watch your face
reacting to what I'm telling you. I can hear your laugh
and see your nose wrinkling in disgust at some of my
stories.*

*Ma is in a lather of excitement over us getting together
isn't she? Don't let her hustle you into anything. She
would like to rush me straight from the ship and up the
aisle. I want our wedding to be when we are both good
and ready when we've got well used to one another again.*

*Dear Fee I do love you and think about you all the
time and think myself the luckiest of men. Take care of
yourself my sweetheart for you are more precious to me
than you know.*

*All my love,
Your Harry.*

It was all right. In a few days she would be over Prince
Charming and be Harry's girl once more.

11

Phoebe was now in a fog. People loomed up at her, then disappeared. Her two constant companions were cold and hunger. One day drifted into another, each one the same as its predecessor. For a week she had stayed in a refuge of some sort, in a long room filled with women, cursing, crying, fighting even. She was reprimanded for wetting the bed. As more of her old life dropped away from her, she began to feel invisible. There were stretches of time when she didn't speak to anyone, and the possibility that she could organise her thoughts into a coherent sentence seemed remote. It was as if her memories were of someone else – a woman with everything to live for. Sometimes she shuffled along to the aquarium and sat outside, if it was not too cold, trying to catch a glimmer of that afternoon with James.

Today, seated on a bench in a park, whose name she could not remember, the idea of letting go of life presented itself. To be released from the effort of hunting for food and warmth, or to search out the means to wash herself, seemed a blessed relief. It was numbingly cold. If she could only turn herself out of the wind and sleep.

From a distance she heard voices in passing.

'Disgraceful state to be in, she ought to be locked up.'
'Poor soul! Put a copper in her pocket, Charles.'

Later another voice drew closer to her. 'God in heaven, it's her. I knows her from the button on her coat, sewed it on for her months ago.'

'Whoever she is, Sarah, leave her be, it ain't our concern.'

Then she was left again to drift and doze. How long after that she didn't know, two people began to haul her off the bench. Phoebe was pulled this way and that until she was dizzy. There were two of them, half carrying, half dragging her along. She had not the energy to fight. If this was to be her end then so be it. Hands stripped her of her clothing. Hands washed her in hot water and helped into a clean bed. For the first time in her life she wanted nothing. There were two different voices, one she knew. There were eyes like shiny currants. Sometimes the two voices would talk across her, and both pairs of hands would help her up into a sitting position against the pillows. It was like being a baby again. The face with the currant eyes would smile and say things to her. During this time of confusion, she was aware of sharing the bed with a big warm body, of hearing prayers said. She couldn't string the words together that currant-eyes said to her, yet the rhythm of them reminded her of a time when she had been happy.

Sometimes she would rise up into wakefulness, with her heart racing and hair slippery with sweat. Always she was running to catch up. There was a fear clutching at her – a crippling doubt. She was caught in the middle. A tall woman in a green silk blouse was angry with her, and there was a man, in evening clothes, creeping out of the door.

There were trays with food: soup and bread, egg custard, glasses of barley water. One morning she sat out of bed and looked out of the window. The sea astonished her. There was something missing on the horizon. It was just the sea and sky, and birds wheeling and crying.

'Tomorrow, Nellie and me, we're going to get you up. We'll sort you out some clothes. You'll feel better when you're dressed, more like yourself.'

What did that mean? Whatever it was she didn't want it.

Washed and dressed, and gripping the banister, she went

one step at a time down the stairs. It was the smallest house she had ever seen. Everything delighted her. She sat in an armchair with her feet on a stool. The room was alive with little home-made curiosities. A crocheted white fringe ran along the edge of the mantelpiece, while in the grate was a spill-box with flowers painted on it. A sampler above the door announced '*God is Love*'. There were strange carved spoons on the wall opposite, with ribbons tied to them, and on the dresser bottles of coloured sand.

'Bet that food tastes better, with you sat up to the table, Miss Phoebe, don't it?'

Was she Miss Phoebe? She nodded, and picked up her knife and fork. It was beef stew and dumplings. The steam rose from the plate, wafting a rich meaty scent into her nostrils. She smiled at the two big women sitting at the table with her. 'You have been kind to me,' she said.

'You were in need and we were passing by, simple as that.' The one with the currant eyes passed her a glass of water.

'Do you remember who you are?' asked the other woman, her expression more curious than friendly.

'I don't know. This is not my home I know that, but you, Sarah, are familiar to me.'

'You used to call me Cook, in them days.'

'And so you are a very good cook,' she replied.

Sarah flushed with pleasure. 'Good of you to say so, madam.'

'So you know who I am?' She watched the woman's face and dreaded her answer. 'Will I like knowing?'

'You are Phoebe Allen and you come from Portsmouth, out Southsea way, in a place called Clarendon House.'

She delayed making any comment. 'How long have I been here?'

'With us it's been two weeks, but how long you bin in Brighton we don't know.'

'Will someone be missing me?' she asked, putting down her spoon. Did she really not remember or was her life so terrible that she had wilfully forgotten? It was like standing outside a half-open door, eavesdropping but not quite hearing, glimpsing but not seeing. Looking down at her left hand she said, 'I am married.'

The woman called Nellie glared at her sister. 'Why don't you tell her? Show her the bits in the—'

Sarah got up from the table so suddenly that her cup rattled in its saucer. 'Miss Phoebe needs to be well in her body before we tamper with her mind. You know what the minister says "Whatever you seek for another let your watchword be – do no harm."'

Looking at them, she realised that her being there had created strain between the two sisters. Nellie wanted her gone, but Sarah, what did she want?

The old cook smiled at her. 'Nellie and me are off to church, won't be gone much above an hour. You sit by the fire and rest yourself.'

When she heard the gate click behind them, she roamed around the room.

'Phoebe,' she said to the woman in the mirror. The face reflected back at her was small. It was her hair that was the most distinctive feature, pale blonde, in tight curls. She wound one of them around her finger, released it and it sprang back into place. Around her neck was a pale stripe of skin. Had she worn a necklace? Touching the hollow at the base of her throat she felt a rush of joy. It must have been a gift. Wound around that feeling was sadness. Phoebe turned away from the mirror, and drew a handkerchief from her sleeve and dried her tears.

She wanted to do something useful, to show her appreciation. There would be dinner later, perhaps she could lay the table. In a drawer in the dresser she found a tablecloth but no napkins. In the kitchen she put together three place-settings of assorted cutlery, then found some drinking glasses and a little china cruet with '*a present from Southsea*' painted across the front. Phoebe knew that the sisters had been servants but she had not realised what that meant in terms of possessions. When she looked more closely at the furniture, cushions, antimacassars, mats and such, the plainness and economy of their living shamed her. What an expense she must be to them, living like a greedy cuckoo in their nest.

At half-past eleven she filled the kettle and set it on the stove. When Nellie and Sarah came back from church they would need a cup of tea. In the larder on a chair was a stack of old newspapers. Idly, Phoebe began to trawl through them. There were items about King Edward and Queen Alexandra presenting medals to heroes of the African war; details of the different catches made by the Brighton fishermen: times of bazaars and concerts, all meaningless to her. And then she saw it: a police notice.

It sounded like a story from a penny dreadful – two socialites on the run: greedy and worthless. Phoebe supposed that there had been hundreds of copies scattered through the town. Now, they would be blowing about the gutters, or hanging on nails in garden privies, being put to good use. Accompanying the article were drawings of Mr and Mrs Allen. Phoebe stared at their faces, hers smiling and vacuous, and James oozing confidence and charm. Words from the past replayed in her head.

'Phoebe, why must you always be grasping at shadows? There is no substance to the man. He is a parasite, living off others, leeching their efforts, their talent.'

Mummy was substance. She painted, did calligraphy, ran committees and wrote petitions. Mummy was elegant and sure of things. She had tried to please her but she was exacting, and Phoebe withered under her criticism. It was cold in her shadow, and she craved light and attention. At parties she flourished. People saw her as decorative, an ornament. She could smile and laugh and flatter, and nothing was required of a pretty girl. James had dazzled her. When she thought about it, her only achievement had been Sophie, her little girl. Sophie had loved her; when she leaned over the cot the baby quivered with joy, her hands reaching up to her. Now, she would love her grandmother, and Phoebe would be no more than a shadowy photograph. For a moment the pain stopped her breath.

The sound of the key being turned in the lock made her scrunch up the paper and push it down the front of her dress. By the time the two women had taken off their coats and hats, Phoebe was in the kitchen spooning the tea into the pot.

Sarah beamed at her. 'It's good to see you up and doing. A bit of moving about will make you feel better. If the weather perks up tomorrow we might venture a trip to the shops down the road.'

'What's cooking in the stove? It smells delicious.'

'A shepherd's pie, all we need now is to get the sprouts done. You could lend a hand there. After dinner we must get started on the puddings.'

'It's Stir-up Sunday,' said Nellie, 'The last Sunday before Advent, November the thirtieth.'

Phoebe frowned. 'Whatever does that mean?'

The two sisters spoke together. '*"Stir up, we beseech, O Lord, the wills of thy faithful people; that they, plenteously bringing forth the fruit of good works, may of Thee be plenteously rewarded; through Jesus Christ Our Lord."* It's the day set aside for making Christmas puddings.'

Phoebe sat with Sarah, cutting the outer leaves from the sprouts and marking them with a cross, so that they would cook more quickly. After dinner she helped Nellie weigh out the pudding ingredients, cut up the orange and lemon peel in tiny strips, and finally give the mixture a good stir.

It was only in the evening, when Nellie went to visit her friend across the road that she thought about her situation. 'I thought I was going to die in that park, you know. Letting go seemed a relief somehow.'

Sarah seemed not to have heard. There was a silence between them for some while, and then she said, 'You need to let go of all that sadness before you can begin to mend yourself, Miss Phoebe. Time, rest and care will have you turned around.'

'You won't tell Mummy, will you?'

'She will need to know that you are safe, beyond that is in your hands. I'll write a note to Fee, you remember her. She can tell madam and set her mind at rest. No need for her to know the address, just that you're being cared for.'

Sarah's warm acceptance of her opened the floodgates, and Phoebe couldn't stop talking. Sarah sat through the long litany of her woes, calmly darning her stocking.

The next day on their way back from the shops Sarah asked her, 'Why was it, d'you think, that you got off the train, when you did?'

'I couldn't bear for Mummy to see me like that, and I didn't want to see her with that look on her face that told me I was nothing. And, there was a wafer of hope that James might still be in Brighton.'

'But you sent her your handbag.'

'Oh, I forgot it in my panic to get out of the carriage.'

Sarah smiled at her. 'P'raps you didn't forget. Unbeknownst to yourself, you sent your Ma a message.'

'Why would I do that?' Puzzled, Phoebe stared into the fire.

The old woman took the wooden darning-mushroom out of the stocking and put it back in her sewing-basket. 'Given time it will come to you.'

'I don't know why I'm here,' Phoebe said, shyly. 'But I'm glad to be with you and Nellie. I'm grateful.'

'That'll be enough to be going on with, don't you think?

Monday 1st December 1902
Dear Fee,
Meaning to write for ages but lost your address so sent it care of the barracks. Me and Nellie are settled snug as two bugs in a rug down here in Kemp Town. Everything rattling along till some weeks ago, we was walking in the park and found this girl half froze to death on a bench.

It was Miss Feeby. I don't know how we got her home she was that trembly. Her clothes not fit for the dustman and her got so thin. She slept and slept. You wouldn't know her, for all the swank has been knocked out of her. Seemingly her husband took off with all her jewels and she'd bin holed up in a hotel till she was almost penniless.

I wanted to write to her mother but wonder if you could speak with her. Miss Feeby is not fit to travel. Perhaps Mrs Mount could come down and see her. She is sorry for all she done but wants to spend Christmas with us. Soon as it is over perhaps you could speak to Mrs Mount and see what she advises.

Hope you will come and see us when all this is settled.
Ever your friend,
Sarah.'

Fidelis had brought the letter to her that morning with her breakfast tray. The relief that her daughter was safe brought Marcia Mount to the brink of tears. 'May I keep this?' she gasped.

'Yes, madam. May I go now, Miss Sophie will be awake soon.'

Unable to speak, Marcia gestured towards the door. As soon as it was closed behind the girl, she covered her face in her hands and wept. She had deceived herself into thinking that she was well rid of Phoebe, but the surge of relief and the tears gave the lie to her indifference. Thank God the child was out of the clutches of that tin-pot gambler and being taken care of. It was not spelled out in so many words, but Marcia knew she would not be welcome in Brighton. What irony it was that Phoebe should be living now in the home of her former servant and dependent on her kindness, when she was, herself, so careless of others' welfare. It was likely that she had not given a thought to what her mother was suffering.

It hurt Marcia to think that Phoebe preferred the company of her cook to that of her mother and her daughter. But what of Sophie, how would she react to her mother's return? Everything would be thrown into confusion. How was it that she could see the solution to any practical problem, but was so inept when it came to matters of the human heart? Well, she would not be precipitate. Dorcas was coming over from the Isle of Wight, so there was much to attend to.

Drying her eyes, she pulled the bell for Eileen to run her bath. Gradually she regained control of the day. There was the orphans' tea-party this afternoon and their presents be wrapped. And then Eileen interrupted her. 'That Sergeant Hankins is here, madam. Wants to see you. Says it's urgent.' Her maid's face was flushed with excitement.

'Show him in, at once.'

As the policeman came into the room she rose, and greeted him. 'Sergeant, do take a seat. Would you like some tea, Eileen will fetch it for you straight away?'

'No, I will not be staying long, Mrs Mount, thank you kindly.'

'Thank you, Eileen,' said Marcia firmly. Once the door

was shut she turned to him. 'You have some new information about my daughter, I believe?'

'Yes, Mrs Mount, she came forward herself yesterday. Called in at one of the Brighton stations and wished to inform you that she is living apart from her husband and in good health. She wishes any reward to be sent to this Miss Sarah Gibbons – the woman who has been caring for her.'

'Thank you, sergeant,' said Marcia. 'I shall do as my daughter wishes. It is a tremendous relief to me, as you can imagine. Thank you for keeping me informed. Is there anything else that you need from me?'

The man got to his feet. 'No thank you, kindly. I will be on my way, Mrs Mount. But, please contact me if there is anything you think I should know. Good-day to you.'

Marcia rang the bell for Eileen. Thank goodness, it had not been necessary to show him the letter from the cook. It would have been too shaming for him to know of her daughter's reluctance to return home. She reached for her pen and note-pad. She wrote a reminder about getting Handleys to send a hamper to Phoebe and the sisters. Perhaps if she were not too fatigued by the orphans' party, she would write a letter to her and enclose a postal order.

12

Daniel handed his mother and Maude into the carriage. Things were going well between them; all he had to do now was to work himself up to a proposal, then he would have his life back on the rails. Promotion was not far off, and Pa and Ma were cock-a-hoop with the thought of a Palmer-Herrick match. If only he could feel something for her other than brotherly affection. He was strung up at the thought of seeing Fidelis at the concert that night. Even though their friendship was at an end, he could not stop wanting her. If he could just see her as the drill sergeant's daughter, one of the numerous lower ranks, and not waver from this, his future would be secured. As they walked to their seats in the front row of the balcony everyone rose and clapped. His father waved them back to their seats, and the concert began. The lights dimmed, and a fanfare announced the appearance of the master of ceremonies, Drill Sergeant Jack McCauley.

'Ladies and gentlemen, I set before you a veritable feast of entertainment: conjurers that will dazzle with the speed of their fingers, dancers that will have you tapping your feet. At vast expense we have secured the services of a lady dear to your heart and mine, Miss Shamrock O'Shea, and at no cost at all the Morgan brothers, princes of drollery. But,' Jack McCauley brought his gavel down with a thud, 'let us dispense with my vertiginous diatribe and present for you – Juggling Jo Johnson.'

Was she on the programme? It was too dark now for Daniel to see. He wrenched his mind back to the man on the stage, throwing balls into the air as if his life depended on it. Desperation rather than gaiety underlined his act, and the audience clapped with relief rather than enjoyment. Two young marines with their faces blacked-up like minstrels tapped their way back and forth across the stage. One behind the other, they moved their arms forward and back in imitation of the pistons of a train. Everyone clapped to the rhythm of the dancers' feet. A shrill whistle from Jack, acting as station-master, brought the performance to a halt. One act followed another in varying degrees of skill: bagpipe playing, singing, even spoon-playing – all had their moment of glory. The curtain came down on the first half, and Daniel's breathing eased.

Maude clutched at his arm. 'It was so good,' she said, smiling at him. 'Weren't the Berry Twins funny?'

'I'm so glad you liked it,' he mumbled. 'Can I get you a fruit cup? You must be thirsty. It's fearfully hot in here.'

'Oh thank you. Shall we step outside?'

Arthur Palmer and his father were laughing together as they made their way towards them. All around, marines and their families laughed and called to one another.

'What's coming next?' Maude asked, as they retook their seats.

Daniel opened the programme and she leapt out at him. Miss Fidelis McCauley with a medley of Irish songs. Christ! Just the name was enough to dry his mouth and churn his belly. He handed the programme back, unable to trust himself to speak.

Fidelis had brushed her hair till it shone, and wore it loose about her shoulders. Afraid to look out at the audience, she had stayed in the dressing-room during the interval. Once the lights were dimmed she would not be able to see him. This was a test of her faithfulness to Harry. If she could get through the evening without coming into contact with Daniel, they would all be safe. Ma would be proud of her and she would get a hug from Auntie Ruby. Afterwards, she could write her letter with no guilty feelings.

'You ready?' called Shamrock, putting her head around the door. 'Come up and stand in the wings. I'll warm them up for you.'

There was a great wave of applause rolling up from the audience as her aunt took the stage. Her smile blazed out across the footlights, as she gave a deep curtsey to her adoring public. She had them eating out of her hand, in a song about a girl who was no better than she should be. With expert timing and a roguish wink she delivered the chorus line: '"*Oh, you don't know Nellie, like I do, said the naughty little bird on Nellie's hat*".' She teased and titillated them until they wept with laughter, and strode from the stage leaving them wanting more.

'And now with songs from the Emerald Isle I give you that red-haired beauty, Miss Fidelis McCauley. Let me hear a real Globe Theatre welcome for her first number: "If I Were a Blackbird".'

As the applause died down, she left the security of the wings and walked across the empty stage towards the footlights. Waiting in the darkness was her audience. Fidelis raised her head and sniffed the air like a nervous animal. It was thick with tobacco, orange-peel, and damp wool uniforms drying out after the rain. As her father sat down her music started. Breathe deeply, she told herself. Don't look out there. The introduction stopped and she began to sing. Her nerves fell away, and the words possessed her. Soon everyone joined in the chorus and she was launched. At the song's end there was a moment's silence, and she waited for their judgement.

Then all she could see were row upon row of clapping hands. She waved to acknowledge the applause from the gallery. He was up there in the front seats with a girl beside him. Just the blurred outline was enough to make her belly lurch and her mouth dry. For a second he looked at her, and then shifted his gaze away. Anger seized her. How dare he ignore her! Whatever it cost, she would make him look at her and want her as she wanted him. The second song, '*She Moved through the Fair*', had no accompaniment. Fidelis licked her lips and swallowed. After a steadying breath, she closed her eyes and concentrated on the intricacies of the tune. The notes spilled out pure and true. This time, when she finished the applause was immediate. As the violin lead her into her last song, she looked up at Daniel and sang only for him.

> '*The water is wide, I cannot go o'er*
> *And neither have I wings to fly.*
> *Give me a boat that will carry two,*
> *And both shall row, my love and I.*'

Between the fourth and fifth verses he raised his head and looked at her, and Fidelis knew she loved him. Her longing fused with the words of the song and the painful sweetness of the violin. She knew he could not look away – he was *ensorcelée*.

> '*A ship there is she sails the seas,*
> *She's loaded deep as deep can be,*
> *But not so deep as the love I'm in,*
> *I know not if I sink or swim.*'

In the stillness between the ending of the song and the applause, he uncurled his fingers from the edge of the balcony and raised his hand for a second towards her.

*   *   *

The hair stood up on the back of his neck, and the purity of her voice pained him with its beauty. There was no hiding the desire that coursed through him. He wanted to kiss her mouth, feel the heat of her and bury his face in her hair. The music stopped and applause burst out around him. She smiled and was gone. The rest of the concert passed in a fog. Automatically, he applauded when required and stood up for the National Anthem. The lights went up and the cast filled the stage. Pa got up and made a speech; the words were meaningless, nothing mattered but his need to see her.

Maude asked him something, and he nodded and smiled without the least idea of what she said. There was a lot of shaking of hands, and acres of nodding and smiling. He found himself propelled out of the theatre and into the night. He was in a fever of impatience. Where was she? As his parents stepped into their carriage and Maude followed them, he saw Fidelis with her aunt walking towards the barracks gates.

'I'll be back in a moment, you go ahead,' he said, turning back. 'I've left my gloves inside.'

He walked back towards the theatre until the carriage was out of sight, then hurried after the two women. They were laughing together. Shamrock walked over to the sentry on duty at the gate and began talking to him. Fidelis followed her.

Daniel fumed. Speaking to her outside the guardroom would be bound to create gossip, and the aunt would, likely, mention it to her parents. As the two women walked through the gate and out of the barracks, Fidelis appeared to look back at him.

He waved his hand. Had she seen him?

'You did well, Fee. I was proud of you, we all were. Ruby was crying, even your Ma had to blow her nose. Mrs Herrick said you were to be congratulated.'

As they stepped into the house, her aunt hugged her fiercely. 'Aren't you a chip off the old block? All those rehearsals paid off, you've a voice like an angel. Isn't that the truth, Mary?'

Ma patted her shoulder, then kissed her. Fidelis knew that she was proud of her but would say nothing. 'Will you fetch the bread-knife, Fee, then we can start.'

She could barely swallow. Food that she had been ravenous for had lost its appeal. Talk passed over her head. If only she could leave. But Ma had worked all day to set such a spread before them, and everyone sat there waiting to share her triumph.

Fidelis laughed at Uncle Norman's jokes and winked at Pa, as he crept up behind Ma with her birthday present, a pair of china candlesticks for her dressing-table.

'Jack, they are very fine,' she said, even reaching up to him and kissing his cheek.

Earlier in the day Fidelis had given her mother a glass flower vase, but now she wanted to round off her day with something more personal.

'It's nearly Christmas, Ma, and I wanted to sing your favourite carol like you'll hear it in church.' She had learnt the Latin words for 'O come all ye faithful' especially for her. Getting up from the table, she stood facing them. Her mother looked happier than she had seen her for ages, even letting Pa put his arm around her.

'Adeste fidele laete triumphantes, Venite, venite, in Bethlehem, Regem caelorum . . .'

To her surprise Pa and Shamrock joined in. When they had finished Ma got to her feet. 'This has been a special day for me, and thank you everyone for your kindness. I am a little tired so I'll bid you all good-night.'

''Night Mary, love,' said Ruby, 'we had best be off. Norman's on duty first thing. Thanks for inviting us, it's bin a rare evening.'

Shamrock was slumped in Pa's chair, boots off and snoring loudly.

'Will you walk me back to Heron Grove, Pa? It's such a lovely night.'

Arm-in-arm they strolled through the silent streets.

'It's a while since I had you to myself, Fee. I need to know how you are faring, out in the wide world. Are you happy?'

'Yes, I love little Sophie, she's coming on so well, now. She seems a different child. Of course, her grandma dotes on her but I think it's because she knows where she is. I have her in a quiet routine. And I get on well with the others. Eileen and Cook are ever so nice and little Midge is lovely. She's got a lad from the barracks comes round the kitchen door. Tommy Jakes.'

'That scamp,' laughed Pa. 'Isn't he the despair of me, and the Sergeant Major? Two left feet and as witless as a pudding, but not an ounce of harm in the fellow.'

She squeezed his arm. 'I love you, Pa.'

'Fee my darling, aren't I the proudest father in creation?'

They walked along the sea-shore towards Southsea. It was a starry night and the quarter moon was on its back. There was no sound save for their footsteps and the lapping of waves on the shingle.

'There's something I want to say to you, while we're on our own, Fee. You're a beautiful, intelligent girl, with your Pa's passion and wilfulness. It's a dangerous mixture and your heart can lead your head astray. Are you certain sure it's Harry that you love?'

Fidelis felt a lurch of alarm. 'I think so, I'm very fond of him.'

'Fee, be very honest with yourself. I know your Ma and Ruby and Norman are all cock-a-hoop about the engagement, but are you rushing into it to please them?' He sighed. 'There's no hell on earth more destructive than a loveless marriage.'

She could feel the tears welling in her eyes. 'Oh Pa, please don't say that.'

'I shan't ever say it again, but I want you to remember.' And then he kissed her on the cheek. 'Fee, you've the voice of an angel. Now, don't you be a stranger to us. When shall we see you again?'

'Boxing Day I think, Pa. Mrs Mount has got all sorts planned.'

'Right my darling, I'd best be off.'

Still upset by her father's words, she crept into the darkened kitchen.

'Hurrah! She's here.' Everyone jumped out at her.

Fidelis laughed, shakily. 'Nearly gave me a seizure. What you doing up so late?'

'How did it go?' asked Cook, sitting there in her dressing-gown.

'Was you nervous?' Midge hopped from one foot to the other.

'Go on,' Eileen sniffed, 'give us one of them songs what you sung.'

'I'd better check on Sophie first, then I'll sing.'

'No need, I popped in on my way down, she's soundo,' said Eileen. 'Come on Fee, let's be having you.'

They hung on her every word as she tried to bring the concert alive for them, laughing as she described the nervous juggler, and impressed by her father's wordiness. Her singing made Eileen cry, and the three of them clapped heartily. It was almost midnight when they all scurried up to bed.

'Thanks for waiting up for me, it was lovely of you,' she said, shyly.

'Why wouldn't we,' sniffed Eileen, 'you're one of us.'

Lying in the darkness, listening to Sophie's steady breathing, Fidelis was too tense to sleep. She was conscious of stepping away from her family and all its security. What she might be stepping towards thrilled and terrified her, but she could no more draw back than stop the tide from turning.

The pitch of excitement the next day, in the kitchen, over the arrival of Dorcas Beningfield astonished Fidelis. What possible difference would she make to their lives, she wondered. However fascinating the woman might be she would still need waiting on, hand, foot and finger. What was she to them? As it happened, Fidelis was kept upstairs nursing Sophie through a feverish cold; she had only glimpsed her in passing. It was over a week before they were properly introduced. One evening, satisfied that the little girl was sleeping peacefully, she went down into the kitchen for a cup of cocoa and a gossip before settling down for the night.

Nobody heard her open and close the door: they were all entranced by the woman in the red satin blouse. Eileen, Cook and Midge were listening open-mouthed. Her voice was husky and she spoke intimately to them, as if they were her closest friends.

'I went out to South Africa last year you know, with my Aunt Millicent. It was to visit the camps where the Boer women and children were kept penned-up like animals. It was horrifying. There were the little ones with measles, lying on the dirt floor. I was in such a rage. They may have been Boer families but for God's sake, they were human beings. There was not enough food, or soap, no way of sterilizing the sheets. Those thin cries of the babies tortured by hunger still haunt my dreams.'

'It's a cruel world and no mistake,' said Cook, blowing her nose.

'Aunt Millicent was magnificent. She rolled up her sleeves and had everyone doing her bidding. We went up and down the veld, by train, visiting one camp after another. I have never attended so many funerals. All the way home from

South Africa to England, she was working on her report. After that we stumped around England talking here, there and everywhere, raising money for the Distress Fund.'

In the sympathetic silence that followed, Fidelis set down her cocoa and drew up a chair.

'You must be Fidelis,' said Dorcas holding out her hand. 'I'm so very glad to meet you. Aunt Marcia has told me so much about you and she didn't exaggerate one bit. You are a beauty, positively Pre-Raphaelite.'

Blushing at such extravagant praise, she held her gaze. Certainly Dorcas looked every inch the artist, with her mane of black hair let loose around her shoulders, and her dark, thickly-lashed eyes dominating her small pale face. In spite of her curiosity there was a bead of resentment that held Fidelis back. What right had Dorcas to swan into their territory, invading their privacy? She had a mental picture of Mrs Mount's reaction if her nursemaid were suddenly to seat herself among her dinner guests and swig the sherry.

'I can't stop, Sophie's not well,' she muttered, not yet ready to pay her subscription to the Dorcas Beningfield Admiration Society. 'I'd better get back to her.'

'Do let me come up and peek at her. The last time I saw Sophie she was a new-born babe.'

'Very well,' Fidelis muttered. This being pally with servants was all one way. They were your chums when it suited them, but you still had to dance to their tune.

Once inside the nursery, Dorcas leaned over the cot and smiled at the sleeping Sophie. 'She is a darling. I look forward to taking her out one day.' She paused at the doorway. 'I believe you sang last night at the concert in aid of the King's Fund for the wounded men from the South African war, another cause dear to my heart.'

Fidelis nodded, and Dorcas took her hand and shook it firmly.

'Good-night to you,' she said, smiling at her. 'I know we are going to be friends.'

Mention of the concert brought Daniel into her mind. Thank goodness she had managed to draw back from the brink of disaster. If her swooning for Daniel had gone any further there would be more than wounded pride to deal with. They had been '*ensorcelées*' as he had said – spellbound. All she had to do, now, was throw away that bottle of perfume.

13

Phoebe was awake early. Gathering up her clothes she crept from the bedroom, familiarity guiding her feet down the narrow staircase. She lit a candle, and by its flame tied an apron over her nightdress. Proud of her new skills, she riddled the ash and clinker from the range and emptied it into a bucket before re-laying the fire with crumpled paper, sticks and lumps of coal. While the water heated in the kettle, she was lost in thought.

The time in Brighton had been a revelation. Privacy taken for granted in Clarendon House was a luxury in Prince William Terrace. Sharing a bed with Sarah, undressing in front of her and using a chamber-pot, were all shocks to her system. That all these things were becoming more and more irksome was, perhaps, a mark of her recovery. On first being rescued she had craved closeness. Now, she wanted to reclaim her life and see her daughter. But Phoebe knew that Sarah and Nellie had saved her life, and she would always be grateful.

She made the tea and while it brewed used the remaining water to wash in. As she lathered soap between her palms she realised it was Christmas Day. All three of them were going to the Methodist church for morning service, after 'wiring in', as Sarah called it: preparing the vegetables, putting the goose in the oven and laying the table.

'Happy Christmas to you, Miss Phoebe,' said Sarah, when she went into their bedroom; blinking at her she struggled into a sitting position and held out her hand for the cup of tea.

'Happy Christmas,' said Nellie, after Phoebe tapped on her door. She was sitting up reading her Bible.

By half-past nine everything was in readiness. Crunching over the frosty streets, they set off for church. Once inside, Phoebe looked about her at the congregation. They were ordinary working people: fishermen's wives, servants from the hotels, labourers and seamstresses. She thought of Mummy and her friends who would be gathering in St Thomas's church in Portsmouth. The women would be assessing one another's outfits, and there would be naval officers reading the lessons and sidesmen taking around the silver collection plate.

Here, simply clad, in front of a plain wooden table, neighbours gathered from choice and conviction. Phoebe shared the hymn-book with Sarah, while the bearded man at the piano began to play. *'Away in a manger no crib for a bed, The little Lord Jesus lay down his sweet head.'*

She could not continue. Tears pricked behind her lashes, and she was pierced with longing for Sophie. The service continued with Phoebe in a fog of misery. While the sisters wished their friends Happy Christmas, she made the excuse to hurry back and see to the dinner. After setting the potatoes to roast around the goose she hurried upstairs. While her courage lasted, there was a letter she had to write.

Mrs Mount called her staff into the sitting-room to give them their presents. Dressed in her party frock and holding her nursemaid's hand, Sophie walked down the last flight of stairs. She had a red satin bow in her hair, and insisted she be held up to the hall mirror so that she could primp and preen in front of it. After she had greeted her grandmother with a kiss, the little girl was settled in her chair with some slices of apple to distract her.

Fidelis looked around her. The Christmas tree was lit with

candles, and on the top-most branch was an angel with gauzy silver wings. She drew in the scents of pine, chrysanthemums and lavender polish, combined with madam's perfume.

'Happy Christmas, everyone.' Marcia Mount stood immaculate in a blue dress offset by a lace collar. 'I want to thank all of you for your hard work and loyalty.' She smiled at Midge. 'Now, I believe there is an extra cause for celebration. Margaret will you come forward, please.'

Unaccustomed to being called by her proper name, Midge blushed and hung back.

'I think Happy Birthday is in order.'

She blushed and twisted a strand of hair between her fingers, while they all sang to her. Mrs Mount picked out a large parcel, and handed it to her. 'For you, Margaret, thank you for all that you have done for me.'

It was a winter cloak complete with hood, and woollen gloves tucked in the pockets.

Midge was entranced. 'I ain't never 'ad a new coat. Ooh, ta ever so much, madam. Mrs Hobbs, Eileen, thank you both more than I can say.'

Cook was given a tea-service, for use in her room, and Eileen a Witney blanket. Each of them of them had an envelope that crackled with paper money.

'Begging your pardon, madam,' said Cook, giving a little bob. 'I'm most grateful but I best see to the dinner, now.'

Eileen followed after her, with the excited Midge.

Marcia Mount shook Fidelis's hand. 'Fidelis, please accept this with my gratitude. You have worked hard and it is thanks to you that Sophie is so happy and secure.'

Unwrapping the red paper, she found a new music case. 'That's just what I wanted,' she said, piling one lie on top of another. Busying herself with folding up the paper, she hid her guilty face. How could she have been so deceitful and foolish? Still, it was all over now, all that madness. There was a letter waiting upstairs from Harry and she had a wedding to plan for.

'I'm off to church now, Fidelis. Please tell Eileen to have the sherry and ratafias ready for our return.'

'Yes, madam.'

After settling Sophie in her pram in the hall with her toys, Fidelis was kept busy in the dining-room, helping Eileen to set the table. Cook, her face slippery with sweat, was setting the Christmas pudding to steam.

'Got six for dinner; madam, Miss Dorcas and four of them Suffagits, them that wants to get into Parliament to give men what for. Rich creatures what 'ave never done an 'and's turn, they don't know nuffink about the plight of ordinary women.'

'But, madam and Miss Dorcas are Suffragists too, and they do more than talk,' Fidelis said, taking up the silver cruet and the serving-spoons.

'Ah, well,' Cook said, turning her attention to the potatoes par-boiling on the back of the range, 'they're out of the top drawer, almost gentry. Knows how to go about things. madam's always sending a sack of coal here and a sack there. Tons of people she looks after, and Miss Dorcas bin out taking round parcels.'

It seemed no time at all until everyone returned from church and dinner was under way. Sophie was back in her chair, the centre of attention, with Dorcas helping her to mashed potato and cutting her turkey into tiny pieces. Eileen and Fidelis rushed back and forth with serving-dishes, and Midge clattered the pots in the sink. Madam's guests were earnest, campaigning women in gravy-coloured tweeds. Their talk was of mission fields, African babies and votes for women. Dorcas winked at Fidelis behind their backs. Then Cook had her moment of glory as she carried the pudding, aflame with brandy, into the dining-room.

Afterwards Mrs Mount said, 'Go now and enjoy your meal. We shall not require you until tea-time.'

Fidelis took the excited Sophie out of her chair and carried her upstairs for her nap. When the toddler's eyes were closed and arms flung back in sleep, Fidelis took up Harry's Christmas letter.

> *November 7th 1902*
> *Dear Fee,*
>
> *I long to see you and hold you in my arms. When I close my eyes I can picture you laughing with your head thrown back and your hair flying all around you. How did the barracks concert go? I have such memories of all of us singing after supper in our house. The audience are in for a treat with you and Shamrock to entertain them. I told you about meeting up with my two brothers in Jamaica three of us all buglers together. Sammy is now a corporal and Peter hopes to be promoted soon. We had such larks teasing one another. There was a wonderful finale to our time together. As a huge orange sun began to sink down in the sky the bugler in each ship took up their positions. From my place on the flagship I could see my brothers each on their bridge waiting for the call to sound alert. One by one we played sunset the notes ringing out across the water. I had the honour, being on the flagship, of sounding the Carry on, before all the others. A proud moment I shall never forget.*
>
> *I am so looking forward to us getting married. Ma used to say that being one another's best friend is the greatest joy in life. Dear Fee have a Happy Christmas and give my love to everyone at home.*
>
> *I am your most loving fiance,*
> *Harry*

Relief flooded through her. Tomorrow she would see Aunt

Ruby and would be able to look her in the eye without squirming.

Footsteps ran up the stairs to her door. It was Midge.

'You comin' down, Fee? Dinner's ready, me bellie's rumbling, what about you?'

'I wouldn't miss it for the world,' she said, taking off her nursery apron and tiptoeing after her.

Cook beamed at all of them. 'I've cut out yer dinners already, don't want all the fantag of servin' dishes. Eat hearty all of you.'

'Our Mum sent some of her raisin wine. Who's for a glass?' asked Eileen, uncorking a bottle.

Midge held out her glass. 'Never had wine.'

Eileen sniffed. 'Don't know about that.'

'Half a glass,' urged Cook. 'She gets tiddly, we'll stick her out in the old kennel.'

The three of them laughed as the red wine glugged into her glass.

'To all of us, our Christmas, bought and paid for.' Eileen gave a rare smile.

'God bless us every one,' said Cook, clinking her glass with Midge.

All was silent, save for the clattering of knives and forks. Fidelis ate slowly, relishing every succulent slice of turkey and crisp golden potatoes. The kitchen was warm and wreathed in the scent of roast meat, spices and heated rum. In the saucepan on top of the stove the pudding bubbled.

'My stars, our Midge, you got the appetite of a navvy,' laughed Cook. 'I don't know where you puts it.'

This was the best part of the day, with them all together, laughing and chatting. By the time the bell rang for tea to be laid in the dining-room, Cook, who had sampled the raisin wine with great zest, was somewhat fuddled. She staggered to bed leaving Eileen, Fidelis and Midge to hold the fort.

Phoebe read through her letter then sealed it away in the envelope before she could change her mind. It was time for new beginnings: she had been a convalescent long enough.

'I'm off to the post,' she called to the sisters, dozing in front of the fire. 'When I come back we'll open Mummy's hamper.'

Promising herself a treat before doing something difficult was an old habit. But this time half the pleasure would be in seeing the sister's faces as she shared the Hundleys hamper with them. Such luxuries would be a revelation. They had worked hard all their lives, smoothing the paths of the rich. Their hands were red and rough from washing-soda, and knees swollen from kneeling, scrubbing floors and doorsteps. But Phoebe knew that once she was away from them and back with Mummy, it would be so easy to slip back into her idle spendthrift ways. In church she had promised Daddy to try harder, but she had made promises before. Quickly she thrust the letter through the red mouth of the pillar-box, before she had a chance to change her mind.

'What shall we try next?' She encouraged Sarah and Nellie after they had feasted on slices of cured York ham from Mummy's hamper. 'Crystallised pineapple or chocolate ginger, violet creams, what do you say? There is of course a plum cake.'

Nellie laughed. 'Miss Phoebe, you'll lead us astray, giving us gentry tastes.'

'I'm going home next week so you won't have time to make a habit of it,' she said. 'I have more than outstayed my welcome.' She waved a hand in dismissal of Sarah's protests. 'I want to thank both of you. I could have died out there in the park and no one would have been the wiser. You have shown me Christian kindness, and I will never forget it.'

'I'll make us some tea,' said Nellie. 'I vote we try the plum cake.'

Sarah smiled at Phoebe. 'That would be handsome. We'll get down the best plates. Fine foods deserve fine china.'

At nine o'clock Nellie went off to bed, leaving Sarah and Phoebe sitting either side of the kitchen fire.

'Did you ever think what could have happened to Master James?' her old cook asked her, when they had sat in silence for some time.

'Do you know something?' Her heart gave a lurch. 'What have you heard?'

'There was a report in the paper, on Christmas Eve, of a man found dead in a London dance hall, near Waterloo station. Seemingly the place caught fire and he was found just inside the door, overcome with smoke. Police wants anyone to come forward who might have known him.'

'But why do you think it was James?'

'It was the things they found in his pocket. There was a photo of a woman with a baby. On the back it said, *"To Darling James with love from Sophie and her Mummy, Christmas 1901."* Then there was a pack of cards and a New Testament.'

'There must be lots of Sophies all over the country,' Phoebe blustered.

'Maybe so, but in the front page of the Testament there was some writing what said, something like, *"To my son James to guide him through his life from his loving father Matthew Allen. Beccles June 1897."'*

'Have you got the paper, Sarah,' whispered Phoebe.

'Here it is my dear, shall I leave you to read it on your own?'

'No, stay with me, please.'

The article mentioned a card for a club in Piccadilly, and a crumpled railway ticket from Brighton to London. He was gone, her second-rate Romeo.

Phoebe wept. 'I did love him, you know, he was such fun.

He always reminded me of Icarus in the story, the boy who made himself wings and flew up to the sun. His wings melted and he fell to earth. Poor darling, he just never wanted to grow up.'

The happiness of the day had evaporated. Phoebe tried to fix images, in her mind, of her husband at his best: James immaculate in bow tie and tails whirling her around the dance floor, James kissing her and whispering words of love, and James, the young father, posing proudly with his daughter. She wept for him and for herself.

Marcia Mount sat with her niece in the sitting-room, staring into the fire, a glass of port untouched beside her. The day had progressed as planned and her friends had departed, fed and wined, effusive in their thanks. Sophie had charmed them with her high spirits – she really was a treasure.

But from the moment Marcia had opened her eyes until now, late in the evening, Phoebe had dominated her thoughts. A year ago, the thought of her daughter voluntarily spending Christmas in the company of her cook would have seemed fantastical. How much had changed in the last year.

'Auntie, you look so sad, what are you thinking?'

'If only Raphael was here,' she said. 'He knew about people; I seem rather to have lost my way.'

'That's piffle. There wouldn't be a Suffrage Society in Portsmouth without you, let alone all the charity work.'

Marcia sighed. 'It's so easy to involve oneself with the needy outside one's door. The needs of Phoebe have always come second.'

'Why do you think that is?' said Dorcas, setting down her port.

'We were always competitors for Raphael's love.' There, she had voiced the nub of the problem around which the relationship with her daughter turned. 'We both wanted to be first.'

'But he loved you both, I know he did, not equally but differently.'

'There is no logic to feelings – if there were, it wouldn't be a problem. Phoebe knew she did not have my love, but was determined to have my attention, for good or ill.'

'But, what do you want for the future? You have Sophie, after all.'

'I want Phoebe to want to come home, for me as well as for her child. I need to know that she has changed, and is ready to take up her responsibilities.'

'Poor, prodigal Phoebe.'

'What do you mean?'

'When the Prodigal Son returned, his father didn't rebuke him for his past failings but welcomed him with open arms, killed the fatted calf and rubbed the slate clean. Phoebe is more than aware of her faults. She is as wounded as you are. What you both need to do is stop rubbing in the salt.'

Marcia stood up and went over to her niece and kissed her. 'What has made you into such a wise woman?' she asked.

Dorcas looked up at her. 'Finding someone to love and being loved in return. The lesson now is to make sense of my life without Mark. Why don't you go and see Phoebe next week? Christmas will be over and then you could bring her home. The New Year is a week away, time for a fresh start for both of you.'

Marcia smiled. 'You are right. I just have to gird my loins, so to speak.'

'Good night, dear Auntie, sleep well, it will all seem better in the morning. I think we should have an indulgent day tomorrow, let charity go hang.'

Marcia sighed. Making a fresh start was so easily said and so difficult to achieve.

Before supper, Fidelis took Sophie upstairs for her bath. The day had lurched from one meal to another. Midge, enveloped in an apron, stood on a box at the sink slogging through the dishes. At ten o'clock, Fidelis left them to their cocoa. 'Good night, God bless,' she said.

'Sleep tight, Fee,' said Midge, rushing over to kiss her.

She was just about to climb into bed when there was a tap on her door.

'Can I come in?' called Dorcas.

Fidelis sighed. 'Yes, of course.'

'I won't keep you long,' she said, perching on the end of the bed. 'It's just that I met a rather splendid Royal Marine, on my way home. He swore me to secrecy and gave me this letter for you.' She put her finger to her lips then crept past the sleeping Sophie, shutting the door behind her.

Fidelis shivered with more than cold as she opened the envelope, and began to read her letter.

> *December 25 1902*
> *Dear Fidelis,*
> *Since the concert I have been in a daze. The purity of your voice cut through my defences and revealed to me where my true feelings lie. I followed you to the gate that night but had not the courage to declare myself. We have unfinished business between us and I need to know what your feelings are for me. I shall be at the Captain's on Boxing Day by three o'clock. If you do not come I shall understand. I will never forget you and always cherish the time we had together.*
> *Ever your fallen angel,*
> *Daniel*

He would be waiting for her tomorrow. Fidelis's resolution ran away like sand through an hourglass. All her other tomorrows would have to take care of themselves.

'Glad you like it,' she smiled, waiting anxiously for her mother's response to the collar she had saved for months to buy.

Mary McCauley unfolded it from its nest of tissue-paper and set it down on her lap. 'From what I can see so far it's a good piece of Duchess lace. Thank you, Fee.' It was praise enough.

'I think I shall save it for your wedding, whenever that will be.'

'What are you talking about, Mary? 'Twill be next year soon as ever young fellow-me-lad is home from sea.'

'Is that what you want, Fee?' Her mother gave her a searching look. 'Are you sure it's Harry you've chosen?'

'Yes, Ma,' blustered Fidelis, 'we've known each other all our lives.'

'That's not an answer.'

Sensing her unease, Pa said, 'This has been all one-sided. Let's give the girl her presents before Ruby calls us in.'

She shot him a grateful look. 'Yes, I can't wait.'

Before her mother could say more Fidelis had the two packages on her lap. Just by their wrapping she knew which was which. The fountain pen from her father was in a satin-lined box. The two of them marvelled at the little lever on the back for drawing up the ink, and the gold nib.

'That is so fine, Pa. Harry won't recognise my writing from its old spider scrawl.'

'We'll fill it in a minute out in the sink and see how it performs.'

The gift from Ma was a stationery box made of green papier-mâché with roses twined across the hinged lid. Inside were sheets of paper and envelopes, plus a small address book and a blotter.

'That is so pretty and useful. Ma, it's lovely.' She went

around to her mother and kissed her warmly. 'I shall feel like a secretary with such grand things.'

Pa looked up at the clock on the mantelpiece. 'We'd better get ourselves into the rig of the day, it's gone six. I'll clear the table while you take your things upstairs.'

When they presented themselves next-door their neighbours were full of welcomes. 'Fee, come in. Happy Christmas, my sweet girl,' cried Ruby, 'lovely to see you.'

She was hugged and kissed and then it was Uncle Norman's turn.

'Hello, Rusty,' he said patting her hair. 'How's the world with you? Looking bonny. Sit yourself down the other side of the table.' He gave a great barking laugh. 'You're the only one skinny enough to sit there.'

Fidelis looked around the little room, so familiar to her from childhood. The walls were covered with paintings of foreign sunsets, of ships the boys had served in, and photographs of Harry, Peter and Charlie in Royal Marine uniform. On the mantelpiece were Ruby's fairings, treasured mementos of days out to seaside towns along the south coast. Unlike Ma's china cabinet and carriage clock, it was all a happy jumble.

Ruby rushed back and forth from the kitchen, while Uncle Norman busied himself pouring them 'port wine for the ladies and beer for the gents'.

Guilt gnawed at Fidelis as she sat there in Harry's house, eating, drinking and laughing as the fiancée, while knowing herself to be a liar and a cheat. If only Daniel were safely abroad and Harry at home, it would never have happened. Then she could have put her whole heart into the party. I love everyone at this table, she thought, and they all love me, yet I am betraying them not for thirty pieces of silver but for what? The feel of Daniel's mouth against mine – the scent and taste of him, and the way he makes my body sing beneath his fingers.

'Fee, more cheese, or boiled ham? What about some of Norman's pickled onions?'

'I'm saving space for your sherry trifle,' she said, passing the chutney to Pa.

'We don't want the girl to get too blown out. Wants her to give us a song.'

'Here, how's little Sophie?' asked Ruby. 'I thought she was a real sweetheart.'

Fidelis let out her breath: this was a safer topic. 'She's walking well and climbs out of her cot now. The other morning she got into bed with me, kept smacking my face. "Get up, Fee," she kept saying. Had heaps of presents, what pleased her most was a bit of red hair-ribbon. Wanted me to hold her up to the mirror to look at herself.'

'Any news of her parents?' asked Norman, spearing an onion onto his plate.

'A policeman came a few weeks ago with Mrs Allen's handbag. Seemingly it was left on a train from Brighton to Portsmouth.'

'What woman can she be, to leave her little girl like that? What's she thinking of?'

'Right, ladies,' announced Pa. 'While us common sea-soldiers clear the table, you get the place set up for a bit of a sing-song.'

Norman played the piano and Fidelis and her father sang.

After two port-and-lemons Mary McCauley began to unbend, and even clapped after Norman recited 'The March of the Dead'.

'Cripes, that's mournful,' protested Ruby. 'Let's finish up with something cheerful. What d'you say, Fee? Something to raise our spirits.'

'What about this? It's Christmassy and you can all join in.'

Fidelis and her parents, with Ruby, sang while Norman accompanied them. '*It came upon a midnight clear, That glorious*

song of old, From angels bending near the earth To touch their harps of gold.'

With many thanks and hugs and kisses the party came to an end. Once indoors, her mother kissed her good-night and went upstairs.

Fidelis and her father sat by the embers of the dying fire, not ready yet to yield up the day. She stared at the spark fairies, lost in thought.

'Remember when you were little, Fee?' he said. 'We used to lay out the matches on the table like they were marines, and go through morning parade together.'

She laughed. 'I can still do all the bugle calls.' Curling her fist in front of her mouth she imitated the notes for the seven-forty instruction: '"Recruits to the edge of the parade ground." I used to call them Daddy's boys. Remember me creeping into the drill shed and watching you raving at them? Don't hold that rifle like a pansy in the chorus, sonny. It's a bloody weapon of war. Hold it like you mean it.'

Pa laughed, 'Happy days.'

'And there's this one.' Again she curled her fist and blew through it. 'Band call, buglers and drummers. "Buglers march forward thirty paces onto the right side of the parade ground. The band will fall in behind them."'

'You had the making of a sergeant major, my girl.'

Fidelis laughed. 'How about Uncle Norman taking the silver bugle and playing Happy Birthday outside Auntie Ruby's bedroom window? She's never forgotten it.'

'What will 1903 bring us?' he said, setting the guard in front of the fire. 'If Auntie Ruby has her way, you'll be down the aisle on my arm and me proud as Punch.'

'We'll see how we feel about each other when Harry gets home,' she said, getting up from her chair and kissing him good-night.

'Time will tell,' he said. 'It's a long time 'til July, so it is.'

15

5th December 1902

  My Dear Mummy,

  Thank you for the hamper and the postal order for
£30. As you advised I cashed it and insisted that Cook
and her sister had twenty-five pounds. The remainder will
be more than enough for me especially as I need to learn
how to manage my money. It has been a simple
Christmas with Sarah and Nellie in their tiny home. We
went to the local Methodist church and the service was
plain but heartfelt. When we sung 'Away in a Manger,' I
was filled with sadness and longing for Sophie.

  Thinking of my failings as a mother made me realise
that, in all my chasing after sensation and novelty, I must
have hurt you deeply and I am truly sorry. There must
have been a wicked godmother at my christening to have
made me into such a wilful and selfish child. The sad
truth is that even when I possessed all the glittering things
I had set my heart on they did not satisfy my craving,
leaving me emptier than before. As you predicted, James
my shining Knight proved to be a hollow prize. He didn't
want a wife and child but a fat purse and a parrot
forever squawking, 'Handsome fellow, clever boy.' Even
Sophie failed to gain her father's love.

  Only Daddy ever made me feel loved and I suppose
that must be true for you too Mummy. What a disappointment we have been to each other.

*Please can you come and see me in Brighton. I know
that we have so much to talk about – practical things and
most important of all, Sophie's well being. Can you give
us warning of your arrival so that we can have a meal
waiting for you.*

With love,

Your repentant daughter Phoebe

Marcia Mount folded the letter back into its envelope. She
so wanted to believe that Phoebe had changed and was ready
to take over the care of Sophie. The little girl was so happy
and settled at Kelmscott. Fidelis had proved herself a responsible nursemaid, but the child's future needed to be put on
a secure footing. Added to that was the question of Clarendon
House. If Phoebe no longer wished to live there, the place
must be cleared and cleaned. Raphael had left it to his
daughter but she did not come into the inheritance until she
was twenty-five, in six months' time. The place must hold
sad memories for Phoebe and had been ruinously expensive
for Marcia.

Now, almost on the point of her setting out for Brighton,
a telegram had arrived.

'Dear Mother, I am requested to attend Portsmouth
Central Police Station tomorrow at 11am please meet me
there. Don't worry. Love in haste, Phoebe'

Don't worry! Marcia had boiled with frustration at the words,
her only comfort being that her daughter's presence had
been requested and not summoned. It was the least likely
place for a reunion to take place. Phoebe had been away
now for over three months. How would she look now, and,
more importantly, what would they have to say to one
another?

It occurred to her that she could meet her daughter from

the train, and thus have the stress of their meeting over before whatever lay ahead of them, at the police station. Marcia gave instructions for the spare bedroom to be made ready for a guest but gave no hint as to their identity; neither did she alert Fidelis to the possible return of Sophie's mother. Discretion was vital. Who knew what the day held for any of them?

Her daughter was barely recognisable when she stepped from the train that morning. It was Phoebe who stopped, started, then smiled as she held out her hand.

'Mummy, how good of you to meet me.'

'Phoebe, is it really you?' Marcia was incredulous.

'I am smaller, paler and certainly less fancy but I am still me.'

'I didn't want to meet you at the police station. Have we time for some tea?' The sight of her daughter shocked her. How plain and hollowed-out she seemed. And those clothes!! Merciful heavens, there was patently much she didn't know.

Phoebe looked up at the railway clock. 'We could have a few minutes in Victoria Park.'

They crossed the road and strolled down the paths between empty flower-beds and naked trees. 'Not a very cheering sight,' said Marcia, as they stood by the ornamental fountain staring into the empty fish-pond.

'It's just resting, Mummy. All the bulbs are there under the earth just waiting for the sun to warm them back to life.'

'You never used to be so philosophical,' she ventured, trying to soften what might have seemed a criticism with a smile.

'I've had a rather harsh education of late but I am through the worst now.'

'Phoebe, what is all this about the police? Why do they want to see you?'

'It's about James. It seems a body has been found in a burned-out building in London and they believe it may be him.'

'Heavens, we are not going to have to identify his body, are we?'

Phoebe shook her head. 'I'm here to see Sophie and to see you. I telegraphed because this is going to be very hard for me and I needed my mother with me.'

Marcia gripped her daughter's hands. 'Of course,' was all she could say; there was much she needed to know but it could wait. Being needed, that was a start.

As they walked through the square and looked up at the lions on the steps of the town hall, Phoebe said, 'Do you remember Daddy had names for them?'

'Aurora and Borealis,' said Marcia.

It hadn't occurred to Phoebe that her mother would have changed, but she had. Sitting with her in the waiting-room at the station she could see that the veneer of confidence was just that – a protective varnish. Was it change, or had she never really looked at her before?

Being there brought back the misery and madness of that September night when James was arrested for common assault. That one punch had broken the grocer's nose and set in train the whole sorry mess. Now the circle would be closed, and she would be back where she had started in the first place. In the time between she had learnt some hard lessons. How would James have acted if he had known he had only a few more months to live? Would he have become a reformed character? Phoebe smiled. It was his wildness that she loved, that flirting with danger and his belief that just around the corner was the bottomless pot of gold. Yet what he left with her was priceless. Out of the wreckage of their marriage had come Sophie.

'How is Sophie?' she whispered.

Marcia smiled. 'She is quite the little girl now, walking everywhere and very like you at that age.'

The question, 'Will she remember me?' hovered and was then abandoned. She would have to win her back by love and patience. But first, she must face the remaining muddle of her marriage and rebuild something with her mother.

Earlier at Brighton station Sarah had said, 'You got to grasp the nettle, Miss Phoebe, you're braver than you think. Here, I made you some cheese and chutney sandwiches. They'll come in handy on the train. There's a bottle of lime cordial, I've stoppered up the top. If you're not back by eleven tonight I shall go on up but you got the key. God bless you. Drop me a line and let me know what happens.'

'God bless, Sarah.' She had leaned out of the window and kissed her. 'You take care now.' When she had tried to thank her the old woman had brushed it aside.

'The thanks I want is to know you're being a good mother to your little girl.'

Dear, dear Sarah, she had been her guardian angel.

At the police station a constable greeted them. 'Mrs Allen and Mrs Mount, this way please, Sergeant Bryan is ready for you.'

The sergeant shook their hands and showed them to two chairs facing his desk. 'Now Mrs Allen, this is a distressing business for you and your mother, and I shall not keep you longer than is strictly necessary. First of all, are you Phoebe Victoria Allen of Clarendon House, Clarendon Road, Southsea?'

'Yes, sergeant,' she managed.

'You are the wife of James Augustine Allen of the same address. Please can you tell me when you last saw your husband?'

Startled, she looked up to see her mother twisting her gloves between her hands. It was a gesture she remembered from Daddy's funeral – the one clue to her mother's feelings on that day. Phoebe had been distraught, but Mummy had been

utterly dignified until the funeral tea when she retired to her bedroom and locked the door.

'On the thirtieth of September last year, we were staying in a hotel in Brighton. It was called Mon Repose.'

'Why were you staying there?'

'We wanted to sell my jewellery in the Lanes and start a new life in America.' She licked her lips. How foolish it seemed, now – the stuff of trashy novels.

'And what were the circumstances of his leaving you?'

'I had fallen asleep in the afternoon and I think he saw it as an opportunity to get away and take my jewellery with him.'

'Strike out on his own, is that what you mean?'

'Yes.' She was acutely aware of her mother sitting there, listening to her misdeeds.

'Did you make any efforts to find him, Mrs Allen?'

'At first I thought he would come back, and then,' she sighed, 'I had enough to do to look after myself.'

'As you have been informed, the Metropolitan Police found what is possibly your husband's body, in a burnt-out dance hall near Waterloo Station.'

'I read that there were some things left in his jacket.'

'We have had them sent down for you to look at. Do you feel able to do that?'

'I would rather face up to it now, than have it hanging over me.'

They were just things after all. She watched the sergeant pull open the desk drawer and take out a paper parcel tied up with string. Phoebe gulped; a whole lifetime reduced to this.

'Do you recognise these items?'

'Yes, all of them, sergeant. My mother has another copy of that photograph.' It had been such a happy day when the photographer came to the house. It was to be a surprise for

James's birthday last year. Sophie was ten months old, wriggling and gurgling in her arms. Phoebe was well recovered from the birth and proud of her new slim figure. She remembered the man disappearing behind the black hood of the camera, and she and her daughter laughing together.

'Mrs Allen, are you able to continue?'

She dried her eyes, 'Ah, yes, sergeant, I'm sorry. The writing in the New Testament, that is his father's. Matthew Allen was a vicar in Beccles, he's buried there.' She looked up at the policeman. 'The cards will be no surprise, from your earlier dealings with my husband.'

'Indeed, madam.' Again he opened the drawer. 'There is also a ring.'

She had bought it for him as an engagement present and was touched that he had kept it, considering the financial straits he had been in.

The sergeant took it from an envelope and set it down on the desk. It was so typical of her husband: twenty-two carat gold with a green jasper stone, a real gambler's ring.

Phoebe nodded. 'Yes, I gave him that ring.'

'How tall was your husband and what size shoes did he wear?'

'Five feet eleven and his shoe size was nine and a half.'

It was all over. She sat there not knowing what she felt.

'I will have to ask you to make a statement to that effect, sign it, and then we will come to the matter of the body.'

'The body, sergeant, what do you mean?' Marcia was on her feet.

'As next-of-kin Mrs Allen will need to let us know her wishes as to its disposal, funeral and burial, you understand.'

'Would it be possible for my husband's body to be brought down to Portsmouth for burial, at our expense?' She looked questioningly at her mother and received a nod from her. 'Whatever he may have done, he was the father of my child.'

'I think we will get the statement taken, Mrs Allen, and then we can contact you tomorrow and make any other arrangements.'

Afterwards, outside the station, the two women stood on the pavement, awkward with one another.

'Phoebe, I think you did well in a very difficult situation.'

She smiled. 'Even at the end, Mummy, he is still costing you money.'

'What would you like to do now? I expect you want to see Sophie.'

'Of course I want to see her but not just yet. I want to do all the horrid, disagreeable things first and get them over with. Let's go to the house and see what state it's in.'

Marcia sat in the cab listening to the horse's hooves clip-clopping towards Clarendon Road. It had all been so different from the encounter she had nerved herself to expect. Phoebe was changed. There was a dignity about her and a different manner in her way of dealing with people. Wanting James to be brought home was a surprise. But then, what did she really know about her daughter's last months?

They both stood in the hallway, looking about them in the cold, silent house.

'How sad and neglected it feels,' Phoebe shivered.

Mother and daughter walked from room to room, opening drawers full of table linen and cutlery, and cupboards full of china.

'I was so lucky and didn't know it,' there was a wistfulness in Phoebe's voice, 'having so much of everything. Poor house, it smells of soot and candle grease and look at the dining-table, it used to gleam, and the mirror is so dull.' She paused at the door of her bedroom. 'I need to be private for a moment. Do you mind, Mummy?'

*   *   *

She had forgotten the chaos she had left it in, the bed unmade and face-powder spilled on the floor. There was her negligee in a corner and James's shirt, the collar bloodstained where he had cut himself shaving. Sophie had been conceived in this bed; Phoebe had sat in it, nursing her while James read the paper. They had fought, made love and fought again. Now it was a sordid testimony to their lost chances.

She looked at her clothes – evening gowns, a long tweed coat, high-necked blouses, and on the floor a dozen pairs of shoes. In the chest-of-drawers were petticoats, camisoles and nightdresses. James's suits and shirts and ties were packed in the other wardrobe. It was like the dressing-room of a theatre, waiting for the actors to return and breathe life into the costumes.

After facing her demons, Phoebe felt tired and hungry. Her mother was in the nursery, looking at the ridiculously expensive rocking-horse that James had bought after a rare win at cards.

'Sophie will love this,' she said. 'In a year or so she will be able to climb up on it. The child is quite tall for her age, you know.'

Sitting down in the bed that Molly had once used, Phoebe opened her handbag. 'Do you know, Mummy, Sarah packed me up some sandwiches and lime cordial, even ginger snaps. I'll just rinse out a tooth-glass and we can have a picnic.'

Marcia surprised her by sitting down on the nursing-chair and holding out her hand.

They ate in silence, passing the glass back and forth between them. Having the advantage of being on her own territory, Phoebe said, 'Why did you never love me?'

It was some while before her mother said anything.

'I had been delighted at the thought of having you, our baby, Raphael's and mine. I had a very sickly time at first, and then in the last few months I was bounding with health.

Your father was sure it was going to be a boy and then came your birth. I was in labour for three days and was terribly torn. The doctor advised against us having more children. We did not get off to a good start, you and I. You would not feed, and turned purple with rage whenever I held you to the breast. We had to have a wet-nurse. But you and Raphael were besotted with each other. I felt inept, a failure as a mother. I was jealous of the love you gave your father, and of his for you.'

Phoebe watched her mother twisting the gloves between her fingers, and felt a great sadness. 'You always seemed a fortress without a single chink of weakness,' she said. 'I tried to please you but could never find a way and, in the end I gave up trying.'

'What a sorry tale it is.'

'I'm sorry, Mummy.' Phoebe knelt in front of her, taking the gloves from her hands and throwing them on the floor. At first her mother did nothing and then slowly, tentatively, she began to stroke her daughter's hair. 'You know, there were days when I thought you were dead and that I'd lost my chance.'

'Oh Mummy, I did love – I do love you,' she gasped, tears pricking her lashes.

'Phoebe, what are we going to do with each other?'

'Let's go home and think of all this tomorrow. I feel as if I could sleep for a week. And I must see my Sophie.'

'What have you agreed with Miss Gibbons?'

'I will send her a telegram and go back on Friday. Whatever happens, I must see the sisters again and thank them properly for all they did for me.'

'Getting the house straight will take some time. But you can probably make one room at least habitable.'

Phoebe was startled. 'What do you mean, I thought I could—'

'I want us to start as we mean to go on. You are a grown woman, quite capable of managing your own house. If you want to make a home of it you must do it yourself. Midge can help you and Dorcas can come over. In six months it will be yours. No, for your sake, I don't want you to come home as the spoilt girl who couldn't cope without her mother. Phoebe, I say this out of love.'

'I am to have Sophie, you wouldn't take her from me.' Her heart lurched. Five minutes ago they had seemed so united.

'Of course you will have Sophie. But you will have to win her back. Four months is a long time in a baby's life, she will need to get to know you. Phoebe, let's not fall out so soon. This is all much too important to rush. I love you, Phoebe. Let's build on this moment. Come along darling, let's go and see her, take the first step.'

Anger and disappointment surged in her, yet she smiled and nodded. Those tactics were now useless. It was her mother who held the trump cards.

'You go up and see her darling, and tell Fidelis I want to speak with her.'

Phoebe knocked on the door of the nursery, sick with nerves.

'Who is it?'

'It's Sophie's mother.'

'Mrs Allen, come in, please.'

She could see the shock and anxiety in the girl's eyes but she could not be distracted, now. 'Hello Fidelis, it's all right, I've only come for a visit while the house is being set straight. My mother wants to see you for a moment.' Seeing the alarm on the girl's face, she smiled. 'I shan't make off with my daughter, I promise.'

'Yes, madam.'

Sophie was sitting on the nursery rug, with her back to the door, playing with coloured bricks, setting one on top of

the other then knocking them over. When they fell apart she gave a delighted, gurgling laugh.

Phoebe edged herself onto a chair and waited to be noticed. Her child had grown. Her hair had thickened and changed from white blonde to gold. It seemed an age before she turned around and looked at her. There was curiosity in her gaze, friendliness even, but no recognition.

16

Painstakingly Mary McCauley pinned out the edges of the Christmas collar, thread by thread onto a linen pad. It really was a fine piece of lacework, and her thanks had been tepid to say the least. Fee must have made a hole in her savings to buy such a thing. Always afterwards she regretted her reserve, but the words stuck in her throat. Affection was something that sat awkwardly with her – a foreign thing she had not the language for. Setting the collar in place distracted her from what was to come later in the day; her visit to the surgery.

It had come about at Jack's insistence. He had been good to her since Fee had gone back into service, and agreed that they should sleep apart. Such a sacrifice demanded an equal response from her – the appointment with Dr Morgan. For months now she had known that her health was deteriorating. The exhaustion, the backache and the persistent cough all combined to remind her of her parents' legacy. It was when Jack found her blood-stained handkerchief that the die was cast.

He had sat on the end of her bed and showed it to her. 'Mary, for God's sake, you must get yourself looked at. How long has this been going on? For Fee's sake, if not for mine, you must get yourself well again.' He had been so concerned for her. 'I don't know what I would do without you.'

'I don't know why,' she had replied in a rare burst of honesty. 'I have not been much of a bargain.' She had seen the tears glistening in his eyes.

'I have been such a disappointment – a rough, ignorant sea-soldier trampling on your fine feelings, not able to control himself.'

'We have Fidelis.' It was all that Mary could think to say. She knew he wanted her to deny the disappointment but she could not speak the lie.

He stood behind her with his hands resting on her shoulders; the weight of him oppressed her, and the heat. 'We have been so tender in our letters, and yet—.' His hands fell away from her. 'I'll care for you, whatever you want or need, anything.'

'To be left alone.' The words hovered on her lips but she did not reply, having lost the appetite for scourging. 'I know you will,' was all she could manage.

Later, seated behind the screen, fastening the cuffs of her blouse, she heard the water trickling in the basin as the doctor washed his hands. Outside in the waiting-room, Jack would be pacing up and down. Taking her seat again in front of the doctor's desk, she awaited his verdict.

'Mrs McCauley, you must have been unwell for some time. Why did you not call and see me earlier? As it is, you will have to go to the sanatorium in Ventnor as soon as possible, if we are to have any hopes of arresting the disease. You know you have consumption?'

'I thought so.'

Doctor Morgan sighed. 'Mary, you are an intelligent woman. Why?'

'There were things I needed to do. I wanted Fidelis to be settled and to put my affairs in order. I don't expect to get well. My parents both died of consumption, so I believe. At least I shall have seen my child grow up.'

'I don't like to hear such resignation,' he said. 'With rest and proper care you could recover, given time and patience. Have you told your husband?'

She buttoned her coat and picked up her handbag. 'He is outside. I will tell him when we get home.'

'I will make arrangements for you to go to the Isle of Wight. In the meantime, Mrs McCauley, I suggest you go home to bed and rest. Is there someone who can care for you?'

'My husband and my neighbour, doctor, that will be enough.'

'What about your daughter?'

'Fidelis is in service. I would not want her to be called away. Besides, I don't want her to be contaminated.'

'Since she has been in constant contact with you, all this time, I think she would have caught it by now. She is in excellent health, I believe?'

Mary nodded.

'Then I think you have nothing to worry about on that score.' He stood up to indicate the end of their interview, and stood at the door ready to shake her hand. 'I will call around to see you as soon as everything is in place. Goodday to you, Mrs McCauley.'

'My darling,' Jack said, when she told him. 'You go straight up those stairs and get into bed. Now we know what it is we can fight it together. You'll get well again, I'll make you well.'

They agreed not to worry Fidelis until she came home the following week, and only then if it was unavoidable.

Mary lay in a stupor of exhaustion, unable to take in the implications of Doctor Morgan's words. All she knew was that the struggle was over and she could be at peace. Nothing would be expected of her and no demands made.

Shamrock stood in her corsets, surveying her bedroom. Clothes wanting laundering were heaped on the floor, and those requiring to be folded away were on the chairs. Come back Fee, all is forgiven, she thought to herself, as she hurried into

the last ironed blouse in the wardrobe. The sight of her own failure to keep on top of things depressed her. No, she would not tackle it now but go out to Eastney and see Jack and Mary. Her brother might stand her a gin-and-pep at the Royal Marine Artillery Tavern across from the barracks. The sight of a few handsome men in uniform would cheer her up no end. Away from Ruby, Norman Dawes was always happy to flirt. They both knew he was well supplied at home – it was just a bit of nonsense. After a stand-up breakfast of tea and Madeira cake she brushed the crumbs from her mouth and hoicked her coat from the hallstand. Jamming a pin through her saucy red hat, she slammed the front door and sallied forth.

'Anybody home?' she called up the stairs.

Looking around her sister-in-law's home Shamrock felt guilt, then irritation. If that Mary spent more time in loving than scrubbing, brother Jack would be a happier man. Well, she'd give her one last chance to entertain her, and then she would stroll around to the barracks. It would be half-twelve soon, first dinner call. She was about to slam the front door behind her when she heard someone coughing from the front bedroom.

'Mary, is that you?'

The coughing persisted. Alarmed, Shamrock climbed the stairs and tapped on the door.

'Come in,' the voice was barely above a whisper.

'This isn't like you, Mary. What's up with you, gal?'

'Fetch me a pillow, please, in the cupboard, top shelf.'

'That's it, let's sit you up a bit. How long you been sick? Honest to God Mary, you look like a ghost. Have you had the doctor to you?'

She nodded. 'Glass of water, please.'

After pouring her some from the jug on the bedside table, Shamrock drew up a chair. 'What's the verdict?'

'I have to go to the sanatorium at Ventnor when there's a bed ready.'

14

He was there waiting on the corner of the High Street. 'I didn't want you to walk to the house alone. Happy Christmas, Fidelis.' He bent to kiss her.

'Happy Christmas,' she breathed, taking his arm.

They walked, heads down against the fluttering snowflakes, until they reached the house. While he found the key, and turned it in the lock, she stood behind him stamping some warmth into her feet.

'I have a surprise for you,' Daniel said, after helping her take off her coat and hat and hanging them up in the hall. 'Close your eyes and take my hand.'

It was cold and dark, and then there was a burst of heat and the scent of spices.

'Abracadabra! Open your eyes!'

She was dazzled. Everywhere there were candles, some in holders, some in cups. On the mantelpiece was a bunch of tapers arranged like flowers, in a vase. The fire had been lit and the wood crackled. Spread on the carpet were the open pages of *The Times*, like a picnic tablecloth.

Daniel smiled. 'We must imagine we are in the country in a grassy meadow and you are my honoured guest.'

There were two plates with large pieces of iced cake and slices of red apples. Beside them were wine glasses. On the fender was a saucepan filled with wine.

Daniel was flushed, and eager for her approval.

'I've never been waited on before,' she whispered. It was

like a dream, but this time her eyes were open and she could see and feel and touch.

Daniel kissed her hand. 'You are well worth the attention. Sit down on the floor and lean your back against the couch. I'll pour you some Christmas punch.'

'You must have come here early to set the scene. It's magical, thank you.'

'I could hardly sleep thinking of today. Seeing your face, full of wonder, makes it all worthwhile.' He set her drink beside her before seating himself opposite. 'To lovers everywhere,' he said, clinking his glass against hers.

'To lovers,' Fidelis whispered. As she bent over her glass, her face was bathed in a cloud of steam composed of nutmeg, ginger and cinnamon laced with port.

'I want to steal time and consequences,' he said. 'I want us to stay in this enchanted cave, with no sense of clocks ticking or people waiting or duties needing to be done.'

'Why did you write to me?' she asked him. 'When I saw you at the concert I knew it was Maude you were with. I thought you were going to propose to her.'

'Let's leave her aside,' he said, staring into the fire.

'But you knew I was engaged to Harry.'

'So,' he challenged, 'why did you come?'

She looked away. 'I couldn't help myself.'

'Nor I,' said Daniel.

She thought of the girl who jumped over Niagara Falls in a barrel. All her life must ever afterwards have been measured by that one event. Fidelis wondered if this afternoon with Daniel would become her Rubicon. Clearing their picnic onto a tray he took it into the kitchen, then held his coat by the fire to warm, before draping it across the couch.

'Come and get warm,' he said, folding it around her.

She lay in a daze, watching him unbuttoning her boots before taking off his own. He went around the room blowing out the candles, save for the bunch of tapers still gleaming in the vase. The room was a place of flickering shadows as they sat drinking the last of the punch. Daniel dipped his fingers into her glass and painted her lips before kissing them. She edged onto her side so that he could lie beside her.

They sipped, and tasted, one another. Fidelis lay with her eyes closed, feeling the heat from his body seeping into her own. Their kisses became deep drenching exchanges, dizzying them both. Touching replaced speaking: stroking, circling and uncovering. Slowly he took off her clothes, unwrapping her like a present, interleaving each discarded garment with a kiss. She watched him as he undid his shirt and slid his cuff-links onto the side table. His body was mysterious to her, the contours blurred in the flickering light. Turning away, he unbuttoned his trousers and stepped out of them, before removing his drawers. How beautiful he was. She studied the sweep of his spine as it curved down his body, bone by bone, then disappeared between the swell of his but-tocks. He danced her slowly, slowly around the room. She could feel her heart thudding, almost hear it in the silence. Daniel laid his coat on the floor by the fire, and pulled her down beside him.

For a moment they lay in each other's arms, and then he began to stroke her neck and then her breasts. Her body sang beneath his touch.

'I want to know every part of you,' he whispered. 'You can touch me, too.'

Fidelis had never seen a naked man, except in paintings, only boys bathing, and then only from a distance. She spread her hand flat across his chest and felt a sprinkling of wiry hair, before pressing her fingers between his ribs. His belly was flat and hard. She hesitated. 'We are so different.'

'We are made to fit together.' He took her hand and placed it around his penis. 'This is my key that fits in your lock.'

It was warm beneath her fingers, and hard.

'Don't be frightened, Fidelis, nothing is going to happen unless you want it to. Let me awaken you.' He parted her thighs and unfolded her secret places, making her shiver at his touch. Delicious waves of feeling washed through her, intensifying with each caress. Daniel turned her onto her back and knelt across her. 'Are you ready? It's for you to say.'

She nodded, closing her eyes.

There was a feeling of tightness as he pressed against her, then a sharp tearing as he thrust himself deeper. The rhythm intensified and she was caught up in it, unable to draw back. Daniel drove himself inside her faster and faster, gasping, groaning, and then she was flooded with a warm stickiness. It was over. He drew away from her.

'Don't move, my darling. Let me get you a cloth. Lie still.'

Fidelis was confused. He had taken her up a mountain and left her on the edge of nowhere. She had felt the power of him but the pleasure had been lost.

'Tell me what you feel,' Daniel said, coming back to her with a towel. He had soaked one end in water and bathed the stickiness away, then dried her.

'As if I was left behind,' she whispered.

'Did you like me stroking you?'

'Yes.'

This time his stroking didn't stop until he had brought her to a dizzying, panting, peak of satisfaction. 'Are you happy, now?' he asked.

Fidelis smiled. 'I'm in heaven.'

'It would be wonderful to fall asleep now, with you in my arms, but I am expected at home by five o'clock, my sweet.'

'I must go, too. Ma will be expecting me.'

'Next time I want you to sing for me,' he said.

So, there was to be a next time. She turned away to find her clothes.

Fully dressed, once again, they busied themselves in setting the place to rights: washing the plates and glasses in the cobwebby kitchen, and collecting up the candles. Daniel helped her into her coat, and she straightened her hat by the hall mirror. When they shut the front door behind them, he drew her arm through his.

'We won't be able to meet for a while. I'll be in Kent but I'll write to you.'

'So will I,' she said, squeezing his hand.

He left her at the South Parade Pier, less than a mile from the barracks. 'I'll miss you, my sweet Fidelis,' he said, as he bent to kiss her.

'So will I,' she said, waving until he was out of sight.

It was cold, and the breeze from the sea scoured her face. It had been her plan to walk home along the beach, but now she crossed the road from the promenade and hurried through the gardens around the Canoe Lake, not wanting to be alone with her thoughts. The park seemed wrapped in gloom, a different place entirely from the summer playground of the day-trippers. As she walked towards home, she heard a dog barking and a familiar voice calling.

'Ebony, come here, sir.'

Fidelis ran towards them. 'Is that you, Pa?' she cried.

'Fee, my love, I was hoping to meet up with you.' He bent to kiss her. 'It's grand to see you. Now our Christmas is complete.'

Fidelis took Ebony's lead in her hand while her father carried her valise, filled with Christmas presents for the family, and together they walked to Gibraltar Street.

'I've been so looking forward to having you home, Fee. It's dismal just the two of us. Ruby and Norman have tonight all planned out.' His voice was anxious. 'You can stay, can't you?'

She nodded. 'Madam said I must be back by eight o'clock tomorrow morning.'

'So, all we have to do is get you home.'

'Hello, Fee.' Her mother looked searchingly at her. 'You're flushed and your breath smells of drink.'

'I had a glass of mulled wine, in the kitchen before I left. Only one glass, Cook said that it was cold out and I should have a winter warmer, as she calls it.'

'I'll make us some tea and find some biscuits. We won't be eating now as Ruby has promised us a feast.'

She went out into the kitchen and left Fidelis standing with her valise, feeling like a stranger in her own home. 'I'll take out the presents,' she said, her voice sounding loud and over-jolly to her ears, as if she were trying to fill an empty space.

'Let's wait for our tea,' said Pa, 'then we can share our presents together.'

She sat next to his chair, on the old leather pouffe he had brought home from Egypt when she was a child. 'I can't wait for you to see it,' she said.

Ma came in from the kitchen and set the tray on the table.

'Get the presents, Mary. I want us to make up for the unwrapping we missed yesterday,' urged her husband.

'I don't know what all the fuss is about,' she said, disappearing upstairs.

When she had filled their cups and they were sitting down at the table, Fidelis watched her parents opening their gifts. Pa tore off the paper and pulled it through the string while Ma untied the knots and folded the paper into a neat square.

'*The Life and Times of a Blue Marine* by Sergeant Major Griffin. Well, isn't that a fine thing. You know I saw that in the bookshop down on the Hard and thought to buy it. Fee, you are a wonder. Did I tell you he was my drill sergeant when first I joined in Deal? Wasn't he a tartar for discipline, but if you put your heart into it he would encourage you to the hilt.' He leapt up, making the tea-things quiver as he came around to her chair and kissed her, his moustache grazing her cheek.

'Jesus! Why did you let it go this far? You don't get consumption in five minutes, must have been on you for months. S'pose 'twas Jack that nagged you in the finish?'

Mary nodded.

'Why in God's name didn't you take yourself to the doctor before?'

'I wanted Fee to be settled, and all my things in order.'

'You know what it'll say on your tombstone? Killed by hygiene and a tidy home.'

Her sister-in-law permitted herself the ghost of a smile.

'What can I do for you? Won't Jack be home in a minute? Should I go around and get us some fish-and-chips?'

'Have what you like. I've some soup on the stove, there's a tray laid already.'

'Right, I'll go and heat it up and see you settled first. Won't be but a tick.' She stood the saucepan on the hob and paced about the kitchen. Poor Jack, to be faced with this. Everyone's sympathy would be with the saintly wife. Well, Mary could go and meet her Maker as far as she was concerned. Never taken to her, she hadn't. That woman had sapped all the juice from her brother, and denied him the warmth and passion he deserved. Still, there was Fee to make up for his disappointment. Wasn't she a grand girl? This would upset her no end.

'Thank you, can you spread that towel over the bed. I'll sleep awhile afterwards, don't bother about the tray.'

Shamrock smiled to herself. She's as anxious to be rid of me, as I am her, she thought.

The sound of the key turning in the lock had Mary starting up. 'Tell Jack I'm sleeping. I'll see him tonight.'

'Hello, me darling, I'm sorry for your trouble. Here, give us a kiss.'

Her brother held her tight and grazed her face with his whiskers. She could feel him trembling. Christ! He was crying.

Shamrock walked him over to the sofa and they sat down together. Not since they were children in Dublin had he wept in front of her. Still holding him she waited, stroking his hair, whispering to him. 'That's it me boy, you let it all out.' Her mind was racing. There was one thing, Jack McCauley could look after himself. There would be no burnt pans or half-ironed shirts with him, and there would be Norman and Ruby to lend a hand. Fee was well settled in her job. Given a few months and it would all be over, one way or another. Mary would be up there singing to Jesus or she would be back home, nagging him for breathing out of turn.

'It's knocked me sideways,' he gasped. 'Don't know why. Looking at her today it was plain for all to see. Thin as a lath she is now, and cough, cough, cough. She's fading away in front of my eyes, not got the strength of a newborn baby. Left it too late she has, going to leave me and there's not a thing I can do about it.'

Shamrock bit her lip. If she didn't get a hold of herself she'd be bawling, too – much help that would be. 'Ah, Jack, don't be burying her yet, she's a long way off her coffin. Good rest and proper feeding, peace and quiet, who knows?'

He gave a shuddering sigh. 'You're right, I'm just getting ahead of myself. She doesn't want Fee brought home, and says she's not to visit 'til she's better. Terrified of her getting it.'

'That's not likely. Fee's been with her all this time and looks as fit as a tick. She would have gone down with it before now if she was going to. Look at us in the Liberties, in Dublin, weren't we surrounded by consumption, right, left and centre?'

Jack gave her a tentative smile. 'We didn't sit still long enough to catch anything. You're a tonic, girl, and that's the truth.'

'I'll nip round and get us some fish-and-chips. You get the kettle on. Mary's had some soup and wants to sleep.'

★　★　★

What Mary minded above all were the neighbours. They would be seeing her carried out of the house on a stretcher – it was so demeaning. If only she could have been taken to a local hospital. The journey she would have to take by boat frightened her. The sea had always been an unknown terror. She remembered at Jack's homecomings, seeing the water slopping against the jetty. It had taken all her will power then, not to run screaming back to the Hard. But worse was to come; she had been expected to go on board the vast ship that he served on. Looking down into the green depths, from the height of the top deck, always made her sweat with fear and yet she couldn't look away.

'Are you warm enough, my darling? Shall I get you a cup of tea, it might be a while before the ambulance arrives.'

She shook her head. 'Just stay here beside me.'

Poor Jack. His face lit up that she should want him and she dredged up a smile. He was probably considered a catch among normal women, even now. The constant need for touching clouded her judgement of him. In all other aspects he was a good husband; a generous provider, clean in his habits and a devoted father to Fee. If only she could have explained, but would he have understood?

The horse-drawn ambulance collected her from home and took her and Jack to the ferry. The nurse from the sanatorium was now in attendance. One of the ambulance men carefully carried her on board. The engines of the paddle steamer seemed to throb through her temples, and there was a smell of oil and sea-water. Voices laughing and talking excitedly around her increased the tension.

'Soon you'll be able to rest, Mary. We'll be there by early afternoon. A room of your own, oceans of rest and good food, and I'll visit you often and often.'

The cold was a shock to her when she was lifted off the boat at Ryde Pier and settled in the special hospital-train with the red cross on the engine. It brought on a bout of coughing that left her weak and sweating. The nurse arranged the back-rest and helped her to sit up against the pillows.

'Ah! Would you look there at the snowdrops, Mary, aren't they beautiful?' Jack pointed out of the window as the train clattered through the countryside.

It was weak and foolish, she knew it was, but the way they shivered on their thread-like stems made her want to cry – brave flowers in a cruel world. She lay with her eyes closed, longing to be there at the sanatorium. Words came to her with the rhythm of the train wheels. 'A room of my own, a room of my own.'

At Ventnor she was lifted into an ambulance and jolted up to the hospital.

'Patient Mary McCauley for Princess Louise block,' the driver said to a porter at the entrance.

Her nerves were taut as fiddle-strings as she suffered herself to be undressed to use a bed-pan, and put to bed. When she was settled, Jack came and hovered in the doorway.

'Goodbye my darling, it's a relief that you're here at last and will be looked after. I'll be over next week.'

And then she was left to sleep in a room of her own. Something she had wanted all her life.

Almost without realising it, Jack found himself walking down Heron Grove and around to the back door of Kelmscott House, and tapping on the kitchen window.

'You must be Midge, I'm thinking?' he said to the little girl, who stood at the door.

'It's not about Tommy, is it?' she gasped, seeing his sergeant's uniform and putting her bitten fingernails to her mouth.

'Would that be Tommy Jakes – appetite like a horse and two left feet?'

She blushed.

'No, I've come to call on my daughter, Fidelis, if that's all right with you.'

'Midge, who you talking to? Get back to the sink and do them tea-things.' The cook gave him an appraising look. 'You must be Fee's Pa, she described you to a T. Sit down. Bet you could do with a hot drink inside you, and whatever I can scare up out of the larder?'

He smiled. 'It's a while since I've sat at a cook's table. Thank you kindly, ma'am.'

'Midge, you get up them stairs and tell Fee as her Pa's here.'

The warmth and friendliness were just what he needed. The journey had chilled him to the bone. 'A good cup of tea, mahogany colour and sweet as a maiden's prayer.'

Cook glowed as she set a plate of cheddar, chutney and buttered bread before him. 'Get outside of that, Mr McCauley, and you won't go far wrong.'

'Call me Jack, why don't you? This will set me up for the long walk home.'

'I'm Mabel.' The cook looked about her as if she had just divulged a secret of national importance.

Jack nodded. 'Well, Mabel, I shall use your name with discretion. I know the problems of maintaining respect among the ranks.' He winked at her and was rewarded by a hearty chuckle.

Fidelis rushed in and kissed him. 'Pa, lovely to see you, what brings you here?'

'I wondered if you had a couple of hours to spare for me?'

'Of course, I'll just ask madam. I'll be down in two ticks, I expect Eileen will listen out for Sophie.'

Jack smiled. Whatever the pains of his life, his daughter always restored him to good humour. She reminded him of the old hymn, 'All things bright and beautiful.' It pained him to think how his news would take the shine from her face.

Coming back into the kitchen with her coat and hat on, she handed him a parcel.

'I've got the evening off, Pa. Are you ready? Oh, yes, I've got a bone for Ebony. It seems a shame to waste it.'

Jack got to his feet. He smiled at Mabel. 'Thank you, Cook, you've put new life in me, so you have. And Midge, I shall tell Tommy Jakes as you send your regards.'

Midge ran giggling out of the kitchen.

'Let's go home and see Ebony.'

On the way they talked of this and that: Miss Phoebe coming back and the eccentricities of Miss Dorcas, anything but Mary. Once indoors, Fidelis was taken up with Ebony's joyous welcome. While she laughed and rumpled his ears, Jack set about making cocoa. 'Take off your coat,' he said, 'you'll not feel the benefit.'

'I just want to go upstairs and get some more things of mine, they'll make me feel more at home.' She was down again before he had organised his words.

'Something's happened. Ma's moved into my room – but where is she, now? I should have known, you calling round for me, like that. Please, Pa, what is it?'

'She's been taken really poorly, Fee, got consumption. Doctor Morgan has sent her over to the sanatorium in Ventnor, for a few weeks.'

'Why didn't you send for me earlier, I could have gone with you?'

'Wouldn't hear of it, she wants you not to visit until she's stronger. Terrified of you going down with it.'

'Oooh!' she shouted, her face flushed with anger, 'why does she do it? Draw away from us, like that?'

'I don't know, my darling.' He was startled by her response, having expected tears. 'Mary has always been a private person, keeping her thoughts to herself.'

'It's so hurtful, as if she doesn't trust us to care for her, or need us, even.'

He reached across the table and took her hands in his, chafing some warmth into them. 'She is as she is, Fee, and we must do our best for her. I shall leave her to settle in and go over again next week.'

'I'll come with you. I'm not letting her shut me out.'

'Why don't you write to her? You know how she loves your letters. Tell her how you feel about things, then you can go, maybe next time. The doctor says as she's to stay in bed and hardly move a muscle. Reading's allowed, and she would love to hear from you. She's that weak that the two of us jabbering on would likely be too much.'

'Oh Pa!' She flung her arms around him. 'What are we going to do about her?'

He stroked her hair. 'You and me, we're going to help her get well in whatever way she'll let us, my Fee. Now, it's a cold night, I want to walk you back as far as South Parade Pier. We'll take Ebony, he's not had a walk today. Have you got everything? Let me tie that quilt up with a bit of string.'

Fidelis looked questioningly at him. 'What will you do, Pa? It's early yet.'

'Oh, I'll go and look in on Ruby and Norman and catch them up with my news. Whatever I hear from your mother I'll keep you posted. Now, find Ebony's lead and we'll be off.'

When they parted, he kissed her and held her close and waved until she was out of sight. Walking back home with his dog reminded him of Boxing Day afternoon when he had met Fee. He had seen her, by the pier, before she had seen him. A memory stirred. It was merely a glimpse of someone and no more – a voice that he recognised, but couldn't yet place. Fee had been lit up by somebody, and it wasn't young Harry.

17

It was the twenty-second of January, a bitter Friday, that Phoebe finally moved back to Portsmouth. She barely had time to set down her valise in the hall before she and her mother set off for James's funeral. The attendance in the Chapel of Rest at Kingston Cemetery was small. It consisted of the two of them, plus some rather seedy-looking men and a blowsy woman in a large hat.

The vicar had never met James, and his eulogy painted a picture of a devoted husband, father and pillar of the community. These words drew sniggers from the male mourners and a frown from Phoebe's mother. During the hymn, the woman at the back sang lustily, covering up the pitiful efforts of everyone else.

Standing at the graveside, Phoebe felt as if she were attending a stranger's funeral.

There were no tears, no sympathetic glances, and the only flowers were the lilies she had sent. What had been the substance of his life, she wondered, as she stepped forward to let loose her handful of earth on the coffin. James had hated her in black.

'It's deadly, my darling. I like you in pale satin with diamonds in your ears. You know me, I love sparkle and shimmer.'

She had fallen in love with him at a party, bewitched by his charm and the way his eyes undressed her. There was an edge of danger that she couldn't resist. But life was more than a party, and James was no good at the long haul. Like a firework, he was spectacular in short bursts. Her memories were mere snatches here and there: his gleeful laugh when he had got away with something, the smell of his cologne, and his appetite for new things and new people. Sex had been thrilling, but sex could not be recaptured; it was a here and now thing that left no memory on the skin.

When her mother strode over to speak to the vicar, Phoebe felt someone tap her arm. She turned to find the blowsy woman at her side.

'I knew your husband, Mrs Allen, I'm sad that he's gone. One thing he had was style, and charm by the bucketful.'

'That's kind of you to say so,' Phoebe said, touched by her words.

'No more than the truth, my dear. Now, I must love you and leave you. Me and his pals will go down the Portland and drink his health.'

Phoebe opened her handbag, but the woman shook her head.

'I wasn't cadging, my dear, just letting you know as we'd be celebrating his life. Shamrock O'Shea's the name. 'Bye Mrs Allen, you get back home out of the cold. This ain't a day to be standin' about.'

'Let's go home, darling, and sit by the fire. I told Cook to have some soup ready, Scotch broth, your favourite.' Her mother led her to the path stretching towards the cemetery gates.

For a moment, Phoebe was tempted to join Miss O'Shea and her chums at the Portland. It would be a more appropriate way of marking his life. But it wasn't James that she needed to impress.

'Think of it as medicine,' Mummy said, handing her a glass of whisky and soda.

Phoebe dutifully sipped her drink, trying not to shudder. Gin with a fat slice of lemon and plenty of tonic water would have been her choice. She stretched out her hands to the sitting-room fire. 'Thank you, Mummy, for giving him a proper funeral. I know he didn't deserve it.'

'Everyone deserves a funeral, it's the least we can do for one another. Now, we've a lot to achieve if you are going to be settled into your home by next week.'

'I thought I would have longer to get to know Sophie again before we moved back to Clarendon House.'

'Longer of course for Sophie – she needs a proper nursery. But you can manage with a refurbished bedroom and a functioning kitchen and bathroom. Living on the premises you will see what else is needed.'

'What do you mean about Sophie?'

'I don't want my granddaughter to suffer any unnecessary anxiety. I want her to acclimatize herself to her new life in easy stages. First she gets to know you again, and then later you may take her home.'

Phoebe gulped down her whisky; this wasn't what she wanted at all. 'It could take weeks and weeks.'

'Very likely, but there is another matter you have to consider – that is, Fidelis. She will need to be asked whether she wants to go with you or stay here. It may be that you will manage your child for a while on your own, and just have a cleaning-woman on a daily basis.' Her mother smiled at her. 'This is all for your good, Phoebe. Think of the next six months as a challenge. On your birthday, you come into your inheritance of one thousand two hundred pounds a year. I want to know that you have a better understanding of the running of a home and the management of your own money, before that happens.'

'I know what being without money is like,' she said, trying to keep the anger from her voice.

'If you are angry and disappointed, Phoebe, use it to prove me wrong. Don't sulk, it achieves nothing and is deeply unattractive. This is a challenge. Do it as if for your father, and to prove to yourself that you are a woman of substance.'

While Phoebe stared into the fire, her mother tugged at the bell.

'Eileen, could you set us both up a tray? We will have our luncheon by the fire.'

The maid nodded, giving Phoebe a speculative look.

'You know, darling, you are lucky to be alive. I could have been attending your funeral today. When you have had your meal, I suggest you unpack your things and have a rest perhaps. It has been a taxing day. Later this afternoon you can see Sophie, and begin to re-establish things.'

Phoebe fell deeply asleep directly she took off her clothes and laid down on the bed. A tap on the door startled her. 'Come in,' she called. It was Fidelis.

'Good afternoon, Miss Phoebe, I've brought you up some tea. I'll be in the nursery with Sophie when you're ready.'

'Oh yes, oh thank you very much, that was kind of you.'

'Right, madam.'

It was difficult to judge what the girl was feeling. Phoebe supposed her return would hardly be a welcome one. She probably feared losing her position.

'This is your Mummy.'

Sophie was sitting in her feeding-chair, with bread soldiers on a plate in front of her and a cup of milk.

'She is so grown-up. When did she start drinking from a cup?'

'I think it's been about six weeks or so. The feeding-bottle got broken and I tried her without it. At first it was a messy business but she does well, now.'

Sophie's blue eyes watched the two women, and then she smiled. 'Fee,' she said, pointing to Fidelis.

Phoebe ached to hold her. This was torture, having to

stand in her own child's nursery like a maid on her first day. 'I've missed so much,' she said.

'Would you like to take her out of her chair, while I clear away her tea-things. There's a flannel and towel on the table there to clean her face and hands.'

Almost everything was different. Sophie was heavier, taller, and no longer her baby. She was a rosy-cheeked little girl who gave her mother equal scrutiny. It was a friendly inspection, as she tugged at her hair and at the wedding-ring on her finger.

'I'm your Mummy,' Phoebe whispered.

'See Gamma.' Sophie wriggled out of her arms and toddled over to Fidelis.

'It's her routine,' she said. 'An hour with madam and then she comes up for her bath.'

'Shall I take her down?'

'Yes, if you like. I carry her to the top of the stairs down into the hall, and then take her hand and we walk down the rest together.'

And so it continued, with her trailing after Fidelis and being fed the crumbs of attention that Sophie chose to give her.

On the following Monday, the child was left in Eileen's care while the rest of the household went around to Clarendon House to do an early spring-clean. Cook was left behind to come along later with a basket of refreshments at one o'clock. Dorcas had come back from a trip to the Isle of Wight, and volunteered to climb up the step-ladder and take down the curtains and clean the windows. Midge and Fidelis were to scrub and polish and set the kitchen to rights. Phoebe and her mother were to go from room to room making lists.

'It's like the story in the Bible of the division of the sheep and the goats,' Phoebe said, consigning a heap of tattered *Illustrated London News* to the rubbish-box.

'Well, there seems to be plenty of bed linen, tablecloths and towels. On a fine day we will open all the windows and give the place a good airing. I have arranged for the sweep to call, and Mr Vivash is coming this afternoon to look at the plumbing and the cooking-range. Now, I'll make a start on the dining-room and perhaps you would like to see what you want from your bedroom.'

Phoebe was relieved that she wouldn't have her mother with her as she dismantled her life with James. She began by opening his wardrobe. He had been such fun in the beginning. Always tempting her to further extravagance, leading her into new risks. But then, he hadn't sulked for days or drunk too much or stolen from her. Taking a deep breath, she began to take the clothes out of the wardrobe and laid them on the bed: James's evening dress, lounge suits, white silk scarves, waist-coats and a heavy tweed overcoat. It was the hairbrush on the tallboy still containing a stray blond hair that brought her to tears. She had loved him once.

'Phoebe?' Her mother's voice was uncertain. She stood in the doorway looking at her. 'If this is too much for you, we could leave it to Fidelis and Eileen.'

She shook her head, and took up one of her husband's handkerchiefs and blew her nose. 'No, I have left too much to them already. It's just the picking over the wreckage. I suppose once it's done I'll have some idea what to do next.'

'What would you like to do? The house can of course be sold,' she said, coming and sitting on the bed beside her.

Always before Mummy had given firm directions, outlined the path she should take. It had been the very firmness that had always driven her in the opposite direction. She looked up in surprise. 'I want to keep the house. It was Daddy's gift to me and I want it to be a credit to him, a real family home for me and Sophie. Perhaps Dorcas could help me decide how it should look, if she is going to stay in Portsmouth.'

Her mother laughed. 'Dorcas is a law unto herself, but at the moment she seems to want to be with us. Losing her soldier has unsettled her. As for Fidelis, I must talk with her and see what she would like to do. She has been very good for Sophie and I don't want to lose her. Perhaps she can still live at Kelmscott and come to you on a daily basis. We shall have to see.'

Phoebe bit her tongue: it was all so up in the air. She was like a plant without a pot, waving its roots, waiting to be planted somewhere. In the nursery she was a visitor. She could bath and dress Sophie, but she had not yet taken her for an outing on her own and at night she retired to the guest room. It was Fidelis who slept in the nursery. Her mother had been right. She needed to be with Sophie in Clarendon House; living in her childhood home, she had no position and was dependent. But tomorrow her nursemaid was planning to visit her sick mother over in the Isle of Wight. Apart from the freedom this gave Phoebe over her child, she felt relief at having some distance from Fidelis. They were awkward and watchful with one another. There were injuries that she and James had done the girl, and she had no idea how the rift could be healed. But she would not think of all the reasons to be dismal: there was a whole day with Sophie to look forward to.

Next morning Marcia Mount felt a need to bring some common sense to the breakfast table. 'Dorcas, taking Fidelis to London for the day would set a dangerous precedent.'

'But Aunt Marcia, she has worked so hard around at Clarendon House and with Sophie. After all, I have no children of my own to indulge.'

'Fidelis has been a saint,' muttered Phoebe, helping herself to the last piece of toast. 'I know they've all worked hard and I intend to . . .'

'You have often said that my staff seem remarkably united and happy, Dorcas, in comparison to other households. Why do you think that is so?'

'Because you are so kind to them and they admire all the work you do?'

'Stuff and nonsense! With me they know exactly where they stand, what their duties are and what their benefits. They know that I am fair and firm. Taking one of them to London would be very divisive. Cook and Eileen and Margaret have all worked equally hard – how do you propose to reward them?'

'I have plans for them, too. A trip to the theatre to see *The Mikado*, it's coming soon to the Theatre Royal, in June. It's just the sort of rollicking thing they'd love. After all, Fidelis will be leaving soon to go with Phoebe.'

'That hasn't been settled yet!' Phoebe glared at Dorcas. 'It may be better to have someone new. Mummy and I have not decided yet.'

'How will it be if I talk to all of them, explain my plans and say that it is my idea entirely?'

'With Fidelis off junketing with you, it will give me a whole day with Sophie and I shall be able to put her to bed on my own,' said Phoebe, spooning the last of the apricot jam onto her plate.

'It's against my better judgement, Dorcas. However, if you are going to be even-handed I can hardly object. But I need to speak with Fidelis in any case. Her position must be clarified.' Marcia looked at her daughter's sullen face and felt a twinge of doubt. If things were to go smoothly she would have to think creatively.

In a berry-red coat she had reclaimed from her wardrobe, Phoebe set out with the pram.

'We are having an outing. Mummy is going to buy you a

new coat and shoes, my lady, and we are going to have fun.'
She chatted to the little girl, pointing out things: seagulls,
ships and a little boy rolling a ball along the promenade.
Sophie was so responsive. Her head turned this way and that,
her eyes searching all the time.

They bowled along to Southsea and the big stores. In the
baby-wear department at George Handley's her daughter
was petted and admired by the assistants. The blue Viyella
bonnet and matching coat looked so sweet on her, and she
was as excited as her mother when held up to the mirror.
Paying for things with Mummy's money was still a humiliation, her own account was not only empty, it was seriously
overdrawn.

Having taken Sophie out of her pram whilst in the store,
Phoebe struggled to get her back inside it. The toddler had
a will of her own, and screamed and thrashed about in
protest. By the time her objective had been achieved, Phoebe
was sweating and scarlet-faced. The child she had longed for,
in Brighton, was a different creature to the one yelling defiance at her now. A toddler's company was not nearly as stimu-
lating as she had expected. All those hours of longing to be
with her, and now she was bored. Phoebe felt ashamed and
unnatural, and not fit to be a mother.

Discouraged, she sat on a bench by the Canoe Lake staring
at the water and the flotilla of ducks sailing past. She was
cold, and the walk to Southsea and back had exhausted her.
Wiping away her tears, she was about to go back to Kelmscott
in defeat when a stout woman in a grey coat and hat
approached, with a small boy in a wicker pram. It was a curious
contraption, with the end dropped down to form a chair.

'Good afternoon, mind if I join you?'

'No, please do,' said Phoebe, glad of some adult company.

'I'm Nanny Hawkins, pleased to meet you, and this is
Master Phillip.'

'Phoebe Allen and my daughter Sophie.' She grasped the gloved hand thrust at her and smiled.

'A bonny little girl, how old is she?'

'Two next August and full of spirit.'

The woman laughed. 'The terrible twos – that's when they learn to say no. Can work you to such a pitch you wants to scream at them.' She turned to her charge and handed him a bag of bread. 'Let's get your reins on and we'll feed the ducks, shall we?'

'Yes, Nanny.' He wriggled his legs impatiently while she clipped him into his harness.

'That's a very good idea,' said Phoebe, beginning to feel brighter. 'Where did you get them?'

'Out at Knight and Lee's, just the thing, they give the child a bit of independence and the mother some control. Like wild animals are children, it's all carrot and stick.'

Sophie watched the proceedings with interest. She bounced up and down in her pram, shouting, 'quack, quack' and pointing to Phillip's bag of bread.

'What d'you mean,' Phoebe asked, pushing the pram to the edge of the pond and taking a crust of bread the little boy handed to her.

'They needs limits – gotta know what they are. When you says "no" you gotta mean "no." Naturally, sometimes you says "yes" and they haves little rewards. The limits makes them feel safe, they knows where they are.'

'Nanny Hawkins, that has been so helpful. Thank you kindly.'

'Not at all, my dear, such experience as I have has been hard-won over the years.' She turned to the little boy. 'Master Phillip, it's time to go home to tea. Say goodbye to Miss Sophie. Perhaps we shall see you again, Mrs Allen. We're hereabouts or on the beach most afternoons.'

'I would like that. Good afternoon to you. Say "bye-bye", Sophie.'

'Bye-bye.' Her daughter waved her hand.

Much cheered, Phoebe made her way back to Heron Grove. She had been too hard on herself, she was a novice after all.

When she pushed the pram into the hall her mother came out of the sitting-room to greet her.

'Phoebe, my dear, you come in and sit down – you look thoroughly chilled. Let me deal with Sophie while you take off your coat. Eileen is just going to bring in some tea and scones. Now, have you been a good girl for your Mummy?'

Sophie turned in her grandmother's arms and smiled at Phoebe. 'Mummy,' she said.

18

Fidelis ran up the stairs, her heart pounding. A trip to London, it was beyond everything – London, the home of King Edward and Queen Alexandra – London with Miss Dorcas – with her anything was possible.

Since she had moved into Kelmscott House they had, amazingly, become firm friends. Mrs Mount's niece simply fizzed with ideas. It was when they all pitched in to clean Miss Phoebe's old home that they had began to talk together.

'You seem to be always on the move, Miss Dorcas. Where do you really call home?' she had asked her, resting back on her haunches and dropping the floor-cloth back in the bucket.

'Although I grew up in Hampstead in London, my first love has always been the Isle of Wight. It's been the family's holiday home since ever and ever. I ran wild with the local children, swimming and climbing trees. Nanny said I had turned into a heathen savage. Last year, in South Africa, I got typhoid and nearly died and, do you know, all my dreams were of Ventnor. I've a fancy to live there all the year round.'

'Would you be there on your own?'

She laughed. 'Who knows? I'm sure many of my friends would like to spend a holiday with me. But I should like to do some writing and get my South African collection together. Fidelis, you must come over and stay.'

'My mother is in the sanatorium there.'

'Oh, I am sorry, this must be an anxious time for you. Perhaps when you are visiting her you might call on me afterwards at Fortitude Cottage. It's not that far from the hospital, you could walk it, or perhaps stay overnight at some time when you are free. Lately, I have felt a real yearning for the good air at Ventnor to build me up, and the solitude to refashion myself.'

'I don't know how I would like living on my own,' said Fidelis. 'I don't think I've ever been alone in a house for more than an hour or so. Probably I'd be bored.'

'You would be surprised.' Dorcas smiled. 'Silence is a very powerful teacher. We are like icebergs most of us, with only a millionth of our potential showing above the water – it's just matter of stretching and daring. But I sense you know that already.'

Often, after Fidelis had settled Sophie to sleep, Dorcas would come and have whispered conversations in the nursery with her. Her talk excited her and was full of questions. What was the purpose of life? Could violence be eradicated from human nature? And why were men and women not equal? Her brain had been turning around a very small circle of thoughts before she met this wild woman.

Later, when she told Pa about the day in London, he urged her to go.

'Sitting looking at your mother will not make a ha'p'orth of difference, whether it's this week or next. I think a postcard from London telling her all about your doings would be the very thing.'

Pa had said that her mother had looked rested, the last time he had been over to Ventnor, but she still didn't want to see her daughter. One of the things they were trying over there was to feed Ma every two hours. Mostly it was milk and eggs, but they even woke her up in the middle of the night to drink beef tea. Fidelis wrote nearly every day, keeping her up to date with the goings on at Kelmscott and the news from Harry.

When Phoebe was settled in Clarendon House and willing to look after Sophie for a day, Fidelis and Dorcas settled on the first Monday in March for their trip.

'Splendid, we'll catch the eight o'clock train and be in Waterloo by eleven. We'll try and pack in as many things as ever we can.'

Sitting in the train, Fidelis effervesced. Everything fascinated her – the other passengers, the countryside rushing past, and most of all Dorcas. Seated opposite in a slim-fitting walking-suit in navy and red topped off with a tiny scarlet hat, she looked stunning, and drew admiring glances from everyone in the carriage. Beside her was a large flat drawing-case in which she kept her designs.

'What would you like to see?' her new friend asked, as the train steamed out of Woking.

'So much,' she breathed. 'The river, the posh shops, Buckingham Palace, the parks and statues, and to just walk about and sniff the air.'

'Well, I think we should take in one gallery, and I have to call in at Liberty's, but apart from that the day is yours.'

Alighting at Waterloo, Fidelis stood watching the stream of people flowing past. What struck her was the sheer variety of human beings swirling around her. Some were questing and confident in fine clothes, and others shrunk in on themselves, shuffling along on the margins of life. Every so often she jumped at a train whistle or had to step out of the way of a porter's cart. The air was coal-laden, laced with the passing whiff of a cigar and a teasing cloud of perfume, here one second, gone the next.

'Exciting, isn't it?' said Dorcas. 'Who are all these folk waiting under the clock? What are their hopes and dreams? What will have happened to them by the time we come back here tonight?'

'What's first on our programme?' Fidelis asked, as they sat in the station buffet eating Chelsea buns and drinking steaming cups of tea.

'Let's see, it's quarter-past eleven. I think a walk along by the river, over Westminster Bridge and on to the Tate. We should be there easily by twelve.'

It was like a waking dream. The Thames was much bigger, much busier than she could have imagined, and there on the other side of the bridge were the Houses of Parliament, honey-coloured in the morning sun. Crossing Westminster Bridge was a wonder to Fidelis. Traffic poured across in a seething mass of horse-drawn cabs, and motor-cars and trams. Never had she seen so many bowler hats, striped trousers and rolled umbrellas. Down below them, the river teemed with life. Barges made their way towards the capital bringing coal from the north, pleasure steamers tooted their horns, and watermen rowed their wherries back and forth as if on a boating lake.

When they stood outside the House of Commons, Dorcas shook her fist. 'Look at her, the Mother of Parliament and not a single woman represented there. I could weep for the injustice of it.'

Not having the vote had seemed a minor inconvenience before meeting Dorcas. Her position as a woman had seemed fixed: now this arty bluestocking was showing Fidelis that it was possible to push out the boundaries. But she was educated and wealthy; what did she really know of the limitations of a nursemaid's life?

As if reading her mind, Dorcas turned and smiled, 'Forgive me, no politics today, our aim is pleasure. We'll stroll along to the Tate, there is something you must see.'

'What's the Tate?' she asked.

'It's an art gallery financed by Harry Tate, the sugar millionaire. It was once Millbank prison, so you see, things can change. I want to show you some Pre-Raphaelite paintings and then we will go to Liberty's, my fabric heaven.'

It was a cold March morning and the wind from the river tugged at hats, pinched fingers and made everyone's eyes water. By the time they reached the Tate Gallery Fidelis was eager to get inside. She craned her neck up at the huge cream stone building, stunned at the thought of the number of pictures it must contain. Walking up the steps between the pillars, she felt as if she were going into church. Inside, that feeling was intensified. Dorcas hurried her past several pictures and then stopped.

'This is it. Do you know, it was painted by Edward Burne-Jones, my father's dearest friend. Ever since I first saw you I've wanted to drag you in front of it. King Cophetua and the Beggar Maid. Take your time, let it seep into you.'

Her eyes flickered over the long canvas. She was intrigued by a strange golden stairway. Two children leant on the balcony above and looked down at the scene below them. There were cloths draped about in muted greys, mauves, fuchsia and apricot. So many of the details intrigued her. Who were the two children? Why did they have a scroll of music? What sort of place was it supposed to be? But then she was drawn to the figure of the beggar maid sitting on a dais above King Cophetua. There was something so sensual and so familiar about the woman. Her dress was a pewter-grey that moulded itself to the woman's body, clinging over her belly and falling into folds to expose her bare feet. Sitting below her was the king in fantastical armour and holding his crown in his hands, gazing in adoration. Fidelis kept being drawn back to the girl, by her beauty and simplicity amid the opulence of her surroundings.

'Don't you recognise yourself? I saw the resemblance immediately.'

Fidelis blushed. Did she really look like that? The Beggar Maid was beautiful.

'It's strange,' she whispered, 'like everything has been turned around. The king is worshipping her, sitting at her feet, and she's raised up above him.'

'Power and riches bow down before the beauty of human love. King Cophetua surrenders his heart to her.'

'I don't think I would like to be worshipped and to be given such power over another person.'

'Or, to be enthralled yourself?' asked Dorcas.

Fidelis looked away, thinking of Daniel and her inability to resist him. It was exciting, but there was a kernel of slavishness in it that sat uncomfortably with her. When she was apart from him, she could see the foolishness of their friendship and yet when she saw him again she was once more captivated. Was it just his charm and his beauty? Or was it because he was forbidden fruit? Only minutes before stepping out for the train that morning a letter had come from him, unsettling all her earlier resolve. It lay unopened in her handbag.

'You said you wouldn't like to be worshipped. What is your idea of love, Fidelis?'

She fiddled with a button on her coat, and Aunt Ruby and Uncle Norman came into her mind. 'I think the way that two people I know love one another. It's easy, warm and comfortable. They seem equal partners yet they are still themselves. They stay together not because they can't live apart but because they freely choose to.'

Dorcas nodded. 'That was my life with a lover some years ago,' she said mysteriously. 'He taught me so much about passion and human dignity and being true to oneself.'

They strolled from one painting to another but nothing had the same intense attraction for her. Besides, her mind was now filled with questions about Dorcas and her lover.

By mutual consent, they left the gallery and caught a tram to Buckingham Palace.

On the top deck Fidelis peered out of the window, as more and more of London unfolded below. The picture she had gazed at on the wall in the schoolroom at the barracks did not begin to convey the splendour of King Edward and Queen Alexandra's residence.

'I shall have to remember every second of today, to tell my mother,' she said, staring through the railings of the vast stone palace. The motionless sentry in his scarlet jacket and bearskin helmet fascinated her.

Dorcas tugged her sleeve. 'You can send your Mama heaps of postcards later. But I have an appointment with the fabric buyer at Liberty's at three. Before then we must have some lunch.'

They strolled through Green Park and got a bus to Piccadilly Circus. It was like the hub of a wheel, with streets radiating out it in all directions, each thronged with horse-drawn cabs and trams, wagons and even sleek-looking motor-cars driven by chauffeurs wearing peaked caps and leather gauntlets. The gleaming statue of the winged Eros enchanted her.

'I must have a postcard of him,' she gasped.

Dorcas laughed. 'He is rather splendid, I grant you, but we must eat.'

They hurried off to the Café Royal in Regent Street and Dorcas breezed through the door. The floors were thickly carpeted and the lift glided them up to the restaurant.

Fidelis was overcome with shyness as the waiter took her coat then held out her chair before handing her the menu.

'What will you have?' asked Dorcas, smiling at her.

'I'll have an *omelette fines herbes* and asparagus,' she said, wondering the French words meant.

'Let's have some wine. I think a Sauterne would be appropriate.'

Fidelis watched the wine waiter hovering as her friend sipped the straw-coloured liquid and nodded her approval, but Fidelis found it sharp and vinegary. The *fines herbes* were also a disappointment being chopped up bits of parsley and such, although the asparagus was wonderfully juicy. But she paid her meal scant attention, being fascinated by her surroundings. In the corner between potted palms was a man in evening dress playing a grand piano. She sat entranced as the keys tinkled under his fingers, and his fake smile gleamed at her.

Dorcas laughed. 'Fidelis, you are so rewarding. I love enthusiastic people.'

'It's such a different world. Thank you for inviting me. I shan't forget this ever.'

'There'll be other times. After lunch we'll whiz along to Regent Street and Liberty's. While I'm busy with the buyer, you can wander through the store. I shouldn't be more than an hour or so. Let's find the Ladies, then I really must dash.'

When she came out of the toilet the powder-room was deserted. After washing her hands and helping herself to some honey and almond hand-cream, Fidelis sat down on a small gilt chair, opened her handbag and took out Daniel's letter.

> *Friday 27th February 1903*
> *My Dear Fidelis,*
> *If I close my eyes I can see you with your great fiery halo of red hair, and your green eyes flashing danger, danger. My Fidelis, you are a wonderful creature and just thinking of you brings me to such a pitch of excitement. I must see you again.*
> *I will be posted back to Portsmouth after Easter, towards the end of April, and wonder if we could arrange to meet and spend one night together. A night that would be*

*printed forever on our memory whatever else happens to
us. I want to have time to make love to you with passion
and tenderness and to have you fall asleep in my arms. We
could go to an hotel and see it as the wedding night we
would have had, were circumstances more favourable to us.
One night and then we take up our duties.*

*Darling Fidelis, please say yes. I shall reserve us a
room at the Queen's Hotel for Sunday the twenty sixth of
April. If you can, and do want to be with me on that
night, meet me at the Harbour Station that morning by
nine o'clock.*

Ever your fallen angel,
Daniel

Guiltily she leapt from the chair as the assistant came into
the room and changed the towels at the basins. There was a
pink saucer for tips on the corner of the dressing-table and
Fidelis slipped a sixpence into it, before putting the letter
back in its envelope. Her flushed face stared back at her from
the mirror before she hurried away. She needed to be on her
own back at Kelmscott, pacing about the nursery, before she
could decide what to do about Daniel.

As she looked about she thought of her mother. Liberty's
was the store Mary McCauley had always dreamed of seeing.
It was where Lady Gordon, her employer, had always shopped
for furnishings and dress materials. Fidelis drifted down the
stairs to the 'Eastern Bazaar,' in the basement. It was a revelation to her. Here were carved ivory ornaments, satin bed-
spreads in jade and turquoise and gold, bamboo tables,
mah-jong sets with curious Chinese squiggles on the creamy
tablets. Fidelis was taken with blue-and-white teasets with
little bowls instead of cups, the chopsticks, fans and carved
boxes. Upstairs she examined the bed linens, the leather
sofas, mahogany desks, and then she found the lingerie

department. There were negligees trimmed with lace as fragile as a spider's web, camisoles with minute pearls as centres to the embroidered flowers. The fabric department was an Aladdin's cave of delights, with every conceivable material from voile and lawn through to brocade and heavy tapestries. Among the dress materials, a length of satin took her fancy. It slipped and slithered between her fingers. She held it up to the light, it was such a delicate colour.

'Do you like that, madam?' the assistant enquired.

'Oh yes,' she blushed, reluctant to part with it, yet knowing that twenty-five shillings a yard was miles past her price range.

Unseen by Fidelis, Dorcas had joined her.

'Two and a quarter yards, please,' she said, taking out her purse.

'But I can't, it's far too expensive.'

'It is my gift. No, I insist, the assistant is right. It's just the right shade of green, eau-de-nil, barely a colour at all.' She laughed. 'I've got a commission for my creation frieze so an extravagance is in order. We will take a growler to Waterloo.'

Jogging along in the London cab with the sound of the horses' hoofs clip-clopping in front of them, Fidelis was in heaven. She sank onto the cushions, sniffing their leathery tang and the smell of tobacco, wondering who had been the last customer. Could it be blowsy Marie Lloyd laughing and singing on her way to the music hall, or perhaps Little Titch with his great long shoes? Her hands clutched the bag carrying her satin. She was itching to search her mother's pattern-box and make a start on her new blouse.

'You mustn't forget to buy your postcard, Fidelis. There is a little kiosk near the station and I have some stamps you may have. Bye the bye, who is Harry that you talk about so much? Is he a special beau?'

'My fiancé, stationed in the West Indies, he'll be home in July.'

'Really, and will you marry him?'

The growler stopped and, while Dorcas paid the cabman, Fidelis looked at the postcards outside the kiosk.

As Dorcas handed her the stamp she repeated her question.

'Of course,' she blustered, staring at the various views, and settling for two of Westminster Bridge.

'How long has he been away?'

'It'll be three years.'

'Do you think he will have changed much in that time?'

Fidelis stood licking the stamps then thinking about Harry. 'He was nineteen when he went away, he'll be twenty-two when he comes back. Went away as a boy and will come back a man.'

'The same must go for you? Do you feel that you have grown into a woman?'

'A lot has happened to me. I must have learnt a few things along the way, made new friends. Perhaps, now, I take my own decisions more than I used to. I haven't given it a lot of thought.'

'Where does that young lieutenant of marines fit into this picture of domestic bliss?'

Fidelis blushed. She had forgotten that Dorcas had met Daniel on Christmas Day and had brought his letter to her.

Dorcas smiled. 'Is he like that length of satin in your bag, a tempting extravagance?'

She nodded, having no words to describe Daniel's particular place in her life.

19

Fidelis lay in her bed in Kelmscott House, savouring the silence of the early morning. She supposed that Sophie would be tucked up in her new nursery, sleeping under the blue ceiling that Dorcas had painted, with silver stars and a smiling man in the moon. Would Daniel be awake in his room in the officers' quarters of the Royal Marine barracks? Would he be looking out of the window at the sunrise? Would he be thinking of her?

She had written and said yes to their meeting, and now it was Sunday April the twenty-sixth. Soon she would meet him with her valise at the harbour station and they would check into the Queen's Hotel as if they did such things every day of the week. It had taken such lies and evasions to steal the time for herself. Mrs Mount believed she was at home with her father, while Pa thought she was at Clarendon House. As long as she was back at Kelmscott by eight o'clock on Monday morning without having been seen by anyone she knew, all would be well.

After standing naked at the washbasin and soaping herself all over with rose geranium soap she dried herself, then took up her scent bottle and rubbed *Ensorcelée* on her neck, between her breasts and on the insides of her thighs. This was the day to be well and truly spell-bound. The eau-de-nil satin clung to her as she tucked it inside the waistband of her black wool skirt. At Handleys she had found some ribbon of just that shade to trim her new straw hat. Not wanting to be seen or questioned, she took up her coat and slipped out of the back door as seven o'clock chimed from the clock in the hall.

They were meeting at eight o'clock in order to wring as much time as possible from the day. Fidelis decided to walk the three miles along the beach from the South Parade to the Clarence Pier, and then through Old Portsmouth to the harbour. She smiled to herself, thinking that she might even pass the captain's house for old times' sake.

On the beach, everything looked different. It was as if she had shed her outer skin and was now acutely sensitive to every sound, smell and touch. The blur of shingle became individual stones formed of different shapes and colours; grey, toffee-brown, mottled black-and-white. They shifted under her boots in a satisfying crunch. The air reeked of seaweed and her lips tasted of salt as she ran her tongue across them. Gulls screeched and the sea foamed at the edges like pancakes in smoking fat. The breeze riffled the ribbons on her hat, and each individual bead pressed against her skin.

Walking past a beach shelter, an old man raised his hat to her in greeting. Did he see? Was it imprinted on her face? This woman is meeting her lover. She walked on towards the Clarence Pier, a great glass and wrought-iron wedding-cake of a building. She slowed her steps, not wanting to arrive at the station first, wanting to savour the moment when first she saw him. Time was a fixed entity, but just for today she wanted gallons of it – sloshing over the sides and forming puddles. As she left the ramparts along the seafront and walked down the High Street in Old Portsmouth, her feelings swung between joy and dread. Would he be there, waiting for her, on the bench beneath the sign that said Portsmouth Harbour Station?

Shivering in the April breeze, she bought her platform ticket and walked onto the station at a snail's pace. At first she did not recognise the figure in a dark-grey overcoat and trilby hat. How vulnerable he looked without his uniform. While his head was turned away from her she stood in the doorway of the waiting-room, watching him. And then he stood up and walked towards her, his blue eyes searching. Watching Daniel stripped of his golden assurance felt like trespass, but she stood treasuring the moment, knowing he wanted her. When she could bear his anxiety no longer she called out, 'Daniel, I'm over here.'

'Fidelis.' He smiled at her, taking her hands in his, squeezing her fingers. 'Darling, thank God you're here, I thought you had changed your mind.'

'Not for one second.'

'I've got a surprise for you.' He drew her into the empty waiting-room. 'Sit here and close your eyes.'

She could hear the rustle of cloth and then a click as if a box had been opened. Daniel took her hand and eased a ring onto her finger.

'Open them,' he whispered.

She stared down at her finger and blinked away her tears.

'My grandmother left it to me. I was close to her, Fidelis, so close. I promised I would give it to the girl I loved. Grammy would have given me her blessing.'

Worn thin over the years, it glinted in the sun. Fidelis gasped. It was meant for life, it was meant for Maude. However much he loved her, she would play the bride for a matter of hours: it would be Maude who wore the wedding-gown and walked down the aisle with him. She struggled not to scream out her jealousy.

'This is not how I wanted our lives to be – you must know that. I want you to have the ring for always, even if we can't be together. All we have is now.' His voice was pleading with her. 'Fidelis, please don't change your mind. I love you.'

For the first time, ever, she did not want to be the one to choose. It was pain now or pain deferred.

'We're booked in at the Queen's as Mr and Mrs Capulet.'

'Romeo and Juliet,' she said, 'the star-crossed lovers.'

She felt as if he had taken her to the edge of a precipice. Yet, she had made her decision days ago: why, now, had it become so difficult? The ring made her into a liar and a thief. But, she was that already. A strip of metal, barely more than a quarter of an inch in width, yet it represented honour and faithfulness. Her very name meant that. The ring was her passport through the doors of the hotel and up into the bedroom. All she had to do was wear it.

'Fidelis, do you want me to leave you here? D'you want me to choose for you?'

'Hold me,' she begged.

They stood with their arms about one another. She could feel his heart beating against her ear, sense his anxiety as he held her in his arms.

'This is our wedding-night. Whatever happens afterwards, it cannot be taken from us. It's what we want, it's what we would have chosen.'

Fidelis closed her eyes, and became aware of her breathing beginning to steady. Love was not forever, it was scattered through life in snatches, not always felt at the time but recognised later. Again she was like a gambler, risking everything for the intensity of the present moment. Here and now was what she could feel and taste: it was what she wanted and what she could not walk away from. She kissed him. 'Yes,' she whispered.

Together they made their way along Western Parade, past the grand seaside villas to the Queen's Hotel. It was a huge brick building facing the sea, surrounded by railings. Catching hold of the brass hand-rail, Fidelis climbed the flights of stone steps to the revolving door at the entrance. Her feet sank into the thick red carpet, and her eyes were drawn to the domed ceiling supported by marble pillars. The signs of the zodiac were painted in gold. She found Daniel's lion, and her own gemini, the twins.

He took her hand in his and approached the desk. 'Good afternoon, we are Mr and Mrs Capulet. I made a reservation earlier in the week.' Daniel took off his trilby and placed it on the desk.

The clerk, in the green hotel livery, took the pen from the inkwell and handed it to him. 'If you would just sign here, sir, and you, madam, I will find the key.'

Fidelis watched the swirling letters emerge from the nib. The address made her smile: '*Sixteen Verona Court, Stratford-on Avon*.' Following his lead she signed her name. Taking up the leather-edged blotter, the clerk pressed it over their signatures.

'Room 450 on the fourth floor, the lift is to your left. Can the porter take your baggage?'

'That won't be necessary,' her new husband said, taking her hand. 'We are only staying for one night, we can carry them ourselves.'

They stood together in the lift, trying to look as if hotels were an every-day, run-of-the-mill part of their lives. As it clanked upwards she felt her stomach clench, and then relax when it reached its destination.

The attendant's face was blank. 'Here we are sir,' he said, 'number four hundred and fifty is around to your left.'

As soon as the lift doors closed behind them Daniel kissed her, his lips warm and salty. Fidelis smiled as the knots of unease untied themselves. They stole around the corner to room 450. He slotted the key in place and it turned sweetly in the lock. Hand-in-hand they walked inside. The sun glared through the slats of the wooden blind. Daniel pulled the cord to shut out the light while she put down her case. At a loss, Fidelis stared at the sand in the seams of her boots.

'Happy wedding, my darling,' he whispered, 'happy wedding.'

She moved around the room in the circle of his arms. They turned ever more slowly. Fidelis closed her eyes, wanting to drift and drift. There was no future, no past, only this moment when Daniel held her to him. He walked her towards the bed and handed her down onto the smooth quilt, then knelt to unbutton her boots. She stroked his hair, warm and silky to her touch.

'This is our kingdom,' he said, 'our stronghold against the world. Here there are no rules but those we choose. No one shall cross the drawbridge, and tomorrow is banished.'

Step by teasing step they undressed one another. She undid his bow tie, while he drew the straps of her chemise down from her shoulders and kissed the tops of her breasts. Teasingly, temptingly, they completed the journey, leaving their clothes strewn across the floor. Fidelis explored him with her hands, tasted him with her lips and whispered in his ear. 'You are beautiful, so beautiful.' How different we are, she thought, walking her fingers down his breast-bone and over his ribs.

He led her towards the window where a shaft of sunlight had warmed the carpet. They lay side by side facing one another: stroking, nibbling and whispering words of love. She took his hands and held them over her breasts, taking his thumbs and rubbing them over each nipple. He descended her body, kissing her skin in minute instalments until she was in a fever of impatience. Daniel probed her secret place with his tongue, making her arch her back and quiver. When he entered her she wound her legs around his waist, drawing him deeper. They climbed together slowly at first, then faster and deeper until she cried out, 'Yes, oh, yes.' Afterwards, they lay on the carpet dazed and spent.

'Are you happy?' he whispered.

Fidelis smiled. 'I'm in heaven.'

'Don't move,' he said, getting up and standing naked at

the washbasin. She looked up at him, wanting to kiss the bones of his spine, to stroke his rounded buttocks. Daniel brought over a soapy flannel and a towel and washed the stickiness from between her thighs. She did the same for him, feeling no embarrassment, more a fascination with how he was made.

'Don't rub any harder,' he said. 'I want to save myself for later.'

'I'm hungry,' said Fidelis, walking naked across the carpet to fetch her case. 'We can have damson wine and some of Cook's fruit cake.'

Sitting up against a nest of pillows they toasted one another, clinking the tooth-glasses. For a moment she thought of the last time she had been toasted in damson wine. It was Boxing Evening at Auntie Ruby's. 'To your future, yours and my Harry's,' she had cried, her face beaming with joy.

'Don't,' said Daniel. 'Today is for us.'

'How did you know what I was thinking?'

'It's a gift given only to fallen angels.' He took the tooth-glass from her hand and set it on the floor. Turning down the sheet he bent over her, licking the cake crumbs from between her breasts. 'Now we need something to round off the meal. There are no brandy and cigars. What do you suggest?'

Fidelis wrapped her arms around his neck. 'Could you see me as an after-dinner liqueur?' she asked.

Daniel awoke sweating and confused. In the stifling gloom he could not imagine where he was, and then he found Fidelis curled against him. Lying there he felt a rush of joy. She was so precious, so beloved. He wanted to stop time, for this to be reality and for his other life to become the illusion. How had he got himself into such an impasse? It was Fidelis that he loved. It was she that he wanted, not dull, well-intentioned

Maude. Why could he not stand up to his father and mother, and tell them what was in his heart? Falling in love was not a capital offence, after all. On next Saturday they were all expected at Admiralty House in the dockyard. There was to be a party. The climax was to be the announcement of his engagement to Admiral Palmer's daughter. He felt as if he were being led to the scaffold. Refusing what had been set in place for him would carry a heavy penalty. The loss of his commission, his mother's disappointment and his father's rage would be just the beginning. He had no private income, and what did he know beyond life as a Royal Marine officer? It would come down to a choice between his family and Fidelis. At the thought of disobeying Jasper Herrick his mouth dried and his stomach lurched. He hated the craven creature he became when facing his father's icy disapproval. Would it be any easier for Fidelis to go through with her wedding to Harry Dawes? Would she have defied both families if he had asked her? There was another shameful aspect to his cowardice. He was accustomed to comfort and deference. The thought of living in one of those wretched little houses, and existing on ale and mutton stew, was unbearable. Once, he and Fidelis had quarrelled about it.

'This is who I am, Daniel, a drill-sergeant's daughter. My mother was a servant and I am a nursemaid. They're honest hard-working people and I'm proud of them. I'll never pretend to be anything different. I may not have the clothes of a lady but I have my own beliefs and you won't part me from them. I love you, but I know you'll let me down.'

'I won't, I promise,' he had shouted, and in that moment he had believed it.

'Daniel, you'll always want to have the cake and eat it. And how could I marry you, knowing how much you had given up for me? Besides, I've promised Harry.'

He dragged on his trousers and crept out to the bathroom.

No, it was not an atom of good scourging himself. He would have to muddle through the weekend somehow, but today was for Fidelis.

On his return she had rolled onto her back. He bent and kissed her face, flushed in sleep. She stretched luxuriously and opened her eyes. Tenderly he drew her hair away from her forehead. He watched her bewilderment turn into delight.

'Is it still our wedding-day?' she whispered.

'Yes, my darling. It's six o'clock. I am going downstairs to order us something to eat. We'll have it sent to our room. Shall I choose for you or bring up the menu?'

Fidelis leapt from the bed and swirled a sheet around her. 'How exciting. Will they bring it up in the lift on a little table, with the food under silver lids?'

'I will demand no less,' he said, touched by her enthusiasm.

'Then I shall dress for dinner. And you can surprise me. Whatever you like.'

She sat on the bed, chatting to him as he splashed cold water on his face and combed his hair. When he put on his trousers she laughed.

'What is it,' he said,' what's so funny?'

'It's just that I never knew what you did with your willy and such. I thought that perhaps you sat on it all. But of course it makes sense to tuck it down one leg.'

'You are making me blush, madam, this is not a conversation for a lady.'

'I was just curious that's all. Really, Daniel it would make more sense for men to wear skirts, don't you think?'

He laughed. Fidelis was so utterly without pretence. 'I think I shall go and get our dinner, madam. While you recover your decorum,' he teased, 'I shall have a drink in the lounge and join you later.'

★　★　★

She crept along to the bathroom, anxious not to meet any of the other guests. Fidelis locked the door behind her and turned on the taps over the bath. An alarming amount of rattling began, then water gushed out and she was enveloped in a cloud of steam. After adjusting the temperature she dipped her toe into the water, then climbed in, luxuriating in the rose-scented steam. This was bliss. She rubbed her flannel over the soap she had borrowed from Mrs Mount's bathroom, watching the bubbles slide down between her breasts. The ring on her finger gleamed. It was meant for her, she was the one he truly wanted. Standing naked, she watched her reflection in the steam-clouded mirror. After she had dried herself Fidelis took her nightgown from the case. It was cream lawn with narrow satin straps. Standing in front of the mirror she saw how it clung to her breasts then flared over her hips. Even with the matching wrapper skimming over the top she was still barely clothed. Taking her brush, she drew it through her hair then twisted it into a knot, pinning it high to the back of her head. In their bedroom she rubbed perfume on her wrists and throat before standing at the window and waiting for Daniel.

'My wife and I would like to dine in our room. It's our honeymoon, you understand.'

'Certainly, sir, I will fetch you the menu. Dinner is served at seven. Shall I bring the wine list, too?'

He chose grilled salmon and new potatoes and asparagus. 'No hors d'oeuvres or soup, thank you. But, we'll have dessert, Charlotte Russe, I think, and coffee to follow. Champagne, please.'

'Certainly, sir, and the room number?'

'Four hundred and fifty, thank you, that's splendid.'

As he opened the door Fidelis turned towards him, and he gasped. Her gown was almost transparent. He could see her nipples pressing against the embroidered bodice and the curve of her belly. Her red hair was swept up above the pale column of her neck, and a cloud of perfume wafted towards him, making him dizzy with desire.

'Fidelis, you are beautiful,' he breathed, taking her into his arms. 'I love you and I don't know how I'm going to bear to part with you.'

'We promised,' she said, 'no talk about tomorrow. What am I having for dinner?'

Her face was flushed with excitement as he wheeled in the table left outside their door.

'Daniel, I think I've died and gone to heaven. This is so wonderful.' She shrieked with excitement when he popped the cork, and gasped at the dryness of the champagne. 'All this time I've dreamt of drinking it and now, aghh! – it's like fizzy vinegar. Give me lemonade any day of the week. But the salmon, it's gorgeous, gorgeous, gorgeous, and the asparagus is wonderful.'

Daniel smiled, it was such joy to indulge her, she was so wholehearted in her enjoyment. Lingering over the meal, they fed each other forkfuls of salmon and drank from the same glass. After he had pushed away the table, she was waiting for him.

Daniel took her to bed. He kissed every part of her from her eyebrows to the instep of each foot. She was everywhere, tasting and touching him, stroking his thighs, taking his penis into her hand and guiding it inside her. They were alternately coarse and tender, laughing and then on the edge of tears.

'I want to sleep in your arms and never wake up,' Fidelis whispered.

He drew her to him breathing in her smell, part perfume, part a deep female scent.

'Dearest girl,' he sighed. Feeling warm and blessed, Daniel closed his eyes.

*   *   *

It was over. Fidelis could not bear to part with him. She bent and kissed his sleeping face. Instead of slowly drawing out the pain she would go now. After dressing she found a scrap of paper in her handbag, and a pencil.

> 'My Daniel,
>   I am leaving you sleeping while I have the courage to go. I shall never again have such a birthday and I want to leave before you see my tears. May you have a good life and I shall try my best to have the same. You have been my bright angel and no one will ever love you as I do. But now I must come down to earth.
>   Goodbye my best love. May God bless you and keep you in his care,
>   Ever yours,
>   Fidelis.

She left the note on his pillow, weighted down with his grandmother's ring. On an impulse she left the half-empty bottle of perfume beside it. *Ensorcelée*, – she had no need of it now. He didn't stir as she dressed and folded away her nightdress. All the while she was on pins, half hoping he would wake up and yet dreading to see her sorrow mirrored in his face. Fidelis kissed him on the lips, then took up her case, closing the door behind her. The clerk was napping at his desk as she passed on through the revolving door and out of the hotel. She walked through the gate and across the road, retracing her steps from yesterday. The beach was deserted save for the gulls fighting over a fish-head, and a dog with its face streaked with white hairs. She sat on the shingle and unbuttoned her boots, and pushed them into her case. Dipping her toes into the water she walked back along the shore, watching the sun rise in the distance over Eastney. It was over, and she didn't know how to bear it. It was the greatest hurt since childhood. Then, she could have climbed

on Pa's lap and wept out her grief. Now there was no one
to console her.

Soon Cook and Eileen and Midge would be waiting for
her, eager to know about her visit to her mother at Ventnor.
Nearing Kelmscott House she sat on a bench and put on
her boots. Soon she must dress in her nursemaid's uniform
and hurry along to Clarendon House. There was one con-
solation: Phoebe Allen never showed the least curiosity in
her servant's lives. She would be ratty as always first thing
in the morning, until she had had her Earl Grey and buttered toast. But Sophie would welcome her with a kiss, and
they would fall into their nursery routine. Today she was
going to Brighton with her mother to visit Sarah Gibbons.
Fidelis had been instructed to make up the bed in the guest-
room as an old schoolfriend was coming to stay. The hours
would creep along. On Wednesday afternoon she really was
going to visit her mother.

Already the week was filling up with activities and Daniel
was disappearing into her past.

20

He didn't love her, and she was undecided about her own feelings. So why was she getting engaged in the big anonymous Admiralty House in the Dockyard? Maude twisted her dressing-gown cord around her finger. Pleasing people, it was her one besetting sin. Mummy had said so, just before she died.

'Darling, you have a right to be happy in your own way – all it takes is courage. Maude, darling, don't live your life to please others, I beg you.'

Mummy had always encouraged her, taught her painting, taken her around the farm and shown her how it worked. They had stood together in the winter store, bathed in the scent of apples, both of them full of wonder.

'Look at them all, the fruits of the earth and the work of human hands – year after year after year. Throughout Kent now, they'll be sliced into pies and puddings, carried to school in children's pockets, pressed into cider vats and poured into tankards. Apples of England, their names run through my mind like beads on a necklace: Beauty of Bath, Egremont Russet, Devonshire Quarrenden, Nonpareil and our own Gascoyne's Scarlet.'

When Daniel came down to Crossways last November, it had seemed a possibility that they could grow to love one another. He and Daddy were easy with each other, walking miles over the wintry fields: and when she had taken him in the trap to the station, he had kissed her on the mouth and squeezed her hand. There had been a letter to thank her for making him so welcome: and an invitation, for her and her father, to stay at the barracks with his parents for Christmas. Daniel would live in the officers' quarters nearby, and there was to be a concert.

She had travelled there with such excitement, but the mood that existed between them at Crossways was absent in Portsmouth. They were both back in their fathers' enclaves. At the Admiralty parties she was at a loss, not knowing how to be glossy and trivial like the other young women flocking around the young officers. The Daniel she had glimpsed in the apple store – funny and interesting – was gone. The Christmas concert had shown her where his affections lay. And she didn't blame him one bit. The girl was glorious, and her voice had brought Maude herself almost to tears. Even though they were in the darkened theatre she could feel his tension, and see by the girl's face, in the spotlight, that she was mesmerised. There was his sudden cancelling of their walk on Boxing Afternoon, and his restlessness afterwards. Then suddenly, on the first Sunday of the New Year, Daniel had proposed to her.

'Maude, I want us to be married. I'm fond of you and we could be friends.'

She had looked up at him, startled at the turn the conversation had taken. Mr and Mrs Herrick were at the Crinoline Church with Daddy. They had walked along to the Canoe Lake and watched the wind riffling the surface of the water. It scoured their faces and made her eyes water. Back at his father's house, he got the steward to serve them tea in the drawing-room, its windows overlooking the beach. Maude sipped her tea and stared out at the sea, grey and choppy. She was startled when Daniel came and perched on the arm of her chair, even more startled at his proposal.

'I don't understand why you should want that. We are

friends, of course we are, but marriage is rushing a long way ahead. Why would you want to do that?'

For the first time she saw him flounder. 'I'm nearly twenty-five. I shall have a captain's commission by the end of the year, it makes sense.'

'Don't you think that is a rather insulting reason to propose to me?' She felt a spurt of anger and knew she must be blushing. 'As if I were an accompaniment to the sword and extra gold braid.'

'I have put it clumsily. I like you, Maude, you're a good person and I trust you. Given time, I could love you.'

'Why don't we give ourselves time, then? Let's both remain free to see how our feelings develop. I don't want you to be held to a promise that perhaps you may regret later. What is behind this? Is it your father pushing you into this? I know Pa is keen for us to be more than friends.' She had looked up at him, and for a moment he teetered on the edge of admitting as much: then he treated her to one of his golden smiles.

'Perhaps they know us better than we know ourselves. Maude, I don't want us to be married straightaway, it's just a mark of our intention to draw closer.'

'Why do we need to make it so public? I can assure you of my affection without an announcement in *The Times* or an expensive ring.'

'I thought you would be excited,' he said.

'If I believed you I would be. Daniel, I'm a country girl, quiet, bookish and shy. I'm neither beautiful nor witty, so why should you want me? I would add nothing to your life apart from the cachet of marrying an admiral's daughter, and I can't believe that you could be that shallow.'

'I need you to be with me,' he was pleading with her. 'I am as you say, vain and shallow. You would demand better of me and I would rise to that.'

'I'm not a medicine to be taken twice daily and swallowed with your eyes closed. What about my feelings? There is no satisfaction in knowing one is second-best.'

'Why do you say that?' He took a log from the basket in the hearth and set it on the fire, nudging it in place with a poker.

'Because, sitting on the chair while others are dancing, plain women notice things. Left out of the conversation at dinner-tables, they pick up the undercurrents. I am not available as your conscience, Daniel, or your hostess. You don't love me, you don't even see me.'

She had run away to the bathroom, her courage at an end, before she mentioned the girl with the red hair. Then it was too late. The parents returned from church, and they were caught up in Sunday lunch. It was only Daniel's mother who noticed anything amiss between them. When she and her father were preparing to leave, Alicia Herrick took her aside and took her to her bedroom.

'Maude, it has been such a joy.' She took her hands in her own and bent forward to kiss her cheek. 'You are such a fine young woman. I have always wanted a daughter, having you with us has shown me what I have missed. Please come and see me, won't you? Before you leave, I have a present.' Alicia gave her a small book of Tennyson's poems. 'There is one named for you, but his Maud has no "e" at the end.'

'That is so kind of you.' She was touched by her warmth and kindness.

'I am perhaps working against my own best interests when I say this, but I want you to have a happy life, my dear. Being without your mother's guidance must be difficult. Maude, if Daniel is not for you, please don't be swept up in the excitement of an engagement. Whatever you decide, I shall always value your friendship.'

But now it was Saturday May the seventh, and she had

fallen victim to Daniel's constant pleading letters. Downstairs in Admiralty House, a party was being prepared and there would be dancing. At some point in the evening the announcement would be made. They would marry in October and go off to the Ascension Islands. Their honeymoon would be spent on the ship going out there.

Maude wanted the evening gone. Ahead of her was the humiliation of standing there, beside her handsome fiancé, watching the other women looking at her and knowing exactly what they were thinking. How could the beautiful Daniel ally himself to such a plain Jane? She knew the second thought. Ah! It's because she's the admiral's daughter. It will give him a mighty shove up the career ladder. But Alicia would be there. She had made sure that her future mother-in-law was seated opposite to lend her courage.

'Come in,' she called to the authoritative tap on the door.

'Hello, my sweet, how are you feeling?' Daddy came over to her and perched on the edge of one of the quilted nursing-chairs she had brought up from Kent.

'Nervous and wanting it to be over.'

He waved his hand as if swatting a fly. 'What nonsense! You have a splendid future ahead of you. Daniel is a fine fellow, he'll go far, soon you'll have a clutch of youngsters, won't have time to be nervous.' He reached into his pocket and brought out a round padded jewellery-box. 'Here, I want you to wear these. Gave them to your mother just after you were born, as a thank-you for giving me a beautiful daughter. Want you to wear them in her memory.'

Maude smiled. Her father so often reminded her of an eagle, with his beaked nose and rangy restlessness, and then he would surprise her with a sudden kindness. She held out her hand, and he placed the pearl drop earrings on her palm. 'They are beautiful Pa, thank you.' He stayed while she put them in place.

'Splendid, splendid! I'll be up to collect you in half an hour.'

'You haven't asked me if I want this engagement,' she said, as the door closed behind him.

His father was proud of him, he could see it in the way he smiled at him. The way he introduced him to others. 'My son Daniel, getting married, don't you know – Palmer's girl, nice little thing. Off to the Ascensions.'

Not even the medal he was expecting from his time in China had bought him such approval. All his striving had been for nothing. Jasper Herrick didn't know his son, and had never shown any desire to find out what moved him. Everyone, even his mother, was simply an appurtenance to further his own ambition. The prize Daniel had striven for all his life had not been worth the winning.

It would not have been so empty if only he had wanted it. But he didn't love her. Maude was intelligent and kind, and he could feel easy in her company. If he were not marrying her he would want her as a friend. She could be witty and wise in her assessment of things. He trusted her but did not love her. Could they, would they, make a go of things?

Only a week ago, he had been with Fidelis. Even now he still had the letter she had left on his pillow. He still wanted her. If he really was the hero she thought him to be, why hadn't he fought for her? Because he was like his father and wanted it all – love and glory. Maude had said he was shallow. And in that moment as he picked up his gloves and glimpsed himself in the hall mirror, Daniel knew it to be true.

'Hello, darling.' His mother took his arm as he helped her into the carriage. 'Pa will be along later, some last-minute thing with the adjutant.' When they were seated she said, 'How are you feeling?'

'Not worthy of her, Ma. I just hope I don't make a mess of things.'

'People have wed happily with far less in common than you and Maude. It's a question of application. Once you've made that promise you must honour it. It's no earthly good looking back on what might have been, and my darling, your mother is not so blind as you might think. I know you have been torn over this and you have had your temptations. But, now your life is with Maude. It's painful, I know, but there it is. Being a man of honour is what I brought you up to be, and what I expect of you.'

Maude felt as if she would faint. The heat from the candles on the dining-table was overpowering. She unbuttoned her long-sleeved gloves at the wrist and rolled them up like bracelets. Her hands were hot, and the wine-glass slippery between her fingers. The soup was peppery, and a sliver of kidney rubbery between her teeth. Opposite her was Daniel, immaculate in his dress uniform, smiling at something his mother had said. He looked across at her and smiled. What did it mean? At the head of the table her father was talking to the chaplain's wife: she knew he was bored and impatient, wanting to engage Captain Percy, across the table from him, in gunnery matters.

As her plate was removed, the chaplain beside her began to speak.

'Miss Palmer, I was so delighted to be invited to your engagement party. I knew your mother.'

'Really, I didn't know that.' She liked his face: it was rosy like a countryman's and there was a hint of an accent.

'I was at Malta when you were just a baby.' He looked towards his wife. 'Meriel and I were newly married and it was my first posting abroad.' He smiled ruefully. 'We were babes in the wood and it was Mrs Palmer who rescued us.

She was so kind and welcoming. We were both most grieved to learn of her passing.'

Maude nodded, and lifted a forkful of salmon to her lips. His mention of her mother would bring on the tears if she were not careful.

'Miss Palmer, isn't it? Congratulations, I was fearfully excited to hear your news. My husband served with Daniel in China. I have not as yet been introduced. You must tell me how you met.' The woman on the other side of the chaplain oozed insincerity.

Maude smiled, then turned to the padre. 'Where is it you come from? I think I recognise your accent.'

'I am from Chatham. I believe your family hails from Kent.'

'Yes, between Cranbrook and Goudhurst.'

'Meriel will be delighted to know that, her father was the vicar of St John's in his early days.'

'Where are you stationed now, Padre?'

'We are about to sail for the Ascension Islands.'

'How interesting, it will be our first posting. We will be there in late October, I believe.'

The padre clapped his hands. 'Capital! Then we shall be your welcoming party. That will give my wife something to look forward to. She was saying, when we arrived this evening, that you reminded her so much of your mother.'

As she looked across the table, Meriel White paused in her conversation and smiled at her. The thought of a friendly face awaiting her lifted Maude's spirits. Dutifully, she asked the pushy naval wife her name, and promptly forgot it. Alicia Palmer was laughing at something Pa had said, and Daniel blew her a kiss.

Her fish course was removed and replaced with lamb cutlets. The dreaded party was becoming, if not enjoyable, at least bearable in the company of the homely padre.

She thought about her engagement ring. They had bought

it in Winchester the day before. Daniel had a ring his grand-mother had left him with the express instructions that it should be given to his future wife. He had been surprised when Maude had refused it.

'Your grandfather chose it for her and I want us to choose my ring together. I shall be the first person to wear it.'

'You are very decided in your views. When I first met you I didn't think you would be, you seemed very much in your Pa's shadow.'

'It's cold in the shadows, don't you find?'

He had laughed. 'Touché. What stones do you favour?'

'I think pearl. It's my birthstone. And when is your birthday?'

'July the twenty-fifth, what does that signify?'

'You are a ruby, rich and red.'

It had been a happy afternoon, such as a brother and sister might spend together. As yet they had not kissed except in their greetings and goodbyes. Daniel had not flirted with her, and it was an accomplishment she had never acquired. Tonight on the stroke of midnight he would put the ring on her finger.

'Shall we do it in public or do you want us to steal away?'

'I am marrying you, not the fleet,' Maude had protested. 'Afterwards, Pa can make the announcement and I will suffer you to waltz me round the room. Or, given my dancing skills, you will have to suffer me.'

She looked across at him and he smiled at her. Could they really and truly make each other happy?

More wine was poured, the dessert was served and then the coffee. Maude, on her father's arm, led the guests into the ballroom. This evening it was the Royal Marines who were providing the orchestra.

When the music started, she was surprised to see Pa leading Alicia onto the floor, then alarmed when Daniel's father took her arm.

'Well, Maude, an exciting evening, what?'

She craned her neck and looked up at him. It seemed that every other sentence was a question and none of them required an answer. His dancing, like his conversation, was jerky and erratic. He looked straight ahead and gripped her hand, steering her through the other couples like a helmsman through a flotilla. It was with relief that she sat down again. And then it was Daniel's turn.

'Hello stranger,' he said. 'I don't think I have spoken to you all evening. Are you enjoying yourself?'

'It has been better than I expected. I had a friendly padre beside me and we chatted away.' She smiled. 'Once my terror subsided I found I was ravenously hungry and ate everything in sight.'

'I had Ma with me and she is a wonder. There was a frightful old bore next to her who blathered on about Nelson. She listened to him as if he were Prince Charming. My partner was a headmistress in a girls' boarding school, a real virago.'

They laughed together, and when the music stopped he led her out to the conservatory. 'Maude, why don't we get engaged this moment? What's so special about midnight? I want us to make our own rules.'

'Yes, I hate all this pressure of the drum-roll and all eyes on me.'

He took the jewel-box from his pocket and held the ring out to her, then slid it on her finger. Maude held up her face to be kissed. His lips were soft and persuasive. She stood on tiptoe and put her arms around his neck. It was a different kiss. His tongue slid between her lips, and she felt a stirring of desire. She was breathless when he released her.

'I think we could be happy,' he whispered. 'What do you think?'

Maude looked down at her ring, wanting him to say that he loved her, but steeling herself against disappointment. 'I don't know,' she murmured. 'Sometimes I feel that we are on the verge of it and then I sense that you draw back. If I could just believe that it was me that you wanted I might begin to . . .'

'There you are, Daniel.' Colonel Herrick did not look in the least pleased to see her. 'I've got Captain Percy at our table. Come along my boy, and you Maude,' he said impatiently.

'No,' she said, 'thank you, I would rather stay here for a moment.' She looked at her fiancé. They had been close in those last few moments, but she sensed that Daniel was setting her aside. Whatever chance of success their future marriage had, it would always founder against the demands of Jasper Herrick. For the first time in her life she experience hatred. Her father-in-law was a schemer and a destroyer. His son might feel compelled to dance to his tune but she did not. Although she had been fearful of going off to the Ascension Islands with Daniel, she now saw it as their salvation.

'Maude, my darling, come and dance with your old Pa. It's that lovely "Gold and Silver" waltz by Strauss.' He kissed her cheek. 'I'll try not to step on your toes.

'I shall miss you, my sweet,' he said, as they whirled around the floor, 'but I must make the most of you while you're here. Six months, it's a very short engagement.'

Daniel was waiting for her when the music stopped, and led her back to his table. She braced herself for another encounter with the iron duke as she secretly dubbed his father, but was pleased to see the padre and his Meriel sitting with Alicia.

They all talked easily together and exchanged addresses, promising to keep in touch. Maude invited them to visit when she and her father went to Kent later in the month. Then it was midnight, after a drum-roll, and her father hurried up to the orchestra.

'Ladies and gentlemen, it gives me great pleasure to announce the engagement of my dear daughter Maude to Captain Daniel Herrick of the Royal Marines. I would like you all to be upstanding and drink the health of the happy couple.' He waved them onto the floor. 'Daniel and Maude, health and happiness.'

A steward filled their champagne flutes and they clinked them together. The orchestra struck up 'The Gold and Silver Waltz'. Setting their glasses back on the steward's tray they began to waltz around the room. Soon other couples joined them.

Maude knew that she should be ecstatic at having become engaged to the most handsome man in the room, but unease hobbled her confidence, like a pebble in a shoe. She glanced at Daniel, and saw that he looked equally uncertain.

21

It was May, her mother's favourite month, with the birthday of the Blessed Virgin Mary and the Corpus Christi processions at her church – May with trees in blossom, daffodils and tulips in the parks, and everything to live for. Fidelis sat in the salon of the paddle steamer and took her father's hand. 'We'll get there in time, Pa,'– but she knew that Dr Freer would not have sent a telegram without good cause.

Why hadn't Ma got better? Four months she had been resting and taking a special milk diet. Prayers were said for her at the Crinoline Church at the barracks and at St Swithun's Catholic church.

The frailty of that figure sitting in an invalid chair, swathed in a shawl, was painful to remember. Ma had been so pleased to see her, and it had been hard not to cry at the unexpected welcome.

'Fee, you look pretty, tell me all that's been happening.'

Holding Ma's hand, she feared to break the bones, and it hurt her to see her wrists no bigger now than a child's. Her eyes were fever-bright, and still there was that cough.

'Is this the blouse you made from the Liberty material?'

'So, you got the postcard from London?'

'Tell me all about it.'

'I'll leave you ladies to chat, and have a stroll round the gardens, be back later,' Pa had said.

Fidelis tried to bring the day alive for Ma. 'It was like a

theatre of shopping with everything arranged to tempt you with colour, scent and feel. You would have loved the materials: satins, velvets, brocade, lace, tulle, organza, Shantung, *peau de soie*.' The words were like the beads of her mother's rosary, constantly passing through her fingers. 'It wasn't just the colours but the feel of them. The way the satin slipped through my fingers, and the delicacy of the voile – it was almost transparent.'

'How is Sophie?' Ma whispered, when Fidelis had thought her sunk in sleep.

'She's bright as a button. Her eyes are watching everything and she has begun to sing now, and in tune. Mrs Allen's moved back to Clarendon House and Sophie's joined her now. At first I stayed at Kelmscott and was a daily nursemaid, now I'm back there, too. The nursery has been redecorated; the walls are yellow and there's a wonderful frieze with animals and birds. Sophie loves it, and I've got my own room.'

Fidelis poured her mother a glass of water. 'It's lovely here, Ma. The fresh air and sunshine must be doing you good. I'm looking forward to us walking in the gardens together.'

Her mother began to cough. Fidelis helped her sit up and take a sip of water, then she handed her one of the hospital spitting-flasks, and paper handkerchiefs. It was so difficult to think of things to say. Every time she visited, Ma seemed more fragile and breathless.

'I'm not getting better Fee, every day I'm weaker and so tired. Fading away, that's what I am doing. Little point in you and your father visiting.'

'We love you Ma, and want to see you,' she protested.

'Perhaps it's all going to take longer than we thought.'

'It won't be long, Father Connor says I am well prepared.' The words were interspersed by bouts of coughing. 'You and Jack will be set free.'

The words were like a blow to the stomach. She gasped. It was as if her mother was looking forward to death. 'I don't want you to die,' she pleaded, unable to check her tears. 'We love you, please try and get better just for us. Try Ma, please, please.'

She closed her eyes. 'I'm so tired, Fee, just go and find your father.'

Fidelis saw him sitting on a bench crying.'

'Pa, what is it? Oh Pa, please don't cry.'

'She's going from us, getting weaker every day. Doctor says she never had the will to fight it. Days, he says, just days.'

Somehow they had dried their tears and returned to her mother's room. They sat and had tea together as if at a garden party. Ma only drank half a cup of tea and refused the sandwiches but they, her visitors, ate and chatted with a desperate gaiety.

And then her father touched her arm. 'Fee, say goodbye to your Ma. I have things to say to her. I'll see you at the bench by the gate.'

Sitting waiting for him, she wondered what she had meant to her mother, that she could so calmly prepare herself for death. Had she even tried to get well?

On the homeward journey they had sat together hand-in-hand in shocked silence. Locked in grief, they had walked all the way across Portsmouth to Gibraltar Street noticing nothing, one footstep following another.

Now, they had been summoned back to the Island with their worst fears about to be realised. At this very moment, as Fidelis sat on board the steamer staring down into the green water of the Solent, her Ma could be passing away from her. If only they'd been able to draw closer. She felt such sadness and regret.

'Fee, I've brought us some sandwiches,' said Pa, coming

back from the buffet on the lower deck. 'We don't know what's ahead of us so we best eat now.'

Fidelis forced herself to swallow down the rubbery cheese. What if they were too late? She had never seen a dead person, and for her first body to be that of her mother was unbearable. How would she cope?

'Fee, darling,' Pa said, 'we'll just have to bear it best we can, there's little chance she'll last until we get there. It'll be one of those days that's lived minute by minute.'

Walking towards the Princess Louise block, fear fluttered in her chest and she wanted to run away.

After the doctor had offered his condolences and left them at the bedside, Jack held his daughter's hand. He looked down at his wife of over twenty years. The disease was well named, for it had consumed her. Ashen-faced in the white sheets, her hair was a startling slash of red. He ached with pity. Mary had gained so little joy from life, and set herself a punishing course towards her Saviour. What would be her eternal reward for such austere devotion?

'I've been a stranger all my life,' she had said, that last time. 'I have never fitted in.'

'Why was that, my darling?' Rarely had Mary spoken of her childhood, and then only in the most general terms.

'My mother said, when they took me to the Sisters, "Be a good girl and don't let them see you cry. Be a proud girl, don't let them see they've hurt you. Remember I'll be looking down on you from heaven, I'll be waiting for you with Jesus."'

'How old were you when your mother died? You never said.'

'I was four, a quiet girl and a private one that never told. Never ever, even when he broke my trust and stole from me.'

He held his breath, fearing to say anything.

'Took the only thing I had. Stole my innocence and trust, broke in and took me. There was nowhere to go, no one to tell. And you know,' she looked at him and there were tears, hovering, 'I was frightened that if I said anything, Mummy would know that I had been a bad girl and she wouldn't be waiting.'

She'd dried her eyes but he had cried for her. 'Sweet Mary, why did you never tell me, darling? I would have tried to understand.' He sat there, lacerating himself for his brute love. All their years together, she must have endured him like a penance.

As if reading his thoughts, she said, 'I don't want your pity. There have been moments, watching Fee grow up, when I've felt happy – scattered moments. But I'm a stranger here – I want to go home. Mummy will be waiting with Pa and Jesus.'

He'd kissed her cheek, and she had not flinched from him. 'I have loved you as best I could Mary,' was all he could manage. On the journey home he had sat shut in on himself – silent and ashamed.

'Poor Ma,' said Fidelis, bending over her mother and kissing her wasted cheek, 'she was so difficult to love.'

'She seemed happy here, the happiest I've seen her in years. I never knew why she married me, you know, Fee, because she surely never loved me. But she has got what she always wanted, she's going home.'

'I don't think she knew how to be close to anyone. She was locked away somehow. Perhaps, being brought up in the orphans' home was a bad start? I wonder if anyone ever kissed or held her there? She was so untouchable. I used to think there was something about me that she didn't like. How I smelled, or how I looked at her, but loving just wasn't in her. Can't remember any time when she really laughed.'

'Fee, the memories will come back. She was reserved in her ways but if anyone gave her joy it was you. You singing that hymn in Latin, that surely made her proud.'

'When you think of Ruby and Norman and their children, they're always laughing and larking and touching and holding. Why couldn't we be like that?'

'That's a cruel question.' He looked away from her, and it was a while before he spoke again. 'You know, when the doctor told me she was dead, I felt a huge relief. Like a stone was rolled from me heart. Isn't that a terrible thing?'

Fidelis gripped his hand. 'Let's say goodbye to her, Pa, and go and ask Sister what we must do next.'

'She told me what she wanted, my darling. It'll be a Catholic service and we'll arrange it with the chaplain. She wants to be buried on the Island.'

'We shall just have to do what she wants, Pa, and then perhaps you'll cry, perhaps not. I don't suppose there are any rules. Ma was the one for rules.' She squeezed his arm, 'We're just the ones for breaking them.'

Fidelis had arranged to spend the night with her father, but on the way home they called at Kelmscott. At their news, Midge burst into tears.

'Mr McCauley, I'm so sorry for your trouble,' said Cook. 'You sit yourself down, I'll get you a mug of ale and something to go with it.'

Fidelis went through to the sitting-room and knocked on the door.

'Fidelis, how nice to see you, sit down, please,' said Mrs Mount. 'How are you settling in with Sophie? I must say that I miss having my granddaughter here.'

'Very well, madam, I have a room of my own and I like it quite well.' She cleared her throat. 'I've come from the Isle of Wight, my mother died there this morning.'

'Fidelis, I am so sorry, my dear. What a blow for you and your father. She was a good woman, I know, you will miss her. Let my daughter know when the funeral is to be, and we will arrange for you to attend and then be home for a day or so.'

'Thank you, madam, I'm just walking back with Father, now.'

'Give Mr McCauley my condolences. Off you go my dear, and God bless you.'

Back in the kitchen, Fidelis saw a letter from Harry perched on the dresser shelf. It had come just at the right time. While she tucked it in her pocket Eileen stood by the iron, sniffing sympathetically as Pa spoke to Cook.

'That was a lifesaver, Mrs Hobbs. I was on my beam-ends, to tell you God's honest truth. I thank you both for your kindness.'

Fidelis shivered and slipped her hand through her father's arm, glad of his warmth. They walked home together in silence. As Pa turned the key, Ebony threw himself at the door, barking a welcome.

'Hello my old feller, I'm glad to see you, and you've Fee to pet you.'

'I'll rouse up the fire and make us some tea,' said Fidelis, 'then we'll just do what feels comfortable, I don't know . . .' Her voice trailed away.

Her father smiled. 'We're a couple of shipwrecked articles and we'll just have to keep treading water 'til we get the hang of it.'

Trawling through the larder, she found a tin with half of one of Aunt Ruby's dripping-cakes inside. She set two large slices on the plates and filled the kettle. By the time she had carried it in by the fire her Pa was asleep. She took off his boots and covered him with a blanket before carrying the tray upstairs to her room. Standing by the window, she heard the bugler play 'Sunset' and saw the flag being lowered at the clock tower. She wept for her mother, and for herself. There were more tears for Daniel, gone now from her life. The *Evening News* had been full of his engagement to Maude Palmer. But she could not regret their time together, for all that it was theft. May seemed a month full of loss, and she longed to see the end of it.

It was, after all, quite a respectable group in the hospital chapel for Mary McCauley's funeral. Jack and Fidelis were the principal mourners, with Shamrock and Norman and Ruby in the pew beside them. The hospital doctor and half a dozen patients attended, and at the back was Dorcas Beningfield.

'I shall be over at my cottage on the day of your mother's funeral. Would it be helpful if I made it available for you to invite everyone for some refreshments – simple food, tea and cider, perhaps? I'll arrange for a cab to be outside the cemetery to bring you over to Fortitude Cottage. I don't wish to intrude if you have other plans.'

'That's ever so kind,' said Fidelis, touched at her thoughtfulness. 'I was wondering what we would do. I didn't want to have us hanging about the hospital. They have been so sympathetic and helpful but I can't be there anymore, it just makes me sad.'

'Well, I shall slip out after the service and have everything in readiness.'

She gasped when she saw her mother's coffin with its wreath of lilies on top. How small it was. Her father took her hand and squeezed it. The sun shone through the stained-glass windows, leaving pools of red and gold and green on the tiled floor. There was an angel in the central window, playing a mandolin. She thought of Daniel and their first meeting on the beach, when he had called himself a fallen angel. Tears welled in her, and she didn't know whom she was crying for.

'Mary McCauley was a woman steeped in faith,' said the hospital chaplain, 'and many is the time she brought me up sharp when she thought I was not fulfilling my duties.' He smiled at them. 'I do hope that heaven is not a disappointment to her, as I believe that Jesus is inclined to give people the benefit of the doubt. But there she will find her parents waiting. Mary was a woman of duty who found love difficult. In Paradise she will leave her pride and hurt at the door and be welcomed as a child.'

Beside her she heard her father gasp, and then reach for his handkerchief. Poor Pa, he would be lonely without his Mary.

What had Ma meant to her? Fidelis wondered. When she considered her own small accomplishments, they were all due to Ma's teaching. Sewing, cooking, letter-writing and reading – all these she had learnt from her. As a small child, she had loved the phrase Ma always said just before she kissed her good-night: '*The Lord make his face to shine on you and be gracious unto you.*' It stopped her being afraid of the dark. What Mary McCauley had been was a good mother – it had not been in her to be a loving one.

As they stood at the graveside, Fidelis threw a spray of roses from the garden at home onto the coffin. Uncle Norman played the Last Post, the notes rising sweet and true over the grave. Fidelis wanted to sing for her but in the end she was too tearful. The chaplain closed his prayer-book and everyone shook his hand. It was over.

'That was very fitting,' said Shamrock, blowing her nose. 'Your Mary would have approved of that.'

'So, what would be suitable for your send-off, gal?' asked Norman, when they passed through the cemetery gates.

'I wants a shillabeer and black horse, brass handles to me coffin and everyone crying their hearts out.'

'What in God's name is a shillabeer?' asked Pa, putting away his handkerchief.

'It's a glass-sided carriage, so it is. Then folks will be able to see all the heaps of flowers bedecking me box.'

They laughed at Shamrock's wild plans as they crossed the road to the waiting cab.

'Good afternoon to you,' the cabman said, as they approached. 'You must be the party for Miss Beningfield up at Fortitude Cottage? Step up then lively.'

Pa climbed up on the outside. 'You'll not mind me riding up with you, squire?' he said. 'It's too good a day to waste shut inside.'

'You please yourself, mister, 'tis no odds to me.'

Fidelis felt a sudden lightness of spirit: there would be no more desperate hoping, no more tearful visits: Ma was at peace. She smiled at Ruby and Shamrock as they all bounced along through Ventnor and on to Wheeler's Cove.

The cab stopped at the back of a solid yellow-and-red brick house with a flight of steep stone steps leading up to it. Dorcas stood at the top to greet them.

'Welcome to you all, I'm sorry about the steps. But come in, do, I have the kettle on, but there is beer or cider and even lemonade.'

They walked through the house, down more steps, and out into the front garden.

'I've set the table and chairs out there. You can see I'm perched near the edge of the cliff. If you want to climb down there, you can paddle in the sea.'

Ruby laughed. 'Look Fee, it's just like one of them chalets from Switzerland, with its balcony and them nice shutters on the windows.'

Taking a seat, Fidelis realised that she was starving.

*　　*　　*

Jack went into the kitchen. 'This is very kind of you, Miss Beningfield. I appreciate it, thank you.'

She turned and smiled at him. He thought her a handsome woman rather than a beauty. There was an easy acceptance in her manner that calmed the chaos in him. He was at full stretch, and no company for anyone at that moment.

'I'm Dorcas and you're Jack, I believe?' Her handshake was firm, and she looked at him appraisingly. 'It's my pleasure to be of use. You look weary. There's a deckchair over in the corner under the tree, why don't you go out and stake your claim.'

She was right, he was weary to the bone. Sinking down into the faded deckchair, away from the others, he closed his eyes. The sun was warm on his face, and bees droned among the hollyhocks. He would have ten minutes shut-eye just to refresh himself, then he would have some of that ham. It was the smell of tobacco that roused him, to find an hour had passed and Norman was smoking his pipe.

'You sunk like a stone, Jack. You must be cold,' said Dorcas, smiling at him. 'Come inside with us.'

He struggled out of the deckchair, cramped and stiff, stamping the life back into his feet and swinging his arms. 'That was good,' he said. 'Doctor Sleep has set me right. Dorcas, I thank you for your kindness.'

She waved his thanks away. 'My house is your house, think nothing of it.'

Jack followed her inside, dipping his head under the low doorway. Inside, the sitting-room was full of books spilling out of shelves, and paintings on the walls. In the kitchen, on the chimney-breast, was a framed drawing of a soldier in his shirtsleeves, caught as he looked up from polishing his boots. The man had a rough-hewn face that was arresting rather than conventionally attractive.

'A dear friend of mine,' said Dorcas. 'Gone two years now.'

'I'm sorry for your trouble. He looked a fine young man, a cruel waste.'

'Isn't war always?' she said, filling three glasses with cider from a stone jar.

He sat between Fee and Ruby and reached out his fork for the ham.

'This will be a great loss to both of you. Grieving is a strange business. It affects people differently, I know,' said Dorcas.

'Well, I wouldn't wish her to go on as she was, Dorcas. It was painful to see the woman I married fading away before my eyes. Still, she's in heaven now and that's what she always wanted.'

'It's her things that bring her close and make me cry,' said Fidelis. 'I can't look in her sewing-basket. Then there's her recipe book, with all the bits of paper slipped in between the pages.'

'I suppose over time, the essence of the person is shown to us. I don't know,' said Dorcas. 'Life is such a mystery, isn't it?'

The kitchen clock chimed five, and everyone suddenly gathered their things.

'Miss Dorcas,' said Ruby shaking her hand. 'It was lovely of you to have us over. Set us up for the journey back, thank you ever so much.'

Shamrock hugged her. 'You did us proud. Jack and me are more than grateful.'

Dorcas kissed Fidelis on the cheek, then turned to her father and held his hand. 'I want to see you both over here again in happier times. Safe journey to you all.'

Shamrock took a cab back to the People's Palace, and the rest of the party walked home from the harbour along the seafront. It was a warm evening, with only a light breeze stirring the black ribbon on her hat. Around them lovers strolled hand-in-hand, dogs trotted, and sailors on the loose eyed up giggling groups of girls.

'It's strange,' Fidelis said. 'June the third will always be a sad date in our family calendar, yet there might be a couple along this promenade tonight who'll get engaged today and it'll always hold happy memories.'

Pa squeezed her hand. 'Yes, Fee, we're just one little speck of humanity among thousands. There'll come a day when it's our turn to laugh again.'

Fidelis held Ruby's hand. 'I'm so glad you came. We couldn't have borne it without you.'

'Your mother left me a daughter to care for, Fee, and that's just what I'll do, my pet.'

'You're a pal, Norman,' said Pa, as they got to the front door. 'Thanks for coming over with us. Mary always loved your bugling. Your playing set the seal on things.'

His friend rested his hand on Jack's shoulder, 'Do you fancy coming in for a glass of Ruby's nettle beer?'

'P'raps tomorrow, thanks, it's been a long day.'

Later, when Pa had gone to bed, she sat reading Harry's letter before following him up the stairs.

March 17th 1903

My Dear Best Girl,

I'm counting the days, less than six months and I'll be home. I was sad to hear that your mother is in hospital in Ventnor, I sent her a little drawing I did of the Palm Trees in Barbados. I hope she gets it soon. Your mother was always kind to me, Fee, and even wrote to say to how pleased she was, about us getting engaged.

Ma, I know is on at you to name the day for our wedding but don't let her rush you into anything. My sweet Fee I'm happy to wait until you're ready, just seeing you, and picking up where we left off, will be joy enough

*for me. I pick up my corporal's stripe soon, and that will
put some more money in our kitty.*

*I long to hold you and show you how much you mean
to me. I want to care for you and make you happy. The
expected day of arrival is July the third. So there will be
no excuse for you to be out when I call. Only joshing my
love, I know that you, too, are counting the days.*

God Bless and keep you safe All my love,
Your Harry

For the first time in ages Fidelis felt anxious to see him. She
wanted to marry him now, to be drawn into his family before
anything else befell her.

22

When she had first suggested taking them to the opera, Eileen had given a sceptical sniff. 'Well I don't know as we'd like that, Miss Dorcas. What's it called?'

'You speak for yourself,' Cook snapped, bashing a block of salt with her rolling-pin. 'I likes a bit of singing.'

'I thought about *The Mikado*. The D'Oyley Carte Company is down at the Theatre Royal soon. What do you say, Midge?'

Busy filling the salt-cellars the girl looked up with a pixie grin. 'I don't care what it is just so we all goes out together. Ain't never bin to a theatre.'

'That settles it. We'll all go up in the gods, and top it off with a fish supper at Cremona's and maybe a sing-song on the way home.'

Eileen blushed. 'I'm ever so sorry Miss Dorcas, got the wrong end of the stick. Thought it was going to be something highfalutin' in Italian, what we wouldn't understand. Yes, please, I'd like that very much.'

'Whose gonna see to madam's supper?' asked Cook, still thumping and bashing while Midge filled the salt-cellars.

'She can go to Miss Phoebe's or even get it herself,' Dorcas had said, knowing they would be horrified at the thought of madam foraging in the kitchen. 'It's settled then. Ladies, you'll have to get out your feathers and we'll sing our hearts out. I shall order the cab to pick us up and we might even manage chocolates.'

'Looking forward to it,' sniffed Eileen.

At a quarter past seven, shy and giggly, the three women stood about in the hall. Tiny Midge, with a large Breton straw plonked on the top of her head, resembled an open umbrella. Square-shouldered Mabel Hobbs was impressive, with her green velvet hat complete with a peacock feather. With ribbons flying behind her, Eileen hurried down the stairs in her cream boater. They were like awkward strangers sitting in the cab together. Only when they joined the queue at the Theatre Royal were the women once again themselves. The crowd were full of back-chat and good humour.

'I bin ter see it three times,' said a woman in front of Cook in the ticket queue. 'Ever so lovely it is and the tunes gets you swaying. Takes you out of yerself, if you get my meaning.'

Moving up and down the pavement was a man in a bowler hat and shabby evening dress, playing an accordion. Midge was fascinated, watching him swoop low and then raise it high, stretch the accordion out to its full extent and then squeeze it up tight between his hands. The music changed from jaunty bits that made her want to dance, and then it turned sweet and sad, making her want to cry. The man held out his hat and nearly everyone tossed in a coin or two.

Eileen sniffed. 'They're going in. Midge, come here with you.'

Up and up they went, higher and higher, past the dress circle and the upper circle and up into the Gods, almost touching the roof. They were swept down the steps between the hard backless benches right to the front row, to be wedged against each other in a simmering stew of excitement. Cook sat with her hat on her lap and Midge stuffed hers under the seat. Eileen clutched her handbag, while Dorcas got out a box of chocolates donated by Aunt Marcia for the occasion, and passed them round.

'Loves strawberry creams,' said Midge, gazing at the scarlet ribbon on the box, and hoping Miss Dorcas might let her keep it as a souvenir. She gazed about, her eyes shining. 'We're all like a lot of bees up here, buzzing. In't they lovely, them gold angels on the ceiling, makes you think of heaven.'

'I'm having a caramel, ta very much, they lasts longer.' Cook dipped in her hand for the square ribbed chocolate, then chewed happily.

'Is there a turkish delight? I favours them.' Eileen searched for her favourite.

Dorcas sniffed the air. The Gods had a particular smell, ripe and friendly, an amalgam of orange-peel, cheap cigars, old clothes and unwashed bodies. There were no little islands of people keeping to themselves as they did in the stalls. Here, there was pushing and shoving, winks and nods, with everyone your neighbour. 'Ssshh!!' quivered Eileen, 'it's starting.'

Shamrock was playing hookey. It was a rare thing for her to do but she felt in need of a night out. Michael, her sailor man, had been posted to Plymouth, back to his wife and children. She doubted she would see him again. In the end, married men were more trouble than they were worth. Flitting back and forth between her and the missus and always wanting a grandstand performance. Tonight, she had been invited out by Dapper Diamond to dine with him at his empire, alias the Cremona Supper Rooms. What could he want? There was no room in his life for casual friendship, and sex he could get at the wink of his eye. Besides, she thought to herself with a rare dash of honesty, there was plenty of younger flesh around. They were two professionals who had dragged themselves out of the gutter. The night promised to be interesting.

She seemed to be in the doldrums of late, what with trying to shore up her brother's spirits after Mary's death, and keep belting out the same tired tunes back at the Palace. What she needed was somehow to freshen up her act with new costumes, and have someone write her some new songs. Perhaps she should leave Pompey and get herself into a touring company. Dashing from one place to another and being up against talented youngsters would sharpen her up no end. She had got stale and bored with life, and it showed in her performance.

Flinging back the door of her wardrobe she scanned the rail for inspiration. The Cremona was as much a stage as any theatre. Wouldn't she go out there tonight guns blazing, and give old Dapper something to fasten his eyes on. There was still some snap in her garter, and the last time she had looked at his arse it had been ripe for pinching. What was she looking forward to most, she wondered, one of his steak suppers or a good romp upstairs in his four-poster bed with the curtains drawn. Of course, one thing often led to another. The path was usually smoothed by drink, but Shamrock was not one to put up with boozy fumbling. She liked a man to know what he was about, and take his time. She also liked to stay to breakfast. Sex always gave her an appetite. No, the best path to her drawers was laughter. A man with wit and daring won hands down every time.

This was going to be a night to remember, so preparation was vital. She went downstairs and set some pans of water to boil while she studied her outfits. The black gown with the jet beads was fetching, but after the funeral she needed cheering up. How about that acid-green one with the deep décolleté? Might as well put her goods in the window while they were still firm and bouncy. A long soak in a hot tub would perk her up no end. Oh yes, and there was the hat with the little veil. What was needed to top off the whole ensemble was a good drench of perfume, and not just dabbed behind her ears.

Thank God he wasn't coming back to Buckle Street. Since

Fee had left it had gone to buggery. As she took up her sponge, Shamrock once more resolved to mend her ways. Either that, or get some woman who liked a challenge and was down on her uppers to come around and give the place a good scouring.

An hour later, Shamrock skewered her hat in position with a pearl-topped pin and surveyed herself in the mirror. I may be the wrong side of thirty, she thought but by God I can teach some of the young things a thing or two. It was sweet Saturday night, and Shamrock O' Shea was out for a good time.

Clutching the rail in front of her, Midge was ready: she was going to remember everything for when Tommy came round to see her tomorrow night. She gasped as the curtain opened. It was like a real place, with the red curving roofs of the house and the mauve flowers trailing down the walls. The girls was so pretty in their costumes, they were like dressing-gowns of different colours, with lovely flowers embroidered down the front. When they turned around they wore big floppy bows at the back, biggest she'd ever seen. Ever so funny the way they moved, slow as slow, like as if they was moving on little wheels. What Tommy would make of the men she couldn't begin to think. Their faces looked like they'd fallen in the flour-bin, and they had stumpy black pig-tails.

'A wandering minstrel I, a thing of shreds and patches, of ballad songs and snatches and dreamy lullabies.' Nankypu's song was so sweet it made her want to cry, but she wouldn't tell Tommy that. Everyone up in the Gods with her swayed back and forth to the music: it was like nothing she'd ever felt before. She was part of it and she wouldn't never forget it. With them, she booed at that bossy daughter-in-law Katisha and laughed at the Mikado's dance. Midge couldn't really make head nor tale of the story and the names was downright daft – Titipu and Yum Yum. Tommy would have a good laugh.

Then Miss Dorcas handed her these opera glasses. They was wonderful. Midge trained them on the stage and all the colour and detail sprang at her. 'Oooh,' she sighed, 'ain't that pretty?' Then Cook nudged her and took the glasses off her and she didn't get them back for ages. Just as she was staring through them again, the curtain came down. 'It ain't over is it?' she asked, wanting to cry.

'There's a long way to go yet,' said Cook, smiling at her.

Around them the crowd swarmed towards the stairs, eager to get a drink at the gallery bar. Some old hands had brought their own refreshment and were uncorking bottles of cordial, beer or gin.

'Cripes,' Cook laughed, 'look at her over there with that parcel of sammidges.'

'Do you want to go and get a drink anyone?'

'We'll have drink enough with our supper,' said Cook. 'Too much of a fag fighting yer way down there.'

'How about you, Midge?'

'No, Miss Dorcas,' she breathed. 'I wants ter stay here forever. When I tells Tom about this he won't never believe it. All them lovely coloured clothes and the way they all moves together. Don't know how they manages to get the fans waving open and clicking shut all at the same time.'

There was just one chocolate each before the curtain rose again.

Dorcas watched Midge's enraptured face. The girl nodded her head in time to the music, and laughed and cried and clapped her hands. Taking up her glasses once more, she trawled towards the boxes near the stage. Adjusting the focus she settled on the blue uniform sleeve of a royal marine officer. It was him, the man she had run into at Christmas, the one that gave her the letter for Fidelis. Certainly he was handsome but a tinge too sure of his charms for her taste, and too young. Beside him was a woman in a blue dress. Shifting the lenses she could see there was a ring on her finger. Two other couples were there behind them. She judged them to be the respective parents. This was the girl he took home, every mama's dream, respectable and well connected. But where did he take Fidelis? Were they still seeing one another? Dorcas felt a twinge of misgiving for her new friend. This man held all the cards: money, looks and privilege. What had the nursemaid got beyond beauty and an untutored intelligence? But intelligence didn't matter a jot when physical attraction was ignited, as she knew only too well. She liked Fidelis, the girl was funny and perceptive, but there was vulnerability too. The fiancé in the background, how did he fit into the picture? Would he come home and take his girl up the aisle, in blissful ignorance of this golden Apollo? And what about Miss Blue Gown beside him? All the ingredients were there for a drama far more compelling than *The Mikado*. Her speculations were interrupted by a sharp dig in the ribs from Midge, who held out her hand for the glasses.

And then it was over. The actors took their bows and the theatre erupted in cheers, whistles and stamping feet. They waited while Cook straightened the peacock feather and skewered her hat back on her head.

Midge burst into tears. 'It was too short, I wasn't ready for the end.'

'Come on love, it's only a make believe,' said Eileen, putting her arm around her. 'We got supper to come.'

Midge shook off her arm. 'I knows that,' she snapped.

'Bet Fee would've loved it,' said Cook, as they made their way out of the theatre and across the road to Cremona's. Around them the crowd, still caught up in the magic of *The Mikado*, were whistling and singing snatches of the songs.

*   *   *

Shamrock watched Dapper Diamond moving through his empire, giving a word here, a smile there, and never stopping at a table for more than ten minutes. She had to admire his style. That satin waistcoat set off his broad shoulders and flat belly, and every now and then there was a flash of his diamond cuff-links. He was bent on having a good time, and everyone was invited to his party. Beneath the chutzpah was a brain as sharp as cut lemon – nothing was left to chance. The napkins crackled with starch, the cutlery gleamed and the waiters were attentive. Intimate dining could be had in the candle-lit booths far away from the door. For a rip-roaring evening out with your pals the cellar provided large tables, large helpings, and waitresses who were never known to blush.

He glided towards her, surprisingly graceful for a large man. 'Evening, Duchess. How goes the world with you?'

'Well now, Dapper, that would be telling. I'm sat here wondering what will be on the table tonight. I've a powerful fancy for a bit of steak washed down with some strong drink.'

'And who am I to disappoint you? Just give me ten minutes then we'll go upstairs. I'll tip George the wink and he'll have a steak fairly sizzling.'

From what she could see the place was packed, and everyone was either raising a fork to their mouth or talking. The smell of hot food had her mouth watering. He made it all look so easy, but she knew he was up earlier and worked harder than any of his staff or competitors. Imitation Cremonas had sprung up now and then but had never had the lustre of the original.

'You know what it's like, Shamrock, you gotta give it one hundred per cent and have an eye for the detail. Everythink gotta work together: the grub, the place, the waiters, so when the customer opens the door he knows he's in for a good time. Then come the end of the evening he'll put his hand in his pocket and feel it's money well spent.'

That was one of the attractive things about Dapper, his energy; the other was his restlessness – always looking out for the next new thing.

'So my Duchess, let's you and I go up to our supper.' He took her hand and kissed her fingertips. 'You know what they say, all work and no play makes Jack a dull boy. I for one am ready for a bit of entertainment.'

When they reached the top of the stairs he took her into his arms and kissed her soundly. 'That's the aperitif out the way. Now let's get to the main course.'

Once they were settled in one of the booths the three women chattered like magpies.

'Our Fee could sing just as good as them girls on the stage,' said Midge. 'Lovely voice she got.'

'Don't reckon she likes it much at Miss Phoebe's,' said Cook, never one to hang back. 'Gets put upon. Reckon if it weren't for little Sophie she'd sling her hook.'

'You know what?' sniffed Eileen. 'I could eat a bloomin' horse.'

Her three guests studied the menu and settled for cod-and-chips and half-pints of ale, with Midge being given lemonade. Dorcas had whitebait and bread-and-butter. There was little chat as they farmed into their suppers.

'You said we could come and visit ya one day when ya goes back over the Island, Miss Dorcas,' said Midge, creating a salt snowstorm over her plate. 'Did ya mean it?'

''Course she did.' Cook wiped her mouth with the back of her hand. 'True blue is Miss Dorcas, there's no flannel with her.'

She blushed with pleasure at the compliment. 'Yes, you must come in August, and we'll have a picnic on the beach. That's a promise.'

When every scrap had been cleaned from their plates with

bits of bread they declared themselves 'full up fit to bust', and pushed back their chairs.

Midge wanted to walk home along the beach. Arm-in-arm they strolled together, singing snatches from *The Mikado*, along Hampshire Terrace with its gentry houses and out towards the seafront. All four of them made a wish and threw a stone in the water. Back on the promenade, they linked arms and sang, 'Three little maids from school are we,' trying to imitate the tiny mincing steps of the actresses from the theatre. It was gone eleven by the time they reached the back door of Kelmscott House.

'Thanks ever so, Miss Dorcas,' said Eileen shyly. 'The best treat I've had in years.'

Cook gave her a beery hug.

'I won't never forget it, not in my whole life,' Midge said, her eyes smiling. 'I remembers everythink and when Tommy comes round I'll tell him.'

'I enjoyed it, too,' said Dorcas, 'thank you for coming with me.'

She went up to her bedroom and realised that she missed those midnight talks with Fidelis. It had been a long time since she had had a real woman friend, if you discounted Aunt Milly. When she had sorted out the cottage she would talk with Aunt Marcia about the girl coming over for a holiday.

Dapper laughed. 'I know you're as curious as a parson at a peepshow. But, the best dishes are the ones cooked slow. Let me cut up your steak, my Duchess. Here, open up, what d'you say?'

Shamrock chewed appreciatively.

Dapper winked at her. 'Reckon that's the best thing bin in your mouth for a long time.'

She laughed. 'You know Dapper, you might well be right. Now, are you going to tell me before the pudding or after?'

He raised one eyebrow. 'Well, I always say you can't enjoy your after unless you've had your befores.'

'You are such an aggravating bugger. I've a good mind to put that steak in me handbag and take it home.'

'Saw you at the Palace the other night,' he said, surprising her with his change of tack. 'Thought you was bored. Didn't have your usual sparkle. Said to meself, that gal needs winkling out of that shell. Needs to sing for her supper someplace else.'

Shamrock put down her knife. 'Bloody sauce! Who are you to judge, music critic of the soddin' *Times*.'

Dapper roared with laughter. 'Smooth down yer feathers. I gotta proposition to put to you.

'I've got a new scheme bubbling gently – a nightclub on the top floor, fancy to call it the Starlight Lounge. A bit of supper, a bit of music, piano tinkling in the background. Somewhere discreet for people to go after the other places shut down. What d'you think? Thought you could maybe sing a bit, talk a bit and give the place a bit of a shimmer.'

Now it was Shamrock's turn to laugh. 'Jesus, Dapper, I'm as discreet as a pair of tart's drawers.'

'New tricks my Duchess, new tricks, there's no rush. You got time to give in your notice at the Palace. In the meantime, how about I show you a few little surprises of my own. It's a long time since I've entertained the aristocracy.'

'Now then Bishop, if you don't behave yourself I shall have to take a pair of scissors to your stipend.'

Giggling together, they left their plates on the table and climbed the stairs.

23

Fidelis rushed down from the nursery to the bathroom on the first floor and vomited into the lavatory pan. It was a week since her mother had died, and she could no longer deceive herself into thinking that her sickness was due to shock. It was seven weeks since the night with Daniel, and waiting in the chest of drawers were her monthly squares, unused since early March. The reason for her sickness could not be avoided, and the knowledge fluttered in her chest like an imprisoned bird. Wanted or not, she was having a baby.

She felt like the woman caught in adultery, waiting while her accusers gathered up their stones. In less than four weeks Harry would be home. A tentative date had been set for their wedding early in December. By that time Daniel would have gone to the Ascensions with Maude. More immediate was the question of looking after Sophie. However tolerant Phoebe might be, Fidelis would not physically be able to remain at her post beyond the summer. By then her predicament would be obvious to everyone. She could not go home and live next-door to Harry's mother, carrying another man's child. And what about Pa, still grieving for his Mary? He would be caught between two families. Ruby and Norman were his friends and neighbours, and had been his lifeline since Ma had been over in Ventnor. Every day, Ruby called to see he was looking after himself properly: at least once a week he was invited in for supper, and he and Norman went dart-playing to the sergeant's mess. Her father loved Harry, and looked on him as the son he'd never had.

The thought of telling anyone brought her out in a sweat, and waves of nausea had her kneeling once more over the lavatory. Soon she would have to take up Phoebe Allen's morning tea. She pinched her cheeks, trying to counteract her chalky pallor.

'Good morning Fidelis, what splendid weather.' Phoebe Allen slid out of bed in her satin nightdress and stared out of the window. 'Mummy will be delighted. Could you start running my bath? Say, breakfast in half an hour?'

For once, Fidelis was glad that she wasn't in Heron Grove, where Cook and Eileen would soon have noticed her washed-out look.

'I will take Sophie out for a long walk this morning. It will help use up some of her energy before the fete.'

'Yes, madam.'

Tipping the lemon verbena crystals into the bath, she knew Phoebe's ploy. By the time she arrived at her mother's garden fete most of the work would be over. All she would be required to do was mingle and show off her pretty daughter. Normally, Fidelis would have been irked by such devious-ness but today she had other concerns.

Soon, whether she told anyone or not, it would be obvious that she was pregnant. If Ma were alive she would have guessed already. What was she to do? The one person she would normally have confided in was Ruby: but now, given the circumstances, she had become the last. If only Dorcas wasn't away in her cottage, finishing some commission or other. She would have listened, and been a bridge between herself and Phoebe. Since her time in Brighton, Phoebe was much easier to get along with, but there were still times when she was peevish and unreasonable.

Fidelis thought of Molly, Sophie's previous nursemaid.

She had been expecting James Allen's child. Molly had told her about going once to this woman, in Portsea somewhere, for some herbs that were supposed to hurry the birth, in the early stages of pregnancy. But she had gone too late and the woman couldn't help her.

'Just as well really, Fee,' she'd told her, when showing off her baby girl some months later. 'After all the shemozzle at the beginning, Ma and Pa worships little Amy, and I wouldn't be without her now for all the tea in China.'

The last thing she wanted was to help at Mrs Mount's fete to raise funds for her Suffragist women. There wouldn't be time to think. She would be back and forth across the lawn, helping Cook and Eileen serve the teas and keeping Sophie out of mischief.

With a feeling of dread, she went into the nursery.

'Fee, Fee,' Sophie cried, bouncing up and down in her cot. 'Me want eggy bread. Bunny want eggy bread.' She clambered over the rails and onto the floor.

She wished they were back in Heron Grove, where Cook would have dealt with breakfasts. Phoebe had a daily woman to do the rough work but everything else fell on Fidelis. The thought of hot cooking-fat and raw eggs made her stomach heave.

'Come on Sophie, let's get you sat on the potty and get your nightdress off, arms up now.' As she bathed and dressed the toddler and answered her stream of chatter, the question pulsed through her. What was she going to do?

Shamrock stood in the wings, trying not to breathe in the stink of animals. Tonight she was going on after Madam ZaZa and her performing dogs. Earlier a nervous Shetland pony, from another act, had peed on the floor. The stench was enough to make her eyes water. She stared moodily at the dogs dressed in coloured skirts, walking on their hind legs for a chocolate, and wondered why she stuck the life. It wasn't even for the applause. In the last few months she knew her star had begun to wane. A new girl had taken her spot – Daisy Devereaux – slimmer and trimmer and always hitting the high notes. Shamrock had become predictable.

'And now are you ready for a rousing number from our own Shamrock O'Shea?'

The applause was tepid. All the time she was prancing about, roaring out the gutsy numbers, then putting a sob in her voice for the tremulous ones, she knew she had lost them. Her audience clapped her off, and then she was back in her dressing-room. Daisy Devereaux had the star spot. The way Shamrock felt, that evening, the girl was welcome to it.

What was wrong with her? She had a new venture starting up with Dapper at the Starlight Lounge. Why hadn't she given in her notice? Walking back to Buckle Street, she was deep in thought. Surely she hadn't loss her nerve, had she? She had a good voice, she could expand her range: it was the new clientele that frightened her. At the Palace you had the stage between you and the audience. It would be people of the likes of Jimmy Allen, who made brittle, meaningless conversation. Whereas at the Starlight they would be up close to her. Those sorts of places hung on the personality of the hostess. Could she pull it off?

As she turned her front door key someone called her name.

'Jesus, Mary and Joseph, you scared the heart out of me, girl. What's brought you up this way? I've not seen hide nor hair of you for months.'

'Let me in, Auntie, it's freezing out here.'

'You put the kettle on while I get out of me glad rags. I'm sung out, and me belly thinks me throat's cut. If I don't get something to eat I'll surely fade away.'

As she sat on the bed and unbuttoned her boots, Shamrock

felt uneasy. It was a funny time for her niece to call, half-eleven at night. What could be up with her? Perhaps she'd lost her job. Well, whatever it was could keep until she had taken off her corset and put on her nightgown and wrapper. A good night's kip was what she longed for, but something in Fee's voice told her that sleep would have to wait.

Yawning, Shamrock wandered back down the stairs into the kitchen. The kettle was just coming to the boil and Fee was standing with the teapot ready to warm. The way she was standing, hunched in on herself, alarmed the woman. 'Somewhere in this god-forsaken hole there's a pork pie and a jar of pickled onions. You make the tea and I'll scare it up out of the cupboard. Ah, there it is, hiding itself behind the cosy. Sit yourself down girl, and join me.' She slapped down two plates and began to cut the pie in half.

'No thanks, Auntie, I don't feel up to it.'

It was then that Shamrock really looked at her. It was obvious. The sight of her lank hair and chalk-white face made words unnecessary. 'Oh, Fee, my darling,' she whispered, 'tell me it isn't true.'

Fee sank into a chair and began to cry, hiding her face in her hands.

Shamrock was stabbed with pity. She pulled up her own chair near and put her arms around her. 'Auntie's got you, just cry it out my lamb.' By God, the child would have a hard road ahead of her, of that she was certain. 'It's a baby we're talking about here, is it?'

Fidelis nodded.

'How far along are you?'

'I think seven weeks,' she mumbled. 'I don't know what to do.'

'Well, child, whatever it is you'll have me behind you, Fee. You won't be alone.'

'I don't want it! I don't want it! I can't have it!' She looked up at Shamrock, her face blotched with tears. 'Isn't there anything we can do to stop it?'

'Ah! No my girl, we're not going down that road. You don't know what you're asking.'

'I've got to. Harry's coming in three weeks or so and Daniel's got himself engaged. There won't be anyone and Pa will kill me. You've got to do something.'

'Fee, now you stop that, right this minute. Nobody is going to kill anyone.' She took the girl's face between her hands, and spoke slowly as if to an infant. 'What you are hinting at is a terrible bloody business. I wouldn't wish it on me worst enemy. And I could never face your Pa if I was party to such butchery. No, no, no, you just listen to me, Fidelis. Your old Auntie will tell you something as I've never breathed to a soul.' She got up and fetched two cups from the dresser and poured them both a cup of tea. As she sipped the scalding tea, Shamrock gathered her courage. It was a part of her life she had not visited in years. 'You must promise me as you'll keep it to yourself. Do you promise me?'

Fee nodded.

'I was younger than you at the time, just seventeen, over from Ireland and starting on the Halls. I was pretty, with long black hair and a waist men could span with two hands, a voice like a nightingale and the confidence of Sarah Bernhardt. I was only a few months in London and green as grass. Didn't this manager flatter me, with his always praising me singing, and saying as he could get me star billing.

'"Shamrock, I'll have you at the top of the bill or my name's not Liam MacCreedy." And it surely wasn't. Later I found out he was called Fred Scrivens and came from Bermondsey. He was about as Irish as Bakewell tart and a liar of the first water.' Ah, success: a faint smile from Fee. 'But, he was beautifully made and I loved just to say things to have him look at me or hear him laugh. If I close my eyes I can see him now and feel that shiver of wanting in me belly. I was in dreamland and waking up time came all too soon.'

While she was listening, her niece began to cut pieces from the pie and to eat them.

'We became lovers and I thought myself in heaven. Then just as he was going to put a ring on my finger, his wife turned up, a big woman with money. My hero crumpled like a sandcastle. Cast me as the villain of the piece and I was out of his bed and back down near the bottom of the bill. And then just as I was trying to get myself back together, I fell pregnant.'

'What did you do?'

'I was in a panic. Miles away from my mother and my home, my brother Jack the other side of the world, I clung to the only friend I had, Vina Manson. She was an older woman, used to have a troupe of performing dogs. Vina had knocked around a bit and seemed, to a frightened seventeen-year-old, to have all the answers. She had a woman she knew, Ma Ferris.' Shamrock wrapped her arms protectively across her chest. 'This woman was going to be the answer to all my prayers. For five pounds she was going to get rid of my little problem.'

'How?' Fee whispered.

'With a crochet hook.'

'What d'you mean?'

'She would put it up inside me and get a hold of the cord and pull the baby out.'

'Weren't you frightened?'

Shamrock nodded, unable to speak. She could smell again the stale odour of Ma Ferris, and her body began to tremble at the memory. 'I was terrified. I screamed out loud with the pain. Must have passed out for a while. Vina was shouting at the old butcher, and all I could feel was the blood pulsing out of me. I don't remember anything more. Seemingly, Ma Ferris ran off, and Vina got me to a hospital saying as she had found me in the street. I woke up in a bed with one of the holy sisters bending over me. Floated in and out of life I did for a long time. One day I looked down the ward and saw a man in uniform coming towards me. I watched him coming closer and closer and I prayed that it would be my dear Jack.'

'Was it Pa?'

Shamrock took a handkerchief from the pocket of her wrapper and handed it to Fee to dry her tears. 'He was my saviour. There's no one as tender and kind as Jack. Came as often as he could and got me fixed up to stay awhile with a couple he knew. I was lucky to be alive. And then when I was stronger came the worst thing.'

Fee reached across and held her hands. 'What could be worse?'

'I went to the doctor and he told me I would never be able to have another child, me insides had been so damaged.'

They were both crying.

It was Shamrock who first released her hands. 'I had to remake my life. All I had to offer was a voice and the gift of entertaining. So I packed me bags and went on the southern circuit – every week a different town all along the south coast. Work rescued me and still does.'

'I can't tell them, I can't.'

'What about Daniel? Engaged is a long way short of marriage. He may surprise you.'

'What am I going to tell Harry? Aunt Ruby is all worked up about the wedding and everything. Thinks I'm going to marry him.'

'I'm not a fortune-teller, Fee. I don't know how anyone will act when you spill the beans. There'll likely be ructions, at least for the first day or so, but leastways you've got people

around that loves you – it's just working up the courage to
tell them.'

'I feel so ashamed.'

'Never be ashamed of loving, my darling. It's what we're
made for.'

'How will I tell them about Daniel?'

'Depends on whether Daniel is going to marry you. If he's
for sliding off out of it there's little point in telling them.
You're grown-up enough to take a lover, you're grown-up
enough to keep your mouth shut. It's Harry that you must
be straight with.'

'I don't know how to do it all. I'm so tired and sick, and
there's my job with Mrs Allen and little Sophie.'

'Look Fee, where are you supposed to be, right now?'

'Back at Clarendon House.'

Shamrock got to her feet. 'I'll walk with you down to New
Road, you'll likely pick up the last bus to Southsea if we're
quick. Whatever else happens, Fee, you'll have me, and your
Dad to fall back on. You're not the only girl this has happened to and you surely won't be the last.'

Fee gave a shaky laugh. 'It just feels as if I am.'

'When are you next at home?'

'On Sunday. Daniel will be back from Kent.'

'Well, that's the first obstacle faced. Who is it, Fee, that
you fear the most?'

The girl looked the picture of misery. Shamrock wanted
to gather her in her arms and say that it would all come right
in the end, but Fee needed more than fairy stories.

'All of them in different ways, I suppose. Daniel because
I want him to say that he still loves me, and that he'll take
care of everything. I know that he loves me but he can't stand
up to his father and he hates himself for not being able to.
I know that but I just can't bear to hear it.'

'Sounds to me as if you've been preparing yourself already.'

'Then there's Pa, he'll be so disappointed. I know it'll hurt him. I'm his princess, and Uncle Norman's his best friend and he loves Harry as if he was his son.'

'Well, my lamb, there's no way forward but straight through. And I'll be standing by with the bandages. What you have to do is take one step at a time. Go back to that little Sophie with a smile on your face. Take some dry bread up to your room at night and chew a piece of it, slowly, when you wake up. Swallow it down with cold water. Leastways then you'll have something to be sick on. There's nothing worse than retching on an empty stomach.'

Shamrock got to her feet. 'You've cleared the first fence, my lamb. If the worst comes to the worst you can come and live with me. We'll likely get on each other's nerves, me being such a slut and you the saintly Mary McCauley's daughter, but I don't think it will come to that.' Shamrock, desperate for half an hour with her feet up, walked her to the front door. 'You're stronger than you think and you've got a family behind you.'

Fee hugged her fiercely. 'Oh Auntie, I don't know what I'd do without you.'

'Well, my lamb, while I've still breath in me body, you won't have to find out.'

Back in her bedroom Fidelis got out her pen and ink. He would not get the letter until Saturday but there would be enough time for him to do as she asked. All her hopes were pinned on him meeting her. But what happened after that was out of her hands.

24

Mummy was coming for a visit that evening and Phoebe was not looking forward to it. Since her return from Brighton things were miles better between them, but there were still areas in which they clashed – money being one of them. When she had protested at the niggardly allowance of twenty-five pounds a month, her mother had made her feel selfish and useless.

'How much do you think the average married woman in Portsmouth has to manage on each week, Phoebe? Thirty-five shillings if she's lucky, and often with less. Your out-goings are minimal. I pay Fidelis's wages and you live rent-free. There is a full wardrobe of clothes that could be worn if you only made the effort to find a seamstress to alter them for you. You really need to take charge of your life. Are you keeping an account book as I showed you? It's the only way to keep a check on things.'

The trouble was she needed someone else to spark her into doing things. Before, it had been James. Now, left to herself, she tended to drift from one day to the next. Once she had settled back into her home, Phoebe had had new calling-cards printed and gone the rounds of her old Southsea chums. The results had been disappointing. The friends that she had previously run with cold-shouldered her with lame excuses.

'Oh, Phoebe, we're just off up to Town. Now we know you're back we'll pop round one afternoon.'

'Are you going to Clarissa's birthday party at the Queen's? Really? I'm sure the invitation's in the post.'

Even had she been invited, what could she have taken as a gift? Besides the lack of money there was her single status. Unattached women upset hostesses' seating-plans and were suspect creatures, often predatory. Wives suspected their motives. Phoebe couldn't decide whether it was the scandal attached to her name, her penury, or her lack of a husband that was the kiss of death to her social life. Being a widow at twenty-four was rotten bad luck.

In Brighton, all she had craved was to be reunited with Sophie: it had seemed the answer to everything. She loved her dearly, but toddler conversation and dolly's tea-parties palled very quickly. What she needed was something to do, but what?

The only adult conversation was with Fidelis, and somehow they had never recovered from the fracas with James. It was getting worse between them. The girl was positively mournful lately. She knew that her mother had died, but honestly, did she need to be so cast down all the time? The other day Phoebe had run into that Nanny Hawkins by the Canoe Lake. It seemed that Master Phillip's parents were off to Singapore where they could get cheap local domestic help. In September she would be looking for a new position. Phoebe liked her. Once she came into her inheritance she would ditch Fidelis. She wished that Sarah lived nearer. Somehow the old cook brought out the best in her. At home, the temptation to backslide was all too easy. In the summer she was going to invite the two sisters to Portsmouth for a holiday. The third bedroom could be refurbished, and there were two single beds that would fit in there quite snugly.

The doorbell rang. Knowing Fidelis was out with Sophie she ran to answer it.

'Do I know you?' She peered at the woman stood before

her. She was familiar, but Phoebe could not put her in her setting. They had never been close friends, she didn't think. Although elegant in a Russian blouse coat and a hat trimmed with flowers, the outfit looked well cared-for rather than new.

'Good afternoon, Mrs Allen, isn't it?'

'Yes, I'm a widow now. How may I help you?'

'I'm a widow too. It's a foul title isn't it? Foisted on one, unchosen, and a ticket to obscurity.'

Phoebe smiled, her thoughts exactly. The woman's voice was younger than her face, but perhaps she had been ill or fallen on hard times.

'Don't you remember me? I had a little shop in Marmion Road: cushions, quilts, lavender bags, potpourri, you know the sort of thing.'

'Oh yes, Mummy and I used to buy things now and then.' Boredom prompted her to ask her in.

The woman held out her hand. 'Daphne Manners, it's kind of you to spare me your time. My husband died last year and left me in debt from which I have been struggling to extricate myself.'

Sensing a sob-story, Phoebe hardened her heart. 'Likewise,' she said. 'I'm sure my circumstances are known to you.'

Daphne laughed. 'Oh no, you mistake me. I'm not wanting money, simply to put a business proposition to you.'

'May I offer you tea? You will have to wait as my maid is out at the moment.'

'I'll come and talk to you in the kitchen, that way we won't waste time.'

Phoebe sat the kettle on the hob and got two cups and saucers from the dresser. 'A business proposition that doesn't involve money sounds fascinating. Do tell me how I am to be involved?'

'I have a great deal of stock but no premises, and you have a beautiful house.'

'But why would I want to turn my house into a shop?'

Daphne settled herself at the kitchen table. 'Now, this is where we use our imagination. Instead of a shop we display my things in their proper setting. Quilts and lace-edged pillowcases on a bed, and cushions in a sitting-room with rugs and candlesticks.'

Phoebe poured the tea. 'How would our customers know of our existence?'

'We would send out cards inviting them to a viewing. When an engagement is announced, a card from *Maison-Belle* would offer their congratulations. When a house is sold, we leave a card, do you see?'

She was excited, but feared being duped by this plausible woman. Being made a fool of once had been painful and expensive. 'I can see what you would gain but how would I benefit?'

Daphne took off her hat and ran her hand through her hair. 'It's a sort of barter to start with, an experiment. I would rent the rooms from you and pay with a percentage of my sales. I haven't, as I said, any capital, simply stock.'

'How would we begin?'

'We would give ourselves three months and see what happens. Success or failure, you would still have your home and I would have whatever things were left. The worst that could happen is a blow to our pride. We are grown-up women, I think we could stand that.' She laughed. 'What's the alternative? Sitting back and waiting to be rescued?'

'Would you like a biscuit?'

'I'd like two, if you please. Now why don't you call around tomorrow and see my things? Basement flat, 70 Waverley Road.'

Phoebe showed her to the door. She smiled to herself; *Maison-Belle* – the name intrigued her, it was the sort of thing James would have loved. Leaving the tea-things in the

sink for Fidelis to deal with, she went upstairs to the sitting-
room. For the first time in ages she realised there was something to look forward to.

Marcia watched her niece haranguing two naval lieutenants,
standing on the fringe of the meeting at Speaker's Corner
on Whit Monday.

'You, Sirs, show me your sleeves – a ring on each one I
see. Did you know that gold braid is sixpence an inch? Do
you realise that what you wear on your jacket is worth more
than one woman's weekly wage, toiling as an embroideress
and badge-maker. Some widow women in this garrison town
have less than twenty shillings to raise their families. You men
who will willingly see thousands of pounds poured into the
building of the mighty *Dreadnoughts* will not put a hand in
your pocket to support our deserving sisters. Will you sign
a petition against the factory owners who sweat these women
in the making of sailor's collars at sevenpence halfpenny
each. No? And you wonder why we want women to have
the vote.'

'Go home and look after your husband.'

'Would that I could, sir, but my man's body lies out at
Magersfontein. Little do you men think of the trail of dev-
astation you wreak when you march to the fife and drum.
There is no glory in war, any widow or orphan can tell you
that.'

The crowd were mixed in their response. Some hardly
gave them a glance, their minds set on ale and winkles. Groups
of men showed off to one another in front of young girls,
out-doing each other in the saltiness of their gibes.

'Men in petticoats, that's what you are.'

'Load of dressed-up parrots, squawk, squawk, squawk.'

Mrs Mount threaded her way through them with her petition. After two hours she had only fifteen signatures. The

citizens' minds were set on celebration; dancing on the piers and watching the Punch and Judy. After the upheaval of the last few months, having some time alone to pursue her interests was luxury indeed. Marcia wished that Portsmouth were a more fertile campaigning soil. It was an impoverished town, with a mass of poor women variously employed in corset-making and naval tailoring. The home-workers, mostly young wives with hungry children, stitched late into the night by candlelight, putting together sailors' collars, intricate garments for a few coppers. Her most passionate interest was in the health of infants. She realised that if help wasn't forthcoming for proper feeding early enough in life, a race of illiterate, rickety children would be the outcome. All of her friends had been horrified at the newspaper articles at the beginning of the war with the Boers, about the poor state of the recruits in the industrial towns.

Stepping through the crowd, she looked back at the striped banners that she and Dorcas had laboured to produce. The colours made a brave show: green for hope, white for faith and red for love. 'Votes for Mothers', 'Votes for Nurses and Teachers', 'Deborahs Awake!'

Recently she had been elected onto a School Board and had been horrified to see at first hand the pale, stunted children of Portsea, the dockland area of Portsmouth. children with twisted, rickety limbs and bare feet. What hope of the Empire's future, with such poor breeding-stock?

It was getting cold and the crowd was drifting away. Marcia helped the women roll up their banners and stow them on their hand-cart. Lady Champney had agreed to let the women keep it in her garden shed at the back of her villa along the seafront. She had also promised tea and buns.

'I don't know about you, Auntie, but my throat is as dry as the bottom of a birdcage. What d'you think? Did we make a difference?'

'Water on a stone, I think, Dorcas, but it was good to be back in harness. I wonder how Phoebe has spent the day. You know, I was dying for her to set up again in her own home and now I miss her. What contrary creatures we are.'

'Come in. I'm so glad you came, and this must be Sophie. Careful of the stairs, they are a bit steep, and watch the carpet, it's rather worn, I'm afraid.'

What a tiny dismal-looking place, Phoebe thought, taking her time to reach the bottom step.

Daphne Manners held the door open to her basement flat. It was in effect one large room, with a bed curtained off at one end and a sink behind a folded screen. It was like an eastern bazaar, packed. Clothes-lines were strung from wall to wall, and hung with quilts and curtains in all possible fabrics and colours. Cushions were stacked in tea-chests, and small items such as pin-cushions and lavender-bags were crammed into baskets.

Her hostess laughed. 'Everyone is speechless when they first come here. This is my little empire. I live, work and have my being, within these four walls. It's cosy, isn't it?'

Phoebe nodded, dazzled by the display.

'Here you are, Sophie, a little chair and table just for you, and what about this, my button-box? Would you like to play with it?'

A kettle was simmering on a trivet over the fire, and Daphne took out some crockery from yet another tea-chest. She opened a window and brought in a milk-jug kept cool on the outside ledge. 'Let's have tea before we get down to business, and I have a special cup for a good little girl.'

Perched on a round leather pouffe, Phoebe let her eyes roam around the room, trying to assess the value of the stock. How would things be priced? Where would they replenish things that were sold? How would the profits be shared?

Sophie rummaged in the box, taking buttons out and putting them back again. She was entranced by the fat-bellied cup with a cat's face on it, and was content to sit and play.

After pouring the tea, Daphne launched into her plan of campaign. 'I suggest we keep things very simple. All moneys made will be divided into three: my share, your share, and stock. At first it will be very little until we establish ourselves. Initially we shall have some outlay in having the cards printed and in serving simple refreshments. There will be receipt books, wrapping-paper and string.'

'What would be the very first step?'

'I think I should come along to your house again and we could decide where to establish *Maison-Belle*. If you used the basement with its separate entrance, it would keep your business apart from your home. There would be no danger of customers trespassing into private territory. Step two, cleaning and moving furniture into place; printing the cards, displaying stock, and issuing invitations to our opening evening.'

Phoebe smiled. 'It sounds terribly exciting.'

'The question is, are you prepared for a lot of hard work, some disappointments and no guarantees? It could all end in disaster. You see, Phoebe, I have a lot more to lose than you have. This little room is paid for with a tiny inheritance my mother left me. All I have is my health and skill. I have no reserves and nobody standing in the wings. This is a real leap in the dark. Can I depend on you not to get bored and leave me in the lurch?'

25

Dear Daniel,

   *I would not write to you except that I am in great
trouble. Being so loving and kind, you are the only person
I can turn to. Please meet me on the beach by the boat-
house at seven, tomorrow morning.*

   Yours in desperation,
   Fidelis

The letter threw him into turmoil. Christ, it couldn't be what
he thought it was. He paced about his cabin. It had taken
him an age to stop wanting her and to get her out of his
thoughts. Fidelis. Simply saying the name brought her vividly
to life; her full breasts and soft responsive mouth. He could
hear her laugh and smell the scent of her filling his nostrils.
Ensorcelée: how apt that word on the perfume bottle was.
They had been bound to one another by mutual fascination.
The bill for their pleasure was about to be presented to him.
What would happen if he just tossed the letter in the waste-
paper basket and ignored it? Self-disgust rose in his mouth
like bile. He owed it to her to be there tomorrow. Besides,
what might she do if he wasn't there? Would she come around
to the barracks and talk to his mother?

After a sleepless night, he dragged on his clothes and left
his quarters, going out of the side gate and onto the beach.
Standing there waiting for her, he remembered the first time
they had met here, accidentally on purpose, in almost the

same spot. Daniel sighed at the memory: she had been like a Burne-Jones painting come to life. He had caught his breath: close up she was even more beautiful than he'd imagined, and she had such sparkle. He looked at his watch – she was late. It occurred to him that their meeting-place was in full view of his parents' bedroom. He prayed that Pa would not take it into his mind to pick up his binoculars as he himself had done, all those months ago.

When he was on the point of leaving, he saw her in the distance. Her upright confident way of walking was gone. Instead she was stooped, with her head down, studying the ground. Drawing level with him she said, 'You came, then.'

'Fidelis, it's so good to see you,' he lied, taking her hand and kissing it. How changed she was from his memory of her, with all that bright assurance. Her skin was pallid and her eyes dull. Even her glorious hair seemed faded.

'Your letter intrigued me.' Even to his ears, the words sounded shallow and insincere.

'Something has happened,' she gasped.

Oh God, she wasn't going to cry. Fidelis looked at him as if she wanted him to finish her sentence. Daniel let go of her hand.

'I'm having your child.'

He stared at a clump of chickweed while his mind recoiled from her words. 'Are you sure?'

'Yes, I have seen the doctor. It will be born in January.'

Still he stared, as if the answer to her predicament lay among the yellow petals. 'There is no possibility that it could be anyone else's, I suppose?'

Fidelis struck him full in the face with the flat of her hand. 'You cruel bastard!' she shouted, running away from him down to the water's edge.

Panic seized Daniel. God in heaven, she wasn't going to drown herself, was she?

'Please stop, Fidelis, I'm sorry, truly sorry. I didn't mean that. I don't know what I meant. What do you want from me? You know that I'm engaged to Maude now. I told you right at the beginning it was on the cards. And Harry, he'll be home soon. He's a good fellow, I'm sure . . .' His voice trailed away. 'I can give you some money.'

Fidelis turned and looked at him, and he withered under her scorn. 'You truly are a fallen angel. All your fine words were moonshine just to get in my drawers.'

She tapped him on the chest. 'It's hollow in there – no heart at all. I feel sorry for poor Maude. You don't love her either, she's just a rung up the ladder. Well, I hope the gold braid and the big house are worth it.' Her face was flushed and she paced before him. 'We had something so special and you threw it away. There won't ever be anyone who loved you like I did. You just didn't have the courage.'

'What about your Harry?' he shouted in panic. 'Poor sap out there, writing to his fiancée, keeping himself pure for her, when all the time she's an officer's blanket. What a surprise he's getting.'

At first, he didn't notice his dog coming towards him. It was Fidelis who turned and spoke first to his father as he came towards them.

'Good morning, Colonel,' she said, and there was some of the old fire in her voice. 'A fine morning.' Only Daniel detected the tremor beneath the defiance. 'I have been talking with your son, but now you're welcome to him.'

The two of them watched her running away.

His father stared at him. Daniel looked down at the shingle, his heart pounding. Why could he never face him? Always, the old man neutered him with his scorn. The men called him 'Arctic', and had no liking for their commanding officer. He wondered what his mother felt for him: perhaps in the privacy of their room Jasper Herrick was different.

'Not a good thing to foul your own doorstep, Daniel. If you must go rutting, restrict yourself to the dock-side, not the drill sergeant's drab.'

'Yes, sir.' Impotent rage seethed in him. Although he himself had insulted Fidelis, his father's dismissal of her rankled.

'I sincerely hope that this is the end of the matter. I'll have no bastards brought to my door. Parade in fifteen minutes. I expect your company to do you credit.'

He was sick of himself. As he walked back to his quarters, Daniel could not see one redeeming feature. How shabbily he had treated Fidelis, how gutless he had been with Pa, letting him speak of her as if she were a common whore. Poor girl, what would she do? She had Harry to face yet. What a sickener for him, stepping ashore to find his sweetheart expecting another man's child. But the rankers settled things between themselves. He would likely come round in the end, and there would be a wedding of sorts and the child given his name.

In the meantime, he and Maude would sail off to the Ascensions and leave them to clean up after him. He realised that already he was looking to his future wife to rescue him. Did she have any inkling of what a poor specimen of a man she was marrying? How could he emerge from this folly with even a shred of honour?

Maude and her father sat in the carriage watching the marines march towards the Crinoline Church, along the Golden Mile in front of the barracks. It was a splendid sight, with the sergeant major with his silver mace, the beating of the drums and blare of bugles. Left-right, left-right, the red-striped legs alternated as the men drew nearer. She could see Daniel marching beside 'A' company. For the first time he resembled the Colonel, looking pale and austere. Sitting beside her in church, he seemed lost in thought. Normally Daniel was so restless, his eyes darting everywhere, and then, afterwards he would make her laugh with his comic observations of the congregation. Now he stared straight ahead. What was it that troubled him?

She found herself looking at the red-haired girl who sat two rows back on the opposite side. She remembered Fidelis McCauley from the concert, and her anxieties about Daniel's interest in her. How different she looked. Sitting down, standing up, hymn-singing and praying, Maude's eyes kept straying to her. She had had such a singular beauty and grace, but now there was a total lack of expression on her face. Was she ill or was she desperately unhappy? What frightened Maude was the mutual discomfort of this girl and her fiancé. Tentatively she looked across at her again. Fidelis was crying.

As the congregation rose to sing, she hurried from the church. Daniel riffled the pages in the hymn-book, and almost without thinking Maude left her seat and followed her out. The girl made her way down St George's Road, away from the seafront.

'Please stop,' she called, running after her. 'It's Fidelis, isn't it?'

She turned and nodded, her face streaked with tears.

'I saw you in church and you looked so unhappy. Is there anything I can do for you? My name is Maude Palmer.'

This was unbearable. She stood there crying, unable to move while Daniel's future wife offered her sympathy, patted her arm and gave her a handkerchief. Maude was kind, and in any other situation Fidelis would have warmed to her but now it was not possible. How could she accept her comfort when she had stolen from her? Whatever Daniel's feelings for this homely girl, she had wronged her. It was just another stone to add to her heap of wrongs.

'Please, Fidelis,' Maude said, touching her arm, 'I know what unhappiness is like, how lonely and desperate one can become.' She was not wearing gloves and Daniel's expensive engagement ring sparkled on her left hand.

'My mother died a little while ago.' Fidelis blurted out the words.

'Oh I am so very sorry. I lost my mother two years ago and it was such a blow to me. She was my dearest friend you know. I still talk to her when I'm alone. It is foolish I know, but it gives me comfort.'

Again she nodded, not knowing how to extricate herself. 'I must go, need to get the dinner ready. Thank you for the hankie, I'll get it back to you.'

Fidelis walked towards Gibraltar Street, her mind in turmoil. Daniel had let her down – but what had she really expected of him? He had never promised more than an affair. And what had she been thinking of, getting involved in the first place? Tears spilled down her cheeks when she thought of their time together, in the hotel, and how tender he had been in his loving. It had been the hardest thing in the world to walk away from the Queen's that morning, knowing it was the last time they would be together. If it were not for the child, growing in her belly, the chapter would have ended neatly with no one hurt. Fidelis resented it, and wished, in spite of Shamrock's warning, that she had had the courage and the money to be rid of her dilemma.

Why had she put herself through the purgatory of seeing him in church afterwards? It was madness, thinking pride would carry her through, and that she would shame him. Daniel had not looked at her once, she was already dismissed from his concerns.

But there were more immediate things for her to worry about. Now there were her neighbours to face. Ruby and Norman had invited the two of them for Sunday dinner, there was no way out of it. How could she sit there between them all, harbouring such a secret? Being alone with Ruby would be the greatest test.

And what about her Pa? At this very moment he would be waiting outside the church, to organise the men for the march-past on the parade ground. Had he noticed her running out earlier? If she went home now, Ruby would be sure to open her front door and ask her in. She could not bear her loving-kindness, alone, but would wait until the men had returned from the barracks. To buy some time, she let herself quietly into the house, took hold of Ebony's lead, and raced him away towards the South Parade Pier. Something Pa had said to her recently played itself back in her mind.

'It's going to be one of those days that's lived minute by minute.'

But this was only one of the days she would have to face. Ahead of her was July the fifth when Harry came home. She dithered about writing to him first, preparing him in some way. Was a letter the coward's way out? What if he was so upset that he jumped overboard or shot himself? At least if she waited he would have his mum and dad to comfort him. Poor Harry, he was such a good man, so kind and loving and larky. Oh God! He would not be feeling larky for much longer. But at least he would have the choice, like Daniel, of walking away. She had no choice but to give birth to this unwanted child. If only she could tell Pa, the only person who would give her comfort and support. But he would be placed in an impossible situation, living beside Norman and Ruby. No, somehow she had to gather some courage and live through the next few weeks, keeping her secret to herself. Facing Harry! Her mind swerved away from the difficulty. But perhaps, minute by minute, she would find the words.

Ebony bounded up to her, standing on his hind legs, barking joyfully. She kissed his muzzle and rumpled his silky ears.

He licked her hands, giving her rough comfort. The two of them left the beach and made their way through the Canoe Lake towards home. Pa was out in the street, seated on the windowledge talking to Norman. Both men were smoking their pipes and 'spinning the dit' together, going over old events and giving them a new twist. As she drew nearer, the old dog gave a last burst of speed and bounded up to her father, barking joyfully.

'Hello my darling,' said Pa, holding out his arms to her. 'I hope you've brought a giant's hunger, for Ruby has a feast in store for us. There's even talk of jam roly-poly.'

Norman bent to kiss her cheek. 'Go on in, gal, tell my Missis if she doesn't get that joint on the table soon I'll be round the RMA Tavern in one, one two.'

'Hello my cherub, and how are you then? You looks proper peaky, not sleeping are you? I can tell. Best have a little nod this afternoon before you goes back.' Ruby lifted the joint from the roasting-dish and set it on the meat platter.

Fidelis watched her stirring flour into the hot fat, then adding the water from the vegetables to make the RBG as they all called it – rich brown gravy.

'Go and give Norman a shout, then get the eating-irons out the drawer and fling them round the table. D'you fancy some dandelion and burdock, there's a jug out there in the scullery. 'Spect the men'll have the nettle beer.' She smiled, her face red from all her exertions, and she combed a stray tendril of hair away with her fingers. 'It's lovely to see my girl again,' she said.

Fidelis concentrated on getting the knives and forks out of the drawer.

When they had all heaped their plates with roast beef, Yorkshire pudding and roast potatoes, Norman passed round the gravy and the other vegetables. 'God bless our innards,' he said, 'tuck in while it's hot.'

Ruby raised her glass. 'To our Mary, a good woman, gone but never forgotten.'

Fidelis blinked back the tears. 'To Ma,' she managed to whisper. At least she thought, her mother had been spared the disgrace of her daughter's unfaithfulness. Fidelis – what a joke her name was now.

Norman leant across the table and squeezed her fingers. 'You gotta look after yourself, Fee, love, 'til my Harry gets back, then it'll be his place to do the caring.'

26

Daphne had assured her it would all go swimmingly on the night, and be tremendous fun. Phoebe was not reassured. So far the launching of *Maison-Belle* had been tedious, and at times exhausting. There had been the arranging for all the stock to be brought around from Waverley Road. Everything had to be priced, and entered into a ledger which was mind-numbing.

'We have to keep track of things Phoebe, you have no idea how items can walk away with some customers. Besides, we need to know what sells and what doesn't, what we need to replace.'

They had decided against starting off in the basement, as it needed to be repainted and carpeted and smelled of damp. She had no money until her birthday the following week. Then if the initial party, to be held in the drawing-room, were a success, she would splash out on the new venture.

She had got Fidelis to give the room a good clean and polish while she took Sophie out, and delivered her business invitations especially to Mrs Marcia Mount and Miss Dorcas Beningfield of Kelmscott House.

Back at home, there was all the fiddle-faddle of sewing on the tickets, and arranging and rearranging the quilts over the chaise-longue and the single bed brought down from the attic. Daphne had transformed the clothes-horse, covering the wooden bars with a remnant of purple satin. Then Phoebe pinned the lavender-bags and potpourri sachets on to it between lace-trimmed pillowcases. She had gone around to Kelmscott and flattered Cook into making some of her coconut macaroons and tiny fondant fancies.

The artificial flowers arranged in vases were quite extraordinary: scarlet poppies, bunches of satin violets and glorious yellow felt sunflowers with orange satin centres.

The date was set for Thursday July the second, and Daphne had arranged to come and sleep there the night before. They had hoped to launch themselves much earlier but Daphne unexpectedly had caught the mumps and everything had been thrown into abeyance. Now, she was back on top form and chivvying Phoebe every five minutes.

'I'll probably stay up all night,' she said,' there's a quilt I want to finish.'

At ten o'clock Phoebe yawned. 'I'm off to bed, darling. I can't keep my eyes open a moment longer.'

'I'll wake you at seven, there's still a lot to do!'

'There hasn't been much fun so far,' she whined, desperate for sleep.

Daphne laughed. 'You're such a baby sometimes. You just want to lick the icing and not take the trouble to bake the cake. Can't you see how satisfying it will be tomorrow, when all our hard work begins to pay off?'

Phoebe wanted to have a monumental sulk, but had found that her business partner did not respond to blackmail.

'Go along, fly up to your nest, and come down tomorrow in a better mood.'

But when she saw everything set out in readiness the next day she had to admit that the painstaking preparations had been worthwhile. 'It looks as if it came straight out of Liberty's,' she gasped. 'I can't believe we did it.'

Daphne winked at her. 'We're almost launched.'

Eileen had been borrowed from Kelmscott to serve the tea, and Midge had been given a new lace afternoon apron and posted at the door. Fidelis promised to keep Sophie out of the way until six o'clock.

Phoebe sprayed the room with her favourite perfume, then screamed with nerves as the doorbell rang for their first guest. Soon the room was crowded with women milling about, peering at price tickets and opening their purses, her mother among them.

'This is quite splendid,' she whispered, 'you have worked hard, both of you.'

Phoebe glowed – such praise was rare indeed. She sat at a table in the corner, took the money, wrote out receipts and collected the sale tickets in a china bowl. Daphne drifted about discussing fabrics and taking orders.

'Every item is unique, madam, only the pillowcases and some of the cushions come in sets. Each sale we have will be different. Commissions? Well, I shall have to discuss that with my partner.'

'Congratulations, Mrs Allen, I have been charmed. I shall contact you soon,' said a woman with a bulging parcel of *Maison-Belle* items. 'Do let me know when the next event will take place.'

By six o'clock the guests had left and the reckoning began. Phoebe totalled up the contents of the cash-box. 'Thirty-five pounds, less five pounds float. That's splendid.'

'Not bad for a beginning,' said Daphne. 'There's an envelope for Fidelis with three shillings and six pence for all the extra ironing.' She called in Midge and Eileen and gave them half a crown each.

'Ta ever so much,' said Midge.

Eileen, with a tray of teacups to wash, nodded.

'What did you want to do that for?' Phoebe snapped, 'they've been paid already by Mummy.'

'It's called goodwill. We couldn't have managed without them. Now, I suggest we have a gin apiece and then clear up. Next week we'll have to go to some auction sales and scout around for bargains. There's often some wonderful lace going for a song, and ribbons and things. Trimmings can work miracles, you know. And how about your clothes, Phoebe, the ones you were getting rid of? I bet your boots we can use them.'

'I thought we could clear up tomorrow,' sighed Phoebe, her earlier excitement beginning to evaporate.

'You can't rest on your laurels in business. No work, no profits. This is expensive stock, we must put it away carefully. As soon as things begin to look creased or faded customers will want the prices reduced.' Daphne gave her a supercilious smile. 'We at *Maison-Belle* have a reputation to maintain – nothing less than excellence.'

Marcia saw it as a milestone – today her daughter was twenty-five years old. It had been a surprise that Phoebe didn't want a party.

'I'm too busy, Mummy there's so much to do. Daphne and I will be going up to London next week to the summer sales. I'll treat us to a slap-up lunch.'

Maison-Belle had come into their lives at just the right time. Boredom had always been a problem with Phoebe, and led her daughter into recklessness and five-minute enthusiasms. But Daphne Manners was a realist, with too much at stake to have a dabbler for a partner. Her brutal honesty had forced Phoebe into doing her share of the work, and she was beginning to take a pride in the venture. The question was, how would coming into her legacy affect her daughter's tenuous hold on reality?

Marcia sat in the drawing-room at Clarendon House, waiting for Phoebe to bring down Sophie for an outing with them.

The door burst open and her granddaughter rushed in and leapt into her arms. 'Hello Gamma, kiss, kiss.'

'Sophie, my dear, what a big girl you are. Now, do you know what day it is?'

The child turned towards Phoebe, 'It Mummy birffday.' Her dark eyes shone, and she jumped off Marcia's lap and ran across the room.

Phoebe held out her arms and swept her up in them, then swung her round the room.

'What are we going to do today?'

'New shoes for me.' She crowed in triumph, holding out her foot.

'I'll get my coat.' Coming back into the room Phoebe said, 'I don't know what's the matter with Fidelis, she looks ghastly lately, and she's almost monosyllabic. If she doesn't buck up soon, she'll have to go.'

'Oh Phoebe, try and have a little understanding, darling. The girl has not long lost her mother.'

'But her fiancé is coming home tomorrow, you would have thought she would be blissfully happy.'

'Do you think she's ill? Would you like me to speak with her?'

'No, Mummy, she's my nursemaid. I will give her another week and then we'll see. But it's my birthday, let's go out and get the shoes and then,' she winked at Sophie, 'then we'll go up the stairs in Handleys and have some cake.'

Her daughter whooped with excitement.

The three of them caught a tram and sat on the top in the front. Sophie was ecstatic. 'Look at pier,' she demanded. 'Beach, beach, look at sea.'

Later, while her granddaughter was absorbed in a cream cake, Marcia broached the subject of the inheritance.

'You'll be a woman of substance, with your own bank account and chequebook. I hope you won't start throwing your money about.'

Her daughter looked mutinous. 'That will be for me to decide.'

'You have a child to rear, a house to maintain and servants to be responsible for. I shall no longer smooth your path. Welcome to the world of grown-ups, darling.' Marcia could feel her temper rising. 'Have you learned nothing from the last time you had money of your own? I would have thought those weeks of near destitution, in Brighton, would have been seared on your memory.'

'I have plans for my business, and I shall set aside money for Sophie and of course housekeeping. But I want to splash out now and then.' She smiled at her mother. 'You will just have to trust me. How will I learn if you're always twitching the reins?'

Reaching into her handbag Marcia slipped a leather jewel-case across the table.

'Don't open it here.' she said. 'I have decided to give you Grandma Mount's pearls now rather than leaving them to you. I want to have the pleasure of seeing them worn. Pearls always suited you, and I feel that you will value them as I did.'

Quickly Phoebe slid the box across the table and into her bag. There were tears in her eyes. 'Oh Mummy, I don't know what to say. They are so special, I remember her wearing them.' She blew her mother a kiss. 'Thank you, thank you.'

Marcia smiled. Her daughter might have chosen to sweep the Brighton episode under the carpet but it had been the catalyst for change. Phoebe would always have to struggle against her inherent selfishness; but there were, here and there, promising signs of maturity. After settling the bill, she got to her feet. 'I must go, darling I'm due at the school for a governor's meeting. Come around on Sunday and we'll have lunch. I'll get Cook to make a special dessert.'

She kissed Sophie's sticky face. 'Goodbye, my sweet, Gamma will see you on Sunday.'

*   *   *

That night Phoebe stood naked in front of her dressing-table, wearing only her grandmother's pearls. They gave off a creamy glow against her skin. All in all, her birthday had been quite splendid. She truly had come into her inheritance. She and Daphne had had a tipsy supper, toasting one another in champagne. Now, after her sending her friend home in a cab, Phoebe padded about in her bedroom, overcome with a sense of anti-climax. It came to her that she had not been kissed, much less had any passion in her life, since James. She had always enjoyed sex, the intensity of it, the total loss of control and the sense of power. Her husband had been such a practised seducer.

Closing her eyes, she sang to herself, drifting across the carpet in a wistful alcoholic haze. Tomorrow she would have to look about her to find out who was available. Marriage was much too much of a gamble. What she wanted was a pleasant diversion with someone who would be as pleasure-seeking and uncommitted as herself. After all, she was a wealthy widow now, and had every hope of being a merry one.

'Aunt Marcia, I'm sorry to be so late, I was waiting for the paint to dry on the window-frames, it's such an aggravation when they get stuck. Everything is ship-shape and Ventnor fashion and I shall take up residence next week. All I have to do is pack my traps here and be gone.'

'Can I pour you some whisky, Dorcas? I'm just unwinding from quite a full day.'

'Certainly you can. Tell me what I've missed in my island remoteness. How is everyone?'

'Phoebe is now twenty-five and very pleased with herself. This *Maison-Belle* venture seems to have fired her enthusiasm and so far it shows no sign of fizzling out.'

'Well, that Daphne Manners is a determined woman with

too much to lose to let it slip away. I liked her and she's good for Phoebe, they're both as bossy as each other. They'll strike sparks off each other for a good while to come, as far as I can see.' She took off her shoes and sat on the floor with her back against the sofa. At first this camp-fire casualness had disconcerted Marcia, but now she was well used to her niece's bizarre behaviour. 'Is there anything else I've missed?'

'Phoebe says that Fidelis is unhappy or unwell. I don't know which. I suggested I might talk with her but it was seen as interfering.'

'I'll go around there tomorrow, shall I? I wanted to say goodbye to her. Well actually, I was going to ask her over to stay for a week or so.' She waved her hand as if to ward off a protest. 'Permission will be asked from my cousin. Some fresh air and sunshine might be just the thing. Though isn't it this week her Harry comes home?'

Marcia frowned. 'Tomorrow in fact, that is what is so worry-ing. One would think she would be bubbling with anticipa-tion.'

'Whatever it is, I'll report back my findings.' She yawned, then set down her glass on the table before kissing her aunt good-night. 'I need a good sleep – who knows what tomorrow will bring.'

27

She had written to him confessing everything and begging his forgiveness but the letter sat un-posted in the drawer beside her bed. Too late now! Walking along the beach to Harry's house, on the morning of his return, Fidelis wanted to die. This was supposed to be a day of celebration, and now it was bitter as gall. Tomorrow she would tell him. Tomorrow she would break his heart. Pa would have to be told and Auntie Ruby. Oh, she would not be smiling tomorrow.

'Fee my darling, you're eager and so you should be.' Aunt Ruby hugged her tightly then held her at arms length. 'What, no pretty frock?'

'I can't come, Auntie. Sophie's not well and Miss Phoebe's away 'til tomorrow, and Mrs Mount's having a garden party, so everyone will be busy.'

'Fee, that is too bad. Harry'll be that disappointed. Can't I send him round to see you, just for a half-hour? He'll be starved for the sight of you after all this time.'

She shook her head. 'Will you say that I'll meet him on the beach down in front of the swimming-baths at eleven tomorrow morning. I need to see him on my own.'

Ruby smiled. ''Course you wants him to yerself, only natural. Come and have a bit of dinner with us after and tell your Pa he's welcome, too.' Again she hugged her. 'You must be so excited. I bet you're counting the hours 'til you sees him.'

Fidelis nodded, trying to smile. 'I'd best be off, I dashed down early to catch you. See you tomorrow.'

Walking back to Clarendon House, she could not stop crying. Here, too, she had to be the liar.

'Fidelis, isn't this the day your Harry comes home? Why are you not down at the harbour waving your handkerchief? My goodness, you look very pale, you're not sick, are you?' Phoebe sat with Sophie in bed with her, looking at a picture-book.

'No,' she lied, 'I'm just disappointed he won't be able to get ashore until tomorrow. If he can't get away, I don't want to see the ship come in.'

'That's horrid for you. Well, why don't you go up to your bedroom and rest for an hour, then you'll feel brighter. I'll take Sophie around to play with Phillip later this morning. You can collect her from there later on.'

In her room, the walls seemed to be closing in on her. What was she going to do with herself until tomorrow morning – hour after hour of waiting to stick the knife in? Harry didn't deserve it. He was so kind and he loved her – not the breathless, bedazzled, greedy, snatching lust she had shared with Daniel, but a day-by-day, faithful and perse-vering love. How could she have been so giddy and foolish?

Returning with Sophie from Nanny Hawkins, later in the day, she saw sailors from the *Ramillies* out with their sweet-hearts. Phoebe was busy with a new friend and didn't take Sophie off her hands until late afternoon. The night seemed endless as she tossed and turned. At one point she thought of dropping the letter through the door, instead of facing Harry, but knew it to be a cowardly thought. He deserved better than that. She woke in the early hours, nauseous and drenched with sweat. In desperation she held her mother's rosary beads, trying to remember the prayers.

Why had they both rejected her mother's faith and gone instead to the Crinoline Church, leaving Ma to pray alone? It was a tangled knot of reasons: something about a priest in

Ireland refusing Grandma McCauley money for her children, and a Christian Brother beating Pa at the school he went to in Dublin. But she remembered as a small child the incense and the Latin, and sitting beside her mother in a daze, looking up at the statues and the bank of flickering candles. It had been such a bone of contention between them. Father Buckley had been kind, and she remembered him visiting an old marine in their street. He had brought him food and sat reading to him from the paper, even played cards. She could have gone with Ma to St Swithun's when her father was away. It would have been a small thing, one hour a week, and have given her so much pleasure. Perhaps she would not have fallen for Daniel if she had been brought up a Catholic.

Phoebe was taking Sophie down to Brighton and all was rush and panic for the first hour, then she was alone in the house, listening to the hall clock ticking away the minutes. It was a still, warm morning: the only sound the crying of gulls as she approached the promenade. In the distance the Isle of Wight was sharp as a snapshot, and the sea a sparkling sapphire. She bit her palm. It was cruel in its perfection. Half-way towards Eastney, faint with nausea, she had to sit down at one of the shelters. When it passed, she walked over the shingle and dipped her handkerchief into the water and bathed her face and neck. Her feet dragging with reluctance, Fidelis neared the part of the beach in front of swimming-baths. Looking up at the clock tower she saw it was ten minutes to eleven.

Harry was waiting for her. At the sight of her he gave a great whoop of joy, and held out his arms. He was tanned and smiling and taller than she remembered. Walking towards him she felt like Judas in the garden, about to betray him with a kiss.

'Oh Fee, I'm that glad to see you.' He spun her round and round in his arms, laughing in his excitement. He kissed her and she clung to him, trying to draw strength for what she

had to tell him. He held her away from him and smiled at
her. 'Let me look at you, sweetheart, let me feast me eyes.
You look tired, love, and you bin crying. They working you
too hard, are they?'

'Harry, I got to tell you, it's why I wanted to meet you
here. I don't think I can . . .' Her words fell over themselves,
mixed with tears.

He held her close. 'Fee, don't cry my love. Whatever it is
can be sorted out. I'm home now, home to take care of you.'

'Oh Harry, I'll never forgive myself. I've been such a fool.'
Fidelis ran from him to the water's edge, her heart thumping.
She took her wet handkerchief and wiped her mouth. This
was harder than ever she had imagined in all her sleepless
nights. Seeing him look at her with such love, seeing his open
honest face, she was ashamed. He ran down the beach towards
her, and she hurtled along towards Fort Cumberland. He
caught her easily.

'Sit down, sweetheart, here, let me take off my jacket and
lay it on the stones, that's it. Now take your time, we got all
day set out before us.'

The only way she could tell him was to stare out at the
sea. 'Happened when Pa came home on the *Terrible* last year.
I met this officer and we were friends.'

'I don't understand, Fee, what's he to us?' Still his voice
was full of concern, yet confident that whatever she would
tell him could be distanced from them by his love.

'We were lovers.' Even with her back to him, she could
feel the impact of her words.

'You better say that again?'

Fidelis heard the chill in his voice.

'We've been lovers and I'm,' she bit her palm, her voice
shook, 'I'm carrying his child.'

'No,' he shouted. 'No!' He took her face in his hands and
turned it towards him. 'You tell me it's not true.'

She closed her eyes, fearful of seeing the damage she had caused him. 'I'm expecting his child.'

'And is this officer going to marry you and raise his child?'

She shook her head. 'He's engaged to someone one else.'

'So, you're both as bad as each other, betraying those that love you.'

'Oh Harry,' she cried, 'I'm so ashamed and sorry and I don't know what to do.'

'I can't take this in. All the time you were writing and telling me what was happening you were seeing your fancy man. Read my letters to him, did you, laugh did you? About the bloody fool half-way across the world, that trusted you.'

'No, of course not, it wasn't like that. I can't explain, I'm just so sorry.'

'Why didn't you write and tell me, Fee? Why let me come all the way home, just months from the wedding, before you crucify me?'

'It was all over but then I found out that, I was . . .'

'So, if you hadn't got caught by him, you would have kept quiet.'

She shook her head.

'What are you expecting from me? What is it, forgiveness, for everything to be forgotten, for me to walk down the aisle with you like nothing's happened? What do we say about the sprog? He some sort of fucking miracle what I sent you in the post?' He gripped her arms and stared at her as if she were nothing to him.

'Harry, you're hurting me.'

'I'm hurting *you*, Jesus Christ.' Harry flung her from him, his voice choked in tears. 'Gotta go, I can't be doing with this.' He was gone from her, running over the stones towards Fort Cumberland, too fast for her to catch him.

* * *

Ruby sat out in the garden, slicing the beans into colander. The bees buzzed around her and the scent from the sweet-peas climbing the trellis was a joy. 'God's in his heaven, all's right with the world,' she thought. Her Harry home again – she couldn't help smiling. What a fine young man he was now, with that extra bit of confidence. She could imagine him pacing up and down the beach waiting for Fee. It put her in mind of her own meetings with Norman after his foreign jaunts – the shyness and then the passion. Not that they didn't now have their times of ardour still. They had been so lucky to find one another. Soon there would be the wedding, it was such a shame that Mary was not alive. She had been a strange inward sort of woman, not in the least suited to the passionate Jack. Idly, Ruby wondered how he coped with such an antiseptic union. She blushed. Perhaps he had a woman somewhere and if he did, who could blame him? It was the warmth and the scent of flowers that was blowing her off course.

Hurrying into the kitchen, Ruby set a pan of water on the stove. Inside on the middle shelf were five stuffed hearts ten-derising with long, slow cooking. There was plenty for the four of them: her and Norman, Harry and Fee, even enough to plate up a dinner for Jack when he came in for second dinner. Soon she would set them on the bottom of the oven and slide an apple pie onto the top shelf. While the water came to the boil for the beans, she laid the table. As the bugle call for first dinner rang out across the garden, Ruby stood out on the pavement looking up the road.

Harry appeared, on his own; she waved to him but he did not wave back. Where was Fee? Her son was walking like a sleep-walker, not looking where he was going. Why didn't he have his head up and arms swinging?

'Got yer favourite stuffed hearts and runners fresh from the garden. Harry, where's Fee, Harry?

He walked past her without speaking, on up the stairs slamming the bedroom door in her face. There was crashing and banging as things were thrown about. She rapped on the door, her heart pounding in alarm. 'Harry, Harry. What's up with yer? Just you stop that.'

He leapt out at her and grasped her by the shoulders. 'Did you know? Did she tell you? Tell me, tell me you didn't know.' His fingers were biting into her skin.

'What, Harry? What you on about? Harry calm down, you're frightening me.' And he was, with his face scarlet with rage and eyes staring. He slumped down on his bed.

'The wedding's off, and d'you know why? 'Cos she's got one in the oven. Couldn't fucking wait for me.'

'Harry!' She sprung at him, stunned at his vulgarity, slapping him hard across the face. 'Don't you dare speak to me like that!'

He began to cry, covering his face with his hands, moaning and gasping. She sat there in frozen disbelief. How could this have happened, how was it that she didn't know?

'Are you sure?'

He nodded.

'I don't understand. Who is he? Is he going to marry her?'

Harry shook his head. 'He's a bloody officer who's got engaged to someone else.'

'Son,' she said, patting his arm, 'honest to God I'd no idea.' And then it came to her. The morning she had gone down to the harbour station to meet her friend from the train. At the time she had thought she was mistaken. Fee had been there but not seen her. She had come out of the waiting-room with a man in a long coat and trilby hat. Tall he was and handsome, put her in mind of someone she knew. Jesus Christ! She could see him now up at the church, reading the lesson like butter wouldn't melt. It was Colonel Herrick's son.

'D'you know who it is?'

Ruby nodded. Why should that dandy get away with it? Let him take his medicine like a man. 'It's Captain Herrick, what was a lieutenant when you went away. You know, his Pa's the colonel.'

'Jesus Christ! All the time,' he gasped, 'all the time she was writing and making plans with me she was whoring with him. Might as well have taken a knife and stuck it in me, been a bloody sight quicker.'

He looked at her, gentle Harry, the easiest and sunniest of her children, his face streaked in tears. 'What am I going to do?'

'Hello, up there, missus, there's a saucepan boiled dry on the stove. D'you want to set the house on fire?' Norman stood in the passage, beaming up at her.

She hurried towards him. 'Something dreadful's happened,' she said.

He bounded past her. 'Harry, what's up? Jesus, lad what is it?'

Ruby took the blackened saucepan from the stove and sat it in the sink and filled it with cold water.

'Back later,' she wrote on a scrap of paper, and grabbed her coat from the hook in the hall. She was possessed by a cold fury. Hands in her pockets, head down, she marched around to Clarendon House and up to the back door.

She hammered and shouted, then a woman came out with a bucket of water and emptied it into the outside drain.

'I want to speak to Fidelis McCauley, and don't you give me no flannel about her not being here 'cos I'll wait all day and all night if needs be.'

'I'll go and see.' She slammed the door in her face and locked it behind her. Ruby paced about the garden, her fury at boiling-point. Beside her the hedge was in flower, and the scent of privet blossom sickened her. The promise of the day lay curdled in her stomach, its brightness tarnished. Flies circled over the ash-can, and she could hear the cistern flushing upstairs somewhere in the house. Minutes later the back door opened and Fee stood there, her arms defensively across her stomach.

In spite of her anger the sight of the girl, her face chalk-white, and eyes puffy with crying, halted her. 'Hello, my fine lady, what have you got to say for yourself? I've just left my lad breaking his heart over you.'

'I can't say anything. I've ruined everything.'

'That's about the size of it. So, why didn't you tell him 'stead of letting him build up his dreams? You are cruel, do you know that? A cruel worthless creature and to think I wanted you for my daughter. You better keep out of my sight, Fidelis McCauley, for it'll be a good long while before I speak to you again.'

Jack McCauley walked home for his dinner feeling light-hearted. This was just the thing he needed, a bit of a cele-bration. He'd seen Harry last night and shaken his hand. By God, he was a man to be proud of, the sort of son any father dreamed of having. It was a mystery to him why Fee hadn't been there. Surely someone could have listened out for the child for an hour or so. Still, she would be there, now, that was all that mattered. He felt a stab of regret that Mary wasn't with him to see her daughter on such a happy day. She had thought a lot of Harry. A greater pity was that she would miss the wedding at Christmas. His poor Mary, well, she was at peace now.

He had been invited next-door to have a bite with Norman and Ruby and his son-in-law to be. Fee was coming too. He tapped on the front door of the Dawes' house then let himself in with the key. Something wasn't right. The table was laid but no sound of anyone. He went into the kitchen; there was a burnt saucepan soaking in the sink and the oven cold. He went back into the hall and was about to call out when Norman came down the stairs towards him, shaking his head and gesturing to him to be quiet. He walked with him onto the pavement.

'What's up, old chum? Where's the conquering hero?'

'Can we go in your house a minute?'

'Right you are.' Jack turned the key in his own front door and held it open.

'Bad business, Harry's that cut up about it, I don't know what to do with him. Should have told me, Jack, it's come as such a shock.'

'Norman, you've lost me, told you what? Where's Fee?' Looking at his neighbour, he began to feel alarmed.

'Christ, you really don't know? Your girl has got herself in the family way with Herrick's son. She told him on the beach this morning.'

'No, that can't be right.' He couldn't take it in: his Fee and the Colonel's son.

'You think I'd make it up? My lad's beside himself.'

'God almighty! I'd best go and see her. I'll talk with Harry later. Norman, I don't know what to say. This has come out of the blue.'

'Your best path is to stay clear of us for a few days. Ruby has gone round to see Fee and she was blazing.'

He shrugged helplessly. 'I'll leave it up to you, Norman. Just tell Harry as I'm sorrier than I can say.'

After getting himself leave for the afternoon he set out for Clarendon House, with no clear idea of what he was going to say or do.

Amazingly she had slept. On waking, she lay for a few blessed moments watching the curtains fluttering in the breeze before the full weight of her situation bore down on her once more.

Poor Harry: how she had hurt him. She smarted from Ruby's furious condemnation. At least Ma had been saved the shame of her daughter's behaviour. She would have been mortified.

Someone tapped on her door.

'Who is it?' she cried, fearful of Ruby's return.

'It's me, Dorcas.'

Fidelis burst into tears. 'I'm in terrible trouble,' she sobbed. 'I've ruined everything.'

'Just tell me, whatever it is. Say it, my dear.' She sat by her bed and listened.

Haltingly, and with many tears, she poured out her story and Dorcas listened until she had finished. 'You are so kind, I don't deserve it. I must go and meet Pa. Goodness knows what Ruby's told him. Then there's everyone else; Eileen, Cook and Midge, then there's Phoebe and Madam.'

Dorcas stood at the window. 'They will keep until another day. But I can see your father coming along the road, now. I'll let him in and make us all a cup of tea. Then I shall be in the sitting-room if you want me. Why don't you wash your face and comb your hair, it'll make you feel better. Shall I send him up when he gets here?'

Fidelis nodded. She made her bed, set herself in order for the next ordeal.

'Are you in there, Fee? Let me in, my darling.'

As soon as he had set down the tray of tea she clung to him, and he held her fast in his arms.

'You know that I love you, don't you, Fee? There isn't anything that you have done or said will change that. Don't be afraid, whatever it is, we can set it right between us.'

'You know, Ma was right,' she gasped. 'She said that Harry was too good for me.'

'Fee, sit down and listen to me, that's a lot of foolishness. I've lived with her all my life and was never good enough, but we rubbed along somehow and eventually fell into friendship. Feeling ashamed of who you are, and what you feel, settles on a person like rust. It corrodes your spirit and steals your courage. So we'll have none of that. It seems to me that things with you and Harry were sweet when I went away, then when I get home again I find you're engaged by letter – big difference between pals and sweethearts. Bet your Ma, and Ruby and Norman were proud as Punch. Made things a bit difficult if you were wavering. Strange to me that you never wrote and told me. But what about this other fellow, how did that come about?'

'I was dazzled, he was so beautiful, and I think he loved me for a little while. And we got very close with one another.'

'Two young people in love with the idea of being in love, and then you went a kiss too far?'

'It was complicated. You won't breathe a word or do anything if I tell you his name? It was Daniel Herrick.'

'Jesus, Mary and Joseph! The colonel's son. Well, I tell you Fee, you don't do things by half.' He smiled at her and took her hand, and then became serious. 'There's a sting in this tale. If it's blown over, why are you still crying?'

'I'm having his baby and Harry will never speak to me again and Aunt Ruby will never forgive me.'

'It's been a rare old day for you, Fee. I don't doubt things have been said, in the heat of the moment, by everyone, and I'm not going to add to them. You need to have a good night's rest and calm yourself. Tomorrow or the next day or whenever, I'll come and fetch you home and we'll talk this out. All I want you to remember is that your Pa is behind you.'

Lying in bed that night, she marvelled that it was only ten months since she had gone down to Farewell Jetty to meet her father from the *Terrible*. Ten months that had propelled her from innocence to experience. It had been such a lesson, not least because of the effect on others of her behaviour. When she saw Harry, laughing and holding out his arms to

her, she had felt such pain. He had loved her with simplicity
and trust and she had betrayed him. Now she saw that what
she had felt for Daniel was a fizzy passion that evaporated
the moment she saw Harry.

28

All night he had lain awake, his eyes gritty from lack of sleep, with questions drumming in his head. Why had it happened? What could she have been thinking of? Why hadn't she written and told him, instead of letting him live in a fool's paradise? Where had they met, and how often had they made love? Harry was flayed with jealousy. He had spent hours torturing himself with wanting her, and all the time she was giving herself away, letting herself be stolen, in spite of knowing how much he loved her.

Ever since their engagement, his every waking thought had been for her, every penny saved was for their life together. His head was crammed with images of the two of them, he and Fee side-by-side walking into the future. There was Fee waiting for him at the door, smiling as he walked towards her. There she was in bed beside him, her red hair spread across the pillow. Then there was Fee sitting with their child on her lap. Yet, all the while she had been with her fancy lover. Captain fucking Herrick had thieved her kisses, smiles and sighs, leaving him, the faithful fiancé, starving for a kiss.

At the sound of the six o'clock bugle Harry dressed and crept downstairs. He swilled his face under the kitchen tap, and dragged on his jacket and cap before leaving the house. The sky was streaked with gold as he ran across the beach and on towards Fort Cumberland, around the point into Langstone Harbour. Gasping, with a pain in his side, he kicked at the stones on the beach then flung them into the water. He roared out his pain into the summer morning.

He knuckled his eyes and dashed away his tears at the thought of yesterday. When he caught sight of Fee, the beauty of her made him want to weep. Standing there, holding out his arms to her, he had felt such joy. For a moment he had held her, and the dream and the reality were fused in the warmth of her body and the scent of her. And then she took it all away. He had been like a mettlesome horse still plunging forward. It had taken time for the bit to cut into his mouth and halt him, shocked and bleeding. In seconds everything was reversed, and love was turned to hate. What were her tears compared to his pain?

Even if he had been able to forgive her for going astray, there was now a child growing in her that Daniel Herrick had planted. He would never have known who his betrayer was but for his mother. Fee could not bring herself to spell it out. 'Fidelis,' he shouted out the name then laughed: Fidelis for faithfulness, what a sour joke.

A dog bounded across to him with a stone in its mouth then laid it at his feet. Harry picked it up and hurled it into the sea.

A voice he recognised from years back called to the animal. 'Tusker, Tusker, come here, boy.'

Jack snapped his eyes open and was instantly wakened by the sound of a stone hitting the window. He drew back the curtain and saw Norman standing in the street below, beckoning him to join him. Dragging on his trousers, he hurtled down the stairs. Ebony leapt from her mat and began scrabbling at the front door. 'Down lad, down,' he said, reaching for his lead and clipping it to the dog's collar.

Stepping out onto the pavement, he looked questioningly at his neighbour.

'Harry's gone off somewhere, we gotta find him. The boy's in an uproar, he don't know what he's about.'

Jack had not seen Harry since his arrival home on Friday, when all was back-slapping, congratulations, and pints of beer. Then there had been the shock of yesterday with the lad heart-broken, Ruby raging, and his Fee so ashamed and tearful.

'When d'you think he went out? Where's he likely to be?'

'Pray to God he's not where I think he is. Ruby let slip that the bloke Fee's been seeing was Herrick's son. If he's gone after him, Christ, it don't bear thinking about.'

'Is Herrick around? Thought he was in Kent?'

'Back last week, he takes that dog of his across the beach of a morning. If they've met up with each other there'll be hell to pay.'

'That where you reckon Harry's gone?'

'Round by Fort Cumberland most likely.'

Once Jack had taken Ebony off the lead the dog sped away from them towards the eastern harbour. 'It's a good step away, pray God we're in time.'

The two men followed Ebony, their boots crunching over the stones. At first rounding the corner, they saw nothing but two dogs bounding in and out of the water. Then higher up the beach, two caps and jackets were flung on the shingle. And then they saw them grappling together, further along the beach. Jack shouted but they were oblivious.

'Jesus Christ,' gasped Norman, sighting his son.

Harry's nose was streaming blood and Daniel was reeling from a punch. Righting himself, he hit back and the two of them gasped and grunted. They circled one another, dodging and diving, hitting and missing, and then striking home. First Harry had the edge and it seemed that Daniel was about to go down; when he recovered his balance and landed a punch that had Harry swaying. As he fell to his knees, the fight went to Daniel who swung back his arm ready for the kill. But Harry recovered himself and dodged the blow. Teeth bared, he brought his fist slamming up into Daniel's chin. The force of the punch had him twisting and falling face downward on the shingle. He tried to rise but Harry was on him, his left hand pressing the blond head into the stones, and his right fist drawn back to deliver a crushing blow.

'Hold hard, that man,' roared Jack, as he and Norman raced towards them.

The parade ground voice connected to the marine in Harry and stayed his hand.

'On your feet and let that man up!'

Norman helped Daniel to his feet.

'Mister Herrick, sir, this is conduct unbecoming to members of the corps and in a public place. A severe breach of military discipline,' barked Jack, stooping to pick up the captain's jacket and cap. 'I take it, sir,' he said, handing him a handkerchief, 'that this is a private matter and will remain so?'

'Quite so, Drill Sergeant, your intervention was timely. I'm sure Corporal Dawes and I, we are grateful to both of you.'

'I believe that concludes the matter, sir,' said Jack.

'And you,' said Norman looking at his son, 'button that jacket and straighten your cap.'

'Good day to you, gentlemen,' said Herrick before calling to his dog. Tusker came running towards him. Turning on his heel and limping slightly, the captain walked away up the beach.

From the clock tower in the distance came the seven-thirty bugle call, alerting everyone to the morning parade. Jack thanked God they were all off duty. 'You all right, lad?' He looked at Harry and hurt for him. What could he say? It would be useless to tell him of Fee's distress when he was drowning in his own pain. 'I'm sorry to see you like this, lad,

I'm sorry for both of you. Want to come back and clean up at my place before your mother sees you?'

Harry shook his head.

'Drop of sea water'll do to mop up worst of it,' said Norman.

'I'll leave you to it, then.' As he walked across the shingle Ebony bounded towards him. 'Hello, boy,' said Jack smiling down at him. 'You don't know the half of it. Let's you and me go home and get out the frying-pan.'

Harry felt empty – even the risk he had run of being court-martialled failed to alarm him. Nothing mattered. He walked down to the sea, and kneeling on the shingle sluiced his face, the salt in the water stinging his cuts. Touching his mouth, he knew that he was going to have a cut lip and thanked God he was on leave, bugling would be out of the question for the next few days. The relief was short-lived. What was he going to do with the next three empty weeks?

'Christ boy, you were lucky there,' said his father, giving him his handkerchief. 'You could have killed him. We could've bin seeing you sent for hanging. Good job old Jack was with us.'

'Don't feel lucky, Dad.' He looked at his father and all his hurt welled up in him. Not since he was small had he wanted to be held by his dad.

'I know, boy. I know, son, you've had a basin-full.'

He leant against him, all fight gone. Oh, the pain would come back, but, just for that moment, the feel of the kersey cloth against his cheek and the smell of his father comforted him.

'Are you fit to walk now, boy? Are you sure? Let's go home and face your mother. I reckon a good breakfast and a soak in the bath-tub will go some way to starting the healing.'

'You think so?'

''Course I do, Harry, you been in the eye of the storm,

knocked sideways – no wonder you can't think straight. Just come home and get your head down for a few hours then you and me will talk things over.'

'Why, why did she do it? All we had, just chucked it away.'

'Whatever she done lad, she's surely going to pay for it. I know it don't feel like it now, but you've got a clean slate and can walk away. Fee got a child to carry and no mother to guide her. She'd want to come to Ruby but there'll be precious little welcome there.'

Harry shivered.

Daniel limped up the stairs to his cabin. His right eye throbbed and he was aching from every joint. A glance in the mirror confirmed his suspicions. He was going to have a black eye. His father had invited an American colonel of marines and his wife to lunch. Seeing him like this would not improve his temper. But when he thought about it, he was lucky to be alive. If Harry Dawes had killed him it would have been no more than he deserved. There was a certain perverse satisfaction in getting his just deserts.

It was Fidelis who would be really punished. Poor girl, her shame would be so public. For the first time since she had told him, he thought about the baby – his baby. The chances were that he would never see him and the child would not know his father. All the privileges of his own life that would naturally have been shared with his own children, would be denied to this unwanted baby. It would be a bastard, its life blighted by its parents' lust. But at the time he had loved her; it had been more than just sex, it had been love, he was convinced of that.

He had lost the chance of seeing his child grow. What if he and Maude were childless? What if this baby Fidelis was carrying was ill-treated by some man, Harry even, how would he feel then? If only, when he had first seen Fidelis, a premonition had warned him of the consequences. But even then, he knew it would have been too late. He couldn't even make some financial amends to smooth her path. The scorn in her face had made that impossible.

It had been a terrifying moment when Maude had followed Fidelis out of church that Sunday. She could have told his fiancée the full story of his deceit, and blown his future out of the water. Waiting for the service to end, he had been in a sweat.

'Poor girl, her mother died last week. Oh, I remember how I felt so lost and grief-stricken. All she was worried about was returning my hankie.' Maude had turned to him and said, 'You know her Daniel, I think she's called Fidelis. She sang at the concert.'

'The drill sergeant's daughter. Oh yes, I've met her once or twice.'

She had looked at him, and he had felt like a worm wriggling on a hook. He shook his head. The question now was, what story could he concoct by the time he walked up the steps at midday to lunch? He had never shown the least interest in boxing, so a tale of a sparring injury wouldn't wash. The worrying thing was that his father had seen him yesterday with Fidelis, and would put two and two together. Whatever else Jasper Herrick was, he was not stupid. Daniel prayed for the inspiration of the moment.

Soon he and Maude would be in the Ascension Islands, where their only problem would be boredom. Oh, he was sick of Eastney and everything connected with it.

At the sight of her son, Ruby burst into tears. 'Harry, oh Harry love, whatever's the matter?'

'Just had a bit of a set-to. What we gotta do now is get some water on. The boy needs a good soak in the bath and some food inside him.' Norman gave her a warning look.

She was fussing, she knew it. But what else could she do? Going and giving Fee a good chewing-up had given her no satisfaction at all. Walking back from their meeting, she had felt ashamed of herself and all that ranting. The worst part of it all was her inability to do anything that would make a difference. Standing on the sidelines was not her style. Being the parent of grown-up sons was far harder than when they were boys. Now she had to guard against being interfering. Harry was a man now, and had to work his own way out of his problems.

'I'll fill the kettle and the saucepans, take too long to get the fire going under the copper. How about you have your breakfast first? What d'you fancy?'

Harry shook his head. 'Whatever, not bothered, going up to get out of me things. I'll be down in about a half-hour.'

Directly she heard his bedroom door shut behind him, she burst into tears.

Norman took her in his arms. 'I know, my gal, it's a bad job all round but I think the worst is over. He went up the beach, ran into lover boy and gave him a right pasting. Thank Christ we turned up when we did or he could have killed him. Had to pull them apart. Jack roared out to them, just in time. Harry had him face-down in the stones, ready to punch his head in.'

''Spose you think I should go and thank him,' said Ruby bitterly. 'It'll be a long time before I talk to either of them.'

'Now that's plain stupid. How's that gonna help anyone? Talk sense, gal.'

'Well, it's how I feel, betrayed by the pair of them.'

'Just you listen to me, my lady.' There was a warning note in Norman's voice. 'We come very close this morning to Harry being court-martialled at the least. We could have been looking at the death sentence. If you hadn't bin so quick to tell him who it was, we'd all a bin spared a deal of trouble.'

Ruby sank down into a chair and cried in earnest. Her getting so riled-up had put her boy's life in danger. How could she have gone on living if he was taken from her?

Norman pulled up a chair beside her, and picking up the edge of her apron began to dab her eyes with it. 'Calm down my Ruby, we've had the fireworks, it's time for dowsing down the flames and taking stock. I expect Harry will want to get away out of it for a while. I'm gonna see if he wants to go down to Plymouth and stop with our Sammy. I reckon his big brother would calm him down, and he's always got on well with Sheila. It all too fresh for him to know what he wants to do. We just got to tiptoe round him for a while.'

'Why don't we all go down? I haven't seen Sammy for ages.'

'Ruby, Ruby, you haven't been listening. If he wants to go down there he'll go on his own. Then he can tell his brother what he wants to tell him in his own time. He's a man now, you must stand back and leave it to him.'

'That Fee needs horsewhipping. I said to her she needn't think she can come round here parading her shame.'

'Stop that talk right now, lady! Whatever's happened, you watch your tongue. What's the good of you going round that church praying, and psalm-singing, and then casting stones right, left and centre. Fee knows she's done wrong and don't need you to tell her. As to you saying she can't come round to her own street and see her own father, that's downright shameful.'

Ruby said nothing, but took up the frying-pan and slammed it on the stove. It was rare for Norman to take her to task, but when he did she knew she had gone too far.

'After he's had his grub I'll get the bath in from the yard and start filling it. In the meantime I'll get out the way. You can put a couple of rashers on for me.'

*　*　*

At eight o' clock on Monday morning, Harry stood at the town station waiting for the train to Plymouth. His rage had cooled, leaving him empty. He would be glad to see Sammy and get away from home. There were so many reminders of Fee around him there: the rockery they'd made with stones from the beach, and over the wall in her garden, the swing that her Pa had made for her. In his bedroom were her letters and the last photograph she had sent him.

His next posting was back at Eastney. Harry had looked forward to living in barracks and seeing Fee every day. Now he wished he could go back aboard the *Ramillies* and steam away from everyone.

29

Every waking thought had been directed to telling Harry about the baby, and she had not thought beyond that. Now there was the day after and the one after that to be lived through. How she was to do that Fidelis could not begin to think. The treadmill of tears and confessions had left her wrung out like a dishcloth. She could bear her own company no longer, and got out of bed wanting to be rescued by the routine of the nursery.

'Good morning, Fidelis, leave the tea on the dressing-table please, and run my bath will you?'

'Feed the birdies, Fofie want feed the birdies.'

'I shan't be back until late so I leave you to organise the day, Fidelis.' After kissing her daughter and checking her reflection in the hall mirror, Phoebe Allen tip-tapped out of the house.

As she washed the breakfast things a plan began to form. By the time she had tied the strings of the sunbonnet under the toddler's chin, Fidelis was ready to put it into action.

'We're going to see my friend and she's got a little girl just like you.'

Sophie would not be deflected. 'See birdies, me take bread for birdies.'

Her nursemaid smiled. 'Yes, today we will do lots of things.' It was a long walk from Southsea to the small streets of Portsea, clustered around the naval dockyard. Being in a different part of town was a relief, and the July sunshine lifted her spirits. The knowledge that she would be welcome was another boost.

'Me and Ma is in all day, we got some sewing work from a shop in Queen Street. Don't be a stranger, Fee, I'd love to see ya,' her friend had said the last time they met.

'Look, chuff-chuff,' said Fidelis, pointing to the train pulling away from the station up above the harbour; but the little girl's attention was drawn to the ragged children slithering over the mud below. 'Wat boy doin?' she asked.

'He wants us to throw him a penny. Shall we do that?'

She took the child out of the pram and held her up to the side of the bridge, giving her two halfpennies from her purse.

The lad grinned up at them. 'Ta, missis,' he called, before dipping his hands into the grey-brown slime and retrieving the coins.

After a promise to see the mudlarks again later on, Fidelis persuaded Sophie back into the pram. Leaving the harbour she followed the line of the high dockyard wall, into Queen Street. Her nose was assaulted by the distinctive smells of the neighbourhood: beer fumes from the brewery, tar and old rope from the dockyard: meat-pie aroma and wet-fish stink greeted her from the doorways of the food shops she passed. 'We've got to find Cross Street, it's not far. Here it is. Ah, number seventeen, shall we knock the knocker?'

'Yes, yes, yes.'

Footsteps could be heard running to the door, and then it opened. 'My stars, it's you, Fee.' Molly's face broke into a grin. 'Lovely to see you, and who's this pretty girl?'

Sophie chuckled.

'Have to leave the pram out there, Fee, ain't got room to swing a cat. Come in and meet Amy.'

They stepped straight into a tiny room where a woman sat at a sewing-machine. On a table were a stack of sailors' collars heaped on brown paper. 'Don't mind me, my duck. I gotta press on. I'm her Ma. You a pal of our Molly's?'

'We used to work together for the Allens.'

'That tripe-hound! If I could've got my hands on him I'd have strung him up.'

Molly shrugged. 'Past history, Ma, give it a rest. Sophie love, come out in the yard and see my little girl, she's playing with her dollies.'

Fidelis stood with her friend, watching the children getting acquainted. Amy, small with dark curls, sat on an orange-box with her rag dolls and their clothes. 'Wat's yer name?' she demanded.

'Fofie.'

'Wanta see me dollies? Gotta sit down then nexta me.'

Obediently Sophie sat beside her, and the two women went back into the house.

'Glad you come, we're going over Victoria Park for a picnic.' She laughed. 'Just be blackberry-jam sandwiches and a bottle of cold tea. Lovely to see ya, Fee, you can catch me up with all the gossip.'

Fidelis smiled. 'I'll treat us to some cake, shall I, or bread-pudding?'

'That'd be champion. Can you stay with the girls while I gets everythink together?'

Soon they were loaded up and on their way. Once in Victoria Park, her friend steered a course past all the flower-beds and Naval memorials to the fish-pond. The two little girls stood at the railings, watching the sun creating rainbows in the fountain's spray, and pointing to the goldfish swimming among the weeds.

Molly spread a blanket on the grass nearby, and they all made a start on the sandwiches. Sophie was fascinated by the purple juice-stained bread, and waved her crusts in the air.

'I've got something to tell you,' Fidelis said, after a swig from the tea-bottle. 'I've fallen for a baby.'

'You gettin' married?'

'No, it's this captain's child and I'm engaged to Harry, he's a bugler and it's all a muddle.' She tugged at a dandelion, fighting off the tears.

'Blimey, a captain! Still, it don't makes no odds if he ain't standin' by ya, could be the friggin' King of England. Oh Fee, I knows just how you feels. I was in a proper panic when I got caught, nearly topped meself, but our mum and dad they was life-savers. Oh, we had a right shoutin' match, and Dad wanted to go round and fix up Jimmy Allen with his guttin' knife.' She handed her a piece of bread-pudding. 'Have you been to the doctor? When are you due?'

Fidelis shook her head.

'Right, I'll come with ya. Soon as you knows your dates you can begin to sort yerself out. Where you gonna have it, Fee?

She poured out the whole story, and Molly listened.

'First off, Fee, you gotta stop being so hard on yerself, speakin' like you was less than the dust. You didn't get up the spout on your own. You can bet your boots your Daniel's not beating himself up over it. Next, you gotta stand up to that neighbour of yours. She got no right ter say as you can't walk down yer own street. Who she think she is, Queen of friggin' China?'

'Oh Molly, it's so good to see you.' Her friend's no-nonsense approach and salty humour was just what she needed.

'I know it all seems the worst thing in the world right now, but once you got that baby in yer arms you'll be the Queen of the May. How far along are you?'

'Three months.'

'You'll be quickening in the next few weeks.'

'Quickening?'

'When the baby starts moving inside, it's like a little ripple across your belly. Lets you know it's real. First off, I thought it was indigestion. But you know, once it happened I felt so different about everything. I even began to look forward.'

Fidelis doubted she would ever feel happy about the baby, but Molly was not one to put a gloss on anything. 'Would you really come with me?'

''Course I will. Meet you tomorrer, half-nine do ya? I'll wait by the Canoe Lake – best not call for ya or our Phoebe will have a seizure.' Her friend laughed. 'If madam Allen knew her little girl was playing with her half-sister she'd have a fit.'

With the sun warm on her back and the scent from the flower-beds wafting towards her, Fidelis felt her terror begin to lessen. A train chugged over the bridge behind the park and high up among the trees. Two o'clock chimed from the town hall tower. She and Molly sat making daisy chains while the girls chased over the grass after the pigeons.

'You haven't told Phoebe yet, have ya?'

'I don't think I can face telling any one else yet.'

'Good, 'cos ya wants ter stay working long as ya can. Got things you'll need for yerself and the baby, and you'll have to pay the nurse. Don't 'spect you'll show for a few more weeks, probbly have to let out the seams of yer dresses.' Molly laughed. 'You're in luck with Phoebe, so wrapped up in herself she won't notice till you drops it on her bed.'

'It's such a relief to have someone to talk to.'

'Well, Fee, anythink what you wants ter know I'll tell yer.'

There were questions teeming in her head, many that she was afraid to ask. But Amy and Sophie came running back to them, having seen the ice-cream man pushing his cart down the path towards them, and their talk came to an end. The four of them had an ice-cream apiece, and Fidelis walked back with her friend so that she could wash Sophie's face before taking her home.

Molly hugged her. 'See ya tomorrer and stop worry-guttin'.'

'Good morning. Miss Fidelis McCauley, I believe, isn't it?' Doctor Morgan stared down at her over the top of his glasses. 'I don't think I have seen you since you were a child.' He smiled. 'One of my healthier patients. Sit down if you please.'

Fidelis swallowed. 'Good morning, doctor.' She stared at the expanse of worn carpet between her chair and the desk, and tried to organise her thoughts.

'I must offer my condolences. You have recently lost your mother, I believe.'

'Yes, doctor.'

'What brings you here this morning?'

'I have been feeling sick and my period, it's very late,' she mumbled, still unable to look at him, and prayed that he would fill in the spaces for her.

'I think the first thing to establish here, Miss McCauley, is how late are we talking about. When did the last one end?'

'The eleventh of April.'

Doctor Morgan looked at the perpetual calendar on his desk. 'So it is the sixth of July, now. If nothing happens in the next few days you will have missed three periods?'

Fidelis nodded.

'Forgive me for my bluntness but you do understand, I presume, what full intercourse entails? A man has entered your body and left his sperm or semen inside you?'

She blushed. How mechanical and devoid of any feeling it sounded, and how shameful.

'Very well, I will just give you an examination. Please go behind the screen, take off your outer clothes, your boots and your drawers, and loosen your corset. After that, lie on the couch and let me know when you're ready.'

Fidelis took off her jacket and hat and set them on the coat-rack before unbuttoning her boots. She thought of her mother having lain on the same couch, only a few short months ago, and felt a twinge of relief that she was not here to witness her daughter's humiliation. 'I'm ready,' she called, staring up at the ceiling.

His hands were cold as he pressed her stomach. Then he left her and went out of the room. Fidelis lay in an agony of uncertainty. Where had he gone and why? The door opened again and he appeared again behind the screen. 'I have asked my wife to come in as I wish to perform a more intimate examination.'

This was excruciating. Only the other week she had sat next to Mrs Morgan in church.

'Good morning, Fidelis,' she said. 'Just part your legs and bring up your knees, that's it.'

If asked, she could have described the cracks on Doctor Morgan's ceiling with pin-point accuracy. She closed her eyes, and her cheeks burned as he probed inside her.

'All done, Miss McCauley.' He and his wife disappeared, and she could hear the door shutting behind her, then the sound of water being poured into a bowl. The fact of the doctor washing his hands, after touching her, seemed to compound her sense of uncleanness.

'When you're ready, Miss McCauley, come and sit down out here and we will talk about what you will need to do.'

'Well now, you are, as you suspected, going to have a child. Your due date will be in or around the sixteenth of January, a long way off yet. Where are you living now?'

'I'm working for Mrs Allen in Clarendon Road. I'm nurse-maid to her little girl.'

'So you will be able to stay there for the next couple of months, I should think?'

She nodded.

'This I imagine has come as rather a shock to you, my dear, and you have not had time properly to assess your situation. The next thing you have to consider is where you will have the child. I believe your home is nearby, and you have your father living there. Is he willing to support you?'

'Yes, but my fiancé lives next-door and he isn't the father. The family are very upset.'

'Things change over the course of time. Now, keep me informed of where you are staying and what your intentions are regarding place of birth. Later you will need to see Mrs Erridge, the woman whom I recommend to assist you at the birth. From what I can see you are a healthy young woman and used to working hard. There should be no problems. If you have a show of blood, go to bed immediately and send for me. Otherwise I will see you in a couple of months.' He stood up and came around the desk towards her and smiled before shaking her hand. 'It's my experience that babies bring their own love with them. Good-day to you, Miss McCauley.'

Fidelis slunk out of the surgery, and Molly followed after her from the waiting-room.

When they were out in the street she put her arm around her. 'I knows just how you feels, Fee – all dirty and shown up. We'll go along the seafront and have ourselves a cup of tea, and you can tell me what he said.'

'Where am I going to have the baby?' Fidelis stirred her tea and watched the whirlpool in her cup.

'You was saying about yer Aunt Shamrock, she sounds all right. Don't matter about her being untidy and that. Tidyness the least of yer worries. Like the doc said, once the baby comes everythink looks different. As to bein' embarrassed! Christ, once you're in labour you won't care who touches ya. Could be the fishmonger or a bleeding archbishop, long as he gets that baby born.'

Fidelis laughed. 'You saved my life, Molly, and cheered me

up no end. I'd better get back to Sophie or Phoebe will be all huffy.'

'I gotta get back down Queen Street and pick up some sewin' for Ma. Drop us a line when you can meet up with us again. In the meantime, keep yer chin up.'

When Sophie was fast asleep that night Fidelis sat writing in her room. She wrote to her father, arranging to meet him at Shamrock's the following Sunday, and to her aunt catching her up on events. Her other letter required more soul-searching – it was to Ruby. When she had settled on the final attempt she sat reading it through to herself.

> *July 8 1903*
> *Dear Aunt Ruby,*
> *I know that I have hurt Harry very deeply and you and Uncle Norman. You were always my dearest friend and my second mother. It may be that Harry will never forgive me and that you won't either. I will have to accept that but please don't take your anger out on Pa. He will need you both as his friends what with losing Ma and now me bringing disgrace to his door.*
>
> *Seeing Harry again I realised that I love him very dearly and that the madness of the time when he was away, was just what I said, a madness. Please tell him that I wish him all that's good in the world and never meant to hurt him. I enclose my ring, which I no longer deserve to have.*
>
> *If you wanted me to be punished for what I did you have your wish. Being separated from you and Harry is a hard thing to bear. I am very frightened of having my baby but hope I will be a good mother so that one good thing will have come out of all this hurt and unhappiness.*
>
> *Please can I ask that you let me know if Pa is ever ill and needing me?*

*Thank you for all the love and care you gave me
Ruby, I shall never forget you.
With love from,
Fidelis*

Putting the letter in her jacket pocket ready for posting the next day, she blew out her candle and lay in the darkness, her mind too busy for sleep. The spell had been broken and now she had to face the reality of carrying Daniel's child. It seemed an enormous task, like emptying the ocean with a teaspoon. Fidelis smiled to herself. If she said that to her friend Molly, she would have said, 'Get a bigger spoon'.

30

Maude stood in her bedroom on her wedding morning, looking out across the orchards. It was August the first and the trees were heavy with fruit. Hanging in the wardrobe was her dress. Alicia Herrick had helped her to choose the pattern and the material at Knight and Lees in Southsea, and a woman in Cranbrook had sewn it for her.

'I don't want a train and a lot of frills and furbelows. Something simple that I can perhaps have dyed and wear later.'

'Maude, you must have whatever makes you happy, my dear. It will be a long day for you and probably a hot one.' Her mother-in-law had smiled at her. 'It is so easy when one is marrying to be swept along by others into a lot of fussy nonsense. I'm so glad that you are having your wedding in Kent among your friends. In Portsmouth it would have become a military affair and have been taken out of your hands.' How kind she was, and how at ease Maude was in her company.

Jasper Herrick had not been pleased. 'I think you're making a grave mistake not marrying in the St Thomas's Church in Old Portsmouth, wonderful setting. There would be a guard of honour and drums and bugles.'

They were sitting opposite one another in the living-room at his house in the barracks. Daniel had been on duty, and Alicia and Arthur were taking a stroll through the officers' gardens.

'I want to be married from my home like any other bride,' she had said, angered by his manner.

'What does Daniel say? I'm sure he would want it to be a royal marine affair.'

'With the greatest respect, you have not the least idea what your son would want.' She was shaking not with fear but anger.

That had stopped him in his tracks. 'You are being impertinent, young woman,' he had snapped, turning from his place at the window overlooking the beach, and giving her the benefit of the famous Herrick glare.

'We are marrying each other, Colonel Herrick, not the regiment. Daniel is a person as well as an officer, as my father is a man first and an admiral second.'

There had been a pause while her future father-in-law digested this further insubordination in the ranks. 'I hope my son knows what he is taking on in you, Maude. It seems that you are set on having your own way in this, so I shall say nothing more. But I warn you, I do not take kindly to such discourtesy.'

And then she had done the unforgivable and laughed. She couldn't help it. Jasper had resembled a turkey-cock with wattles trembling. 'I am not afraid of you, Colonel. I don't know why but I thank God for it. I don't like you either, you are a bully and too used to your own way. If you will forgive me, I shall go and join my father in the garden.'

Later, thinking about the scene Maude laughed again. If only she could get Daniel to stand up to him as she had. It hurt her to see him so unmanned by his father. Sometimes, when they were alone together, she glimpsed what her future husband could become away from his malign influence.

'I have been so unthinking, when I look back over my life,' he said, 'like a blinkered horse following the path set out before me. It would be good to look up over the hedges occasionally and see what other paths there are.'

He had surprised her with his interest in Crossways. Down in Kent he was lively and interested in everything about him. Here, he was her Daniel, the man she wanted to marry. How could she help him to strike out on his own, away from the pattern laid down by Jasper? Maude sipped her morning tea and wondered whether his affair with Fidelis was truly over. Certainly, with his posting to the Ascensions there would be a safe distance between him and her red-haired rival. Looking at the islands in the atlas, they were miles away from everywhere – a mere pin-prick in the Atlantic, half-way between Africa and Brazil. There was something unfinished between Daniel and that girl; what it was she was afraid to guess. The girl was beautiful, and had seductive qualities she herself had never possessed. She knew her tears that Sunday had been for more than her mother's death, and Daniel had been distracted, frightened almost. I do love him she thought, and I know that he likes me – will that be enough?

'You ready for me to help you with your dressing, Miss Maude?'

'Come in, Mira, please,' she turned and smiled at her. 'I'm so glad you're here. You can set me right and make sure that I go out looking my best.'

'You'll be a handsome maid and that young man should count himself lucky. You're a treasure, Miss Maude and that's the truth. I'll just take your tray downstairs and 'fore I forget, I got a letter for you what was left in my keeping when your dear mother passed on. Told me most partickler to give it you on the day you was to be married.'

> 'My Darling Girl,
> I am so glad that you have found a man to love and I hope with all my heart that he loves you in return. Missing your wedding is one of my many griefs but I hope this letter will be a small presence on the day.

*I so want you to be happy as I was with your dear Pa.
What can I tell you that will be of any use? Being happy
is such a fleeting here and there thing that cannot be
pursued of itself. I think wanting one another's good is a
start. Becoming a couple requires a lifetime's effort on
both sides. All sorts of things come into play, loyalty,
humour and commonsense.*

*If it is a Service marriage other factors intrude, not
least being the constant moves and the challenge of
making whatever quarters you are given into a home.
But, I know that you are a born homemaker Maude. Be
one another's best friend and confidant and remember
secrets are the death knell of true intimacy.*

*I want you to know that I consider you a fine woman
and a daughter to be proud of and that in some way I
shall always be somewhere in your heart. As you see I
have enclosed my little cross and chain given to me on the
day of my confirmation. I would so like you to wear it
now and always as a reminder of my love.*

*To the apple of my eye,
Mummy.'*

'You have a good cry, Miss Maude, and get it out the way,
don't want you grizzling in church.'

She hugged Mira.

'Let's be getting you into your finery. Jonathan's been up
early getting everything up to the mark. The sun's shining
and it's going to a real country wedding.'

Maude smoothed down the folds of her dress and looked
at herself in the mirror, before Mira fixed the veil in place.
She was surprised to find that she was pretty, with her face
flushed and dark hair shining. Her mother's cross glinted
against her neck, and the bodice of her dress was like a satin
skin, emphasising her breasts and the neatness of her waist.

She even moved differently. On the dressing-table was a bottle of Lily of the Valley perfume that Daniel had given her. Experimentally, Maude dabbed the stopper behind her ears. 'How do I look?' she asked the woman who had known her since childhood.

'A picture, that Daniel will be overcome, I'm thinking. Now, your father wants a word before we sets off, so I'll give him a call before we fixes on your veil.'

'Oh, my Maude, you look so lovely. How are you feeling, happy I hope?'

'Pa, you remembered, I didn't want you in uniform,' she cried, rushing into his arms.

Her father looked utterly different from the military figure that everyone was accustomed to seeing in Portsmouth. Instead of the gold braid and navy-blue cloth of the admiral he was in a grey flannel suit and matching waistcoat, and looking every inch the country gentleman.

'This is your day, in your home among friends, my dear girl. The navy has no place in it. I would have walked down the aisle with you dressed as a chimney-sweep if needs be. Are you nervous?'

'I'm not now – not with you here, Pa. Do you know Mummy left a letter for me with Mira? Wasn't that wonderful?'

He smiled. 'How typical of her, even when so ill to think of her daughter. You are very like her, with the same sweetness and underneath that, a steely determination. She was my love and my conscience, always requiring the best in me, and I think you will do the same for Daniel. He is a good fellow who needs to get away from his father, an ossified armadillo if ever I saw one. Your foreign posting will give you breathing space, and by the time you return the old man will be retired.'

When Mira had fixed on her veil, Maude picked up her bouquet of roses and maidenhair fern and walked carefully down the stairs.

Awaiting her in front of the house was Jonathan, resplendent in a yellow waistcoat, a new jacket and riding-breeches. The little trap had been polished and white ribbon plaited through the pony's mane. Horse-brasses gleamed.

She kissed him. 'Jonathan, it looks splendid. Thank you so much.'

'Morning, sir, morning, miss.' He smiled, and raised his ribboned whip in greeting. 'Miss Maude, you looks a proper Kentish maid. Are we ready?'

Sitting up in the trap beside her father, she gripped his hand before turning to take a last look at her home. 'Drive on,' she said.

Daniel had not slept. He stood at the mirror, razor in hand, staring at his lathered face. He wanted to marry Maude for all the wrong reasons. She was his dear friend and his shield against his father. Was friendship enough? And, what of desire? They had kissed now and then, hugged each other even, yet he had had not the slightest wish to carry things further. Well, it had gone too far now to pull out, and on what grounds could he do so? What he needed was distance. In the last few weeks he had been filled with anxiety. Making decisions of any kind seemed impossible. He had to get away.

After their honeymoon, a weekend in Plymouth, they would board the ship for his posting to the Ascensions – a small space of time between one life and the next. He vacillated between desperately wanting to marry her and wanting to escape, with an equal frenzy. Lying in bed at night he would wake suddenly, his pulse racing and his body covered in sweat. What was wrong with him? He had desired Fidelis but when he had last seen her, looking so pale and sickly, he had been revolted. Her news had panicked him. He was ashamed at his relief when she rejected his offer of money. Then had come the fight with Harry Dawes. He had Fidelis's father to thank that he was here at all. Daniel remembered the ill-disguised contempt in Jack McCauley's eyes when he handed him his jacket. All in all, he had made an unholy mess of things.

A knock on the door had him leaping in alarm. Christ! What if it was his father wanting to give him advice?

'Come in,' he called.

'Hello darling, may I come in?'

He sat down, weak with relief. 'Mother, how good to see you.'

Alicia bent to kiss him, then laughed as she wiped the shaving-soap from her mouth. 'Are you feeling panicky?' she said, taking up his razor. 'You were always keyed-up before going back to school. Is this standard panic or something more serious?' She slid the razor smoothly down his cheek.

'I wish I was going back to school now,' he sighed.

'I think that you and Maude will do well together. She understands you better than you know yourself.'

'I just don't feel worthy of her.'

His mother laughed, and some of his anxiety leaked away.

'The thing to do, Daniel, is to become worthy. Try and focus your attention away from yourself, think what she may be feeling. Consider what is in her best interests instead of your own.'

'There's something else.'

Alicia swished the razor in the water before shaving the other side of his face. 'I rather thought it was *someone* else.'

'You knew?'

'One doesn't have to be Sherlock Holmes to pick up clues, here and there. The barracks is a small incestuous world and there are many windows. It is Fidelis McCauley, I think. She has recently lost her mother, I believe. What has she to do with today?'

'She's having my child. I tried to offer her money, I know

that she will be in difficulties because of me but she wouldn't take it. I honestly thought that I loved her, but I never said that I would marry her.'

'Actions have consequences, Daniel. She will feel shamed by you, and her child will have the stigma of illegitimacy. I don't think there is anything you can do in regard to Fidelis, you have done more than enough. Fortunately for you, she has a good father and will not be left destitute. I believe there is a fiancé in the background. Who knows? He may prove to have the maturity that you are lacking.'

He winced under her reproach.

'What you must do now is study Maude's happiness. Try to be a good husband to her. You never know, one day you may come to love her and in the meantime you might develop some self-respect.' She handed him the towel. 'I will see you in church, Daniel. A few prayers may not go astray.'

And then she was gone.

In spite of her rebuke he felt a sense of relief. He could breathe more easily – yet nothing had changed. His mother had just altered the focus of his thoughts, as if he were a pair of binoculars needing repair. She was right – Fidelis was in the past. This was his wedding-day and Maude was waiting.

Daniel dressed carefully before going along the hotel corridor to his best man's room.

'Guy, are you there?'

'Come in, Daniel, my word, how dashing you look. Miss Palmer will faint at the sight of you. You look the very model of a model major general.'

'So speaks the debonair Captain Margrave. I shall have to protect the bridesmaids.'

The two men walked down the stairs and out of the hotel and followed the road towards the church.

'Have you seen the bridesmaids, Daniel? Am I likely to be overwhelmed?'

'They are a mystery to me, Guy. Maude has kept them a closely guarded secret.'

The church was full, and he could feel everyone watching them as he and his friend walked up the aisle and took their seats. He knelt in the front row and closed his eyes, trying to gather his thoughts. The organ wheezed out the wedding march, and a ripple of expectation passed through the congregation. Getting to his feet, he stepped out into the aisle and waited for Maude to join him.

31

Fidelis lay awake, listening to the sound of the sea washing the shore below her window. It was the one connecting thread between her new surroundings and her old.

She was on holiday. Normally her one free week a year would have been spent at home, but she was not living in normal times.

'When is your holiday, Fidelis?' Dorcas had asked, one day soon after Harry's return.

'It's the first week in August. I don't know what I'll do. I would have gone home and had a day out with Pa or met up with Shamrock, or even gone out with Ruby but,' her voice trailed away, 'I don't know.'

'I wondered if you might like to spend it with me on the Island? I had planned to have your friends from Kelmscott over for a picnic.' She laughed. 'It promises to be a lively time.'

'I've never had a real holiday, not going away and things, that would be lovely.' It had been something to look forward to, and now it was here. This was her first night in Fortitude Cottage. Taking a blanket from the bed she stood out on the balcony, listening to the waves rising and collapsing on the beach below. The sea had always been a part of her life and she could not imagine living away from it. Dorcas had spoken of bathing naked, and the silky feel of the water against her skin. The thought appealed to her, but would she ever feel comfortable enough with her new friend to try it? Feeling chilled, she went back to bed, leaving her curtains and window open.

On wakening in the unfamiliar bedroom she was seized by a nameless anxiety. What would she do with herself? Never had she woken without knowing what the day held for her. She longed to fill this shapelessness with something, anything to distance herself from her treadmill thoughts. When was she supposed to get up? Could she make herself some tea? Would it be all right if she wandered out onto the beach? Although she and Dorcas had often talked for hours together, here she felt shy with her. What, apart from being two unmarried females, had they in common?

Slipping her feet into her boots, she crept down the stairs. The wood-stove had been cleaned out and relit, and a full kettle set on the hob. Fidelis was surprised to find the back door wide open yet no sign of her friend. After hurrying across to the privy, she returned to the kitchen and made a pot of tea. Carrying the kettle upstairs she washed and dressed, then tidied her bed.

'Hello Fidelis, I've been up since dawn, walking. I've brought you some cowslips. Aren't they glorious? See, the dew is still on them; they smell divine.' She took up the teapot. 'Good, you have made yourself at home. Ready for breakfast?'

She nodded, feeling the shyness slipping away.

'What shall it be? Bread and honey, or how about a Beningfield throw-together?'

'What's that?'

'It consists of whatever is to hand, well-seasoned and fried together.'

'My Pa would call it "banyan".'

'There you are, we shall take turns in cooking, and by the end of your stay the Fortitude Cottage cookery book will be mightily expanded.'

She watched Dorcas in a faded blue dress, her hair tied back with a piece of string, assembling her dish. There were eggs, some cold potatoes, mint leaves, tomatoes and a few mushrooms and marmalade.

'Don't look so scandalised. I have an adventurous approach I grant you, but some times the result is quite wonderful.'

'How about the other times?'

Dorcas laughed. 'A cowpat would be more appetising. But experimentation is my watchword.'

'My Ma used to make everything so carefully, weighing and measuring, but Pa used to do cooking by pinches and handfuls.'

'Exactly so. If you will get down the plates from the dresser and cut us some slices of bread from the crock over there, we'll be well on our way. The butter is out in the garden in the safe.'

The throw-together was delicious, but Fidelis could have done without the marmalade. She ate two slices of bread-and-butter and rubbed the crust around her plate. While Dorcas tended the garden, she washed up and swept out the kitchen.

'I'm going to do some writing now for the next couple of hours – you are free to do whatever you like. This afternoon we can go into Ventnor and get some fresh supplies. We can go swimming or fishing, there are a hundred things to do here.'

'Can I sort out the kitchen?'

Dorcas laughed. 'If you want to, but I'm getting you out in air this afternoon. I want your father to see a change in you when you go home next Sunday. Holidays are about doing different things.'

Fidelis boiled up some water on the stove and, while it was heating up, took down the curtains and carried the chairs out into the garden. It felt like play rather than work, since it was self-chosen. Soon the curtains were washed and spread out to dry, one on a lavender bush and the other on a clump of rosemary. There seemed no rhyme or reason to the cupboards, and after she had scrubbed them out she imposed her own idea of order. On top of the book-case in the sitting-room she found a straw hat and tied it under her chin. Mixing up some vinegar water, she cleaned the windows. Bees buzzed about her and a butterfly flitted past. Fidelis felt a lightness of spirit and a shifting of the dread that had lain coiled in her stomach. The worst had happened, and she had not been struck down by a thunderbolt. Pausing between one task and the next, she rested in the moment. Being there was enough.

'It smells wonderful: beeswax polish, lavender and rosemary and just clean,' said Dorcas, standing barefoot in the doorway. 'Sit down, Fidelis, while I draw us off a bucket from the well. You will be amazed at how cold the water is.'

'That was so fresh,' she gasped, 'and like ice.'

'Are you ready for shopping? We'll take plenty of bags and buy up whatever Ventor has to offer.'

They climbed down the steps at the back of the house, and up the hilly road into the town. The afternoon was hot and Fidelis was glad of her hat.

'When we've got our supplies I think refreshments will be needed so we'll go to Graham's Buttery: the cakes are divine. Speaking of which, I thought we might get some baking things, you might like to make something for when our friends come.'

'I'm feeling a bit anxious about that. I haven't been to see them in ages, and they don't know about my baby,' she said, when they stopped to rest on a bench.

'This will be the perfect time to tell them, don't you think?'

Fidelis squirmed. 'It's not just the baby, it's that I carried on with someone else while Harry was away. What will Eileen think? She's ever so funny about that sort of thing. And, Midge, she thinks I'm special.'

'They're your friends, Fidelis. Granted it will be a surprise but I'm sure they'll support you. Cook will likely make some clothes for the little one. And after all, Mabel Hobbs was a married woman and there's little that would make her blush.'

'I'm frightened they'll judge me and think I've been deceitful.'

'So it's pride talking here. You have been their beautiful talented friend, and now they are going to find out that you have fallen off the pedestal they put you on.'

'Something like that,' mumbled Fidelis.

'You'll survive. You're tougher than you think, I'm sure of it. Ready for some more walking? Remember, we've got Mrs Graham's cakes to look forward to.'

Dorcas strode on with no sign of tiring, and soon they were in the little hilly town, walking down from Albert into Victoria Street.

'Mad for the royalty are the people on the Island, what with the family spending so much time over at Osborne House. It's brought a lot of trade and visitors over.'

It took an hour or so to gather together vegetables, meat and bread from the small shops in the high street, and then it was off to the buttery.

'Take your time, Fidelis, there are so many cakes to choose from. I could recommend them all,' Dorcas said, as she studied the menu.

'Lavender sponge, please, it sounds like something out of a book. What colour will it be?'

'Wait and see.'

When it arrived it was a normal sponge cake with white icing streaked through with lavender flowers. The flavour was intense, and she could not describe exactly how it tasted except that it left a gritty feeling in the mouth. She looked around her and saw that there were paintings on the walls. Some of them were enthusiastic daubs and others quite skilful. Her eye was drawn to the one above the empty fireplace. It was of a child of perhaps nine years old, a dark-haired gypsy-looking girl holding a shell in her hand. She was studying it with great attention. Fidelis could see that the painting was exceptional. The detail was astonishing; the traces of sand on one bare foot, the way the seaweed looked freshly pulled from the water, and the sense of total absorption of the child in the shell. She got up and went over to read the title on a gold tablet set in the frame: 'Dorcas' by Sir Marcus Beningfield R.A. 'It's you,' she cried, delighted at her discovery.

'Yes, on the beach here during one of our endless summers. Daddy painted it. We were more or less on our own that year. Mummy was a doctor in the East End of London and had caught the measles from one of her patients. She was in the cottage all the time in a darkened room. Mrs Graham was a great friend of ours, and looked after Mummy while I played with her children.'

'Did you have a happy family?'

'Oh yes, indeed, I was an only child but there were always aunts and uncles and cousins. Our house was always full of exciting people. You would have loved Uncle Raphael, Phoebe's father. He was very kind and told wonderful stories. There were painters and writers, and I was like a sponge soaking up all the ideas: socialism, home rule and free love. Sometimes I would go with Mummy and see the poverty among the people she visited. Children with no clothes, let alone shoes, whole families living in one room, and the mothers under-fed and exhausted. Even then I wanted to change things.'

'Do you think they can be?'

'Yes, they must change, and those of us who have come

from privileged homes owe it to our neighbours to fight for them, don't you think?'

'I suppose so,' she said doubtfully. Her own experience of the rich had shown her that Dorcas and Mrs Mount were the exception in their interest in the poor.

'We must get things changed so that women get proper child-care. The need for clean water and proper housing requires us to campaign out on the streets, outside Parliament. If women get the vote and get elected to Parliament these things can be changed, must be changed.'

Fidelis licked her fingers and ran them over the plate to rescue the crumbs. She could see that Dorcas would set people on fire with her enthusiasm. Most of the speakers she had heard in public either got ignored or ridiculed.

'Fidelis, you must stop me when I get on my hobby-horse. This is your holiday. We'll go and sit on the pier for a while then walk home in easy stages.'

They sat in deckchairs with the shopping at their feet. Fidelis had severe indigestion and regretted her lavender cake. 'You said something about the Undercliff. What is it?'

'It's a natural terrace, formed millions of years ago when the whole face of St Catherine's Down fell into the sea. We'll walk the road along it one day. It's seven miles long and quite wonderful, winding up and down along the ledge and full of surprises, sudden woody areas and then rocky drops with great boulders lying about.'

'It seems strange to me looking out at an empty horizon. Walking along the seafront at home, I have the Isle of Wight on one side and Hayling Island on the other. How far away is France?'

'About sixty miles, beyond the reach of the pier telescope, certainly.'

'All these grand hotels, who stays in them?'

'Wealthy invalids, some of them attending the sanatorium

on a daily basis, and of course, people visiting patients there. A whole host of different folk, I should think. Young couples on honeymoon, and families glad to escape from the cities.'

Dorcas got to her feet. 'Fidelis, you're beginning to look quite pink. We should get into the shade.'

They walked home in easy stages, resting often on benches by the roadside. By the time they climbed up the steps from the beach to Fortitude Cottage, Fidelis felt sleepy and her indigestion had passed.

'I'd better get the meat into the wall-safe or it will be quite spoiled. Pour us some water, will you please.'

The cottage was dark and the water wonderfully fresh.

'Fidelis, go and have a sleep. I'll have our dinner ready by six. Open the window and close the curtains and it will be cool.'

She lay in her shift on top of the covers, feeling luxurious. Fancy lying in bed in the afternoon and not being sick. The morning had been fun, and there were five and a half more days.

As she was drifting between sleep and wakefulness she became aware of a faint stirring across her belly. Was it the lavender cake? Or was it quickening? Fidelis lifted up her shift and pressed her fingers across her stomach, and concentrated her attention. For a while nothing happened, and she had almost thought it was her imagination when there was again a fluttering. It was her baby, a real live being. The realisation that she was its mother and that its life depended on her was overwhelming. She cried with pity for her child. All her thoughts had been for herself and how she would be affected. All the time her baby, unwanted and unloved, clung to life. Lying there, something her own mother had said to her came to mind.

'You have it in you to be such a fine young woman.' What did that mean in her present situation?

'Hey, sleepy-head, supper's ready. It's way past six but I didn't want to wake you.'

Fidelis was stunned. Hastily she dressed and joined her friend at the table in the garden. 'Ooh! It's delicious, the lamb chops are so sweet. I didn't know I was that hungry.' Later she washed up while Dorcas poured them both a glass of cider.

'Something happened today,' she said shyly, when they sat together with their drinks in the cool of the evening. 'My baby moved.'

'How wonderful, how did you feel?'

'Frightened at first, then everything became real and it was – I don't know. My feelings changed towards it, my baby.'

'How had you been feeling?'

'Angry, disappointed with myself, and bitter towards it.'

'So how do you feel, now?'

'I realised that I was its mother, and my baby depends on me to look after him.'

'Did you love your royal marine, Fidelis, and did he love you?'

'Both of us loved each other, I know we did. I can't say that I'm glad it happened or that I'm not still frightened, but I feel more hopeful of being able to cope.'

Dorcas looked thoughtful. 'How would it be if you came and stayed here until your baby is born? You could house-keep for me, which would not be very taxing, and I'm sure you could do some washing or sewing for one of the ladies hereabouts. The sort of thing your mother did, delicate things.' She waved her hand. 'Don't make up your mind yet, sleep on it and speak with your father when he comes over.'

That night she slept soundly; and the days flashed by, filled with walking and talking. One afternoon, she went up to the cemetery and took some roses and honeysuckle from Dorcas's garden. Kneeling by her mother's grave she no longer felt angry, but sad that she was no longer there to guide her.

She thought how, if the baby were Harry's and he were away from her, she would be writing to him about all the minute changes in her life and about the holiday. Instead she wrote to him every day, as a friend, pouring out her feelings, good and bad, and sealing each letter in an envelope although she knew she did not have the courage to post them. But writing them seemed to help.

And then it was Friday and the picnic.

'Cor! Don't you look well, Fee,' said Cook, giving her a hug when she went to meet them at the station. 'Air over here must agree with ya. Put on weight, too, if I'm any judge.'

Fidelis blushed, and busied herself talking with the old cabman who had waited outside the cemetery on the day of her mother's funeral. 'Dorcas wants you all to stop off at the cottage first and have a cup of tea before going down to the beach.'

'Good idea,' sniffed Eileen. 'I'm that thirsty. Hello Fee, good to see you.'

'I'm busting for a wee,' said Midge, hugging Fidelis enthusiastically.

Arriving at the cottage, Midge leapt out and rushed over to Dorcas.

'Likes your place, it's like out of a storybook. Can I use your privy? Then, can I look round the cottage?'

She laughed. 'Of course you may. Cook, Eileen, all of you, welcome, welcome. The kettle is boiling. Let me show you where the toilet is. It's a long journey.'

After their tea all three of them processed through the cottage, exclaiming at the views through the windows, admiring the paintings, and giving it their approval.

It was quite a performance getting the bags of food, sunshades and rugs down onto the sand, but by twelve o'clock they were settled. Midge used a trowel and became absorbed in building a sand-castle, while Cook brought out her knitting.

'It's another world over here,' said Eileen. 'Even smells different.'

Dorcas followed later with a jug of tea.

'You got a little bit of paradise here, Miss Dorcas,' said Cook, helping herself to another cucumber sandwich. 'This is a rare treat.'

'You make this cake, our Fee? asked Midge, spraying crumbs everywhere. 'Can I have another bit?'

Eileen smiled. 'You looks ever so well. How's your Harry?'

It was a shock to find out that none of them knew about the broken engagement.

'Won't be long,' said Dorcas. 'I'll go back up and bring us some fresh tea. The salty air gives one quite a thirst, don't you think?'

Fidelis seized the moment to tell them what had happened. 'I've got something to tell you,' she said. 'I'll have to leave work soon, because I'm having a baby.'

'My stars,' said Cook, 'you're a dark horse. How d'you manage that with your fiancé over the water?'

'Mabel!' sniffed Eileen, indignantly, 'that's not your concern.'

'Blimey, who was it?' Midge asked, her face alive with curiosity.

Fidelis blushed. 'It doesn't matter now, because he's gone away.'

'Oh, Fee, you silly girl,' Cook said, looking as if she were about to cry. 'That poor Harry, he must be that upset. What was you thinking of?'

Fidelis blushed, and felt that she had somehow let them down. 'I just wanted you to know before I speak to Miss Phoebe.'

The thought that they had been taken into her confidence seemed to pacify them.

Cook reached forward and patted her arm. 'Well, my gal, you'll have your work cut out looking after a baby on your own.'

'I expect I will, but my Pa and Shamrock will help me.'

'He came round the other night, did your Dad. Lovely feller. If I was a few years younger, I'd snap him up.'

Everyone laughed and the tension eased. By the time Dorcas returned with the tea they were once more chatting happily together.

Dorcas insisted on travelling back with them to the station, while Fidelis cleared the tea-things and began to cook the supper.

They all three of them hugged her, before leaving.

'Bye, Fee, see you over the other side,' said Cook. 'I'll get something for your nipper started soon as I've cast off what I'm doing.'

'You take care of yourself,' Eileen said, 'and don't let Miss Phoebe put on you. I know what she's like.'

'You'll let us have a hold of your baby when it comes, won'tcha?'

''Course I will, Midge, 'bye now.'

Suddenly the rest of the week rushed by, and she was standing at Ryde Pier saying goodbye to Dorcas.

'It's been just what I needed,' she said. 'I feel tons better and able to cope.'

''Bye, Fidelis. I have so enjoyed your company. We've become firm friends, haven't we. Now, don't forget to think about coming here when you finish work, and your father can visit you as often as he likes. Think of it as your second home.'

Sitting on the steamer, watching Portsmouth harbour drawing nearer, she felt all her responsibilities falling again on her shoulders. In Ventnor it had been so simple – but that was just a holiday; now she must face real life again and the vagaries of employment with Phoebe Allen.

32

Phoebe blushed: this was ridiculous. She turned away on the pretext of studying her programme, and then when she looked up again he was still smiling at her. Who was he? It was a charity event for the South African Women and Children's Distress Fund, for goodness sake. Her mother and Dorcas were there. How was it possible at such a dull event that someone could be flirting with her? The man was decidedly handsome, and had an air about him that indicated an appreciation of women and what pleased them. Once this awful matron had finished desecrating 'One fine day in spring-time', it would be the interval, and everyone would start circulating.

It was so strange. She had had no intention of attending, but then Daphne had come up with this wonderful idea.

'We have to speculate, Phoebe. A big event at the Queen's Hotel: all the monied people will be there. It will be the perfect occasion to throw the spotlight on *Maison-Belle*.'

'But everything will be for fund-raising, we shan't make a penny.'

'Ah! This is where it we show ourselves to be a little business with a big heart. There will be at least a hundred people there. We will get there early and leave a business card on every seat. Then comes the climax. We'll auction one of our best quilts for the cause, and do *Maison-Belle* no end of good. Our next party is only weeks away in October. Think how many potential customers may be there.'

She had to hand it to her, Daphne was a marvellous businesswoman, and their little enterprise was beginning to reap rewards. There were tedious aspects to it, like the preparation and clearing up after parties, but soon she was going to employ a live-in maid who would help with all that.

It was lucky Fidelis was back from her holiday and could look after Sophie tonight. Phoebe smiled. She had a feeling she might be out rather late.

'Ladies and gentlemen,' said her mother, 'it is now the interval, and after you have partaken of the excellent buffet generously provided by our hosts, the Queen's Hotel, we will hold the auction. It is with great pleasure that I introduce to you Mr Paul Velmar, who will be appearing at the Theatre Royal next week, who has generously agreed to be our auctioneer.'

The rest of her mother's speech passed her by. It was him – the man who had winked at her. Phoebe could barely control her excitement. She got to her feet and drifted towards the buffet table with as much nonchalance as she could muster.

'May I help you to some food, dear lady? It looks delicious, doesn't it?'

His eyes were the colour of the Amontillado sherry, and his voice was deeply seductive. She nodded her consent.

'I always think one eats with one's eyes, don't you agree? How cleverly they have arranged the delicacies, contrasting the pink salmon with the green asparagus and the quails' eggs. What can I tempt you to, or shall I choose for you?'

'I am in your hands entirely,' she said, enjoying herself hugely.

They stood in a corner slightly apart from the rest of the audience, in an enchanted bubble.

'You have the advantage over me of knowing my name. What shall I call you?'

'I am Phoebe Allen.'

'How appropriate, Phoebe the sun goddess, with your

golden tresses. Tell me what does a goddess do on a Saturday evening? Where should we go for further delectation?'

She giggled, he was utterly absurd. There had been an article in the paper about a discreet little club above the Cremona Supper Rooms. It catered to the late-night crowd, and was more exclusive than the downstairs facilities. What had intrigued her was the glass roof enabling one to dine beneath the heavens. 'There is a new place that I have heard about called the Starlight Lounge. It sounds fun.'

'Darling, come over and let me introduce you to a potential customer. Do excuse us, Paul.'

Phoebe could have hit her mother. Obediently, she prattled on about *Maison-Belle*, all the while desperately trying to extricate herself. At any moment the interval would be over and Paul Velmar would slip through her fingers.

As she was about to resume her seat in a fury of disappointment, he passed close by her and slipped a piece of paper into her hand. All through the auction she was conscious of it nestling in her pocket.

At the end, Phoebe kissed her mother. 'It was a triumph, Mummy, and I'm so glad that it went well for you. Two hundred pounds is splendid and, of course we have given *Maison-Belle* a little spotlight. Lots of the cards have been taken up, and Daphne says there were ten people during the interval who said they would come to our next party.'

'Darling, that's splendid. Come around to lunch on Sunday with Sophie. Dorcas will be with me. She was so interested in your new venture.'

'Yes, of course I will. Must go now, I'm frightfully tired.'

'Phoebe, where d'you think you're going? There are things we must decide.' Daphne had that sour look that made her want to hit her.

'Have breakfast with me tomorrow, my sweet, and you shall have my full attention.'

Having to run the gauntlet of her family and of her business partner, she almost didn't make it to the cab around the corner in Nightingale Road, where as promised in his billet-doux, Paul waited for her.

'What a popular woman you are, Phoebe,' he said, as he helped her into the seat beside him, 'but I want a piece of you, too. I presume you are a night-owl — or shall we have to be home by midnight?'

Careful, you know nothing about him, a voice warned her. Don't let him know where you live just yet. 'Oh, I am a creature of the night,' she said, feeling again that tingle of excitement that she had not experienced for a very long time. She was getting into deep waters. Paul was dangerous, but that was part of his charm.

'Very well, the Starlight Lounge it is.'

Phoebe almost walked out when she saw Shamrock moving between the tables. But having committed herself thus far she could not draw back. She was not ready for Paul Velmar to know any more about her than she chose to tell him. Certainly he must not know she had money, or that there was a child in the background. Her address must remain a secret until she knew where this tentative liaison was going.

Looking around the dimly-lit room she did not recognise anyone she knew. James's old cronies would be at some gaming club. Her escort helped her out of her coat and held out a chair for her.

A waiter came to their table, and Paul ordered them both a double gin and tonic.

'I had gone there this evening expecting to be bored silly, and then I saw you.' He took her hand and twisted her wedding-ring around her finger. He gave a regretful frown. 'All the most desirable people one meets are spoken for, don't you find?'

Phoebe smiled. She was not going to be drawn. 'It depends

on what you want,' she hedged. 'Desire is such an individual thing.'

'It's a mixture of things, isn't it?' He kissed her fingers one by one. 'It can be the eyes or the voice, a perfume, or a certain air of something promised and something withheld.'

She felt like a swimmer being drawn away from the shallows towards deeper, less certain waters. 'Perhaps it's better left unsaid.' She looked away. He really did have the most mesmerising eyes.

'Is Portsmouth your native soil?' he asked, as the waiter arrived with their drinks.

'My parents came from London but settled here before I was born. But I don't want to exchange histories. Let's be mysterious strangers a while longer.' Phoebe knew that the more enigmatic one was, the more certain one could be of landing a catch.

Her companion smiled. 'Don't worry, my darling, I am in no hurry, no hurry at all. Shall we try some of the Starlight's steak patties? They sound divine.'

Shamrock watched Phoebe Allen with a certain misgiving. She was a lamb playing in front of a lion with Paul Velmar. There had been trouble at the People's Palace with that snake in the grass. One of the dancers had been taken in by his fake charm. The police had been involved, but didn't the silly girl get talked out of bringing charges at the last minute? Pretty thing she was, not unlike Mrs Allen. Shamrock sighed. Why should she care? What was the woman to her? Only that she had admired her for having Jimmy's body brought home and giving him a decent funeral. Warning her off would be difficult. The attraction of the Starlight Club was its air of being slightly beyond the law. Names were never given out to others and conversations not repeated. She and Dapper were just feeling their feet in a new milieu, and must tread carefully. If confidentiality could not be counted on they might as well shut up shop. And the last thing they wanted was failure rubbing off on his well-established supper rooms.

She was on the verge of making some risky investments; one by slipping her shoes under Dapper's bed and the other by lending him some money. That was why she was relieved to know that Fee was going to be settled elsewhere. If the worst came to the worst she could sell her house in Buckle Street now, without leaving her niece in the lurch.

'Hello, my gal, how's it going, are you making my fortune?' Dapper slid through the door and kissed her on the cheek, before glancing around the room.

'We're shifting those patties of yours. Funny how just making them smaller and charging twice the price works up here. See Velmar sweet-mouthing Jimmy Allen's widow?'

'How long's his run at the Theatre Royal?'

'Six weeks, I think.'

'I'll be glad to be shot of him, the reptile. If there's any trouble, just blow that whistle. I'm only next-door in the office. We'll shut at two.'

Shamrock blew him a kiss. Dear Diamond, there was much more to him than sparkle; how much, she was beginning to find out. Watching Velmar go off towards the gentlemen's washroom, she walked across to Phoebe, uncertain as to what she should say.

'It's a long time, Mrs Allen, since I saw you. How is life treating you these days?'

'Very well, you must come to one of my parties, I'm sure we would have something to interest you among our stock.' Well, at least she was sober, and hopefully able to accept some friendly advice.

'Now, Mrs Allen, I want you to tread very carefully, there are some rough people about, people who don't take no for an answer. As to your parties, you just give me one of those fancy cards and I might drop in one day. 'Bye for now.'

A couple of naval officers toddled in and wanted a song, and so she did not see the going of Phoebe and Velmar. By three o'clock she was tucked up with Dapper and lost to the world.

When they got to Clarendon House it seemed churlish to leave Paul Velmar standing on the pavement. After warning him to be quiet, they crept into the sitting-room and she offered to make some coffee. By the time she came back from the kitchen with a tray he was sound asleep on the couch.

Slightly foozled, Phoebe shut the door and crept upstairs to bed. What fun it had been, her first foray into the world of men. She must wake up early and get him out of the house, or she would scandalise Fidelis. Laying her clothes on the chair, she slipped into her nightdress and fell thankfully into bed.

It was such a muddly dream: James was there with her, kissing her, but somewhere in the back of her mind she knew he was dead. He felt so real, the weight of him. She fought her way up out of sleep. Something wasn't right. It was his smell. James hated gin, and would never kiss her if she had drunk it. First, she must rinse her mouth and clean her teeth and even then . . .

'Sweetheart, don't struggle we're nearly there, nearly there.'

'Aaghh!' It wasn't James. Gasping and pushing against the man in her bed, Phoebe was terrified. He smelled sweaty and was so heavy. She must get him off her, she must.

'Lie still! Lie still!'

'No, no,' she screamed. Her arm waved about over the bedside table, trying to get hold of the lamp. If she could just push it onto the floor the noise of breaking glass might alert Fidelis, sleeping across the passage, to her plight. Paul was grunting with the effort of hauling up her nightdress, while still crouching over her. As he wrestled it free, his fingernails scraped her thighs. Phoebe turned her head from side to side trying to break loose of his hand, now clamped across her mouth. She tried to punch his back but her blows bounced off him. In desperation she bit his hand.

He reared up and shouted, 'Bitch, I'll have you.'

Again she pushed against the lamp and it fell to the floor, but not before Paul Velmar had slapped her with all his strength.

Phoebe fought against the dizzying blow – she must stop him. As he punched her full in the face the door opened.

Suddenly the weight lifted, and there was roaring and shouting and doors slamming.

'Get out! Get out! Fetch the police I will!'

Fidelis was there, talking to her. At first she couldn't make out what she was saying. 'He's gone, now, yes he has. Listen, Mrs Allen! I hit him with the water jug and he cut his feet on the broken glass.'

Phoebe burst into tears. 'Oh Fidelis, I've been so foolish. Such a stupid, stupid woman.' She couldn't stop shaking.

The girl sat with her holding her hand. Just her presence was reassuring.

'Don't worry, I shan't tell anyone. I'll run a bath for you and you can soak it all away, then I'll bring you up some hot milk.'

By the time Phoebe had scrubbed herself clean and put on a fresh nightdress, Fidelis had changed the sheets and swept up the glass. Her face was creased with concern as she said, 'Why don't you sleep in my room for the rest of the night?'

'I don't deserve your kindness,' Phoebe whimpered, sitting up in her maid's bed, sipping the milk.

'We all make mistakes. I've made a very big one.'

Something in her voice cut through Phoebe's distress, and she looked at Fidelis.

'What do you mean, Fidelis?'

The girl stared at the floor. 'I'm going to have to leave you soon, on account of my having a baby.'

Phoebe was confused, perhaps it was the smack that Velmar had given her. She could still hear a ringing in her ears. 'But, I thought your fiancé was away.' She blurted out, amazed at the girl's revelation. 'Oh, I'm so sorry.'

For the first time in their five-year relationship, Phoebe touched Fidelis. Her words connected in Phoebe's mind with her own time in Brighton. She reached out and patted her shoulder. 'What will you do?' she asked.

'I'm going to live in Fortitude Cottage with Miss Dorcas, 'til after the baby is born. Then,' she shrugged, 'who knows?'

'When do you want to leave?' she asked. 'It's possible that I can find someone by the beginning of October. Will that suit you?'

'Yes, Miss Phoebe, that will be just right.'

'We shall miss you. You have been very faithful to me in spite of my foolishness.'

Fidelis smiled. 'She is a little love. I'll remember her always.' She took the cup from her and stood in the doorway. 'You'd best try and get some sleep. Good-night, madam.'

'Good night, Fidelis, and thank you so much.'

Lying in the little single bed after drinking the milk, Phoebe lay still shaking. What a worthless creature she was. So full of her own importance and then, just like before, she over-reached herself and left others to pick up the pieces. Somehow she had got to grow up.

33

It was November, and still Harry had not written to Fidelis or called around to see her. His rage had burnt itself out, and what was left was emptiness. There was no purpose now to his life beyond the Royal Marines. He was relieved to settle back into the barracks, and immerse himself in bugling and the training of his recruits. But now and then someone would ask the dreaded question.

'How's the missus? Heard you'd got spliced, how's it panning out?'

'Didn't work out,' he would pin a smile on his face. 'Lucky escape, mate.'

Walking down to Gibraltar Street was the real test of recovery. He dreaded and yearned to see Fee in equal measure. His mother never mentioned her, and Fee never visited her father, as far as he could see. It was as if she had died. Relations between the Dawes and the McCauleys were cool, to say the least. He knew that Ma had taken against Fee with a fury that astonished him, and had even told her she was not welcome, in her own street.

It had just made matters worse. Now he felt he had lost his mother as well as his fiancé. That warmth and closeness he had had with her all his life was gone. There was a side to Ruby Dawes that he had never thought to see; a harshness and self-righteousness that sickened him. Norman, caught between the two of them, was the Dad he always had been, and Harry went home as much to see him as anything else.

Every day he saw Jack McCauley, who greeted him with his usual friendliness. He wanted to ask him about Fee, but could not seem to create an opening whereby her name could be mentioned.

She had always been a part of his life, and he grieved for her. Every day of his childhood they had seen one another, and had probably waved from their prams as babies. It was only when he said goodbye to her three years ago that he realised their friendship had turned to love. That kiss on the jetty had been their first. Now, it was likely it would be their last. The hatred that had burned in him that morning on the beach had gone. He just wanted to see her and find out if there was a friendship worth rescuing. It was the fact of the baby that he couldn't grapple with. Every time he brought himself to the point of writing to Fee, or even calling on her, the unborn child stayed his hand. It was the undeniable proof of her unfaithfulness that would not go away.

Day by day, the lack of any resolution to his feeling wore away at him. He did his work, marching, bugling and training, with his usual thoroughness and pride. It was his only pride. But, there was no zest or enthusiasm in his life, no larking or back-chat, just a weary plodding.

One Thursday afternoon, late in November, he had some free time and wandered aimlessly out of the barracks gate.

'Harry, Harry, Jesus man, got cloth ears, have ya? I bin calling to you for the last five minutes. Where you off to?'

His spirits lifted at the sight of his old sergeant, nicknamed Daddy Gibb. He had been a stern but fair taskmaster, and winning his approval had been Harry's keenest wish as a young recruit. 'Hello, Sarge, it's good to see you. Let me buy you a pint.'

'That's the best offer I've had all day. Ya looks down in the mouth, lad. What's up with ya?'

'It's a long complicated story.'

'Well, lad, make it simple. Break it down for me. One thing I got is time, and you don't look to be going anywhere.'

Sergeant Gibb watched his most promising recruit, and thought about the bits of gossip that had come his way, and mulled them over. All the fire had gone out of the man. He hated talent wasted, and could see that things were critical. Lucky the pub was half empty and he had time to spare.

'Cheers, Harry, now what's been going off? I heard you was getting married, and then you wasn't, what's the truth of it?'

'While I was off in the West Indies she met this other bloke, and things got hot between them and now she's having his child.'

'That's a real facer. How long you known the girl?'

'All my life, we grew up together. She's Jack McCauley's daughter.'

'What, young Fee? So you was pals before you got to being sweethearts?'

Harry nodded. 'Only had one kiss before I went away, and then I proposed in a letter and sent her a ring. We were all set for the wedding in October.'

The sergeant paused to drink his pint, and wiped the froth from his mouth with the back of his hand. 'So as far as I can see it was all done on paper. You're old pals then all of a sudden you're getting married. Missed out a bit here, haven't ya?'

Harry frowned. 'Dunnow what you mean.'

'Getting to know each other, talking things over. Christ, Harry, there's a deal of difference between being pals and being sweethearts. Where did the getting engaged spring from? Strikes me that you knew her when she was a bit of a kid but you never got to know her as a woman, you left that for someone else to find out. She's been just a picture in your head, lad. This Fee is flesh and blood, and open to temptation same as all of us. And how about you out in the tropics. Don't tell me you didn't lust after some of those dusky maidens?'

'I kept myself for Fee,' said Harry defensively.

'Well, that was bloody noble of you, but you can't look me in the eye and say as you didn't think about it. How did this engagement malarkey come about?'

Harry paused before answering. If he were honest, he had drifted into it, as a way of making her exclusively his girl, and because of Ma's nagging letters. His girl – what a joke that had been. 'My Ma and Dad were pleased as Punch, and Fee's old man as well. Her mother even wrote me a letter saying as she would be proud to call me her son.'

'My God, Harry, are you wet behind the ears? For a grown man you take the bloody biscuit. Gonna be crowded walking up the aisle with your Ma and Pa, Aunt Fanny, and Christ knows who else. What about Fee? What did she have to say about it?'

'She was surprised and said she'd think about it.'

'All the while she thinking about what she felt, there's all the relatives stirring the pot. Let's back-track a minute. You said you picked out a ring and sent it her. How did you know what she wanted?'

'I didn't, I just thought . . .'

'Well, that's where you went wrong, all along lad. Went at it half-cock and it's blown up in your face.'

The talk with Daddy Gibb had not gone at all as he expected. It had not been a sympathetic hearing, more like teeth-pulling. 'Well, it's dead and buried now, what with her having his child.'

'So you've chucked in the towel? What's the other bloke going to do?'

'Got married, and gone off to the Ascensions, but I gave him a good hiding first.'

'You took a risk if it was the man I'm thinking about. Lucky you wasn't both court-martialled.' There was a pause, as he took out his pipe and tamped down the tobacco before lighting up. 'The real question in all this is, do you love her, and if you do, what are you going to do about it?'

'Can't stop thinking about her. It's just the baby.'

'Yes lad, but it's her baby, they come as a package. There's a sight more to being a dad than just dipping your wick. If you're the man I think you are, you'll take her and her child. If not, stop belly-aching, get on with your life, and leave her to someone with a bit more about him. While you're chewing on that I'll get us another drink.'

Later he walked along the beach, turning over what Daddy Gibb had said. It was true he had taken things for granted, and thought that friendship flowed seamlessly into love. All his thoughts still stalled at the thought of Herrick's child growing day by day, as a reproach to him and all his starry plans. But the old sergeant had opened up other aspects of his dilemma, ones that he had not even considered.

After chewing things over for another week, Harry decided to act. He had to do it straight away before he had time to think. There was enough wasted time already. Walking towards Clarendon House he rehearsed what he was going to say. In the end, he hoped that simply seeing her would drag the right words from him. What did he hope for? At the least, he wanted to see Fee and talk with her. Just being friends would do for a start. Perhaps that was all they should ever have been. Daddy Gibb's words had stung. If it had been anyone else, Harry would have hit him.

How had things been for Fee since their meeting on the beach? It was something he had not thought about. One by one, she had lost almost everyone who was important to her. What with Mary McCauley's death in May, his furious rejection of her, and then his own mother's vociferous scorn, the girl must be heart-broken. Well, at least she would be able to count on his friendship. All they had to do was get over the first hurdle, seeing and talking to one another.

As he drew closer to Clarendon Road his resolve began to weaken. What would he do if she didn't want to see him? Are you a man or a mouse, he chided himself.

'Yes, what d'you want?' The girl was sharp-faced, and not in the least friendly.

'I want to speak with Fidelis McCauley.'

'She's not here, wasted yer time.'

'When she likely to be back, then?'

'Gone, left, got a job over on the Island.'

For a few seconds he stood there, unable to think. It was as if the air had been sucked from his lungs. What could he do now?

She was about to shut the door when he put his foot against it.

'I want to speak with Mrs Allen.'

'What she want to see you for? Here, what you doin'?'

Harry pushed his way through the kitchen and into the hall. 'Mrs Allen, are you there?'

A voice from the top of the stairs called down to him. 'What are you doing in my house. If you don't leave this minute I shall call the police.' A slim woman with blonde hair peered at him over the banisters.

'Mrs Allen, I'm Harry Dawes. I was Fidelis's fiancé. I want to see her but she's gone.' His voice trailed away.

'Well, Harry, you had better go into the sitting-room and I will be down in a moment. Phyllis, bring us in a tray of coffee, if you please.'

He perched on the edge of a chair, sick with disappointment. It just felt such a waste of time, on top of all the days and weeks he'd wasted already. Why had she gone there, of all places?

'Good morning, Harry. I suggest you don't come striding into my house again, uninvited. However, as you are a friend of Fidelis I will say no more.'

'I'm very sorry, Mrs Allen, it was just that I'd got myself all keyed-up to see her.'

'Thank you, Phyllis, that will be all.'

He twisted his cap between his hands. Where had his impulsiveness got him, sat here like a stuffed dummy? Now that he had made up his mind to see Fee, all the delay was agony to him.

'Fidelis has been over in Ventnor now for over a month. What is your business with her?'

What did she mean? 'I just want to see her, Mrs Allen, to talk to her and explain how it's all been a bit of a shock and to see if we can be friends.'

'I see.' She poured the coffee into tiny cups and then looked up at him. 'Do you take sugar?'

'Two please.' He didn't even like coffee, and when he tried to drink it he almost gagged with the sweetness. Well, if he wanted to see her he would just have to suffer this genteel torture.

'I have a great deal of respect for Fidelis. She has been a most loyal and responsible nursemaid. I have come to like her very much, and I want what's best for her. Do you?'

'Of course I do.' He could see that she was just as Fee had described her, pretty in a dainty-doll style, and used to getting her own way.

'Well, Harry, I am a person who has made many mistakes and most of them have been brought about by impetuosity.' She smiled at him. 'I owe it to Fidelis to protect her, and to make sure that she wishes to see you before giving you her address.'

'I see.' Harry got to his feet wanting to slap her. 'I won't waste your time then, Mrs Allen.'

'So you are giving up, are you, without even trying to persuade me otherwise?'

'I want to see her, you won't tell me where she is, so it's stalemate.'

'I might remind you, Harry, that she is in Ventnor because she does not feel able to return home. I believe your mother has something to do with that? Sit down, please.'

'I'm sorry, I was just so disappointed.'

'Do you love her, Harry?'

'Yes, of course I do.'

'In that case you will have to be patient. Fidelis has made a mistake that has cost her dearly. She has been let down by those in whom she had put her trust, and is well aware of the hurt she has caused. Have you not made mistakes, Harry?'

'Of course,' he mumbled, angered that whatever he said seemed to put him in the wrong.

'What is needed now is compassion, not judgement.' She smiled at him. 'I will write to her and tell her of your wish to contact her. It will then be up to Fidelis to contact you. And now I should like you to leave.' Phoebe Allen tugged the bell-pull beside her chair. 'Goodbye, Harry. Remember a faint heart never won a fair lady.'

Ruby Dawes looked up from her ironing, as the front door was slammed shut. 'Hello Harry, what's up, you looks like a thundercloud.'

'I want to say something to you, Ma, all the way through with no interruptions. So, sit down and hear me out.'

She set down the iron and sat facing him across the kitchen table.

'I looked forward to coming home and seeing you and Dad and most of all, Fee. Then it all fell apart, what with

that Herrick bloke and the baby and the fight and everything. It took me a long, long time to calm down and begin
to sort out what I wanted to do about it. You thought you
was acting for the best by storming around to Fee's work
and tearing a strip off her, even saying as she shouldn't walk
down her own street.'

His mother's mouth was set in a firm line, and her eyes
glinted with suppressed anger.

'All that's happened now is that she's had to go and work
over in the Isle of Wight. You've made everything black-and-
white, and right and wrong, with me on one side smelling
of roses, and Fee on the other side tarred and feathered.
What's up with you? I always loved the way you thought the
best of everyone, I was proud of you. There was no one like
my mum. Now you're hard and angry and unforgiving.

'Now, I don't know what is going to happen between Fee
and me. Perhaps nothing, maybe friendship, maybe more, I
don't know. One thing I do know, I owe her a hearing. We
need to talk to one another, to get it all out in the open. I'm
not a saint, and she's not a bad girl. I'm going back up the
barracks and I'll see you on Sunday. Let's hope you'll have
had time to think about what I've said. I want my old mum
back, and I know she's still there, somewhere.'

He bent to kiss her cheek, then shutting the door quietly
behind him he marched up the street.

34

Fidelis looked at her efforts with satisfaction. All the decorations were either from the seashore or the hedgerows. There was a jug crammed with silver honesty leaves and orange Chinese lanterns. There were shells heaped along the windowledges and a tree decorated with red berries, fir cones and jasmine flowers. Branches of rosemary crackled on the fire, and a rabbit stew simmered in the stove. It was Christmas Eve and Dorcas had gone to meet Pa, leaving her to nap by the fire.

Life had settled into a routine, with Dorcas writing and sketching while Fidelis did the housework. There was also the washing she took in for one of the ladies at Steephill Castle. Fidelis had never seen the woman in question, but collected and returned the garments to the Lodge in return for her wages of two shillings a week. In between tasks she made clothes for her baby. Early in her stay, she sewed them on the balcony while listening to the sea. In the last couple of months, the colder weather drove her indoors by the fire. In those moments she was closest to her mother. Fidelis had thought herself so much her father's child, yet now she was moving very much to the ordered rhythm of Mary McCauley.

Still she kept up the letters to Harry that almost filled the box Dorcas had found for her. It was a deep sadness not to have heard from either Ruby or Harry, in all the months since his return. She placed her hands over her belly and said, 'Never mind, my pet. You and me have got each other and you have a dear granddad waiting to see you, and Auntie Dorcas. We shan't want for love.'

She wished that Ruby would come. Kind as Dorcas was, she had never been a mother. Having someone near who had given birth would be so reassuring.

May Goodale, the local woman whom the doctor had recommended she talk to, was not one for delicacy. When she enquired, shyly, where would the baby come out, her answer was blunt. 'He'll come out the same place as he was planted, my girl.'

She must have looked alarmed, for May grinned and patted her hand. 'It's what we're made for. You'd be mazed at how that body of yours can stretch itself. No need to be feared. It's hard labour and I 'spect you'll scream and curse, but once you hold that child in your arms the birthing of him will fade away like summer mist. That friend of yours is a good strong woman. We'll fetch him out, no trouble.'

Looking out on the grey December afternoon she was cheered to see a robin perched on the bird table, tugging at a bacon-rind she had put there earlier. 'You've got such treats to come, my little lamb. I wonder what you would think of this little robin with his cheery waistcoat.' She didn't know when she had begun talking to her baby. The habit had stolen up on her. Like thawing snow, her bitterness had melted, and now she was looking forwards to her child being born. Perhaps not the birth, that still filled her with vague forebodings, but seeing her child and naming it.

A rapping on the door roused her from her reverie.

'Come out, come out, wherever you are,' called her father, through the letter-box. Fidelis laughed at him as she swung back the door, and he took her in his arms.

'Hello my darling girl, and what a bright smiling creature you are.'

'Pa, it's lovely to see you. Now, Christmas can really start.'

Behind him was Dorcas, looking equally excited. She seemed to have become a part of their family.

Her father bent to kiss her, his face icy against her cheek.

'Oohh, step inside quick. You're letting in the cold.'

'Good, you've laid the table, I'll just put the shopping away and then we'll eat.' Dorcas bustled about, while Fidelis lit the candles on the table.

'It's good to be here,' said Pa, as he poured out the cider, 'in a safe billet out of the cold. And I tell you I'm raring for the feast I've been promised.'

'A one-pot meal, as always when I do the cooking,' smiled Dorcas. 'But Fidelis has excelled herself with the trifle.'

All three of them chatted together, exclaiming at the food and toasting one another. While Dorcas and Jack washed up, Fidelis lay dozing on the sofa. When the clock chimed ten she got Pa to help her to her feet, and waddled up the stairs. 'Don't forget to leave a mince pie for the reindeer,' she said kissing them both good-night.

In the morning Pa tapped on the bedroom door. 'Happy Christmas, my darling,' he called, before coming in and setting a tray on her lap.

Breakfast consisted of two pieces of toast cut in the shape of Christmas trees thickly spread with honey, and a cup of hot chocolate.

'How are you feeling, my Fee?'

'Happy-sad,' she said, knowing he would understand.

'Tell me.'

'I'm happy to be here and have you and Dorcas with me, but I want Ruby to come. I need her.' Fidelis began to cry, and her father set down the tray and took her in his arms. 'Ruby said to me last time, "now your Ma has died I'll be your mother,"' Fidelis burst out. 'I feel abandoned by her and Harry. It hurts that they won't forgive me. And other times I want to go over there and bang their heads together.'

'It seems to me that you're all waiting for the other one to make a move. They'll come round, I feel it in my bones.'

'Happy Christmas, Pa,' she said. 'I'll sing out when I'm ready for the inspection.'

The rug was warm under her bare feet and the fire crackled. Rubbing a soapy flannel over her body, Fidelis felt her baby moving beneath her fingers. Was that a knee or an elbow, she wondered, as her belly rose and fell. Smiling to herself, she dressed slowly and refilled the kettle.

'I'm going to give you a present, little one,' she said, and began to sings carols while dancing slowly round the room.

Dorcas appeared and then her father.

'Are we ready?' said Pa, taking the key of the shed from a cup on the dresser. 'You stay in the warm while we carry them in.'

The presents took her breath away. 'How did you make them without my knowing?' she gasped. 'They're beautiful.'

Set before her were a nursing-chair and a wooden rocking-cradle. The chair had been covered with material she had seen in Dorcas's room one day.

'The design is called the strawberry thief, it's one of my favourites.'

She hugged them soundly. 'I'm afraid my presents won't last, they're in the larder.'

Her father laughed at his cake made in the shape of a marine's pill-box cap with red and blue icing. 'Well, isn't that fine, and haven't I often said that I would eat my hat.'

For Dorcas she had constructed a bright yellow sun with a smile on its face. 'Because you are always lighting up our lives,' she said shyly.

'Thank you,' her friend said, 'thank you, both of you, for adding so much to my life.'

The two days of Pa's visit passed quickly, full of laughter, song and feasting. And then it was over and he held her in his arms.

'Goodbye, Fee, I'll be over for my birthday, just you hang on to the baby 'til then. No, don't come out in the cold, you stay in the warm. 'Bye my darling.'

She went upstairs to wave to her father from the back window until he was out of sight.

On the fourth of January, Dorcas was off to London to attend a meeting of the newly founded Women's Social and Political Union. She spoke constantly about the Pankhurst family who were the leading lights.

'They are so inspiring, especially Sylvia, the younger sister. If you saw the wonderful banners she has made you would know what I'm talking about.'

Although a little anxious about being left on her own Fidelis knew how important such meetings were to her friend, and had not the heart to dissuade her.

In spite of her eagerness Dorcas hesitated at the door. 'I'll go and leave a note for May Goodale on my way out, just to say that you're on your own. Failing that, there's Mrs Peters along the lane.'

Fidelis laughed. 'I'm not due for eleven days, yet. May says first babies are never in a hurry.'

'I'll be back first thing. Are you sure as sure that you've felt no twinges?'

She smiled at Dorcas's anxiety. 'Not a sign, it's much too snug inside to come out yet. 'Bye,' she said, pushing her down the path.

Singing to herself she washed the dishes and swept the floor. Upstairs again she looked at her baby clothes. Fidelis held a little jacket up to her nose and sniffed the new wool. Soon it would be buttoned across her baby's chest. She fell into a daydream, imagining holding the infant warm against her breast. Tears came into her eyes. Poor babe, how little it had been welcomed. Shame and condemnation were the responses from most people. Whatever she felt now towards Daniel, her child had been conceived in love. If it had been Harry's baby, Ruby would have guided her every step of the way. She could not fault Dorcas or May Goodale for their support, but what she had craved was Ruby's reassurance.

'I must give you a name, little one. What shall you be? Jack for a boy, I want you to be jolly like your Granddad and to have his tender heart. If you're a girl, I think Dorcas Mary, after my dearest friend and my mother. She was beautiful and full of skills, baking, sewing and gardening.'

By nine o'clock she had Pa's birthday cake out of the oven and cooling on the window-sill. As she walked across the kitchen, a rush of water ran down her legs and into her slippers. Fidelis stood looking at the puddle on the stone floor, feeling both excitement and terror. Soon May would call and if the worst happened she could ring her bell. It would have to be a dire emergency for her to call Mrs Peters at the end cottage. On glancing at her bare left hand, the woman had glared at her.

Fidelis told herself to be calm, there was plenty of time. Keeping busy would distract her. She made her bed, putting on the old sheets put aside for the birth. By eleven, both bedrooms were tidied and the furniture polished. She put the jam between the layers of her father's cake and dusted it with icing sugar. Her only sign of things to come was a low back pain, probably due to her frantic housework. After eating some soup and bread, Fidelis fetched her mother's rosary and she fell asleep on the sofa clutching it in her hand. A feeling that her stomach was being held in a vice wakened her. What should she do? After an hour or so free of pain she felt her fears were groundless. May Goodale would be calling soon, full of humour and good sense.

On a whim she got out the clothes-horse, then carried the cradle downstairs and hung the tiny clothes on the rails to warm. Whatever the turmoil ahead, there would be a child at the end of it needing something to wear. She was drinking some raspberry leaf tea when a strong muscular spasm gripped her. Fidelis didn't know whether to go to bed and lie down again on the sofa. Whatever she did her body was in control and the birth process had taken over. By half-past three she was exhausted and panicky. After filling her hot-water bottle she changed into her nightdress and went to bed. Fidelis clutched the rosary and prayed that someone would come.

When she opened the front door, Ruby was embarrassed to see Jack McCauley standing there. The sight of him always tugged at her conscience.

'Good morning, Ruby, may I come in?'

His question underlined the distance that had grown up between them.

'Is anything wrong?' she asked, feeling a twinge of fear. If anything happened to Fee she would never forgive herself.

He shook his head, 'Only this coolness between us. Ruby, I know Fee wronged Harry and hurt him deep. I don't excuse what she's done. But she's my girl, and I feel for her without a mother to show her the way of things,' he said.

'Her friend is away in London today and Fee will be on her own until I get there tomorrow. Could you find it in your heart to go and see her? I know Mary would have appreciated you giving her a bit of care. It would set my mind at rest if you went today.'

On the train from Ryde she thought about her neighbours, remembering the four of them in married quarters together, young newly-weds. Mary had been the dead spit of Fidelis, but without her warmth and the humour. But they had been friends.

As she walked up the path to the cottage her mouth felt dry with fear. How in God's name were they going to talk to one another? The front door was open. She walked through the kitchen and sitting-room, calling as she went. 'Fee, it's Ruby, where are you? Your Pa sent me.' Cautiously she climbed the stairs. The first bedroom was empty, and then from across the head of the stairs came the sound of crying. Pushing open the door, she looked down at the girl on the bed.

'Auntie Ruby, I prayed you'd come.'

'Hello Fee, tell me what's happened. D'you think the baby's coming?'

'My waters have broken, that was at nine this morning. Dorcas left a note for the nurse this morning and I don't know where she's got to.' Fidelis burst into tears. 'I'm so glad to see you, Aunt Ruby. I know I don't deserve you, I'm so sorry.'

It was gone – that hard knot of anger had dissolved the moment she saw her. 'I'm here now, my pet. So tell me, have you had any pains yet?'

'I had one about half an hour ago but nothing since, it seems they are about that time apart but I don't know.'

'Wouldn't you like to get up and wash your face and I'll plait your hair up out the way, make you feel nice and cool? While you're doing that I'll slip down to this May Goodale's and see if I can stir her into coming. Don't worry, my pet, I've helped a good few babies in my time. Just give me directions and I'll be back in a jiffy.'

When Ruby got to May Goodale's there was a note pinned to the door. *Over at Niton for birthing of twins left at seven this morning. Be back soon as. In emergency call Mrs Cleaver.*

Not knowing who or where the other nurse was, Ruby wrote on the bottom of the page, '*Come soonest Fortitude Cottage, labour well advanced. Mrs Dawes.*'

'I thought I should go back to bed until it came,' Fee said, when she went upstairs to look for her.

Ruby laughed. 'It's not going to be here in five minutes, love, you've got hard work ahead. Let's get you up and walking about a bit. I'll fix us both a sandwich.'

Fidelis felt weightless with relief. She had forgotten how comforting Auntie Ruby was. 'I prayed for you to come. There wasn't anyone else I wanted, just you.'

'Fee, you'll have us both blubbering, and a fat lot of use that would be.'

'I need to go down to the privy.'

Before going down to the kitchen, Ruby looked around the bedroom. It was cosy with its patchwork quilt and rag rug over the varnished floorboards. The walls were a cheerful yellow and there was a pot of white hyacinths on the dressing-table. Beside it was a carved wooden box. Curiosity had Ruby taking off the lid. It was filled with letters. She listened at the door before reading the name and address on each one of them.

'Auntie Ruby, I've forgotten, do you take sugar?' Fidelis called from below.

Hastily she replaced the top, her mind in a turmoil.

Fidelis wandered about with Ruby beside her. The pains came closer and lasted longer. 'When will it be over?' she gasped, as her belly was gripped and squeezed.

'Don't know pet, you've a way to go yet. Nature takes its course.'

'How's Harry?' she gasped. 'I think about him every day.'

'Hurt bad, Fee. Why did you never write to him? If you could have explained how it happened, it might have gone some way to helping him understand.'

'I write to him every day, Aunt Ruby, there's a box upstairs full of my letters. I'm just too ashamed to post them.'

'You are a silly girl, what good they doing up there? What I need to know is, how you feel about my Harry?'

Fidelis began to cry. 'Directly I saw him again I knew he was the one that I really loved, but it was too late.' She rubbed her eyes with the sleeve of her nightdress. 'Even if he could forgive me there's the baby to think of. What I want more than anything is for him to be my friend again. Hoping for anything else is moonshine.'

'How would it be if I gave your letters to Harry and left it up to him what he does next?'

'I don't know. Aahh! D'you think you should go again and see if May's home yet?' She clutched her friend's arm. 'You don't think it's dead, do you?'

'I dare say we'll manage 'til she gets here,' said Ruby, sounding calmer than she felt. 'As to it being dead, that's stuff and nonsense.'

'It hasn't moved all day.'

'Oh Fee love, it's resting up for the journey.'

'I wish,' she gasped, 'that we were all friends again.'

'We will be, darling, given time. Now, let's have you upstairs in bed. I'll bring you up a fresh hot-water bottle. You'll need the chamber-pot up here after.'

'What time is it?' she asked later, when she came out of a doze to be gripped and kneaded by another fierce spasm.

'It's half-five. While you sit and drink that water I'm going to get a fire going in this grate. Have you some clean rags and scissors and twine to hand?'

Fidelis was alarmed. 'In the top drawer. You don't need them yet, do you?'

Ruby held her hand. 'You're a strong girl, and being frightened will tighten up those muscles and won't help an atom. Those pains are pushing your child out into your arms. If you feel better walking, we'll walk, if you'd like your back rubbed, that's what I'll do. You and me, we'll work together.'

'I'm so tired.'

'You know Fee, I was there when you were born. Your mother screamed the place down. But when you were put in her arms she was weeping with joy. Then, when he crept up to look at you, Jack was like a dog with two tails, that excited.'

Fidelis smiled. 'Could you rub my back, please?' Soothed by the rhythm and warmth of Ruby's hands, she drifted into a doze.

Awakened by a strong clenching of her belly, she saw May Goodale staring down at her. 'Well, Miss, you bin busy. Let's see how things is looking.' She flung back the bedclothes. 'Part them knees, no good being dainty now, we've a way to go yet.'

'How were the twins?' she asked.

'Fine little scraps with good pairs of lungs, the two of them. I'm just going downstairs to fetch us a cup of tea. Birthing is a thirsty business.'

'Where's Aunt Ruby? Aaaahh!' A wave of pain had her gritting her teeth.

'Making us all a cup of tea. You was lucky she come over.'

'What time is it?'

'Half-nine, Miss. I'll be up with us drinks in two ticks.'

Then everything gathered pace. Fidelis had no will in the matter, as her body heaved and retreated, leaving no gaps between. She clutched Ruby's hand.

'You're doing marvels, Fee. Sip this water and let me sponge your face, we're on our way. I've knotted a sheet to the bedpost, pull on it when you gets the urge.'

And then everything seemed to stop and she fell into an exhausted doze.

'Happens like that sometimes, but don't you fret none, we're on our way.'

'What time is it?'

'Gone twelve. Be a birthday present for Jack,' said Ruby, squeezing her hand.

'So tired,' gasped Fidelis, 'I want it to stop.'

It seemed she had barely closed her eyes when she was pounced on again.

'That's it my pet, grab a hold of that towel and push. Scream if you wants to, it's coming now for sure. That's it, darling.'

'On the verge, my girl, nearly there, you grab a hold o' that sheet now.'

Grunting and groaning, she was servant to her tyrannical body which thrust, and thrust.

'Pant, girl, pant there, I got his head in sight. Right, off you go now.'

After a mighty heave, she was conscious of something warm and slippery resting against her thigh, then a cry that made her snap open her eyes and reach towards it.

'Fee, it's a little girl. Oh she's bonny, just let May cut the cord and clean her up a bit then you shall have her.' Ruby kissed her. 'Congratulations, my pet, you've got your reward. Bet this will be the best present your Pa has ever had. You shall have your little maid any minute now. Just one more push and we'll be rid of the afterbirth.'

The weight and warmth of the baby lying against her breasts was a wonder to her. Fidelis touched every inch of her child, marvelling at her perfection. How round and neat her head was, how daintily her ears were set. She cried at the minute toenails.

'What you gonna call her, Fee?'

'She shall be Dorcas Mary McCauley, after my best friend and my mother. What d'you think?

'That's beautiful.' Ruby sat next to the bed, mopping her face with her hankie. 'I've been so miserable, Fee, and ashamed of myself. Will you forgive me?'

Fidelis smiled. 'If you bring me a cup of tea.'

May Goodale washed little Dorcas, dressed her, then settled the baby in her basket.

'I'll be in later to see how you're both faring. If she cries you can try her at the breast but she's wore out with the birthing. And you, missie, tuckle down now and get some rest. Babies is demandin' once they gets going.'

Ruby helped her to wash, and changed the bed for her while she sat in the chair by the fire. Fidelis drank the tea, declaring it the best she had ever tasted. Going over to the dressing-table she opened the box that her friend Dorcas had given her. 'You might as well take these back with you,' she said, handing the letters to Ruby. 'It will save me buying the stamps.'

35

Jack was returning from giving Ebony a good early-morning run along the beach before setting off for the Island. As he approached Gibraltar Street, he saw Norman knocking at his front door. Oh God! What was up? He couldn't bear for anything to have happened to Fee. Ruby had not returned from Ventnor last night and he had lain awake, his thoughts in turmoil.

'Here, Norman, I'm here,' he called. Ebony raced ahead of him barking excitedly.

'Happy Birthday, Granddad,' called his chum, slapping him on the back. 'Our Ruby managed to get a message through to the barracks about ten minutes ago. Good news at last, Jack. A little girl, Dorcas Mary.'

'Thank God, oh, thank God,' he gasped, shaking Norman's hand and trying fish the key-string through the letter-box at the same time.

'Give it here, mate, you're all of a tremble, and rightly so. Not every day you gets to be a granddad. You sit down and I'll stick the kettle on, we'll lace the tea with some rum, seeing as it's a bit of a celebration.'

Jack sat down in the kitchen and passed his hand over his eyes. He felt blessed. There were no words to describe the relief and joy that flooded him. Fee was safe, and there was a new life to think about – a new life and a new year, what could be better? While he sat there absorbing his good fortune, Norman pottered about the kitchen, spooning the tea into the pot and searching out the rum from the sideboard in the sitting-room. 'You needs some grub inside you before you sets out for Ventnor. Let's see what you got.' With the familiarity born of long friendship, his neighbour rummaged in the cupboard, and found the bread-bin and a pot of beef dripping. He hacked them both a doorstep of bread and spread the dripping generously.

'You're a pal and no mistake,' said Jack, settling himself at the kitchen table. He sipped the rum-laced tea appreciatively. 'Ooh, that's put a bit of new life into me and no mistake.' After making inroads into his breakfast he paused. 'Norman, I'm just sorry it's not your Harry's child. I know this has hurt him bad. I wish it had been different.'

'He's a young lad with all his life before him, who knows what's round the corner. Least, now our Ruby's thawed out we can get back into the old routine.' He got to his feet. 'I'd better get my skates on, there's parade in half an hour. 'Bye me old pal, see you when you gets back. We'll wet the baby's head good and proper.'

''Bye Norman and thanks for everything.' Jack didn't quite know what to do with himself beyond squaring the kitchen away and packing his things together. The ferry didn't leave until a quarter to nine and it was now only half-past seven. He could have caught an earlier boat but he had arranged to meet Dorcas and travel over with her.

Taking up his bag and clipping Ebony's lead in place he set off to make a detour.

Shamrock was intent on her pleasure, and did not take kindly to the insistent rapping on her door. Whoever it is has no sense of timing, she thought. 'It's no good, Dapper, you'll have to tie a knot in it. Whoever's down there means business.'

'And so did I,' sighed the regretful Dapper, rolling away from her.

Shamrock laughed, as she dragged on her wrapper and hurried barefoot down the stairs. 'Hold your noise, I'm coming,' she roared. 'Jack, Jesus! What's up with ya? It's only quarter past eight.'

Her brother seemed to be dancing on the spot. 'It's Fee, hasn't she had her baby, little girl, Dorcas Mary. Can't stop, I'm off to Ventnor right now.'

'Oh, Jack, isn't that the grandest news.' She hugged him fiercely. 'Send her my love and say I'll be over next Sunday rain or shine.'

Once the door was closed she burst into noisy tears. Fee was safe and sound and with a baby to love. Praise the angels and saints.

'Shamrock?' Dapper rushed down the stairs towards her. 'What is it, my babe?'

'Fee's had her child and all is well. Ooh! Give me a kiss, you great lummox.'

Dapper grinned at her. 'What you bellerin' for? I thought someone had died or summat.'

''Tis such a relief, Dapper darling, it's a real weight off my mind. What a grand start to the year. Can you search out some booze, I'll put on the frying-pan, nothing less than a bacon sandwich will do it.' While the fat sizzled, she marvelled at the twists and turns that life threw up from time to time. Last year had been rough as emery paper, with Jack torn this way and that, what with Mary withering away in the sanatorium and Fee in desperate straits. Shamrock herself had been on the skids, with the audiences turning against her and Michael swanning back to his missus. She had been heart-sore, and everything had seemed tasteless and insipid. If only she had known that Dapper was round the corner. Their lovemaking was simply the icing on the cake. What was so important to Shamrock was their partnership in all the other areas of her life. The profits from the Starlight

Lounge were split two ways, and from the supper rooms as well. In a few days, her home in Buckle Street would be put up for sale after a monster clean-up, and the money ploughed into their joint ventures. Together they would choose a new home. At his insistence, she was slowly getting to grips with her sluttish ways, but it would take time.

'There's an inch of rum in one bottle and a mouthful of gin in the other but—' like a conjuror, he took his other hand from behind his back and produced a bottle of sparkling wine. 'Not quite champagne, my darling, but it'll have to do.'

'To Fee and little Dorcas,' they cried, raising a couple of smeary glasses in the air.

Dapper took her hand. 'There's a question I've been meaning to ask you. Now what was it?' he said, grinning at her.

Shamrock slapped his hand from where he was about to place it. 'You had better remember, Dapper Diamond, quick, smart, or you'll be singing soprano after I've finished with you.'

Jack and Dorcas hurried up the lane, eager to see Fee and her baby,

'Fancy naming her child after me, it's such a generous thing to do.'

'You more than deserve it,' Jack said. 'Didn't you rescue the girl and look after her like she was one of your own? And I, for one, am deeply thankful to you.'

'Oh, stuff and nonsense,' blustered the woman. 'Fidelis has become a dear friend and such good company.'

As they went through the gate to Fortitude Cottage, Ruby was waiting for them. She rushed up to Jack and hugged him. 'Hello, Granddad, Happy Birthday,' she cried. 'You know I couldn't be more pleased if that little girl up there was one of my own.'

'I wish she was, Ruby, with all my heart, and I thank you for being with my girl. It was you she wanted, no one else would do.'

Ruby beamed at him. 'Birthing is a miracle, Jack, and I felt privileged to be there. I'm off home to my Norman now, and that son of mine. Need to knock some sense into him.'

He smiled at her. 'You just let things take their course, Ruby. If it's meant it's meant, otherwise no power on earth will change things.'

His neighbour winked at him. 'Sometimes life needs a little nudge and I've got just the thing.'

''Bye Ruby, and thanks again.' He waved her away and then rushed through the cottage and up the stairs.

Fidelis floated up from layers of sleep to find her father sitting on the bed watching her. She smiled at him, and he leaned over and kissed her face.

'Hello, my love, how are you on this wonderful morning?'

'Pa, it's so good to see you. Happy Birthday, your present's downstairs.'

He went over to the crib and peered inside. There were tiny snuffling noises; he bent down and lifted back the covers. She watched the delight on his face as he looked at his grand-daughter. Pa raised his eyebrows and she gave an answering nod. With great care, he wrapped the baby in its blanket and carried her to the window. She watched his tender smile as he studied the little girl.

'She is a wonder so she is, and the image of you, Fee. Look at those little sandy eyebrows, straight as if they'd been drawn with a ruler. I love touching that little soft spot on the top of her head. It's fragile as gossamer, yet I can feel a pulse beating there steady as a rock.' He laughed in delight. 'Her little tongue is seeking her mother, I'll bring her to you.'

They sat together examining Dorcas Mary, and exclaiming

as she curled her fingers around Jack's thumb, laughing at the downy hair on the edge of her ears and her slate-blue eyes that seemed to stare straight at them. It was some while before they noticed Dorcas standing in the doorway with a tray of cake and tea.

'Come in, Dorcas, I'm so glad to see you. Look at my baby – isn't she the most beautiful you've ever seen?'

'Fidelis, you're so clever. She is glorious, I shall have to draw her portrait. I've brought us all some tea and birthday cake. Thank you so much for naming her after me, it's a great honour. It will be such a pleasure watching her grow.'

'I want you to be her godmother, there's no one who deserves it more. You have been so good to me, just like a sister.'

'It's been my very great pleasure,' her friend said, her face pink with sudden shyness.

After singing Happy Birthday and drinking their tea, they kissed her and left her to tend to her new infant.

Fidelis was fuzzy with tiredness, but she begrudged the time away from her baby spent in sleep. It seemed unbelievable that only yesterday she was unborn, folded inside her, and now she was a separate being. Dorcas Mary wrinkled her brow and quested with her tongue before beginning to cry. Unbuttoning her nightdress, Fidelis tried to position the baby at her breast. It was some while before they were comfortably placed, and Fidelis's heart was thumping with alarm at her daughter's demanding squawks. Snuffling and gasping, the baby settled to her task. Her jaws worked steadily and after a while at each breast her head lolled drunkenly in satisfaction. By the time Fidelis had changed the baby's nappy and re-buttoned her nightdress, she was exhausted. Clambering back into bed, she lay against the pillows with Dorcas in the crook of her arm. They were both sound asleep when May Goodale looked in on them later in the day.

It was a time of intense swinging emotions, as she and her baby settled in with each other. Sometimes her daughter screamed for no reason, reducing Fidelis to a jelly, and at others she slept soundly, not wanting to wake even when her mother's breasts ached with fullness. All the while her friend Dorcas brought her trays of food, kept her company, and alternately commiserated and rejoiced with her.

Soon it was time for Pa to go home. It was on one of her tearful, inept days and Fidelis clung to him.

'I'll not be gone long, my pet. Sure, I'll be over next weekend and Shamrock is coming to play the grand-aunt. By that time you'll be much more on an even keel, so you will. Don't you worry, now. You're just an apprentice mother still, you'll get your papers soon, and will be dishing out advice with the best of them. 'Bye, my sweetheart.' He bent over the crib and stroked his granddaughter's cheek. 'Goodbye, my little rosebud.' And then he was gone.

Sometimes Daniel floated into her mind. She wondered how she would feel if he were suddenly to appear. Fidelis could not deny that she had loved him, and for a while, she was convinced, he had loved her. It had been a mutual fascination, intense and illusory but as insubstantial as a soap bubble – here one moment and gone the next, but when you saw it you marvelled at the rainbow colours caught within its fragile globe. Did he wonder about her at all or think of the child they had made together?

She thought about Harry, and mourned their broken friendship, for that was all it had been. All the while she had seen him as a boy, and only in the moment when she walked towards him on that July day did she realise the falseness of her image. He was a man, tall and broad and confident. A man she could desire, and a man she had thrown away. Harry knew about love, for he had been one of Ruby and Norman's treasured children; listened to, laughed with, and held close.

Fidelis felt a twinge of alarm as she thought of the letters that Ruby had taken to him. Would they make a difference, would he understand? Sometimes she thought of her mother saying that she was not good enough for Harry, and wept.

At other times, she was so absorbed in little Dorcas that everything else ceased to matter. She wrote to Molly and to everyone at Kelmscott House. How far away they seemed. Her whole world was now encompassed in that one small bedroom: feeding her baby, sleeping, eating and talking with her friend – everything else seemed unimportant. Soon she would venture downstairs, and even have an outing into Ventnor. But for the moment she was content.

36

It wasn't until the early hours of the next morning that he opened the box. At the sight of Fee's familiar handwriting he shut it again, his stomach churning. All these months he had been longing to hear from her, and now he was afraid. In a fit of rage he had torn up all the letters she had written to him while he was away, as well as the special ones he'd kept from earlier times. In the end, curiosity overcame him. Opening the first one he smoothed out the paper and began to read. There were no dates on the letters and so it was difficult to know if they were in any order. He just picked them at random from the box.

Dear Harry,

I know that I have broken your heart and the sight of you has broken mine. Seeing what I have risked and lost has been the greatest pain I have ever known. The moment I saw you again I knew it was you I loved.

Now I must pay for my folly. Soon everyone will know my shame and the child I am carrying will share it too. I don't want it but I have no choice in the matter. It has been such a time of sadness, beginning with the loss of my mother, and now, the loss of you and Ruby whose love has always been so precious to me.

I don't know what I shall do or where I will go to have my baby. If you are wanting me punished you have your wish in full measure.

*I love you and wish that I could turn back the clock
and have a different ending with me running into your
arms, free of guilt and full of love, but what I have sown I
must now reap.*

Yours in sorrow,

Fee

The shock of that morning, when he had waited so eagerly
for her, struck him afresh. He had held her for less than a
minute, overwhelmed by her beauty and his love for her. It
was the moment he had dreamed of in all those months and
months apart from her, then it was snatched from him.
Reeling, disbelieving, he had been unable to take it in. Rage
followed and the need to hit out, to smash something, anything to deflect the pain. Harry was shaken at the effect of
reading that letter. But now he could not stop. Riffling through
the envelopes, he picked out another at random.

Dear Harry,

*I have cried all my tears and suffered shame and
regret, but now I must survive in some way or another
for the sake of my baby. Writing to you has become a
habit and gives me some comfort, as it makes me feel
that we are still friends, even if I never post these
letters.*

*We were true children of the barracks, weren't we? Do
you remember that feeling of walking down the road with
our fathers, how tall and strong they seemed? Then there
was that thrill when they swung us up onto their shoulders and raced one another down the road to dinner. You
are threaded through my childhood in almost every
memory.*

*How about when you had measles and I crept up to see
you with a frog in my pocket. What a jumper he was. And
then you come to see me with a beetle in a matchbox that*

died by morning. Then there was our excitement when my Pa brought home Ebony as a tiny puppy.

You were always two years ahead in everything and I was convinced that I would eventually catch up those years. Do you remember learning to read? You rushed around the room, picking up things and calling out their names; Stephen's Ink, Robin Starch and Swan Vesta matches. Aunt Ruby burst into tears, she was so proud of you.

When the magic moment happened that all those black squiggles on the page became words, I couldn't wait to get home and ran across the Parade Ground to tell my Pa in front of all his recruits. When he shouted at me to go home I was in a fury. Oh, he tried later to explain that the Parade Ground was the holy-of-holies but I was having none of it. All evening he tried to win me round but I was determined to have an apology from him. And in the morning a note was slipped under the door.

How I loved being in your house with Aunt Ruby. She was so cuddly and happy all the time. What a good mother she was with that little notice pinned inside the front door, Remember you are our boys and we love you. I know now that my mother loved me too but I wanted to feel that love and to be held by her.

Harry had not expected this vivid torrent of memories. He put the letter back and closed the lid. How could he have thought it possible to wipe her out of his life? But how could he take back what he had said, or, how could he heal the hurt inside him? The fact that it now depended on him to make some move frightened him. He had to be certain that he could forgive her and let go of the past. But all the time there would be that baby between them, living proof of Fee's

unfaithfulness. Having started to read he couldn't stop. He
picked letters out at random.

> *My Pa read me the story of Rapunzel the princess in*
> *the tower with the golden hair. Straight away I wanted to*
> *climb inside the clock tower at the barracks and push my*
> *hair though the window and have you climb up it to*
> *rescue me. I always wanted to be the centre of attention.*
> *This memory makes me sad as I still need rescuing from*
> *myself and I realise now that you will not come.*

From across the back garden came the six o'clock bugle call.
He knuckled the tears from his eyes and shut the box. All
day, he could not stop thinking about her. What was stopping him going to see her? Christ, he was gutless. Standing
in the pub that evening laughing, joking, throwing darts, she
was there still, in his head. In his room unable to sleep, he
once more drew out a letter.

> *This week I am having a holiday in the Isle of Wight.*
> *It is a welcome space in my life, giving me time to rest*
> *and think how best to live the life that I now have.*
> *Today has been a small turning point for me when I felt*
> *my baby move inside me. It was such a tender feeling*
> *and I was filled with such pity for it. Ever since I knew*
> *that I was pregnant I had been filled with such desper-*
> *ation and dislike of my coming child that I felt quite*
> *ashamed..*
> *I have been selfish thinking only of myself and resolve*
> *to be a good mother come what may. I got up and stood*
> *on the balcony with my hands over my belly and prayed*
> *for my child's well being.*

His mind shied away from thinking of the baby. It was
Herrick's child that had come between him and Fee, stealing
their future. Where everything had been fixed in his mind,

now there was uncertainty. Another voice had entered his head and was pleading to be heard. Whilst he was relieved that Ma had shed all that bitterness, and that Fidelis was well and safely delivered of her child, Harry needed time. He had to be sure what he was feeling. Again, he riffled through the box.

> *Dear Harry,*
>
> *Today I woke up in such a rage with you and Ruby – how hard and unforgiving you are and how goody-goody. I want to come over there and shout and scream at the pair of you. How dare you both condemn me, and my child. We will manage without your approval, thank you very much. I have given up scuttling about the place and apologising for my existence. I am determined to make a good life for myself, and my baby. It will be a different life from the one I planned but it will honestly lived and I shall regret nothing.*
>
> *What makes me the most furious is that I still love you.*
>
> *Fee*

Harry could see her with her red hair flying, marching about and shouting for all she was worth. He was angry too at loving her, still. The letters had stirred up so many feelings and had brought her so vividly to life. What was he doing dithering about like a love-struck schoolboy? He was a man, for God's sake. Compulsively he picked up another envelope and began to read.

> *Dear Harry,*
>
> *I have been thinking about how little prepared I was, by my mother, for being your fiancé. She was not a cuddly, affectionate mother or a loving wife. I was un-prepared and unaware of how my body could lead me*

astray. Always my mother turned her face away from kisses, and lived inside herself, hardly ever letting Pa and I know what she was feeling.

I think I was like a firework waiting for someone to set a match to me. This does not excuse what happened, Harry. But whatever giddy excitement I felt has now proved to be a false trail leading to me into my present difficulties. I do not ever want to see Daniel again and will not inform him when my baby is born. His part in my life is at an end. If my child has to grow up without a father I will just have to love it twice as hard.

You must decide whether or not to believe me. Since you will never see these letters, and have quite made up your mind about me, this little confession is worthless.

I hope you will have happy life. It's strange that Ma always said you were too good for me and now she has been proved right.

Your friend
Fee.

He so wanted to believe her. Fee was wrong. She was miles better than him, braver and far more honest. It was strange, looking back, how awkward he had felt about calling Fee's mother Auntie Mary. He remembered her always straightening pictures, and searching out specks of dust. Yet she had thought to write to him when he was away. He would shut the box soon. He was on duty tomorrow and it was now one o'clock in the morning.

Dear Harry,
I miss you tonight and feel full of love for you as I go into the New Year. How many parties we spent in your house, laughing and singing. Do you remember how we ran into the street at midnight? We were such firm friends,

*knew so much about each other, and now we are
strangers.*

*You were my perfect family, warm and loving and
close. I think I fell in love with your family and wanted
the engagement as a way of being part of them. I don't
know. Certainly when I saw you on the beach, looking so
much a man and not the boy I had waved away three
years ago, I felt differently towards you. I saw that I
wanted you as more than a friend. But it was too late,
and I shall always regret losing you.*

*Harry I feel very frightened about giving birth to this
baby. I so want to love it without the shadow of how it
was made creeping into its life. What if I die, who will
love my child? I feel so lonely tonight and so sad. Your
forgiveness would mean so much to me at this moment. I
am such a coward. Just to know that we can still be
friends would give me courage.*

*It is very difficult to explain to you how it feels to
carry a child, being such a close relationship, really flesh
of my flesh. The body takes over and whether I'm ready
or brave enough it will push my baby out into the world.
Then it will be a separate being yet still dependant on
me. I do hope and pray that I will love it and be a good
mother.*

Always your loving friend,
Fee

The words began to run together and he set the box down
beside his bed and closed his eyes. What breathed through
the letters was her courage and her pain. Fee had opened
her heart to him with no reservations, now it was up to him
to answer her. Harry had wanted to hold back until he was
sure of his feelings, but now he realised that until he saw Fee
again he would never know.

The next morning he dressed and hurried along to the barracks, dropping the letter he had written that morning into the post-box, before he had a chance to change his mind. Slowly a plan was forming, the time for words was over. He had been a faint heart too long; something bold, heroic even, was called for.

37

Each day her daughter was a fresh wonder to Fidelis. As she sat feeding her she would uncurl her tiny fingers or stroke the heel of her foot. Touching the soft patch on the top of her head, and feeling the pulse beneath beating against her hand thrilled her. How could she have doubted loving her? She was now Cassie, and Dorcas Mary would be used for special occasions such as her christening, to be arranged soon, but Cassie would be her bread-and-butter name. May Goodale was right, all the pain and anxiety of her birth had faded in the pleasure she brought. The little bedroom facing the sea was like a cocoon to them for the first week or so. Her nurse was most adamant about her not stirring from it until the tenth day. This morning, Dorcas was going to heat up the water and unhook the tin bath from the yard. She would tend to Cassie while Fidelis had a long luxurious soak and washed her hair. The sheets would be changed, and she was going to get dressed. There was so much to look forward to.

Pa was coming over tomorrow with Shamrock, and Aunt Ruby would follow on the Monday. There had been a letter from Mrs Mount enclosing a postal order for ten pounds. Phoebe had written and sent a silk christening robe. Surprisingly, she had had a letter from Alicia Herrick. It was most carefully worded. The gift of twenty-five pounds was for her to spend, as she wished. It was sent, alledgedly, in recognition of her mother's last few years working for the Herrick family. At first she wanted to throw it on the fire.

'Don't do that, Fidelis.' said Dorcas 'That money was owed to your mother, she worked for that. When you're up and about, we'll get the train to Newport and get you some new clothes.'

The letter she wanted had not come. What had he done with her box? Had he even opened it? All the ups and downs, the hopes and fears of her time in Fortitude Cottage were in those pages. If he could not see that she loved him, then he was not worth the paper. It had been a time of trial; and she had come through it, much to her own amazement, stronger and more determined to make a life for herself and Cassie. If Harry wanted to be a part of it she would be glad, but if not, she was not wasting any more tears.

Fidelis lay in bed in the darkness, listening to the snuffling and squeaking sounds of Cassie stirring in her cradle. Getting out of bed she opened the curtains and daylight flooded the room. This was her favourite time with her daughter, the dawn feed.

'Good morning, my darling, how snug you look wrapped round in that sheet like a little caterpillar.' Settling in her nursing-chair she unbuttoned her nightgown and guided Cassie's seeking mouth to her breast. The intimacy of feeding pleased her. It was a closed circle between mother and child, a giving and receiving. There were times when things did not go well, then Cassie screamed and she did not know what was wrong, but those moments of closeness each morning were treasured by Fidelis.

When her daughter relinquished her hold, she changed her napkin then wrapped her in the rainbow blanket that Dorcas had made.

'Let's tuck you up warm and we'll go out on the balcony and listen to the sea. Isn't it a lovely sound? Soon, I shall show it to you. We'll go down the steps and walk along the beach. When you're a little girl we'll paddle together. There's no end of things we'll do, just you and me.'

'Good morning, Cassie my sweet,' said Dorcas, dropping an envelope onto the bed. 'Let me take you, while your Ma has her tea and reads her letter. Don't be too long, the bath is just right.'

Fidelis stared at the handwriting she had been waiting for. No, she would have her bath first and work up to Harry Dawes later. Nothing must spoil this longed-for treat.

She left the envelope on the bed and padded downstairs to the kitchen where the tub awaited her.

Lying in the steamy water she wondered what Harry would have to say for himself. In the weeks of waiting she had persuaded herself that she didn't care, but now she found that she did. Feelings were such unreliable things. Your thoughts could tell you one thing and then smack, up came fear and joy and tears leading you up quite a different path.

She worked up a lather with the soap and dug her fingers into her hair, then rubbed at her scalp. Soon, pink and glowing, she climbed out of the water and towelled herself dry. As she went back upstairs she could hear Dorcas in the living-room singing to Cassie.

'Now Harry Dawes, what have you got to say for yourself?' she said tearing open the envelope.

> *January 12th 1904*
> *Dear Fee,*
> *I am very nervous about writing to you in case I make matters worse. I was so shocked and roaring with rage and hurt that morning on the beach that I did not know what I was doing. I wanted to hurt you back. Another feeling was jealousy that another man had touched your body and seen you naked when I had only ever kissed you. That feeling was boiling in me when I saw him later on and I might well have killed him if your Pa and mine had not dragged me off. Afterwards it didn't make me feel any better.*

*Pride is a real difficulty for me, and letting others see
my weaknesses is hard. I want to forgive you but I don't
know how to do it. Perhaps my pride has blinded me to
the faults on my side and I need you to forgive me. I feel
very sad at the difficulties you have had and want to
make things right between us. Your letters brought you so
close to me and I realise that I am in danger of losing
you because of my bone-headedness.*

*I am glad to know that you are well and have had
your baby safely. Ma never stops talking of you and
Dorcas Mary.*

*I hope we can be friends because I have missed you so
much.*

With Love,
From Harry

'Oh, Harry,' she gasped, between tears, 'you are such a
fool, holding back and doubting.' While proud, honest men
fumbled their way towards women, dazzlers like Daniel
stepped in and carried off the prizes. He had been like a
golden magnet, drawing her to him with his devastating
smile and silken words. She had been *ensorcelée*, she couldn't
help herself. All the while they had been spell-binding
one another, Harry had been waiting and hoping and
trusting. It was the false-hearted who won fair ladies, not
the true.

What did '*I hope we can be friends*' mean exactly? She was
glad to have the letter, but where did it lead? Was he going
to come and see her, or was he waiting for her to come to
him? Would she forgive him for his fumbling, bumbling way
of going on? Well, that rather depended on his next move.

'It was from Harry,' she said. 'He wants me to forgive him
and for us to be friends.'

Dorcas laughed. 'He'd better hurry up, I'm thinking,

time is wasting.' She put her head on one side and looked speculatively at Fidelis. 'I wondered if you would like a little outing this afternoon. I've arranged for a cab to come and collect us at two o'clock. Where does the fancy take you?'

'I promised myself to visit the cemetery and take some flowers for my mother. But, there's not much around this time of the year, and then I fancied to go to the Buttery. Is that possible?'

'Trust you to want two things in opposite directions. Of course it's possible. As to flowers, there's a pot of hyacinths in the shed, just peeping up out of the soil.'

'That would be just right. Let's do the cemetery first.'

The afternoon was cold and clear, and Fidelis felt a sense of release being out in the air again. She looked around her at the bare trees and hedgerows. In a few more weeks there would be buds and shoots appearing. Snowdrops would be nodding in the grounds of Steep Castle, and in the front garden Dorcas had promised daffodils. Cassie gave a little chirrup.

Handing the baby to her friend she walked up the path to Mary McCauley's grave, carrying the pot of flowers. Kneeling down, she set it on top of the earth facing the stone cross that marked her mother's resting-place. 'Here I am, your rebellious daughter, half-way towards being a fine woman. I didn't think so but there is a lot of you in me and I thank you for it,' she said. After a moment or so she got to her feet. Before leaving, she repeated the prayer her mother had said to her each night at the bedroom door. *'The Lord bless you and keep you. And the Lord make his face to shine on you and be gracious unto you.'*

Feeling at peace with herself she walked back to the cab and climbed inside. 'You know, I think what I would like would be to take some cake home. As Ma would have said, I've overreached myself.'

Dorcas laughed. 'What do you fancy?'

'I think a slice of cherry cake would be just right.' She tucked the blanket around herself and Cassie, and waited for Dorcas to return with a large paper bag.

'No nibbling 'til we get home,' she ordered.

The outing had tired her more than she realised, and after feeding and settling Cassie she opted to have a rest and eat her cake later. Undressing seemed an enormous effort and she was grateful for the hot-water bottle Dorcas had made for her. Soon she drifted down into sleep.

Slowly, insistently, the sound of a bugle pierced her consciousness. The notes were so sweet and true. It was the sunset call. For a confused moment Fidelis thought she was back in Gibraltar Street, and then she opened her eyes. It was only half-past three: what was happening? Getting out of bed she found her slippers, and wrapping a blanket around herself she stepped out onto the balcony. There below was a Royal Marine Bugler, immaculate in number one uniform. Seeing her, he raised a white gloved hand.

'Hello, Fee.' He smiled ruefully. 'I got my courage up at last,' he said. Then he took up the silver bugle again and played the sunset call for her alone.

Fidelis stood there with tears rolling down her cheeks. He was so handsome. Why had she never seen it before? Hope flickered in her heart. Surely, wearing his best uniform and bringing the silver bugle must mean something.

'Oh, Harry,' she said. 'I had nearly given up on you.'

He smiled. 'I got there in the end, Fee, and that's all that matters. You know I love you.'

From inside the house came the sound of a baby crying and still Harry looked at her.

Fidelis nodded and smiled in return. 'You'd better come in,' she said. 'I think I can find a piece of cherry cake.'